Empire in Pine

Book Two

The Red Fury

Empire in Pine

Book Two

The Red Fury

By

Naomi Dawn Musch

Empire in Pine

Book One: The Green Veil
Book Two: The Red Fury
Book Three: The Black Rose

Desert Breeze Publishing, Inc.
27305 W. Live Oak Rd #424
Castaic, CA 91384

http://www.DesertBreezePublishing.com

Copyright © 2011 by Naomi Musch
ISBN 10: 1-61252-929-1
ISBN 13: 978-1-61252-929-5

Published in the United States of America
eBook Publish Date: October 15, 2011
Print Publish Date: April 2013

Editor-In-Chief: Gail R. Delaney
Editor: JB George
Marketing Director: Jenifer Ranieri
Cover Artist: Jenifer Ranieri

Cover Art Copyright by Desert Breeze Publishing, Inc © 2011

All rights reserved. No portion of this book may be reproduced or transmitted in any form or by any electronic or mechanical means, including photocopying, recording or by any information retrieval and storage system without permission of the publisher.

Names, characters and incidents depicted in this book are products of the author's imagination, or are used in a fictitious situation. Any resemblances to actual events, locations, organizations, incidents or persons – living or dead – are coincidental and beyond the intent of the author.

Dedication

For Jesus, the definer of friendship, and to my friends and sisters in Christ:

My pal Vickie Lintula has prayed for me and with me, and she has rejoiced and sorrowed with me as we live our strangely parallel lives. She is always game for an adventure. She even endured me fleshing out my WHOLE idea for this story to her on a weekend road trip to Peshtigo (where she bought me a great book that helped immensely with my research). What a cherished friend and good listener! Bless you, Vickie. "...there is a friend who sticks closer than a brother." Proverbs 18:24

To the Johnson ladies, Tammy, Stephanie, and Emily, who've always been among the first readers of my books or manuscripts, and who never fail to encourage me and share my excitement. Tammy, we think so much alike it's scary (in a good way)! You guys bless me. "Therefore encourage one another and build one another up, just as you are doing." I Thessalonians 5:11

Chapter One

1870

Elaina Kade blinked twice and stared at Jed Clark as he ripped her heart free from its roots. It wavered and crashed in her chest with the same swift roar as a white pine in a violent wind, shredding into pieces, casting debris through every part of her -- body and soul.

He broke their engagement, right out here on her own front porch, with her family sitting inside, maybe hearing every word.

Jed's gaze fell away as he said it. "Maybe we'd just better call it quits. I can see now you're not the girl for me."

She gripped the arms of her mother's old rocker while Jed sat there on the porch rail, playing with his hat, either refusing or too embarrassed to look her in the eye. "Is that what you think, Jed? I'm not fit to marry you?"

He shook his head, but unconvincingly. "Well, considering..."

"Considering?" Her voice lifted. "What's that supposed to mean?"

His glance darted up and his eyes narrowed. "Considering you're not the easiest girl to get along with."

She flushed and sat up straighter in the rocker. "What do you mean? Just because I don't let you tell me what to do? The trouble with you, Jed, is you expect a few strong words and a pat on the head now and then will keep me lined up to your liking. Well, I'm not a fence post you can steady with a few good whacks!"

"You don't ever listen to anybody, Lainey, especially me."

For a moment she gawked, certain what he said was untrue, unreasonable even. Tears welled, blurring her vision, and she despised them. "You think you're too good for me?"

"Course not, Lainey. That's not it at all--"

"Most men would tell a girl *they* weren't fit for *her*. They'd at least have the decency to say, 'I'm not the man for you.' Even Owen gave me that much. But not you." She stuck out her chin and spat the words. "You have the gall to tell me I'm the one with the problem. I'm not good enough or woman enough."

Jed's brow furrowed and his face reddened beneath his short dark beard and tanned skin. "No, *no*! Now don't go twisting my words around to mean something they don't! I'm only trying to say that I just don't think we're meant for each other."

"But we prayed, Jed!"

"Yeah, we were wrong, I guess."

"Wrong to pray?"

"No, course not. Just wrong in thinking we knew God's answer."

"Could we have been so wrong? Whatever happened to the mighty Jed Clark who was going to 'tame that little filly Lainey Kade'?" Her voice rose up another notch. She barely noticed the curtains twitch on the front room window. "What's the matter, Jed? Did you think I didn't know how you bragged all about how you were going to settle me down? Course I heard. My brothers heard and my cousins heard. Seems like everybody heard!" She jumped to her feet, flinging the creaky rocker backwards. Jed reached out to her but she backed away spouting the gossip back to him. "'That Lainey Kade, she's a shrew all right. Not ever going to marry, likely,' they said. But then you stepped up to the task." Lainey stuck her fists into her hips and mimicked Jed. 'Oh, you wait and see. I'll settle her down all right. I'll have that girl eating right out of my hand, just like a chickadee.' Yes, Jed, I heard all the talk. But I thought maybe you were worth it, so I didn't care. I see now how wrong I was!"

Jed grabbed her wrist and hung on, even as she squirmed to break free. His voice clamored for superiority. "Now you just wait a minute! I never said anything at all to make it sound like you were something to be won, like... like a trophy or something! It was only talk with the fellows, that's all."

"Ha! I guess that tells me how highly you think of me."

Jed released her arm and threw his hat down on the rocker. "That's not what I mean, Lainey, and you know it. Course I always thought you were something, like a real prize, but not like getting you was some kind of game I had to win or a mountain I had to conquer."

"I think that's what you thought of it the whole time. Just a game where Jed Clark could prove to the fellas he had the charm to win the unwinable Lainey Kade!"

Jed picked up his hat and slammed it on his head. "Trouble with you, Lainey, is you want me to be Bobby, and I'm not him. Bobby Braedon's dead, and he isn't coming back."

The blood drained straight down to her feet. She dug her fingernails into the palms of her hands. "That's a lie, Jed."

"Is it?"

Her heart pounded. "You've got no right to bring Bobby into this."

"Why not? You said you were gonna marry me. Doesn't that give me some kind of right to tell you I can't compete with ghosts?"

"Nobody's asking you to compete. I'm -- I'm not looking for anybody to be Bobby."

"Aren't you?" Jed harrumphed. "Then you've got me and Owen and everybody around here fooled." He thrust a finger at her. "I think that's exactly who you're looking for, but you'll just have to keep on looking, because no man I know wants to step into the shoes of a dead man in order to convince a woman to love him."

Humiliation gored her. Shallow gasps lifted her chest as she fought both tears and rage. "I don't know why I ever believed you when you said you loved me. Makes me wonder who was the bigger fool, you for pretending, or me for believing you!"

Jed's face twisted. He opened his mouth and closed it again. "Oh, forget it, Lainey! Just forget it!" He stomped down the porch and tramped across the lawn to his buggy, flinging a few last words over his shoulder as he leapt up onto the seat and laid the reins hard across his horse's neck. "Forget everything about us!"

*****

The heat of the day surrendered to a cool evening breeze as the sun set over the Chippewa Valley. With a few quick flicks of her hand, Colette Kade drew the curtains against the twilight. Eleven-year-old Kenton moaned. "Can't we leave 'em open? And open the window too?"

Colette smiled and her gaze drifted to her husband Manason as they shared an unspoken understanding. "Lainey and Jed don't need us listening in on them. If you're warm, go out and sit on the back step for a while."

"Check," said Kenton, as he maneuvered a rook into a deadly position on the board between him and his pa.

Manason returned his son's grin. "You aren't going to win that easily."

Colette realized Kenton barely heard her. He focused on the chess board, determined now to beat his dad. She sat down in her chair and sighed, resolved to finish her mending. Lainey's plaintive voice sounded through the window at her back. A rustle of unease stirred through Colette. Then followed words from Jed which didn't sound happy either.

Kenton lifted his head, his ears and eyes a bit too keen. "Uh-oh."

"You never mind. Sometimes courting couples need to air out a few disagreements when they're getting to know one another."

"Lainey's got more airing to do than most, I reckon."

"That's enough," Manason said softly. His glance slid over at Colette and he grinned. "Least we know what they're doing out there."

"Nase! What a thing to say."

Kenton laughed, but stifled it quickly as the argument between the lovers out on the porch rose to a more intense pitch, one voice climbing atop the other.

"They'll wake Grandma."

Colette turned to the window, wanting to pull back the curtain, but fighting the urge. She heard Manason's nervous foot-tapping beneath the small table where the pieces on the chess board quivered. "Your move," he said, his voice sounding tight.

Kenton sighed and maneuvered his king behind the safety of a knight.

Outside, footsteps barked across the porch floor and down the steps. Colette peeked between the curtains, holding her breath as silence fell. She watched Jed climb up on his buggy and whip the reins across the back of the horse. A moment later the door flew open and Colette dropped the curtain, turning in time to see her daughter slam the door and spin away from it. Elaina paused and looked at them all. Her blue eyes glistened like clear gemstones. Then she hiked up her full brown skirts and ran up the stairs.

Colette looked to Manason. He frowned as Lainey's bedroom door slammed shut above them.

"Not again," said Kenton. "This is the third one. She's going to wind up an old maid for sure."

Manason's gaze dropped from Colette and he looked at their boy. "Why would you say such a thing?"

"It's what some of the kids think."

"The girls or the boys?"

"Both." Kenton shrugged. "Just ask Eldon or Gray."

Colette jammed her sewing needle back into the pin cushion. "We will. We will ask them." She set the mending aside and stood. "I think I'd better go talk to her."

A crash from Lainey's room upstairs quickened her steps.

*****

Elaina gazed at the shards of her looking glass strewn across the bureau and the floor. Later she might regret smashing the precious mirror, a birthday gift from her pa several years ago, but anger and hurt burned through her, and she really just wanted to break something else. She wished she could take Jed's heart and dash it against the wall instead of the pretty piece of crystal quartz he'd once given her.

Instead, Lainey threw her body across the bed and let the grief and rage swirl like a river inside her. She plucked at the threads of the hand-pieced quilt her grandma made and pummeled her fist into her tick as angry sobs broke free.

She didn't bother to answer the soft tapping on the door. A moment later, the bed dipped as Mama sat down beside her. Her long, graceful hands glided over Lainey's back in a gentle caress.

Long minutes passed silently until Lainey's quiet tears stopped and her breathing evened.

"Did you break up?"

She turned onto her back, pushing strands of her black hair out of her face. She gazed fully and sorrowfully at her mother and nodded. "How could it have happened again?" she whispered. "Everything's ruined."

"It isn't."

"Oh, yes." Elaina sat up and leaned forward. She let her mother hold her. "Jed's made it very clear. He's done with me." The final, ragged remnant of her heart clenched tight inside her chest, making it hard to breathe. She pulled away and lunged off the bed, nearly stepping into the glass.

"Lainey, honey, you don't really believe it."

"It's over, Mama." She plucked the remaining hair pins from the tumbling knot at the nape of her neck and tossed them on the bureau among the glass. "It's over and what's more, I'm glad."

"I don't think I believe you."

Lainey threw a look at her. "Why? Because I'm crying? I don't even know why I am." Tears kept erupting despite her fight against them. She wiped at them.

"You love him."

Lainey harrumphed.

"Well, Sweetheart, don't tell me you've been planning all spring to marry Jed without loving him."

Lainey said nothing. She turned away and unhooked the buttons on her shoes.

"Careful of the glass."

She didn't care if she cut her feet to ribbons. Her heart already lay in shreds. Trying to love Jed had been a bad idea from the start. Far too different from one another, Jed always thought he could change her. He'd as much as admitted so in his constant boasting. He arrogantly believed he could bend her to his will just by making her swoon over his charm and good looks.

No. She didn't want to change Jed. It was Jed who wanted to change her.

She kicked her shoes across the floor and began undressing as thoughts of Jed's courtship burned inside her. Truth be told, he'd done a better job of settling her than Owen Steckler had last year. Blind and numb over Bobby's death at the time she met Owen, she let her relationship with him get much too close to the altar. At least when Jed came along, he made her think love was possible again.

But not anymore.

Now it was hopeless. She should be glad. With nothing left of her heart to crush, hope became obsolete. Her heart was turned to little more than lifeless tissue inside her, no longer a feeling, blood-pumping organ, but a pitiful pile of rubble like her mirror -- brittle and useless.

"I suppose if you don't feel like talking about it then I'll leave you get changed. But I'm here if you need me."

Lainey raised her eyes and looked into her mother's. "Yes, Mama, I know."

Mama smiled and left, shutting the door with hardly a sound. Lainey sighed, her tears dry. She tried thinking about the whole affair reasonably, assuring herself it was best after all. At twenty-one, she ought to be mature enough to thank Jed for pointing out the truth. They really had little chance of loving one another for a lifetime like her folks did.

Still, what if they had tried harder? What if she could give Jed her whole heart, complete and full, like it had been when Bobby Braedon owned it? Jed's accusations rang through her thoughts, and tears flooded her eyes again.

No matter how she kneaded the what-ifs in her mind, or how she mulled over all the charges they made toward one another and whether or not they were valid, it still added up to their break-up being a good thing.

But it didn't take away her shame. A vast lump of it settled like a boulder in her chest.

Lainey didn't come down again that evening. Late the next morning her appetite finally beckoned her from bed, so she rose and calmly cleaned up the broken glass and clothing littered around her room. Noon passed by the time she went downstairs to face the world again.

Her eyes felt puffy and strained. She imagined the look of their redness and the white, washed out pallor of her skin, even without the benefit of a mirror to glance in. Her hair hung limp and oily from hours spent worrying her hands through it too. But what did it matter?

She found both Mama and Grandma eating lunch in the wide front kitchen of their log house. Her brothers, Grayson and Eldon, left hours ago to work at the mill with her father, and Kenton had long since gotten shed of the house and his school work too. He never lingered around the house, especially since Pa brought him the new gelding to train.

Lainey smelled yeasty bread rising in pans on the warming shelf above the cook stove, and her stomach growled. She lifted a lid on a pot of venison stew and helped herself to a small plateful.

"Feeling better?" asked Lavinia Palmer, Lainey's seventy-five- year old grandmother who had moved in with them after grandpa Eldon passed away ten years ago.

Lainey took a seat. "I suppose I wouldn't be able to eat otherwise."

The old woman laughed. "That's my girl. Strong like your mother was at your age."

"I never was," said Colette, breaking a piece off her bread and adding another swipe of fresh butter to it.

"Fooled me then. You always seemed confident as any young thing -- you and Joe and your friends. Took confidence to marry a big man like Lainey's father, and courage to move up north being a widow with a child. And, it was your spark and initiative that captured the heart of the man you're married to now."

Lainey's mother blushed and dabbed her mouth with a napkin to hide it. "It wasn't confidence, Ma. It was impetuosity."

"Nevertheless..."

Lavinia smiled and lifted her glass of milk in hands twisted by age. The skin stretched taught and papery across her narrow fingers, but

Lainey thought them beautiful. Even their blueness looked lovely to her.

"Mama?"

"Yes."

"Thank you for last night. I'm sorry if everyone was upset."

"We weren't upset. We just hoped you were okay."

Lainey took a bite of her stew, turning over her thoughts for the thousandth time. "Could you hear us out there on the porch?"

"Only a little."

"Not me. I slept like a log." Grandma pushed herself up from the table to pour them tea, her movements labored.

Lainey and Colette smiled at one another, and Lainey sighed. "We were pretty loud."

"We tried not to notice, but we really didn't hear much."

She shrugged. "We quarreled. He said we weren't meant for each other."

Lavinia puffed as she set the tea kettle on a trivet and took her seat again. "Oh, now, how could he know that?"

Mama spoke carefully. "I thought the two of you had that settled, and that's why you decided to marry each other. We talked about how important it was that you both be sure."

Lainey looked at her mama for a moment then shrugged. "We didn't know what we were talking about, I guess. Oh, Mama, I just wish..."

"What, honey, what do you wish?"

"I wish I could get away -- away from everything."

"That's how everyone feels when they break up. You'll feel better soon. I know you will. And besides, I bet Jed will come around and regret what he said. I don't think he'll give up on you that easily."

"He didn't give up easily, Mama." She fiddled with a tea cup between her hands. "He's been trying hard. It was me. I made it impossible. He told me the truth. He could never live up to Bobby."

"Bobby! Bobby Braedon?" Lavinia gasped. "Is that what your quarrel was about? He's upset about that poor dead boy?"

"No, Grandma." Lainey caressed her grandma's hand and tried to smile. "He's not upset about Bobby. It's me. I can't let go of what it felt like to love somebody the way I loved Bobby... with all of me."

Both ladies stared at her. She'd probably shocked them with her candor. They should be used to her frankness by now.

Colette cleared her throat softly. "Well, honey, I think I know something about losing someone you love."

"My father? But you loved Pa first." She meant Manason. He'd always been Pa to her, her true pa, even though she didn't own a single drop of his blood. "That made it different."

"It took a long time for love to grow between your father and me, that's true. But it did happen. I was devastated when he died. I never thought for a moment Nase would come back into my life or that I'd be able to let go of the past, but I did."

Lainey frowned and pushed back from the table. "Well, I'm certain Bobby won't be coming back from mine." She went to the sink and jerked hard on the pump handle until water gushed into a basin. Splashing some on her face and patting it dry on a towel she went on. "Even if I could, I know now I don't ever want to love someone again. I've never felt so beat up inside. I can only think that if Bobby hadn't gotten killed, I wouldn't be in this mess right now."

Grandma's eyebrows jumped. "What mess, suffering, you mean?"

"This mess of feeling like I'm stuck. I can't go back and, much as I'd like, I can't go forward. I'm stuck here in the Chippewa where everybody knows what a shrew I've turned into. Jed's gotten his fill of me same as Owen did. There isn't another man around this country that'll want to put his name next to mine once word gets out. Not that there's a one of them I'd want my name next to." Lainey flipped the towel over a rack and leaned against the dry sink, crossing her arms. "I hate how endless and stagnant the future looks."

Colette sighed and straightened up in her chair. "You're right, Lainey. Something has to change because you're becoming morbid. I don't think the future looks as bleak as you think it does. You just need to put your mind on something else. The Independence Day festival in Eau Claire will be here before you know it. That ought to give you something to turn your mind to."

"Oh, Mama, you surely don't think I want to go to the festival after what's happened!"

"It'll be good for you to have some fun without Jed. Wallowing in self-pity won't help. It won't stop the rumors you're worried about either. Enjoy your independence for a while until you both can get your perspectives straight."

"My perspective is just fine, Mama. I can't go to that festival. I'm too ashamed. Don't you understand? Jed's made up his mind!"

She turned away and stared out the window above the sink.

Mama's tone was firm. "I understand. You're young and your heart aches. But it'll get better. You'll see. You need to trust the Lord. Now hang that towel straight so it won't mildew."

Lainey scowled as she took out her frustration on the crooked towel. Her heart didn't ache. It was far beyond that. She'd left most of it behind with Bobby, and the rest she let Jed ruin. Maybe she ruined his too... Mama's overt optimism nagged at her.

Lainey bowed her head. The answer certainly didn't lie in waiting around for Jed anyway. 'Trust God,' Mama always said. Her mother may as well hand her another bitter pill to swallow.

Mama spoke to Grandma. "Nase plans on sending Grayson to Chicago on business after the holiday. Says it's time to put him to use. He's old enough."

"What's Nase need in Chicago?"

"He's got contract business with one of the shipyards. Nothing serious. Just paperwork. It'll be good for Grayson. Nase was his age when he started out."

Lainey frowned as the older women's conversation wormed through her. She turned to face them. "Grayson's going to Chicago? On his own?"

Mama sipped her tea and set it down. "That's what your Papa says. I don't think he's told Gray yet."

Lainey lifted her shoulders as doors to escape swung wide in her thoughts. "I'll go too." She rushed over to the table faster than Mama could speak. "You're right. I need to put my mind on something else. I'll go along with Grayson. I'll shake the sawdust of the Chippewa off my feet, if only for a while."

"Oh, Lainey," Mama began shaking her head. "I don't know. I think you're getting ahead of yourself."

"Getting ahead of myself?" Lainey bent close, clutching Mama's arm. "Mama, look at me. I'm a grown woman. I'm not ahead of myself. I'm behind. And what do I have for prospects? Nothing. I've no work to occupy me, and as far as finding a husband..." She shook her head and stood straight as a rod, determination running up her spine. "I can't wait to get away." She paced around the table. "It's exactly what I'll do."

"Sounds an awful lot like running away if you ask me."

She scoffed. "I'm sure that's what Jed will think. But I've every right to go on a trip with my brother and see Chicago. I'll get away long enough to catch my breath and find a way to live without the idea of marriage."

Grandma *tsked*. "Another way to live? You talk as though your life is over. Jed's bound to settle down and come around. I bet he's already sorry."

Lainey glanced at Grandma then back to Mama, drilling her with her gaze. "'Don't wallow in self-pity. Enjoy your independence.' You said those things just a few minutes ago."

"I know, Sweetheart. I did. But I meant you should spend time with your friends. Have some fun with Katie and Ginny. Go out into the community and help everyone see the wonderful Lainey we know. Remind Jed of who she is. You can prove away any silly rumors. Remember, I also said to trust God."

Lainey slapped her palm on the table. "The rumors are true! And Jed's right! Bobby does haunt me. I imagine him lying out there, crushed under that tree." Her gaze dodged back and forth between the women. "I trusted God and He took Bobby. I trusted Him and now Jed's given up on me. You tell me to keep trusting God! For what? I have to get away. I have to!" A giant fist squeezed her chest, pinching the air from her lungs, and her eyes burned again.

Mama's brow furrowed. She took another sip of coffee. "I'll talk to Papa."

Lainey sucked in a sharp breath and let it out slowly. She stooped to kiss her mother's cheek. But her thoughts drowned in the shambles her life had become since Bobby died. She had to get away, or she might never be able to breathe again.

Chapter Two

Zane Beaumont stared, choked by the sight of blood turning the shirt of the dead man dark. It soaked the ground, glistening in the mud beneath his feet. A sob wrenched out. "Pa!" Zane tumbled to his knees at his father's side and clutched his father's shirt, twisting it, wringing the blood into his hands. Smoke from gunpowder blasts hung heavy in the air, stinging his nostrils and tearing his eyes. His own blood ran from the gash on his head.

He knew he dreamed it, but he couldn't pull himself out of it. Explosions rocked the earth around him. Bullets whizzed past his ears. More men cried out and fell.

He held his father, crying until the blood ceased streaming from his chest and bubbling out his mouth. His eyes stared up and through Zane.

"Run! Run, Zane!" Suzanne's voice called him and he looked up to see her standing there on the battlefield, her dress in tatters, blood streaking her cheeks and matting in her long, red-blond hair. She stretched out her hands, shooing him. "Run, Zane!"

She stood in front of him now, at his side, pulling him away from their pa. She cringed and tripped over his leg when a cannonball fell close. Her face twisted and she pulled on him. "Get up, get up!"

Kelly's voice came through the smoke and the haze. "Time to get up 'less you want to end up in St. Paul." Zane felt his leg jerked again.

The haze evaporated and shafts of light pierced his brain. Suzanne and his pa disappeared, but Zane's head throbbed like it had been hit by the butt of a Yankee rifle."C'mon now." Kelly's patient chiding. Zane cracked open one eye. The silhouette of his giant brother stood over him against the sun. "Boat's docked. Passengers are ready to unload. You want to get trampled?"

He slid himself up against the wheelhouse and rubbed the heel of his hand into his eyes. Lifting his hat, he pushed fingers through his stringy hair.

"I bet you feel just about as bad as you look. I could use a bath too. Think you can hurry it up so's we can find one?"

"Yeah." Zane pulled his long legs up and teetered to his feet, leaning hard into the wheelhouse until he felt steady.

"You were dreaming?"

Zane glanced at his younger brother and barely nodded. Kelly always knew when the dreams came, and how he woke each time feeling like he'd been through Bull Run all over again.

"Well, let's get off this boat. Walking will feel good. Been so long, I forgot what Illinois ground feels like."

Each hoisting a carpet bag up over his shoulder, the brothers disembarked at Rock Island. While the other passengers gathered with families or collected their trunks, the Beaumont boys made long strides through the pack and into the main town.

"You get any rest at all?" asked Kelly.

Zane lifted his chin in the direction of a tall gray building with the faded red word *Hotel* arched across a sign dangling from the eave. "Rest enough."

"Well, maybe once we get shaved and have food in our bellies you'll feel perkier."

He didn't argue with that or with Kelly's big grin. His "little" brother carried big shoulders, a big smile, and a bigger than life kind of heart.

"Let's start with the first one."

An hour and a half later Zane felt like a new man. He knew he smelled better after his bath, and he figured he looked human again after putting on a clean change of clothes. The sun already stretched a long way across the sky and his stomach beckoned for a hot meal.

"I'll take the biggest steak you've got," he said to the plump waitress taking their order, "as fast as you can bring it."

She snapped up the menu from his hands. "I imagine the cook will take as long as he has to."

Zane looked up at her and put on a smile. "I don't know that I was done looking at that."

"It comes with potatoes and green beans." She turned to Kelly. "Same for you?"

He nodded and handed her his menu.

"I'd like mine medium well," Zane said.

She glared back. "I guess you'll get it however the cook decides to make it."

"Well, ma'am," Zane leaned back and held her eyes with a bigger smile, "I reckon you must have some cook back there. I guess I'll take it any way you want to bring it to me since that's the case. And I'll trust your judgment on dessert. Bring whatever you've got."

Her lip twitched and he thought she might roll her eyes, but she turned on her heel and marched off through the swinging door to the kitchen.

Kelly chuckled. "Keep working at it. I'm sure you'll win her over."

"I can only try."

"Her type's always softened up by gentlemanly behavior."

"Well, that's you then."

"Listen to you. You are feeling pretty good tonight, aren't you?"

Zane pulled out a watch and glanced at the time. "I should be able to find us a game in this town, don't you think so?"

"Money's running pretty low. After we eat these steaks, we'll only have enough left for bed money. I sure do relish the idea of a night in a real bed."

Zane nodded. "I'll try and add to it."

"So long as you don't lose it."

Zane tapped his fingers on the table and looked across the room out the window. "I don't plan to."

The waitress served their steaks almost twenty-five minutes later, and if not the most tender they'd ever eaten, they weren't the worst, either. The pile of potatoes and steak covered in gravy went down with complete satisfaction.

Zane stuck a toothpick in his mouth and stretched his legs out under the table. "Feels good to be on land again."

"I'm with you there, brother. So, when you figure on finding that game?"

"Well, let's just take us a little walk down the avenue and see what Rock Island has to offer."

Kelly slugged back the remains of a cold glass of milk and rose, crushing his hat back on his blond head. "Lead the way."

An hour later they laughed over whiskey and cards in a local saloon. Kelly ended up excusing himself as soon as his small stakes disappeared. But as Zane's winnings stacked up, he planned to take advantage of all the evening offered. Having already broken even on the bed money, he slipped a few bills to Kelly before he left.

"Make sure the bed's soft," he said. Kelly nodded and touched his hat as he sauntered away toward the bar to inquire about a room.

*****

A long-legged, lightly clad female sidled up beside him. "If it's a room you need, I'll show you mine."

Kelly turned sideways, leaning onto one elbow on the bar. He tilted back his hat and gave her an appreciative perusal. "Well, now, it's not that I wouldn't mind taking you up on that offer, but you see, this dollar bill is about all I can afford to spend tonight."

"Oh... too bad," she purred and turned to walk away, her hand drifting across his shoulder as she did.

Kelly watched her move across the floor. *I hope you fill the coffers tonight, Zane.* He turned away reluctantly. "A glass over here, bartender."

The man filled the glass and took his money, the bill just enough to cover the drink and the room. Kelly kept two other bills pocketed and out of sight. Something small to fall back on in case Zane's luck at the table turned.

"Thanks." He nodded at the barkeep as he downed the drink and took to the stairs to find their room and call it a day.

He roused sometime later, not sure of the hour, but sensing dawn wasn't far away.

"Kelly, get up."

"Get some sleep, Zane."

"Come on. Get up."

"What for?" Kelly turned and buried his head beneath his pillow.

"Because there's a man downstairs who's gonna come busting in here any minute and put the fire under you if you don't."

Kelly's eyelids slid open a crack and he peaked out from beneath the pillow. He groaned. "What did you do?"

"I won, that's what. Now come on."

Kelly harrumphed and pushed himself up off the bed. He fumbled with the pants Zane threw on his lap.

"Can you hurry it up a bit, Kell? That fellow's got some friends." He went over to the door and cracked it open an inch.

Kelly could hear a general commotion taking place downstairs. He yanked on his boots, and rose to button his pants.

"You can do that later. We have to git!" Zane shut the door and hurried over to lift the window sash.

"You won, huh?"

"Fair and square." He swung his lanky legs over the sill and looked down to the ground below. "Some guys are just sore losers."

Zane jumped to the ground, hitting the dirt with a grunt and rolling sideways.

"I'm getting tired of this," Kelly mumbled as he let go of the window, and the ground rose up to meet him. "Ouch." He pushed himself upright and let Zane pull him up off the ground.

"It was a soft bed, too, Zane. Don't think I'm going to let you forget that for a while."

"Yeah, well, at least you got to give it a try."

A disturbance in their room drew their eyes back up to the window.

"They're gone!" a gruff voice hollered. But whatever else they said faded in the distance as the Beaumont brothers headed toward the train station, hoping for a quiet alley where they could get a few winks before morning and trouble fell upon them.

The next morning they boarded a train heading east to Chicago. Kelly finally rested his guard, but he still felt groggy after spending the night in a boxcar. "So, how much did you win anyway?"

Zane opened his jacket and pulled out a wallet. Discreetly he opened it and fanned a thick cluster of bills so that Kelly could see what they had. "You want to take it now?"

"Wait until we stop." It looked like a small fortune. "You're sure it was fair and square?"

"Sure was. Course, that no-good loser who busted into our room didn't think so. Unfortunately, he had lots of friends who were easily persuaded."

Kelly chuckled. "At least it wasn't over a girl."

"Well... I did win a kiss."

"What?"

"Once that fellow -- Reed was his name -- ran out of money, he got the idea to wager a kiss. He was a local. Promised that saloon gal he'd pay her back later if he lost."

"And he lost."

"It was a sweet reward. Course, now Reed's in debt."

Kelly shook his head. "To think I could've afforded more than just the bed."

Zane leaned back and tucked away his billfold, laughing. He reached over and mussed Kelly's hair. "Sometimes you fold up too soon."

"Yeah, I guess."

*****

It was nightfall again before the Chicago Rock Island and Pacific brought them into the city. This time both Beaumonts were too tired to spend the night on anything other than sleep. Zane promised Kelly a full night's rest in a fine, comfortable establishment, and handed over the kitty so that Kelly could do the choosing.

The next morning, fully rested and with a breakfast of steak and eggs and griddle cakes weighing heavily in them, they set out to explore the bustling city.

"Been a long time since we last saw Chicago," said Kelly.

Zane heard the nostalgia seeping out of his brother's thoughts. Though Kelly was taller than Zane, with muscles stretched over his shoulders like cordwood, moments like these made Zane feel more than only two years older. The gentle yearning in Kelly's voice almost made him sound like a youth again.

"Yeah, it sure has. Looks changed."

"Remember when you and I and Suzanne came here with Ma and Pa that summer I was twelve? Didn't seem like so much to look at back then."

"Everything's different since the war."

"Is it the war that changed it?"

"No, not just. People are moving west for lots of reasons. Everybody scattering to the winds."

"Like us."

Zane nodded, but said nothing. They'd been scattering and never settling for five years now. He didn't like to think about it. Even as much as he missed the rest of his family, he didn't like to think about them. Memories of days like those spent here in Chicago were best pushed forcefully out of his thoughts.

"Say, Kelly, how about some new clothes? You've been wearing that same pair of long johns since December."

Kelly chuckled. "Yeah, they're not much more than a few threads strung together now."

"I noticed that when you were scrambling into your britches yesterday morning."

"I don't think you could rightly call it scrambling."

"No, not rightly."

"Sure, I'd like some new clothes. These have nearly grown to my skin."

"Then let's find a shop that has stuff pre-made."

Two hours later they were both suited up in new underwear and shirts and jeans. They even had a couple of extra changes and a new carpetbag in which to keep them.

"I feel like a real gentleman."

"Me too," said Zane. "And it didn't cost as much as I thought it would. Hardly put a kink in the stash."

"As if you'd care."

"Well, we did all right, didn't we?"

"We sure did."

Kelly slapped him on the shoulder and Zane grinned. "That's why you're the banker."

Kelly's lifted his brows. "I thought I was the preacher."

Zane looked at him closely, thinking how much he sometimes wished he'd spared Kelly this path they'd been on since leaving the army. He wouldn't want to be separated from Kelly, but their closeness cost his younger brother much. Zane regretted Kelly's losses, even if he didn't regret them for his own sake.

"You are the preacher now and then, Kell. Now and then."

Chapter Three

Lainey lay on the bed in the hotel room she shared with her cousin Katie and gazed up at the ceiling. Rain slashed against the window pane in a deafening downpour. Thankfully, they'd decided not to go out earlier today. The clouds portended the impending storm, and it would have caught them.

Katie hummed as she bathed in the tub behind the screen.

Lainey called to her. "Are you shriveling up in there?"

"Yes I am and loving it. Do you suppose it will rain all night?"

"It might. What will we do if it doesn't stop by tomorrow?"

"Pooh! Don't say such a thing. I have the perfect new dress all picked out in my mind, and it may take us hours to find it. I can't wait to visit all those lovely shops. I do hope Stephen and Gray are resting. They will need all their strength to drive us around Chicago."

Lainey laughed. "I'm sure they are. There isn't much more they can do. I need to buy some more charcoal for my sketches."

"I'm sure we'll find some. For myself, I intend to spend as much money as possible on new hats and clothes and souvenirs."

Lainey rolled onto her side and tucked her arm beneath her head. She thought about her escape. Papa understood so well. He told her it was about time she and Grayson got to see what happened after all those big trees left the camps and mills of Kade Logging. He didn't act at all surprised about her wanting to go along. It was his idea to send her cousins Stephen and Katie along too, using the excuse that Stephen might as well get used to his role in the family business as well. But good reasons aside, Lainey thought Papa understood her need to get away from all the gossip around Chippewa Falls. Papa was the best.

"I'm so glad Papa told us not to rush. We have an entire month. A rainy day to rest won't really interrupt our plans at all."

Water sloshed in the tub behind the screen and Katie heaved a sigh. "Weren't the Dells fabulous? I'd like to go there again sometime, perhaps for my wedding trip."

Lainey raised her brows. The things Katie said! "Your wedding trip? And who are you planning to marry, pray tell?"

Water trickled, and Lainey pictured Katie's shoulder shrug. "Oh, it doesn't matter who. Just as long as he takes me on a glorious honeymoon."

Lainey sat up and pulled her sketch pad across the bed, carefully flipping back the pages. "I suppose the Dells would be a romantic place to spend it," she said, almost absent-mindedly as she gazed at the drawings.

Her favorite part of the trip so far had been their tour of the

Wisconsin Dells three days ago. They took a boat tour in the Dells and found themselves awestruck by the bizarre, almost haunting sandstone rock formations looming over the Wisconsin River. For a single day they'd stepped into another world, from another time. Drifting along in the hired boat, tranquility captured Lainey unlike any other time in the past month. Even looking at the images now helped her recapture the serene spirit she had possessed while she visited there.

Papa reminded her to take her sketchbook along. "Capture your vacation," he said. Papa always knew what to say to put her mind off one thing and onto another. Still, her latest dashed romance didn't leave her mind so easily.

"If I didn't have my sketches, I might think I'd imagined our four days at the Dells."

Katie murmured her agreement. "It was pretty. It was a long enough visit for me though. By our last day I felt quite ready to set off on the next adventure. I'm glad we're finally getting to see the big city."

Lainey stared at another picture of Grayson lounging on a rock, gazing at the clouds. A long piece of grass stuck between his teeth waved upward. Lainey would have been just as content to relax in the countryside around the Dells for a month. No one intruded upon her there. She could easily fill her entire book with sketches of the scenery or of her brother and cousins taking delight in the attractions.

"What about your honeymoon?" she asked smiling. "What if your husband doesn't want to do anything but keep you there for a month?"

A loud splash answered. "That, my darling cousin, is different. If I get a husband, then I'll gladly keep him to myself for a long, long time."

Lainey laughed.

"Lainey, do you think maybe with time away, things might be different when we get back -- things between you and Jed, I mean?"

She flipped the sketchbook closed then turned over and jammed the pillow under her arm. Her thoughts seared at the memories of the Independence Day festival. Grayson had convinced her to go though she didn't want to. He insisted her lack of attendance would only give rise to more gossip and speculation. So she'd piled into the wagon with her family and endured the three-day event in Eau Claire with sheer agony. She'd hoped to avoid Jed completely, but that had been asking too much. She cringed when she remembered the governor's ball. Jed had made it a point to ignore her, though he cast a glance her way more than once, always making sure she noticed while he danced with other girls. Even Katie. Katie, to give her credit, looked stricken to think she might have hurt Lainey by dancing with Jed. She insisted she only did it to wheedle facts out of him about how heart-broken he was over Lainey. But it turned out he never mentioned her to Katie at all.

"No, Katie. Things won't change. And even if he wanted them to -- which he won't -- a girl can only endure so much humiliation."

Small splashes sounded as if Katie was getting out of the tub.

Lainey stood up to pace. "If he thinks for even a moment that I miss him, he's mistaken. And mind my words, Katie. I may be drenched in humiliation, but I'm certainly not jealous. Anyone who wants Jed Clark can have him..." She paced to the other end of the room. "Arrogant, self-absorbed, insensitive brute that he is."

Katie sounded subdued. "I'm so glad Stephen took him to task."

Lainey's gaze drew to the rain streaming down the window pane, streaming memories of the final night of the festival back into her thoughts. Stephen tried to help. He took Jed to task outside the hotel, with Jed's friends looking on. Jed made some remark about her -- Stephen kept the specifics to himself -- and he gave Jed a split lip in rebuttal. But even Stephen's defense left her conflicted somewhere between satisfaction and mortification.

Lainey's righteous indignation drained out of her body as quickly as it filled it. "Yes. Stephen tried."

Katie stepped from behind the screen dressed only in her bloomers and camisole. She dabbed a towel against damp curls at the nape of her neck.

"And really, Katie," Lainey said, picking up her sketchbook to put it away, "I don't even like to think about it. Getting away has given me space to breathe easily for the first time in days. I felt everyone's pity at the festival, or in some cases, their derision." She lifted her chin. "I'm looking forward to our little outing tomorrow, and to being on our own for the rest of the month. No more looks of pity from everyone I meet. No reason to avoid public activities. No more wondering what Jed is doing or if he misses me even a little."

She shrugged her shoulders. "Certainly, he doesn't. What kind of man misses a woman who only makes him miserable and spiteful?"

Katie stared at her, but strange, satisfying resolution flowed through Lainey. She hoped she was done crying for good. The remnants of her heart lay too weary and hardened by pain to shed more tears. The effort of caring even a little just took too much strain. She gladly embarked on this vacation and every pleasure it afforded. She fully intended to enjoy the next few weeks and put thoughts of her failed relationships far out of mind.

Lainey pursed her lips and clasped her hands. "What'll we do for an hour or so tomorrow while the boys take care of the logging contracts?"

Katie seemed to realize Lainey's resolve and almost be relieved by it. She tossed the towel aside and retrieved her skirt and blouse off the back of an upholstered chair. "Maybe we can get some lunch and plan our afternoon shopping agenda."

"Sounds like a good idea. We'll mention it to Stephen and Gray."

"I just hope the rain stops. I don't know what I'll do with myself if I have to spend another whole day in the hotel."

In the past Lainey might have been just as restless as Katie, but these days she cared little for crowds. The sites would be there to see anytime. Lainey Kade was in no hurry.

She wandered to the window to peer out, but rivers of water streaked the glass, obscuring her view. She took a deep breath, thankful there would be no chance of running into any acquaintances during their shopping spree.

*****

The skies cleared pretty as a bluebell the following morning. They all woke up early, anxious to see Chicago after their day spent in repose. Grayson found a driver to take them to an attorney's office to deliver a packet of papers for his father. He and Stephen stepped off there with instructions for the driver to leave the ladies at the small café up the street.

"We'll meet you there in less than an hour."

"All right. Don't hurry. We'll be fine," said Lainey.

A barrage of delicious smells greeted them as they stepped inside the small, bright café and found a table. They each ordered chicken and dumpling soup and a roll to eat then passed the time pleasantly sipping tea while they waited for their food to arrive.

Katie leaned back and glanced around at the other customers. "We're so far from home. Not a soul in sight whom we'll recognize."

Lainey nodded. "Or who recognizes us."

"No. Doesn't it make you feel... exotic?"

"Exotic? Well, no. Not exactly."

"Foreign?"

Lainey laughed. "No. Not foreign."

"What then? How do you feel, knowing that everything and everyone we know is hundreds of miles away, and we are totally on our own here in this unfamiliar place?"

"I don't know that I feel anything in particular."

"Nothing at all?"

"Contentment, maybe."

Katie scooted forward, her brown eyes flashing. "Do you, Lainey? Feel content, I mean?"

"To a degree."

"To what degree don't you feel content then?"

"I don't know. I guess that I've lived with a certain expectancy for so long, now that I've nothing to expect, it leaves a little hole."

"What did you expect?"

Lainey shrugged and leaned back, making room for the waitress to set her soup before her. She spread a napkin over her lap. "Nothing much. Just the usual anticipation of things. You know, like loving someone, marrying them, or starting out on my own path apart from my parents."

"And we are starting out."

"We're taking a vacation, hardly starting out on our own. And you know I no longer have any expectations about the other things I mentioned." She nibbled on a gooey dumpling, hoping the food would take away the gaping spot inside her.

"Things won't be the same after this," said Katie. "We'll both want more."

Lainey nodded. Yes, she would want more. She would want to experience this kind of freedom again, someday. Already nearly August, they could spend a week in Chicago before beginning the trip back up north. They'd already decided to take an alternative return route north to Milwaukee and Green Bay and then venture on a less traveled route to the central part of the state, briefly visiting their relation in Grand Rapids. Other sites to see and things to do awaited them on the return journey. The places would be more rustic and even primitive, perhaps, but they were country folk, used to such things. Lainey wanted to compare the sites they saw up north in the eastern parts of Wisconsin to the places she knew at home in the Chippewa Valley.

She focused on her meal. "I don't hardly like to think of going back, so let's not."

The waitress returned, smiling. "Excuse me." In her hands she carried two plates of apple dumplings with cream. "Dessert for you both," she said, setting the plates before them, "with compliments from the gentlemen in the corner."

Katie smiled, but when Lainey turned slightly and caught the gazes of two men watching them, she flushed and turned away.

She looked back politely at the waitress. "I don't believe I can eat another bite. Tell the gentlemen I'm sorry."

Katie stared at her for a moment then looked back up at the waitress. "Tell them thank you. I'll enjoy mine."

The waitress walked away, taking Lainey's dumplings with her. Lainey's mouth watered slightly as she watched them disappear.

"Elaina Kade, since when do you turn down sweets?"

"Since two strangers just bought them for us, and I have no idea what they expect in return."

"Oh." Katie set down her fork. "I should probably send mine back."

"No." Lainey waved off the suggestion. "It's too late now. They're probably harmless enough anyway. Just don't keep looking over there at them."

"I can't help it, Lainey." Katie leaned forward and whispered, "They're not bad looking."

Lainey chuckled. She saw no sense in ruining Katie's fun just because she had no desire to make friends herself.

"Well, we'll see how interested they are when Gray and Stephen get here."

As if on cue, the two strangers picked up their hats and sauntered over.

"Hello, ladies. I hope we didn't offend you by buying dessert." The man who spoke was tall and thin, but solid, like a young maple. Reddish blond hair swept back from his face and waved just slightly behind his ears. His skin, sun-kissed and ruddy, showed early signs of lines at the corners of his silvery-blue eyes.

He looked rugged like an outdoorsman, a woodsman even, though he dressed with more style.

The other man must be some relation, a brother perhaps. Enough of a resemblance made Lainey think so though he stood a couple of inches taller and looked broader across the chest and shoulders. His blond hair contained no strawberry highlights. His face appeared fuller, his smile more open.

Lainey's eyes drew almost irresistibly into the light ones of the first man. "I'm sorry I was too full to accept your kind gesture."

"I was afraid you didn't like apple dumplings."

"Who doesn't like apple dumplings?" asked Katie.

"Well, that's what we thought."

"We're new in town, and we were a little bit bored," said the taller of the two, "and thought maybe we could sit with you and talk for a few minutes, if you don't mind."

Katie smiled a bit too welcomingly. "Well, Lainey and I--"

"I don't think we have much more time," said Lainey, throwing a sharp glance toward her cousin. Sometimes the three years separating their ages showed up in Katie's inexperience in such situations. She didn't appreciate any stranger from who-knows-where knowing her name here in Chicago.

Katie's smile fell. "That's true."

"We're meeting someone," said Lainey, purposefully not mentioning she expected their brothers.

"Oh, then we're intruding."

"Not really--"

"Well, like I said," Lainey shot a glance at Katie, "we haven't much time."

Just then the bell jingled above the door. Gray and Stephen stepped inside.

"Ah, here they are now." Lainey tried not to let the relief appear too evident in her voice.

Instantly the demeanor of the two men changed. They stood straighter and stepped back from the table.

"Well, we won't keep you," said Silver Eyes, "seeing as how you're indisposed."

"Enjoy the dumplings," said Brawny.

Katie looked just a bit disappointed. "Yes, thank you. I will."

Grayson Kade came over and pulled out a chair next to Katie.

"What was that all about?"

Stephen sat down beside Lainey.

Katie pouted. "Oh, nothing. Just that they wanted to be friendly and you two had to come in and scare them off."

Both Grayson and Stephen studied the two strangers.

"Well, it's probably a good thing we came when we did."

"Yes. I, for one, am glad," said Lainey. "And, Katie, don't you ever tell strange men that these two are our brothers. Let them think differently and we'll be all the safer."

"Oh, pooh. What's the fun in that?"

Grayson laughed and Stephen patted Lainey's hand. Later, as they strolled up the boardwalk toward one of the many fancy shops lining the streets, Katie complained to her cousin, "The thing is, Gray, there was a time when Lainey would've enjoyed the attention just as much as I."

And Lainey knew it was true.

*****

"I'm getting tired of Chicago." Kelly tapped his foot against the boardwalk, and then paced past Zane. "I didn't want to say anything back in Rock Island, but you know, it wouldn't take more than a couple of days to get to St. Joe. What do you say we head on home to see Suzanne and the kids?"

Zane rested with his hands laced across his mid-section, tipped back on the hind legs of a chair parked outside the doorway of the Ramblers' Saloon. Tired from another bad night's sleep, he pulled his hat down to shade his eyes.

"Don't want to."

Kelly stopped walking. "Think you'll ever want to?"

Zane warded off the immediate sense of irritation Kelly stirred in him by bringing up such a notion.

Two weeks after arriving in Chicago, Zane's winnings at the poker tables kept stacking up. But despite their financial comfort, Kelly grew restless. Zane didn't mind moving on, but restless or not, he refused to go back home. Five years away seemed a long time, but it remained too bitterly short for Zane.

Kelly kept silent, waiting. Zane felt his brother watching him, as though staring him down would draw an answer out of him.

He sighed. "Hard saying. No one's stopping you if you want to go."

Kelly didn't respond. Zane didn't open his eyes or lift his hat. He didn't need to in order to tell Kelly bored a hole through him with that thundercloud look of his. By golly, he should've been a preacher. Kelly's look alone might scare young kids out of hell if his preaching didn't. Unfortunately, it didn't have the same affect on Zane. Not much did since the war. He'd seen hell already, and God hadn't done anything for the poor boys who suffered in it and died, even as they cried out to Him. And when Zane and Kelly cried out, their pa still died.

Zane had been doing battle with God ever since. Twice now, God scored against him. First with his pa, and then with his sweet mother. Kelly saw it that way too. But apparently Kelly hadn't figured out yet that if they went home now to see their sister Suzanne, it would likely just end up as another chance for God to strike them a blow.

Suddenly the chair flung out from beneath him, sending him down hard on his backside as the chair clattered on the planks. He yanked away his disheveled hat and clamored up from his sprawled position, scowling back at Kelly.

"What'd you do that for?" As if lack of sleep wasn't bad enough, now Kelly goaded him.

"I'm sick of sitting around day in and day out waiting on you, Zane!" Kelly's raised voice drew stares from passersby.

"I don't know what you're complaining about," he growled back. "We got money to eat with and a clean bed every night to sleep in, and you don't have to do nothing to get it."

He dusted off his hat and brushed a hand through his lank hair before he nestled it back on. He picked up the chair, scraping it back into place.

Kelly leapt toward him and shoved a finger in his face. "Don't talk to me about having to do nothing! If I didn't look after you, we'd be dead or in jail or just plain broke from your devilry!"

Zane fell back, struck silent for a moment. Then the fire kindling inside fell out of him and his eyelids drooped along with his voice. "And I ain't your babysitter either, so maybe you should just start earning your own keep and deciding for yourself where you want to go instead of expecting me to keep leading you along." He pushed past Kelly and stepped down off the boardwalk into the street.

*****

Zane sauntered up the street, looking as casual as ever, but Kelly recognized the kettle brewing beneath his brother's calm exterior. Several moments passed before he noticed his own fists clenched. The frustration still churned like hot steam inside him.

Well, what did he expect? He figured if he mentioned the idea of going to Missouri, Zane would choke. Kelly didn't even feel like going there himself until just lately. Though they swung by every major city west of the Mississippi since the war, and a few to the east, they studiously avoided their home state. Memories haunted too deeply. Going there again meant seeing blood on the fields and in the streets. It was possible they might never go home, and Zane would never be able to forget.

A flash of fresh anger rose up inside him. Well, so be it! It didn't mean he couldn't go himself and see the sister he hadn't visited in nearly six years! He might just go ahead and let Zane wallow here in his own misery.

He stepped down off the boardwalk and started up the street after him. Zane's long strides already covered a good distance, but Kelly's limbs were even longer. He'd just catch up and let Zane know he was taking his share of the money and going home, like it or not.

He picked up his pace, walking right down the middle of the street, side-stepping puddles and jumping out of the way of the occasional horse or buggy. Up ahead, Zane took the bend toward their hotel. Yeah, Zane would hole up there until evening, sleeping or fuming, until the sun set and the raucous call of the saloons beckoned him. By then, Kelly might already be on a train.

And the trains -- that was another thing. Men laid track everywhere these days, north, south, east and west. There wasn't any place it wasn't aimed at touching. Sakes alive! Since last year it had been possible to ride clear across the continent! The two of them didn't need to keep living like they were. They could get jobs with the railroads any day. They could make honest money, and then maybe hard work would help them move beyond the pain of the past.

Kelly slowed as he lunged back up onto the boardwalk and took the corner, excusing himself to a group of church ladies walking by. They must've just come from the church across the street. Was it really Sunday? Must be. Kelly glanced over at the white-steepled structure and winced at a twinge of sorrow or guilt or some other kind of gut-wrenching he couldn't exactly put his finger on, then pushed the feeling away. His pace slowed as he stared at the place, unable to draw his eyes away.

A preacher stood out front, shaking the hands of his congregation as they emerged in small groups and slowly scattered. And just that quickly, all Kelly's energy and defiance toward Zane dissipated along with the Sunday crowd.

Pulling away his gaze, he kept back on course toward the hotel. But the effect of the past moments was complete. He already knew once he got to the hotel he'd not say anything to Zane, and he wouldn't be leaving his stubborn, broken brother behind after all.

Chapter Four

The bed jiggled and Kelly sensed Zane's movements even before he opened his eyes. About now his brother was tugging on his boots. Then he stood, offering stillness, but Kelly heard him buckling his belt, getting ready to head out someplace, so he finally pried one eye open. The day must be really late, because Zane never woke up until close to noon. He would play cards until the saloon closed up, then he'd wander sleeplessly or try to go to bed and toss for several hours more. Zane often wasn't able to fall asleep at all until the sun began to peek above the skirt of the horizon. By then he would tumble into bed exhausted, possibly drunk, but hopefully dreamless. Unless Kelly found his own late-night entertainment, he usually had his breakfast done and the morning paper read before Zane saw the light of mid-day. Maybe Kelly might even have had a pleasant stroll in a park, making the acquaintance of some lovely ladies. So, for Zane to be up before him, it must be late indeed.

"What time is it?" Kelly murmured.

"A little past eight. Go back to sleep if you want."

Kelly blinked, ungluing his eyelids a little more. "Did you say eight? As in eight a.m.?" He shrugged onto his side and saw Zane running a comb through the strawberry-blond hair that had grown out past his collar.

"Yeah. Breakfast time."

"Couldn't sleep?"

"Slept okay," he answered, but shadowy rings under Zane's eyes told Kelly it wasn't true.

"Hold up and I'll join you." Kelly stretched his legs over the side of the bed, "If that's all right."

"Sure. Let's go."

Less than half an hour later, not yet nine o'clock, the Beaumont boys ate platefuls of bacon and eggs and fried potatoes at the nearest diner. Zane hadn't said anything about the previous day, so Kelly decided to go straight at it.

"Sorry about knocking you out of that chair yesterday. Guess my foot was just a little itchy."

"Both feet more likely." Zane gave Kelly a grin that let him know all was forgiven.

"So, anyway, I've been thinking. I don't suppose it was a very good idea about going to St. Joe. It would be... you know... difficult still."

Zane nodded, glanced out the window.

"Just thought I'd let you know." Kelly mashed some more of the eggs into his mouth.

"I've been thinking about that too," said Zane, almost startling Kelly. "You know, I'm just not ready." His voice sounded thick, and the words clearly forced. Zane never really talked about his struggle, he simply dealt with it in his own way.

"Yeah. Me either."

"Maybe someday. Maybe just to see ma's tombstone. It wasn't up when we left."

"Suzanne will be taking good care of her resting place."

"We can count on Suzanne."

"Sure."

They continued their breakfast in silence for a while then Zane spoke up. "I got up early because I wanted to do some thinking about things. I wondered what you might think of heading up north a ways, into Wisconsin. I hear it looks a little like home the way home used to be."

Kelly nodded, taking a slosh of milk. "I hear some parts are like that."

"Gets cold up there."

"I heard that, too."

"Maybe we could find us a little town to rest up in for a while."

Kelly locked eyes with Zane. "And?"

"Maybe you could find something to put your hand to. You know," Zane grinned wickedly, "to keep you out of mischief."

"I was thinking about a job. I think I need to do something."

"Maybe you'll find somebody's chickens to butcher, or a cow to milk or something. I hear tell there're lots of cows in Wisconsin."

Kelly laughed and flicked a piece of potato at Zane which hit his shirt front. Zane laughed and flicked it back, and they fell back into their meal.

"So you're feeling like putting your hand to some real work. Next thing I know you'll want to take up your old habits."

Kelly stilled and looked straight into Zane's soul. "No," he said softly. "I don't think I'll ever be in that place again."

"No... I reckon you won't."

They finished eating, their conversation going on to other things. Then they paid their bill and headed back in the direction of the hotel.

Kelly kicked at a rock. "Should we find out when the next train leaves?"

"If you're ready."

"I've been ready for days, brother. I've been that ready."

By mid-day they'd bathed, packed their bags, and purchased their tickets. The next train left at 3:00, so they wouldn't have to spend another night in Chicago.

"I should get up early more often." Zane tucked his bag into the seat next to Kelly. "A person can get a lot done in a day this way."

"Now don't start saying things you'll never likely do."

A sense of adventure washed over Kelly like clean water in a bath. He and Zane had been traveling a long time, but it had been quite a spell since he'd felt this way about moving on. He credited it to the idea that they might be sitting still for a while, and probably, too, because he was thinking about finding some gainful employment, something he could put his mind and heart into for a while. It didn't matter if he washed dishes or laid track, or even milked a Wisconsin dairy cow. Maybe the work, the steadiness, would help him to settle some of own demons, finally.

*****

Zane looked out the window at the streams of people moving up and down the boarding platform. Tearful partings, well-wishers, passengers of every ilk stepped up the narrow metal stairs onto the train. He cottoned to the idea of getting clear of the crowds again. Chicago was no place to stay for too long. He was likely to get into trouble if he did.

Maybe this trip north would be just the thing for both of them. Kelly would benefit from the change. For Zane it might be another matter.

He didn't know how long Kelly would stick to the notion of work. After living life on the edge for so long, it was hard to imagine the drudgery of routine holding onto his strapping younger brother. But who could tell?

A lot of wilderness shrouded Wisconsin. Maybe the two of them would get back to their country roots. They could do some fishing and camping. Perhaps even a little hunting if they stayed until fall. They hadn't done those things in years, not since before the war when toting a gun felt good, and lying all night on the ground was something you did because you wanted to. If a thunderstorm came you covered your head, but you didn't hear cannon fire, and when the lightning flashed it didn't make you think of rockets or the flash of fire in the pan.

People said the rivers and lakes in Wisconsin led from the heart of the country into the rest of the world. What Wisconsin didn't touch by train it definitely touched by water. He saw folks building homes out in Nebraska with lumber from Wisconsin. The very shipyards here in Chicago stacked with acres of pine boards likely swelled to size because of trees up north.

"I can't wait to see some of those trees." He spoke just barely loud enough for Kelly to hear him.

Kelly gave him a bemused glance. "Yeah. There are lots of trees there."

Shortly after pulling out of the city, Zane fell asleep. He slept deep, soundly. A couple of times he vaguely felt someone touching his chin. Kelly. Some inward voice finding its way through his muddle of unconsciousness told him he must be snoring. He knew it was true when he finally woke up and saw Kelly looking at him with a humorous smile, and he tasted the sour dryness in his mouth. Zane rubbed his hands over his face, scratching at the red sparkle of day old stubble on his jaw. Then he pulled himself up and glanced around.

He looked to his left, across the aisle, just in time to see a pair of brilliant blue eyes avert themselves from a perusal of their own.

*****

Lainey didn't know where to focus her attention after the man across the aisle caught her watching him. She glanced at the back of the seat ahead of her, and then her eyes flicked past her seat mate Stephen to catch a glimpse out the window. The other man, too, the big blonde on the other side of the sleeping fellow, caught her looking and grinned at her unabashedly. She wished, not for the first time, that she had her cousin Ginny's dark, native complexion so that she could hide the blush creeping up her pale throat and cheeks. Try as she might, there seemed to be no place to direct her eyes, and they kept flitting back at the passengers next to her across the aisle.

Finally, feeling awkward and ridiculous, she offered what she hoped was a mere neighborly smile, convinced that these were the same men who'd offered her the apple dumpling dessert in the café a week ago. As she tipped her head in a brief nod and smiled benignly, the man with the silvery blue eyes propped them a little wider.

So, he remembered as well.

Lainey tried, then, to go about her own business, leaning over to ask Stephen if he had finished with the newspaper. She planned to read every last article and editorial, hoping it would swallow away the miles and help her avoid strangers who might be more than willing to make conversation.

As had happened so often during their weeks of travel, Lainey's past experiences crashed into her thoughts, and like it or not, she thought about Jed. Still sorry for how things wound up between them, she'd begun to get over her anger. The hurt, though, was different. It was much more difficult to bandage her lacerated pride over being cast aside, not by one man, but by two. And a second rejection on top of the pain of losing the one she truly, unreservedly loved to an untimely accident in the woods still stung.

As the train chugged along and the forests and fields blurred by, Lainey clearly recalled Bobby Braeden's endearing face, the lines around his mouth when it widened into a smile able to sweep her breath away and send her heart skittering out of time. She tried vainly to focus on the words in the paper, but instead she kept seeing Bobby flipping back the brown lock of hair that tumbled over his hazel eyes. She could hear him saying her name, the way he said it, melting her heart.

Tightness squeezed the air from her throat and she closed her eyes against the memories, but still it was almost as though she could feel his hand falling over hers, calloused and warm.

"Excuse me, Miss."

Lainey jerked her eyelids open, jarring her body rigid and pulling her hand into her lap where it crushed the newspaper.

She stared first at her hand, then at the man across the aisle who'd touched it with his own. Her heart pounded and she caught her breath.

"I'm sorry. I didn't mean to frighten you. You dropped this." The man with the strawberry blond hair and silvery eyes held her small reticule in his hand and offered it to her.

"Oh... Thank you," she stammered. "I didn't realize I'd dropped it." She took her purse and looped the strings over her wrist. She made a commotion of organizing the disarrayed newspaper while Stephen tried to help and the stranger looked on.

"I didn't wake you, did I? I apologize if I did." He spoke with a pleasant southerly accent.

"No, not at all. I was merely... thinking."

He stretched out his hand. "I'm sorry. My name is Zane. Zane Beaumont."

She glanced at Stephen and then quickly back at Zane. "I'm Lainey. This is Stephen." She made it a point not to offer their last names.

Zane Beaumont stretched further and grasped Stephen's hand. "A pleasure."

Katie and Grayson, sitting in the seat ahead of them, turned around to see who spoke.

"So it is the same foursome we met in the café last week," said Zane. "Allow me to introduce my brother Kelly." Kelly Beaumont stretched out his hand to shake Lainey's and Stephen's and Gray's. He couldn't reach Katie's, but nodded.

"I'm Grayson Kade. Folks call me Gray. This is my cousin Katie."

"Katie..." prompted Zane.

"Katie Gilbert," she said, beaming and totally ignoring the wide-eyed hint Lainey tried sending her to not be so gullible.

"Ah, Gilbert." Zane scrutinized Lainey with his cloudless eyes.

"Yes. I'm Lainey Gilbert," she said quickly before the others interrupted. She caught the quick exchange of looks between Katie and Stephen, and Gray's questioning gaze settled on her, but none of them contradicted her.

"I see." The way Zane said it sounded as though maybe he really did see.

"So, Mr. Beaumont," she said, bracing up, not caring which Mr. Beaumont she addressed, "will you be traveling all the way to Fort Howard?"

"It's possible." Kelly's blue eyes danced in his handsome face. "We haven't seen Wisconsin, and it remains open as to what places we might want to visit now that we've finally come here."

"You travel often?"

"You could say so," Zane said, still studying her, with only a brief gaze at Stephen. He was obviously trying to gauge their relationship. Were they husband and wife? Brother and sister? It piqued Lainey's humor to realize he puzzled over it, and she favored this more-than-adequate entertainment for their journey. She settled back to enjoy the conversation and do some investigative questioning of her own to turn the attention away from herself and her companions.

"Then you're salesmen perhaps?"

"No. How about you, sir?" Zane looked away to Stephen.

"I'm a logger. We're from Wisconsin. On our way home now."

"Then you live in the town you mentioned? Fort Howard?"

"No. We're from the Chippewa country on the western side of the state. We're just enjoying a little tour before we return." Stephen patted Lainey's knee. "Lainey, dear, if the porter comes along, stop him, will you?"

Lainey smiled inside. Ah! Stephen was onto her charade and could be trusted to play along. Katie's dark eyes darted between them and she turned and whispered softly to Grayson. His head nodded slightly.

Gray would think she was crazy for putting on such a show, but she didn't care. He'd go along, just because she was older and, he'd wish, wiser.

The fellow, Zane, leaned a little further away when he heard Stephen's term of endearment, and the other man, Kelly, made some quiet remark in his ear that Lainey couldn't discern.

She pushed on. "Have you gentlemen ever engaged in logging?"

"No. It's not the sort of work we've ever done," said Kelly. "We have tried mining, though."

"Really? Mining for lead? Iron?"

"Gold," said Zane. "Out in California."

"Don't forget about that bit we tried out in Dakota Territory."

"We didn't stay long enough to count the mining there."

"No, you're right," said Kelly. "Not to mention that the Indians in those parts are none too friendly to the miners or nearly anybody else."

Lainey quirked a brow, wondering if they were being honest. Stephen spoke up. "So you gents mined for gold. Find any?"

Zane's gray eyes took on a level, almost steely look when he spoke to Stephen. "Not in the mines." Lainey waited for something more, but the two simply held one another's gazes.

"Can you elaborate?" She waved her fingers as he looked back at her. "I'm sorry. I have no business asking. Never mind."

A lazy smile lifted one corner of Zane Beaumont's face, and Lainey wondered how he could be so bold in his obvious interest considering that she was pretending Stephen to be more than a friend or relative.

"I won my share," he drawled. "Playing cards, mostly. And some I got as pay doing other honest work."

She wanted to pull back her gaze as any lady might at his confession, but truth be told, Lainey wasn't that dainty of mind. If he intended to impress or shock her, she wasn't going to give him the satisfaction of either.

"So you're good at it then, Mr. Beaumont? Playing cards I mean."

"Passing good."

"And what is it that you do, Mr. Beaumont?" Lainey asked Kelly. "Are you a card player, as well? That is, if you don't mind my asking."

"No ma'am. You can ask, and no, I'm not much of a gambler. I've tried it. I'm just not good at it."

"So you've been traveling for quite some time then by this means?" asked Gray, and Lainey smiled at her brother's intuitiveness.

"Quite some," said Kelly.

"The world's an interesting place, Miss Gilbert. My brother and I want to see all we can of it while the opportunities afford themselves."

She didn't correct him on his use of the term "Miss", but pretended she didn't notice. "Well," she said, tiring of the game, "I hope you enjoy our fair state. We haven't any gold to mine here, though you may find your pleasure at cards when the boys come into the towns on a Saturday night."

"I'm sure that Wisconsin will keep us fully delighted by all it has to offer." The expression Zane wore when he spoke said more than mere words.

Lainey turned aside and pretended to look out the window, signaling that their conversation was at a close, and thankfully, the Beaumont brothers kept to themselves.

Stephen leaned close. "Do you want to explain some of that to me?"

"I think you understand enough already."

He shrugged slightly. "They seemed harmless enough."

"They always do Stephen. That's the problem. At first... they always do."

Chapter Five

They spent the night in a Milwaukee hotel. Grayson asked the girls if they wanted to stay for another day or two and see the sights, tempting them with descriptions from Colette about the wonderful German architecture in the growing city. But Katie deferred to Lainey, and Lainey had had enough of cities. She wanted to go north, to have a closer look at the Lake Michigan shoreline and see the much heralded Green Bay. If she'd only thought sooner of it, she might have spoken to her parents about sending her from Fort Howard by steamer across Lake Michigan to spend a year with her aunt Annie in Michigan. It was too late for that now. But maybe next summer, if she still felt so unsettled, perhaps then she would suggest it.

"Let's not go directly to Fort Howard, though," she said, bringing a light to Katie's eyes. Let's stop in Sheboygan. We can go swimming in Lake Michigan. It might be our only chance. We can picnic like we did in the Dells, and I can draw some pictures. It will be relaxing, I promise."

"That sounds like a great idea." Grayson looked at Stephen. "What do you think?"

"We may as well. It'll be a full day by coach to get there, and we'll want to rest up anyway." He gave them a conciliatory smile. "It's your trip, ladies. Let's do it your way."

Katie cheered, and she and Lainey fell into a quick embrace.

They left Milwaukee later that morning and arrived in Sheboygan in the afternoon. The blossoming city offered them more than pleasant accommodations after their trip. They took rooms in the elegant Sheboygan House where they rested and decided on events for the coming days. An evening stroll after dinner helped settle their stomachs and gave opportunity to plan a picnic on the white, sandy shores of the lake the next day. As dusk covered the town and the girls settled in their room for the evening, Gray and Stephen knocked on their door to let them know that they were going out for a while.

"Don't be too late. We've got a big day tomorrow, and we don't want you two just lying about on a blanket on the beach behaving like complete loafers," Lainey scolded.

"Only an hour or two," said Gray.

Lainey grazed him with a warning look. "Promise?"

"He promises," said Stephen. "Don't worry. I'll look after us both."

"That's what worries me."

Lainey watched for their return, peeking out the door every now and then as she heard someone on the stairs, but it was three hours before they returned. Tempted to chide them for the lateness of the hour, she quietly closed the door and breathed a sigh of relief instead.

She found the men up and ready when she tapped on their door the next morning. "Well, I'm impressed. I didn't actually expect to see you two awake and alert. I'd planned to pounce on the bed and shake you out of it. Now you've ruined my fun."

Gray laughed and pecked her on the cheek while he buttoned the cuffs of his shirt. "So, are you girls ready to go on a picnic?"

"No breakfast first?"

"Of course. But after that, we're off."

"What about lunch? We have to buy some provisions for the picnic. I'm sorry we didn't get a start on it yesterday."

"No problem. We have it all taken care of." Grayson's eyes sparkled.

Lainey raised her brows. "Is that so?"

"Oh no!" Katie slipped in behind Lainey and threw her hands up in dismay. "Don't tell me! They're planning to catch fish for our lunch. We'll starve," she moaned, plopping onto the bed beside Stephen.

He laughed and put an arm around his sister. "Now, Katie. Why would you think that? It doesn't show a great deal of confidence in our angling ability, now, does it? But before you protest any louder," he placed a finger on her pouting lips, "rest assured, we are not planning to catch our dinner. No, ma'am, we have lunch well in hand."

"What is it?"

Gray and Stephen cast each other a conspiratorial glance. "Well... that does remain a bit of a mystery." He rose as he spoke and picked up the blanket one of them had folded and lain on the corner of the bed. He tucked it beneath his arm and led the way to the door.

Gray followed, but both girls stayed put. Lainey's hands went to her hips, and Katie's arms folded across her chest.

"So you don't have anything planned... really," said Lainey.

"Yes and... no," said Gray. "We've left that matter to the friends who'll be joining us."

Lainey dropped her hands and frowned. "What friends?" Skepticism swelled in her chest. She didn't like unknowns, and she liked less the feeling that Stephen and Gray were up to something. Just the way that they were handling the picnic now, with their secrets and smugness, told her that she wouldn't like whatever it was they'd planned.

"Just those two fellows we met on the train coming from Chicago, the Beaumonts. You remember them, Kelly and his brother Zane?"

Katie clasped her hands in pleasant surprise, but a growing annoyance straightened Lainey's spine. The last thing she needed was to have the peace and tranquility of her day ruined by those interlopers, those gamblers. Strangers they didn't even know!

Yet, she tamped down the protest threatening to erupt. "They're here? I thought they were going further. Where did you see them?"

"We were just watching Zane win a few hands last night, that's all."

Lainey shot a withering look at Gray. "You were in a saloon last night?"

"Well where else would I go after dark?" He glowered at her, unhappy to have her mothering him.

She reproved Stephen with another look. "You're supposed to be the older, more mature of the two of you."

Stephen approached her slowly and reached for her elbows, but she yanked them away. He abandoned his gentle effort at appeasement. "Lainey, it wasn't like that, and you know it. Gray didn't drink and neither did I."

"It's not a place for either of you."

"Don't be such a scold," he said, his voice souring.

Lainey felt as if he'd dashed frigid water into her face. A scold. Another appellation to add to the growing list. First they called her a shrew and now a scold. It was as if, despite her desire to forget the past she ran from, she remained doomed to flounder in it and become everything her tormentors named her: a scornful, hateful, embittered old maid. A carper. A biddy. Anyone who made the mistake of thinking they wanted her companionship would find out her character, and they'd cast her off for the ill-tempered woman she was. They'd grow tired of her strong will and bossy tirades just as Jed and Owen had.

Tears lodged in her throat.

Even Stephen and Gray. I'll turn them all away.

She looked at her feet, waiting for the clenching grip around her throat to subside before she whispered. "I'm sorry, Stephen. I know you wouldn't drink." She lifted her eyes to his and then to Grayson who stared at her. "You, too, Gray. I'm sorry I treated you like you were Kent's age. You're both grown men... I..."

Grayson reached over and grabbed her hand. "Aw, don't worry about it. C'mon. Let's go."

Katie looped her arm through Lainey's and they followed the men from the room to collect the girls' bonnets and some items from their own room. "It'll be fun," Katie said. "If you don't want to talk to them, you don't have to. Just leave them to me."

Lainey smiled ruefully at Katie and pressed her shoulder against her cousin's. "I'll try to be nice. I promise."

*****

Lainey stretched her legs off the blanket onto the warm sand, tugging her skirts down over them. She shielded her eyes with her hand and looked out into the gently rolling surf where Grayson and Stephen and the two Beaumonts laughed and dove, their voices muted by the rushing wash of the Lake Michigan surf against the shore.

"They seem very nice," said Katie. "Don't you think?"

Lainey dropped her hand and looked at Katie, then reached for a pickle. She shrugged. "I suppose they are."

"The tall blonde has a nice smile."

Lainey didn't respond. How could she without getting caught up in Katie's hopeful evaluations?

Katie was watching the swimmers, too, as Lainey crunched on the pickle. "Zane seems like he's trying to have fun, but it isn't as easy. He's..."

Lainey brushed her hands together. "What?"

"Oh, he's handsome too."

"That's not what you were going to say."

"He has stormy eyes."

"What does that mean?"

Katie swung onto her side, cradling her head in her hand. "His eyes change like the water."

"Explain what you mean."

"You know, the way the water can look clean and clear, or like slate when the weather turns. Remember the day it rained in Chicago, and the way the water on the lake looked so mysterious and violent the evening before?"

Lainey nodded. "I see what you mean."

"But Kelly's eyes always look clear and blue, just like this day."

Lainey rolled her eyes and swatted Katie's arm out from under her. "You're a romantic."

"Well, it never hurts."

Lainey looked back out at the swimmers. She said nothing to Katie, but her heart answered. *Yes, it hurts, Katie. It really does.*

*****

Zane sluiced water off his arms. The wind kicked the sand against his wet calves as he shuffled up the beach toward the women on the blanket. He shook his head, spraying water out of his hair, and pushed it back from his sunburned face. Several feet away from them, he stopped.

He bent, reaching for a towel. "Have you had enough to eat?"

"Yes." Lainey barely glanced at him. "We're quite satisfied."

"What did you call those sausages again?" asked Katie.

"I was told they're called bratwurst. The German immigrants make them."

"They were wonderful. I hope we'll get them in Eau Claire sometime."

Zane folded his legs under him, dropping comfortably into the sand. "In due course, you probably will."

"You'll have to go back in to clean off," said Lainey.

Zane tried not to study her as he answered that he didn't mind, though the temptation to stare had been with him all day. She was bewitching, this Lainey Gilbert who pretended to be married to dark and handsome Stephen. But if Stephen was her husband, why had he gone out and left her alone last night? No man in his right mind would do so with a girl like this black-haired siren waiting for him. Her vivid blue eyes reflected the blue green of the water. If he believed in myths and fairy tales, he would say she was a mermaid, come from the depths of the Green Bay itself.

She'd given up holding her bonnet in place against the shore wind, and now it sat on the blanket with a rock settled on its rim, just like the other girl's. Barely bound, her silky black hair tumbled about her neck and shoulder line in a drooping bun, and tendrils of it clung to her neck and forehead as she perspired in the sun.

The sun had kissed the paleness away from the bridge of her nose and cheekbones, and they would be tender tonight from the sun, just like his own.

The temptation pulled at him to reach out and touch her long fingers, or draw them to his lips as some women liked. But an inner warning told him that this one would not, so he denied such urges as they arose.

"You should try the water," he said, admiring the idea of seeing her lift the edges of her skirt to wade ankle deep in the surf, her bare toes wiggling in the wet sand beneath her.

She leaned back on her hands and smiled, a little twist in her expression as though she considered it. "I'm afraid, Mr. Beaumont, that if I were to go in, I might not want to come out again."

"There's plenty of the day left."

Her gaze fascinated him, made him wonder what she was thinking and what she would say. What came out next surprised him.

"I wonder if you would teach me to play cards."

He gaped then chuckled when she lifted a brow and smiled.

"Really? What sort of cards?"

"The sort you play best."

Challenge sparkled in her blue-eyed gaze.

"Why should a lady wish to play poker? It isn't normally done in polite society, though my understanding of Wisconsin womanhood is... uncultivated."

"I have three brothers, Mr. Beaumont. I would like nothing better than to be able to challenge them in a friendly game when I return home, and to shock them with my skill."

He laughed again and she joined him, though not robustly. Yet, the sound of even her small chortle thrilled him with anticipation.

"And what of your Stephen? He would not be opposed to your learning such an art form?"

Her dark brows lifted, two perfectly etched lines above her eyes. "I should hardly think he would care."

Zane tried not to let his expression show that he'd realized her series of blunders. Three brothers. And Stephen shouldn't care?

He watched her for a long moment, noticed the way she stiffened her back in pride when challenged about Stephen. Slowly the dare drifted from her expression.

"I would gladly teach you to play -- and even to win -- but I have one condition." He paused dramatically. "You must stop calling me Mr. Beaumont. My name is Zane."

"All right. If you insist. I wouldn't want to miss out on such an opportunity because of formality."

"Nor would I. So -- Mrs. Gilbert--"

"Lainey." She swallowed, and he focused for a moment on the movement of her throat. "I would prefer it if you called me Lainey."

"Lainey," he said, finding pleasure in saying her name, and in knowing how closely he'd come to flushing her out, "are you sure you're up to the challenge?"

She sat up straighter and looked dead into his eyes as she began unfastening and pulling off her shoes.

"I'll let you be the judge of that." She jumped up on the blanket and, hiking her skirt well up past her ankles, ran down the beach and into the water, stumbling and running forward until it caught at her legs and she tumbled in.

For a moment he couldn't believe his eyes. Then Zane laughed and clapped and whistled across the sandy expanse.

Katie perched to her knees. "I don't believe she did that! But then, I don't know why not!"

Zane laughed louder, wondering only slightly at Katie Gilbert's comment as he lifted himself out of the sand and ran down to the shore in Lainey's wake.

Diving in the cold water a second time after being wet earlier, shocked him. But Zane ignored the icy grip of the deep lake as he stroked hard and fast to catch up to the girl. How she kept going in those long skirts, he didn't know, but he believed that it involved a distinct lack of petticoats. Finally he approached her, standing in shoulder deep water with the others, her gay voice laughing as she splashed at Grayson Kade.

"I knew you'd come in," he caught Gray saying. "What took you so long?"

"I had to get warm enough."

"Sure. Well, I'm ready to get out."

"Go ahead. It looks like Katie's thinking of getting her feet wet. She'd probably like some company."

They all turned their heads to watch Katie wading along in the water's edge, her sleeves pushed up past her elbows and the hem of her skirt dragging in the surf. They all looked except Zane, and Kelly quickly brought his eyes back to the bathing beauty in their midst as well.

Gray decided to head in toward shore, and the others splashed about a while longer. Finally, tired and chilled, Stephen suggested they head in. They all turned to follow him, but after a few strokes, Zane noticed Lainey wasn't beside them.

A moment of worry ripped at his chest, and he turned around to help her, but she wasn't there. He looked about and finally spotted her more than thirty yards away, heading into deeper water.

Lainey? Her name washed silently off his lips. "Lainey!"

She didn't look back, but kept up her long steady strokes. The others stopped and looked behind. Then, as one, Zane, Kelly, and Stephen turned about to follow her, pausing occasionally to tread water and call her name.

"Where's she going?" Kelly hollered out.

"Who knows, probably to Michigan!" Stephen's answer came as nothing less than a growl, and Zane wondered why this man who pretended to be her husband didn't sound more concerned.

"Lainey! Come back! We're all getting cold."

A buoy rocked in the distance, and Zane wondered if that wasn't her goal. He swam forward with Kelly close behind and gaining.

"What's she doing?" Apparently Kelly wasn't satisfied with Stephen's previous answer.

"Heading for the buoy, I think." Zane grimaced, fatigued to be talking while he swam. If weariness dogged him, how tired must a woman in a sodden skirt feel? She may be enjoying herself, but any moment now her energy might deplete, and worse, she could get caught in a riptide.

"I'll catch her," said Kelly, and with stronger strokes, he pulled ahead. Zane pressed on more slowly, and Stephen fell even further behind.

"She'll be okay," Stephen called. "She's the best swimmer in the family!"

Zane grimaced again. "I'll bet she is," he said, but not so Stephen heard.

The next time Zane lifted his head, she hung onto the buoy with Kelly beside her, and they were talking calmly when Zane swam up to them.

She smiled triumphantly, not looking at all like she'd just swum a quarter of mile with a dress wrapped around her legs. "Ready to head back?"

Zane gripped the buoy's edge and Kelly steadied him. He spoke between ragged breaths. "Is all this just to say that you're up to my offer?"

"It may be, though not necessarily."

"As I thought."

Kelly looked between them with a special penetrating look reserved just for Zane. "I can't wait to hear what this is all about."

"Let's go," said Lainey. "It's a wonderful day for swimming!" And before Zane could say anything she plunged away from them toward shore.

Chapter Six

Kelly could tell Lainey's tenacious spirit impressed Zane, despite his brother's surprise. And though his elder brother appeared somewhat annoyed at having to chase the woman out into the dangerous water, it impressed Kelly as so like something Zane might have done that he figured Zane wouldn't hold onto any irritation. His older brother meant something behind those words about a challenge, and it intrigued Kelly to know what it was.

He left Zane at the buoy, still catching his breath, and pulled up in strong strokes beside Lainey. If he didn't know better, he'd think she was actually racing him. Though fatigue was starting to slow her down, she didn't stop to tread water until they reached a place shallow enough to stand in. Then he could see that she was almost out of breath. Her chest rose and fell in quick time, and she'd lost her bun completely so that her black hair ran in literal rivers down her back.

Kelly admired the way her flowered blue and white dress clung in all the appropriate places, and when he reached out and took her arm to assist her, she didn't resist.

"You're quite a swimmer. Can't say as I ever met a gal who could swim so well."

He caught the satisfaction in her quick glance as they treaded up onto the sand. Most women would have lounged beneath a parasol all day, trying to look cool and calm, daring the wind to touch one crimp of their hair. But this woman -- this woman defied everything Kelly presumed women to be -- delicate, predictable, needy. And to top it off, she appeared more stunning the way she looked now than any belle he'd ever seen twirling across a ballroom floor.

"I didn't grow up in a large town." She drew away from him to find her own balance. "I'm a country girl, and my brothers and I had to make our fun where we could find it. If I couldn't keep up with them swimming in the creek or climbing trees or hunting squirrels, then I'd be left behind."

"I see. No girls to play with?"

She shook her head. "Not many. Just Katie and her cousin Ginny. But I didn't see them every day. My brothers, on the other hand, were always around."

Her smile and jeweled blue gaze wound their way through him, stirring crazy thoughts. "So may I ask about this challenge my brother spoke of?"

"He's going to teach me to play cards."

Kelly did a double take, looking at her, and she slowed her walk.

"Are you sure you want him to do that?"

"Of course. I think it will be fun. Do you play, Mr. Beaumont?"

Kelly glanced behind and saw Zane making his way into the shallows and trudging toward shore. Up ahead were the others. Kelly wished he could get her to stop, right here, and maybe take a longer walk with him up the beach, just to be alone with her. But she was probably more tired than she looked, and besides, her husband kept his eye on them.

He intended to do one thing, though.

He touched her shoulder and she stopped for a moment at his touch. "You have to call me Kelly. I'm far too young to be Mr. Beaumont to anyone except Sunday school children."

She seemed to consider that. "All right," she said finally. "And you may call me Lainey. But then, you already have." Her smile caused his chest to swell. She stepped forward again, but stumbled on the wet, sand-laden hem of her dress. His hand shot out to hers. She blushed and kept going, but he still had her hand. So what if Stephen Gilbert and her brother Gray watched his smart move. Even dark-eyed Katie bored a hole through them that reeked of shock. He was stronger than either of the two men, for sure. If Stephen wanted to challenge him, he had his excuses, and if those failed, he had muscle.

But Lainey deftly slid her hand from his, and so his imagination needed to spread no further.

Gray grinned wildly. "So, did you have fun?"

"You could have drowned!" shot Katie. "What were you thinking?"

Stephen said nothing, but warning flashed in his eyes. Still, to Kelly, it seemed gentle enough.

Katie began gathering up their things. "It was a good thing the boys were out there, in case anything might have happened."

"Oh, stop fussing." Lainey took the blanket that Stephen offered her to wrap in.

Kelly doubted that Lainey was cold, but she probably did perceive how she appeared in her wet clothes. Stephen, at least, cued in on it.

Zane came up then, seeming slightly winded, but no more worn out than Kelly felt. Kelly was fast and strong, built differently than Zane, but his older brother possessed a rock solid, lean prowess of his own.

Tall at just under six feet when he stopped growing, Zane had to watch Kelly shoot up and finally stall out nearly four inches past him. And Zane's long, wiry muscles rippled in the sun, but his shoulders didn't bunch in great knots the way Kelly's did.

Why Kelly sometimes caught himself making comparisons between him and Zane, he couldn't figure. No fierce competition ever existed between them. Squabbles were infrequent and seldom of importance. And in most things that mattered, they shared the same views. But Zane was two years older, and being the younger brother, Kelly sometimes couldn't avoid making comparisons over the years. Kelly admired nearly everything about Zane, and even when Zane made mistakes,

Kelly found it easy to forgive him and see him instead as a hero.

But at the moment, he found strangely, he couldn't read the expression registering on Zane's face. Was it chagrin, intrigue, or just plain weariness? With all they'd been through together, the war, the loss of their parents and some close friends, leaving home and traveling all over the country, the fights and scrapes, the drinking and women, Kelly could usually tell what was on Zane's mind. But not this time.

Was Zane thinking about Kelly's attempt to get closer to Lainey Gilbert? "Glad to see you made it back," he said smiling.

"And you." Zane looked first to Kelly, but more pointedly to Lainey.

"Thanks for going after her," Stephen said, his hands on his hips. He nodded at Kelly. "You're a stronger swimmer than I am."

"I've always been a bit of a bull. Just ask Zane."

Zane's smile lifted in a lopsided fashion. "I haven't challenged him since he was twelve."

"Well, it looks like we've eaten all your sausages," said Gray.

"Bratwurst," Katie corrected.

"That swimming will take its toll. I think we'll be hungry again in a couple of hours. Will you men think about joining us for dinner?"

"I know I will." Kelly's eyes kept pulling back to Lainey. He couldn't help watching her, his mind not releasing itself of expectations.

"That would be fine." Zane shook Gray's hand and then Stephen's. He turned to Lainey. "And I'll bring along the cards."

She smiled a purely mischievous smile encompassing both Zane and Kelly. "I can hardly wait."

There was a time when, looking at the face and form of a beautiful but married woman, Kelly Beaumont would have fought down the thoughts that skittered around his mind. But those days and those convictions no longer held much sway over him. They died with the idealistic young man he used to be before the war. Now he knew the truth. You might only live a little while on this earth, and even then your days could be filled with pain and sorrow. Best to take your pleasure where and when you could, and not to think about right, wrong, or consequences.

So as Lainey walked away, cocooned in the blanket with her brother on one side of her and her husband on the other, Kelly let those thoughts roam free.

*****

"She's not his wife."

Zane dropped the bombshell on Kelly later as they dressed for dinner. As he expected, the announcement gave Kelly considerable pause while he finished his toilet and turned from the mirror to peer at Zane.

"You're talking about Lainey?"

Zane stood up from the bed and tugged on his shirt sleeves, giving his brother a look that registered neither surprise nor question.

"Did she tell you that?"

"She didn't have to."

"Why do you conclude it?"

"It seems obvious." Zane adjusted his tie. "She makes her own decisions, never deferring to him. He's a little bit protective of her, but not in any husbandly way that I can tell. And she's made mistakes when she's spoken about herself."

"What sort of mistakes?" Kelly ran a comb through the bright blond hair that brushed against his collar.

Zane shrugged himself into a jacket. "Well, she doesn't seem quite comfortable with the title of Mrs., for one."

"How do you know that?"

Zane only looked at him.

"It doesn't seem like much to go on."

"I know a poor bluff when I see one. I'm telling you, Kell, she isn't married."

Kelly slipped on his jacket and reached for his hat. "I may have to test your theory."

Zane led him out the door. "Be my guest, but I thought you'd done that quite competently at the beach today."

*****

Lainey slipped her arm from Kelly Beaumont's and allowed him to pull out her chair at the table in the intimate, curtained, dining room. Then he sat to her right at the head of the table. She looked across the table where Zane pulled out his own chair after helping to seat Katie. He caught her eyes and she found his gaze unfathomable. He had that ability to mask his thoughts and emotions. She could see that, if nothing else.

She half jested when she mentioned the idea of learning to play cards. Now, knowing he would teach her, anticipation flitted like a kite tail on the wind inside her.

Who was Zane Beaumont, and what made his eyes look like clear water one minute, and dusky steel the next? No doubt, if he played his opponents with an expression as unreadable as the one he wore watching her now, he must be a gambler to contend with.

Their evening passed pleasantly enough. Several times throughout the meal Lainey had to remind herself to behave as though she were Stephen's wife. He'd been gracious enough to keep playing along, but she wondered how long she would have to keep up the charade. Surely, only another day or two. They would be on their way to Green Bay, and the Beaumonts would travel on elsewhere.

As dinner drew to a close, Katie admitted she was tired.

"We'll head up to our rooms." Gray stood to pull out her chair.

Lainey brushed an imaginary crumb off her skirt. "I'm not tired. I'd rather hoped to see if I might be much of a student at cards." She turned to Stephen. "You don't mind, do you?"

"I'll stay with you, if you really mean to learn."

"You can stay if you like." Zane's intrusion into their discussion sounded conciliatory. "But I promise that your, um, wife... is completely safe with me. We won't leave this room. You've my word as a gentleman."

Stephen hesitated and Lainey took his hand, applying light pressure. "Really, Stephen, I won't be able to concentrate if I'm being watched. Go ahead. I'll be up in a while."

She watched him vacillate between responsibility and the force of her will, and finally he conceded.

He leaned in close to her ear. "I don't like to leave you."

She turned him aside. "Please go, Stephen."

"What are you doing, Lainey?"

"Breaking the rules."

"You're up to something."

Her ire rose to a simmer. "No I'm not. And I'm not romantically interested in either of these men if that's what you think. But they seem willing enough to entertain, and that is something I do desire."

"I'll just wait outside."

"Go to bed, Stephen. Katie's ready to drop, and Gray too. I'll be fine."

Stephen grazed the Beaumonts with one more glance. "What about Kelly? Is he staying too?"

She turned toward Zane. "Will your brother be staying?"

"Not unless you wish it."

"I'm a little nervous about being watched while I learn."

Her eyes fell and Kelly stepped forward. "I don't often stick around for long when Zane plays, though I'd much prefer to tonight. But if it makes you uncomfortable, I'll head off too."

"You don't mind?" He softened at her gaze. She liked Kelly. She didn't want to use her charm on him this way, but it was working.

"I'll see you tomorrow," he said, and made it sound like a promise.

When the others had gone, Lainey sat back down and waited for Zane to address her. For a long while he shuffled cards and said nothing at all. Then he stopped, cut the deck, and began to deal. When he finished and they both picked up their cards, he stared at her long and hard. She waited for him to speak. He didn't even blink. She finally dropped her gaze and squirmed beneath his silent examination.

"Are we going to play?" Her voice sounded breathy and slight in her ears.

He lifted a one-sided smile at her, and his eyes slipped into a dreamy gaze. "Sure we are. The first thing you need to learn, Lainey, is that you should never let someone disconcert you the way I just did. If you can hold steady under scrutiny, then you're a long way towards a better bluff than your opponent."

She took a deep breath. "I see."

"You understand that half of the game is the ability to bluff and to read your opponent."

She nodded.

"I don't know if you do."

Something in his tone pulled at her. "I think I do."

"But you're not a very good bluffer."

"I've not had the chance--"

"Haven't you?" He leaned forward on his elbows and perused her face so closely that her skin felt hot. She pressed back in her chair and frowned.

"You're not married, are you? Stephen isn't your husband. He isn't even your betrothed."

Lainey's mouth fell open and snapped closed again.

Zane smiled. "I thought not."

What was the point in arguing? He'd found her out. "How did you know?"

"As I said, you don't bluff as well as you think, but I can help you with that." His steady smile finally reached his eyes. They were clear again and sparkling and Lainey had the distinct feeling that she'd crossed onto more dangerous ground.

But she liked it.

"All right, Zane. Then teach me how to bluff."

*****

Her heart was far from mending. But for the first time in many weeks, Lainey felt that she could replace it with something less fragile. She could pour something more vital and less susceptible to pathos into the gaping hole God carved inside her when He stripped her heart out. Lainey often thought about last June's conversation with her mother about God lying to her. She blamed Him for all her heartache as much as the mere human men who blundered in and out of her life. In fact, the more she analyzed it, the more the entire blame belonged on God. If only He hadn't taken Bobby...

She decided to fill her empty space with other things -- nothing that would torture her emotions, but instead replace them. The death-defying swim in Lake Michigan exhilarated her. Equally so, she delighted in the improprietous thrill she got playing cards with Zane.

After leaving Sheboygan, Zane and Kelly Beaumont tagged along to Fort Howard on the Fox River and Green Bay. Somehow, inadvertently, the Beaumonts became traveling companions to her party. For almost two weeks, Lainey remained Zane's diligent student, playing cards together every chance they got. Lainey's distraction bored Katie, but nevertheless, Lainey stuck to it. The other men eventually joined in, and pretty soon they spent their evenings playing for nickels and dimes, small stakes to Zane for certain. Sometimes Kelly stood behind her and offered his advice. He knew more about the game than he let on, but insisted he'd never been able to hold his own in a real high stakes game like Zane did.

Kelly liked her. Once the charade of her being married was dropped and they discovered she was really still Lainey Kade and not Lainey Gilbert, and that Stephen was really her cousin, Kelly made no pretense of shying away from his romantic interest. But one thing Lainey was very sure of, she wanted only to be friends. Besides, Lainey had a pretty good notion that any interest Kelly revealed was no more than drew him to any summer fling in any of the hundred other places he'd roamed.

In further fact, Lainey found herself liking both Beaumont brothers a great deal. They were becoming her friends, good friends, and she didn't want to jeopardize their relationship together by turning either of them into the next Owen Steckler or Jed Clark.

They were like her.

Zane and Kelly looked for fun and diversion, nothing more. They, too, were wandering, perhaps running from something. Though they hadn't said so, Lainey sensed it -- the kindred nature of their friendship.

When not practicing her card game or wandering idly about the town with her brother and cousins, she drew. Several sketches of her companions filled the pages of her sketchbook. Some portrayed them lounging on the lake shore, others playing cards. One she really loved depicted Grayson looking out over the bay, a wanderlust of his own shining in his deep brown eyes.

She drew ships at harbor, flatboats poling up and down the Fox, and just lately, a scene of men working in a lumberyard. It reminded her of home. She missed that sight, but not enough to return. She didn't know when or if she'd ever feel like going back. Yet, time was running short. September fast approached. Katie and Stephen started talking about the visit they anticipated with their grandparents in Grand Rapids. They intended on leaving in a day or two because the fall cutting season encroached, and Stephen and Gray would soon be needed at the mill.

Lainey set her pack of charcoal on the sketchbook to keep the pages from fluttering and leaned back against a tree where she watched the mill workers from afar. Her bosom lifted with a sigh.

"Excuse me."

She startled and turned swiftly at a stranger's voice behind her. He took his hat off his balding pate and stepped nearer, almost standing over her.

"I didn't mean to startle you, but I couldn't help noticing your work. I'm sorry. I was watching you from over there." He pointed to cluster of oak trees a few yards away. A friendly smile lit his face. "You've captured the scene very well."

He wore a suit and held a bowler hat in his hand. Fine beads of perspiration dotted his brow. He stretched out his hand. "My name is Arthur Frayman. I'm a newspaper man from New York."

She took his hand and shook it. "Pleased to meet you, Mr. Frayman."

"May I?" he asked, indicating the drawing pad beside her on the grass.

With only a moment's hesitation, Lainey handed him her sketches and he studied them. One by one he turned the pages, taking in much of what she'd done over the course of the summer. Finally, he flipped back to the one of the men at the mill.

"Would you be willing to sell this?" He handed it back to her and she looked from the drawing back to Arthur Frayman again.

"You want my drawing?"

"I work for a paper that will want it. I'm here doing stories about Wisconsin life. People out east want to know what it's really like before they let their sons and daughters come to the frontier. They want to see the lumber districts, the farms, the mining towns -- all of it. You have some other drawings there that interest me as well. Might you consider selling your work?"

Lainey held the drawing pad close and shrugged, but with the uncertainty of some new excitement. "I don't know. I suppose I would." She stood, Mr. Frayman offering her his hand.

"I think we can agree on a satisfactory compensation." He pulled a wallet from his pocket and began counting out bills. Lainey's eyes grew wide.

"Would fifteen dollars be enough for the first one, with the contingency that I get the first chance at any others you might wish to sell?"

Fifteen dollars? Lainey's heart began to throb. She fought to keep her voice steady.

"That would be more than sufficient. Would you like to take it with you now?"

"I need something to store it in safely. Tell me where I can find you later this afternoon."

Lainey thought quickly. "I could meet you at the café on Main Street at three o'clock if you like."

The round-faced gentleman smiled. "Perfect. I have a room near there." He handed her the money. "In good faith," he said, and they shook hands again.

"Thank you so much, Mr. Frayman."

"The pleasure is mine, Miss--"

"Kade. Lainey Kade."

He gave her a slight bow. "I'll look forward to seeing you at three o'clock."

Lainey returned his parting smile, pleasure filling her.

Her work, published in a New York paper! She hardly dared imagine it. As the man strolled away, Lainey's heart slowed its racing. She decided to hurry back and tell the others. She picked up her charcoal box and wound her way down the lane toward the hotel. Part way along the path she paused.

No. She'd not tell them yet. She would wait until after her meeting with Mr. Frayman.

By two-thirty the day had turned sultry. After a mid-day spent outdoors and a full evening with the Beaumonts planned ahead, the Kades and Gilberts decided to take the afternoon to rest. Katie wrote a letter to Ginny, and Stephen took a nap. Grayson announced news of an invitation to have lemonade at the home of a young woman he'd met clerking in one of the shops.

Lainey quirked a brow at her younger brother. "When did this happen?"

He smirked. "While all of you were otherwise occupied."

"What's her name?"

"Her name is Lucy. And she knows I won't be here much longer, but doesn't mind us having an afternoon together."

Lainey hummed. "Would you walk me to the café on Main Street if it isn't too far out of your way?"

"You're hungry?"

"No. I'm going to sit there and do some more drawing."

"All right. Let me get my hat."

An hour later Lainey pored comfortably over her drawings with Arthur Frayman. He bought three more, paying her ten dollars apiece. Lainey felt like a rich woman. Even more compellingly, he promised to contact her for more in the future.

"You may sign them if you wish," he added.

Lainey reached for a piece of the charcoal she kept wrapped in paper in her dress pocket. She poised to sign the first one, a sketch of a farm they'd passed south of the Black River just after leaving home, but hesitated. When the charcoal touched the paper instead of writing *Lainey Kade* as she had been about to, she put down *E. Eastman*.

"Eastman?"

"My full name is Elaina Eastman Kade, and I think I shall stick to this part of it for the drawings."

"I understand. Notoriety is sometimes difficult to deal with, and as a woman your work could be difficult to sell. Now if you'll give me an address where I can contact you again."

Lainey thought quickly. She liked Mr. Frayman. He seemed like an honest, kind man.

"Well, sir, at the moment I am also a visitor to Fort Howard. But if you will send anything to the post office here, I will be sure to leave an address where it can be forwarded."

His brows lifted, arching his forehead with lines. "May I ask where you are from?"

"I'm from the western side of the state, the Chippewa Valley area near Eau Claire. But I won't be returning there. In fact, I hope to stay here a while longer."

He smiled again. "Then I will send further requests to the post office as you suggest. Perhaps we'll be able to meet again, for I plan to be in this part of the state a while longer still." He rose and shook her hand. "It's been wonderful to meet you, Miss Eastman."

"You as well, Sir. Thank you."

He placed his bowler on his head and tugged on the rim. She watched him leave, her hand slipping to the folds of bills in her pocket. *Forty-five dollars.* She'd just made forty-five dollars with her drawings! She could live in Fort Howard for a long time on forty-five dollars.

Chapter Seven

Grayson stalked across the carpet in front of Lainey, his brows bent in two deep furrows and his jaw set in a way that made him look an awful lot like Pa when she sassed him. Stephen wore his "wait and see" expression, standing silently with his arms folded while Grayson had his say.

"Lainey, you've not been yourself for a long time now, but this beats all! You know I would support you in just about anything, but an unmarried woman living all alone in a strange town, how can I explain that to Ma and Pa?"

She rubbed her temple. "Stop shouting, Gray. You won't have to explain anything. I'll write them a letter and they'll understand."

"You don't honestly believe they'll be all right with this notion of yours?"

"I'm twenty years old. Ma was a mother by my age -- and living alone -- and traveling alone. She understands me better than you think."

"Yeah, and what about Pa? He'll feel compelled to come all the way across the state to bring you home because I couldn't, right at the start of the cutting season."

"No he won't. He'll let me make my way."

Grayson ceased his pacing to stare at her. "He holds me responsible, Lainey. You know it. He'll think I failed."

Stephen stepped forward. "Lainey, Gray has a point. And since I'm the oldest of this Kade-Gilbert clan, and I have a lot riding on this trip, you need to understand it from our side. I'd be a fool if I dared take this excursion too lightly. Your pa may call it a vacation for your benefit, but for Gray and me it's an extension of trust. Uncle Nase is looking toward growth and productivity for his company. He and my dad expect your brother and me to take our responsibilities seriously now. The chance to settle this little bit of business for Kade Logging in Chicago, and the duty laid on us to take good care of you and Katie on this trip is a step of faith in us." He stepped a little closer. "Why do you want to make our job difficult?"

Stephen's words crushed, but she pushed herself up from under their weight. He didn't mean to wound. He only wanted to shoulder his responsibility in a way that made her pa proud.

"That's right, Lainey," said Grayson. "Sometimes you just need to listen. You always keep your own counsel, but slight anybody else's. Katie might be impetuous and a little immature, but she's manageable."

Lainey cringed. Isn't that what Jed wanted her to be -- manageable? She ignored it. "Is that what you really think I mean to do, Stephen? Make your job difficult? If you understood my pa, you'd realize how well he knows both of us. He already trusts you and Gray. And he let me go on this trip because he knows I mean to get beyond the past. I can't do that in the Chippewa. And Pa doesn't expect you to manage me."

She threw a look at Grayson then stepped closer. She took his shoulders in her hands. Frustration vibrated through them and she squeezed gently. "You haven't failed, Gray. I have. I haven't been able to face the thought of going home again."

He rocked his head at his shorter, more stubborn sister. "I just don't get it. What could possibly keep you here?"

"Nothing."

"Then why stay?"

"No, Gray, I mean *nothing* is exactly what does keep me here. I don't have friends or obligations or any past to contend with. "

"And you hope you'll find your way into the future by closing yourself off to everyone?"

She shrugged as she turned away and took a few steps. Then she turned to face them again. "I don't really know about a future. I only know I don't want anything waiting from my past back home. Even in the unlikely event Jed would change his mind about me, I can't say I'd want to try again. I've come to face the truth that I gave my whole heart to Bobby, and there's nothing left of it for anyone else."

"I know you feel that way now, but--"

She held up her hand. "I know my mind on this. I'm just the woman they say I am, that even you think I am, and I don't want to go back there to hear it all again. I'm staying in Fort Howard."

"Lainey, I don't want you to take this wrong," said Stephen. "I'm proud of you and respect your backbone because you're as close to me as Katie is. But it makes me a little nervous when you get that challenging glint in your eyes like I've seen you have with the Beaumonts.

"If you're willing to let me speak plainly, I will. You can be a loose cannon sometimes. The fact that you're hurting -- probably more deeply than any of us know or can even understand -- makes me think you're willing to fire a little more easily. The way I see it, and the way I think your pa might see it, is that your fuse is short. It's short enough and frayed enough to ignite. It looks to me like its burning now. I don't know if I can stop you from making this decision. You're right, after all. You're old enough to know your mind. But it makes me wonder if you're headed toward an explosion."

Grayson stuck one hand on his hip and rubbed his brow with the other, but Stephen ignored him and went on.

"Lainey, we love you. But we all know when you ignite, there's no telling what you might do. I think we can even take Jed Clark's word on that."

She didn't say anything, but his gaze worked through her, allowing her time to consider his words. After a bit she shrugged her shoulders and forced a smile. "Then all I can ask for is your support. I guess I just don't want anyone to be caught in the fallout."

Stephen stared back at her for a long moment. Finally his gaze dropped and he gave a curt nod. The first bit of relief washed over Lainey.

A miserable sort of concession struggled on Gray's expression. "Fort Howard's so far away, Lainey. Why not come with us at least as far as Grand Rapids. You have roots there without the complications, and it isn't so far for me or Ma and Pa and Kent to see you sometimes."

He offered an idea worth considering, but she held back.

"I can't argue your point, but for some reason -- call it my stubborn will if you want -- I don't want to go there either." She looked to Stephen, but his eyes had lost their conviction and she forged ahead. "I don't want roots."

Grayson clutched both hands behind his neck and rolled his head back, moaning. "Lainey, you got no place to live! What'll you eat? What'll you do for money? Who'll take care of you? There are rowdies in this town, same as any lumber town. There are vagabonds and stragglers of all sorts. What'll folks take you for?"

Her brother's anguish nagged at her. She had to do something to make Gray comfortable with the idea. Stephen might be ready to concede, but not if Grayson got him worried.

"I have something to tell you."

His eyes opened even wider and he dropped his arms. "Something else? You're killing me!"

She opened the wardrobe and reached into the pocket of the dress hanging inside. Like a magician, she produced the roll of bills and held them up before their eyes. They narrowed.

"Where'd you get that?" Grayson's stare slid from the bills in her hand to her face. "Lainey, you haven't started playing cards..."

She rolled her eyes and slapped his arm. "Of course not." She handed the wad of cash to Stephen who counted it. "It's even better, but I want it to be a secret for now. You can tell Ma and Pa, but no one else yet." She sighed, drawing out his agony just a little longer.

"Well?"

She did a little dance and went to her sketchbook. "It's my drawings. I've sold four of them, and I'm likely to sell more."

"What?"

Thrilled by Gray's awe at her accomplishment, and by the appreciative look on Stephen's face she told them about the meeting with Arthur Frayman and his interest in her work. She told them about opportunities to do more drawings for his newspaper back east.

Grayson stared, wordless. She watched his dark eyes spark as he tried to understand all the implications of her plans and the sale of her drawings. She could live independently, at least for a while. Maybe it would provide her with the healing time she needed. Slowly she saw him not only concede, but become excited for her.

"What about Katie? She'll have the same questions."

She looked at Stephen. "Tell her later. There's no sense in upsetting her for the rest of the trip. When it comes time, just tell her it's all settled and figured out."

He nodded, his lips set in a straight line as he handed her back the cash.

Grayson's brown eyes narrowed again. "What about the Beaumonts?"

"What about them?"

"They haven't said anything about traveling on. They're getting to know you pretty well. Do you feel safe being left here with them, not knowing anyone else?"

Lainey hadn't given them much thought; that was true. She wandered back to the wardrobe and tucked the money away. Walking to a desk that sat beneath the window in her room, she pulled out the chair and sat down, drumming her fingers against the smooth wood.

Finally she shrugged again and looked between her brother and cousin. "I don't mistrust them. They've been gentlemanly in their conduct toward me so far. As it is, I think they'll remain my friends as long as they stick around."

Stephen's eyebrows twitched, but Grayson nodded, less reluctantly this time. "I think you're right." Then a slow smile stretched across his face, wiping the tension away. "I'm pretty sure, in fact, they'll be more than glad to hear you aren't leaving with us. Maybe Kelly will look after you as well as Stephen or I."

She blushed and *poohed* him with a wave of her hand. "Now don't go getting notions. You know what I said. I won't be risking those boys finding out what a dragon Lainey Kade is."

As much as she tried to joke, an uninvited emotion rose into her throat. Thankfully, Grayson stepped over and wrapped her in his arms, giving her time to swallow it away.

*****

In their home on the hill above the Chippewa, Manason and Colette stood close, reading Lainey's letter between them. Manason wrapped his arm more tightly around her, offering strength she needed.

"I couldn't make her come, even though I tried," Nase muttered, reading the final line of Gray's missive.

"What on earth is that girl thinking?" His hand went to his forehead as he dropped into the chair by the table, pulling Colette onto his lap. She laid her head against his shoulder.

"Oh, Nase. She's still hurting."

"But to stay in a foreign town alone?"

"It's still Wisconsin."

"She's never been there before. The place is full of strangers and foreigners and trouble-makers--"

"And churches and women and children and hard working men like you and the boys... and God."

He kissed her cheek and smiled. "Sorry for forgetting."

She sat up and looked into his eyes, still drawn to them after all the years. She stroked his bearded cheek. "We have to let her go, don't we?"

He sighed and nodded. A little chuckle escaped him. "To think what's come from her love of drawing."

"God's taking care of her."

"He is, isn't He?"

"She doesn't see it that way."

"She might."

Colette shook her head, sadness etching her brow. "No. If she did see it, she would be ready to come home. She'd trust Him with her heart."

He patted her shoulder and she stood to her feet, taking his hand. Nase leaned to blow out the lamp and let Colette lead him toward their room. "We'll just have to be thankful that she's safe."

"I wish there was something we could do."

He jolted to a stop, pulling her to a halt. He looked into her face. "Colette, what about that piece up near Marinette?"

"What are you talking about?"

"The land. Remember that piece you bought with Harris's money back in '59, the one up the Peshtigo?"

"What about it?"

"You said yourself that all the money you invested from Harris would be Elaina's dowry someday. Maybe she could use a little of that now."

Colette's blue eyes brightened and Manason squeezed her hand.

"What'll we do with it?"

"We won't do anything. But we'll tell her about it and about the other property that's to come to her too. She'll be twenty-one in a few months. If she needs something to do to keep her mind busy and to set her heart on, maybe it's about time we told her about this inheritance. She can do with it as she pleases."

Colette fell into Manason's arms and hugged him. She landed a kiss on his lips that grew long and loving.

Her breath whispered against his neck. "You are my hero."

"I always did like that you thought so. We'll write to her in the morning." He kissed Colette again and ushered her into their room, closing the door.

*****

Lainey sat in the shade on a small knoll wearing a navy blue swimming tunic and bloomers. She leaned her back against an oak tree and threw acorns into the current of the Fox River while Zane and Kelly whooped and splashed in the water. She glanced at the portrait in her lap of them acting like young boys instead of grown men, and she smiled. Glancing about, she spied more nuts.

"How's the drawing coming?" Kelly called.

Lainey scooped and emptied a fistful of acorns into her skirt beside the sketch pad. "I'm working hard."

Not too hard. The money she earned from Arthur Frayman would last a long time. Plus, he wrote again hoping to purchase a drawing of the new train track inching toward them from the south. Her memory quickly recollected the sights of men sweating in the sun while they drove spikes into rail ties, and she had no trouble reproducing a vivid depiction for him. Her untroubled lifestyle endured in the promise of income, just like the Beaumonts'.

Zane continued doing well enough at the card tables on Saturday nights, and Kelly talked about getting a job, but didn't seem in any hurry to do so when it took away from the carefree days the three of them spent together. Whatever skills he and Zane might have learned in the army, they kept to themselves. She wondered, but didn't pry. If they had any talents beyond those Zane taught her in cards, they decided not to use them, and she for one wouldn't be telling them to stop living for the joy of it.

She tossed a few more acorns, but they fell wide and the boys didn't notice. Then the sun brightened a subtle nuance of Zane's face and caught her eye, so she grabbed up her charcoal, deftly applying strokes to the image in her lap.

There now. Better.

The Beaumonts had such interesting faces. Untapped secrets lay behind the depthless blue of their eyes, things that happened to them during the war, perhaps, or in their travels. Things they didn't talk about.

She didn't care if they kept their past to themselves, just as they let her do with her own. She leaned over to reach for more acorns burrowed in the thick grass. She aimed for Kelly, but the acorn plopped well short. He grabbed it before it raced away in the current and threw it back at her, plunking it on the ground beside her. Kelly waited for her to throw it back, and he lunged into the water to catch it.

He still held her in a more than friendly regard, and at times she saw a glint of interest in Zane's unreadable gaze, too. But in as lighthearted fashion as she could, she made it clear she was through with romance and relationships without telling them any of the sordid details that brought her to this point. From that time on, they kept their insinuations to themselves and didn't press her for a more personal acquaintance.

One of her acorns finally came close enough to bounce off Zane's shoulder, and he stopped shaking the water from his hair to look over at her. A dangerous grin filled his face right up to his eyes. "You better watch it, Miss. You know how to swim well enough for me to risk tossing you in." He moved as if he might come after her, but she called his bluff and threw another acorn at him, missing him by a wide mark. He fell back into the water and laughed.

"You'd better watch yourself," she hollered. "I'm on to your bluffs."

"You think so, but I've still got ways of keeping you from reading my mind," he said.

Heat climbed up the back of her neck, headier than what the sun produced. A fire burned in her raging as red as autumn's crimson leaves filling out the trees around her. She liked solving Zane's bluffs just as well as she liked engaging Kelly's fun spirit.

Kelly had taken her for a late night of dancing. When all the polite girls went home, she stayed, laughing and swinging around the plank floor with him while his blue eyes danced before her.

She'd spent another long night with Zane, watching him play cards in a gambling house. She never thought to enter such an establishment before, never in her life. But she wanted to see him play the way he really played -- with winning intent, and for much more than her nickels and dimes. She wanted to feel the tension of the kind of game that sent fires burning in him.

He'd agreed to let her come.

No man she'd ever known would have let her do that without a fuss. But Zane saw she meant it when she said she wanted to see him play and, without her asking first, he invited her to come with him that Friday night.

He would let her go again if she wished it.

She didn't owe either of the Beaumonts any explanation for anything she chose to do, which was just the way she liked it. And they accepted her partaking in their schemes without comment. In fact, she looked forward to their next escapade together.

What was this thirsty fire burning inside her that only daring, risk, and adventure sated? Katie would never abide it, and Stephen would be troubled by some of her actions too. Gray might join her in the fun as soon as he realized he couldn't stop her.

What drove her to behave this way? She didn't know if it had a name, but as she brushed debris from her lap and rose to join the men in the water, she decided whatever this desire for risk, this desire to exchange one new adventure for another was called, it claimed her, and she wouldn't let it go.

*****

The swimming season ended after that. Autumn's chill descended, and they spent more time walking in the woods or sitting by the hearth. Lainey found a regular residence in a room owned by the butcher and his wife willing to take a dollar a week plus twenty cents a day for meals. Later, Lainey traded some of the price by helping the Mrs. with small tasks around the home and garden, which she didn't mind doing in the least. Helping out didn't take much of her time, and the kindly German couple didn't pry into her personal life.

Late one morning near the end of September Lainey stopped by the post and found a letter waiting from her parents. She strode out onto the boardwalk and ripped it open, mindless of passersby stepping around her as she walked slowly down the middle of the walk, reading.

She scanned the pages quickly, then went back and read them again.

And again.

An inheritance?

She stopped and stared hard at the words, wondering if she really understood. But it was explained quite plainly.

"*Your mother invested a small fortune during and shortly after the years she was married to your natural father. Much, though not all, of this investment was in forest land throughout the territory. After statehood, settlers began flooding into Wisconsin and, as you know, land values have been increasing ever since. Some of the land that your mother purchased, sight unseen of course, is not far from where you are. It's on a tributary of a river called the Peshtigo, near a place not far from Marinette, north of you. Nearly all the rest of the property she invested in is in or near villages on the Wisconsin, the bulk of it being near Bull Falls. I will look into it further if you like, but it is your land, Lainey, to do with as you wish. We would have waited for your birthday to tell you, but thought that now might be a better time...*"

She lifted her gaze from the pages and stared up the street. She owned an inheritance in the land. Something left from the father she never knew, who'd judged her mother wise enough to use his money as she saw fit. Like wings lifting her off the ground, she soared inside. First the sale of her pictures, and now this opportunity.

She might never marry, might never have a family of her own or the life that other women seemed to want. But if Lainey could never have forever with Bobby Braedon, she'd find other ways to pour zest into her life, other ways to feel *something*. And going to see this land and this place she'd never heard of before might just open up the doors to doing it.

Throwing caution and decorum to the wind, she ran up the street, her bonnet falling off and her hair tumbling down as she headed for the place she was sure to find Zane. He'd be sleeping in his room above the Buzz Saw Saloon.

*****

Since it was still only a little past ten in the morning, only three souls lingered in the saloon at the time, one of them the owner who stood behind the bar polishing glasses. Nevertheless, a young lady none of them knew, running through the barroom and up the stairs to the floor where all manner of worldly characters snored off their whiskey, drew their rapt attention. But Lainey paid them no mind. She knew which of the windows overlooking the main street belonged to Zane and Kelly.

Finding the door most likely to be his, she gave a few quick raps. When no one answered she pounded harder.

"Yeah." She had to press her ear against the wood to hear the muffled reply.

Opening the door a crack, she peered into the room. The window stood open and a breeze lifted the curtains, washing the room in a chilly but fresh scent of pine resin from a fresh layer of saw dust on the street below. Her eyes scanned quickly to the bed and took in the lump that must be Zane buried under a pillow and blankets.

She pushed the door open wider and let herself in. "Zane?"

The pillow flipped over and Zane's head sprung up at her voice. With his hair pushed all around his head, he squinted at her a bit bleary-eyed, but in a second his eyes opened wider.

"For heaven's sake, Lainey! Shut the door before somebody sees you in here!"

She closed the door behind her and strolled over to the side of his bed, beaming at his flustered look. He swung his legs over the side of the bed, keeping the blankets wrapped around them. He pushed a hand through his disheveled red-blond strands.

"What on earth are you doing here?"

A momentary chuckle rose to her lips to think about Zane worrying over her reputation. It wouldn't have surprised her so much had it been Kelly, but Zane? She grinned at him.

"I've come to get you out of bed. I have news and I'm bursting to tell you about it."

"Well let me get my pants on."

She hesitated a second and he stared at her. Then, grinning broadly and biting her tongue about having lived with three brothers all her life, she turned away and moved to look out the window. She heard him jump to his feet and scramble into decency.

"Seen Kelly?" he asked.

"No. Not yet. He always gets up earlier than you, doesn't he?"

"He has a hard time sleeping in." He still didn't give her permission to turn around.

"You're opposites in lots of ways."

"I don't sleep at night. He doesn't sleep once the sun comes up. That's about it."

She shook her head, uncertain if he watched her. "No, there are lots of things. Kelly's..."

"Kelly's what?"

She turned around. Zane wore a pair of denim pants. His hair was combed and he stood there buttoning up the final buttons on his shirt. A two-day growth of red beard made him look ruddy. Suddenly Lainey realized she really was alone in a room with man who wasn't her brother. A handsome man who felt dangerous and compelling.

"Happier, I think."

"Kelly has his demons, same as me. He's just possessed by them differently."

"Why do you say that?"

"Call it something in our natures." He walked over to the pitcher and basin on the washstand and filled the bowl. Rolling up his sleeves, he splashed water over his face and dried on a towel.

She watched the process just as she'd seen her father and brothers and uncles and cousins do a hundred times. But something in Zane's movements belied a difference. The way his jaw worked, the lazy gaze of his gray eyes when he looked at her, the movement of the muscles in his forearms just doing this simple task of washing his face.

She pulled her perusal away forcibly, but she didn't blush. "I'd like to hear more about your family sometime, if you want to talk about them."

Zane stilled. Holding the towel, he looked hard at her. He started to open his mouth, to say something. Pain flashed for a moment in his eyes, turning them to pewter.

"Did I hear Kelly say something once about a sister?"

The pain in his gaze ebbed away, but she could tell that thoughts haunted him. She had no right to crowd in on them any more than she would want him crowding in on hers, but she didn't withdraw the question.

He nodded. "We have an older sister. Suzanne. She's married and lives in St. Joseph, Missouri with her three children and husband who's a doctor."

"Is St. Joseph your home too?"

He threw the towel onto a chair and unrolled his sleeves. "Used to be. I don't have any desire to make it so again."

She understood the look in his face as he said it. She felt it as well.

"What about Kelly?"

"Kelly would like to see Suzanne. But as for St. Joe, he feels about like the place as I do."

She nodded, his emotions driving deep inside her. He didn't want to go home. Neither did Kelly. Neither did she.

"Now what did you come bursting in here to tell me? A lady doesn't just saunter through a saloon and into a man's bedroom without something important to say."

"You speak from experience," she said, grinning.

His eyes lighted and he smiled dreamily, but didn't acknowledge her remark. She noticed that when he smiled, deep lines dented his cheeks and defined his jaw.

"Well," she said, clearing her throat, trying not to waste time noticing such things, "Neither you nor Kelly nor I have to think about returning to our homes for a while longer."

He sat down on the edge of the bed crossing his arms over his chest. "And why is that?"

"Because we have a new adventure ahead of us." She flourished the letter before him. "It appears that I am a land owner."

He frowned, waiting for her explanation.

"I just received this letter from my parents who've informed me that before I was born my mother claimed a piece of property north of here, not far, and it now belongs to me. I suggest that the three of us go up there and see what it looks like."

"The three of us?"

She nodded.

"Why me or Kelly?"

"Well you can't expect me to travel alone, unprotected."

"I hardly imagine that your folks would consider my brother or me to be proper chaperones. Probably the opposite, in fact."

"I'm not asking for their opinion. And no one in the Peshtigo country knows you're not qualified to chaperone me either."

"Oh, that game again." His voice dropped a notch while his eyes gleamed at her.

She warmed. "Well, I hadn't exactly thought of *that*."

"Come here." He patted the bed next to him.

She drew back, hesitated, and then boldly sat beside him.

He turned to face her, his arms still crossed tightly in front of him. "What do you want to do with this land?"

"I don't know. I don't know what it's like. It's probably woods. Most of the properties the cruisers locate for the mill owners are heavily wooded. But it could be property that my mother expected to be platted for towns someday. Either way it's probably worth a handsome bit of cash. Doesn't that interest you?"

He held her gaze for a long moment. "Why should it?"

She stammered, glancing at her hands in her lap. "I... I don't know. I just hoped maybe, since we've been having such fun, you and Kelly might..."

He picked up her chin. "Stop worrying. Of course we'll come with you. We've nothing better to do."

Suddenly the door swung open and Kelly stepped into the room. Zane dropped his hand and Lainey stood up quickly. Kelly stopped mid-stride, regarding them both.

"Lainey, what are you doing here?" Obviously filled with the same shocking thoughts as Zane's earlier ones, he frowned at her, and he threw Zane a speculative look.

"Kelly, I'm glad you've come." She sounded excited and breathy, even to her own ears. But wasn't her news plenty to be excited about?

"Lainey's getting big ideas in her head, Kell. She's come over because she couldn't wait to tell us about them."

Kelly's shoulders drop a fraction. In relief perhaps? Why else did he think she'd come? What did he imagine that she and Zane were doing, sitting so closely together on the bed, his hand cradling her face?

Quickly, she explained everything about the land to Kelly.

He tossed his hat into the chair where Zane's towel had landed earlier. "I thought you wanted to stay here for the winter."

"I did, but not now that I've found out this news. Now I want to go see the land, see what might become of it. What's the difference if I stay in Fort Howard or in some other town up north?"

"None, I guess. Zane?"

"I told her we'd go along. She can hardly travel up there into that country alone. She'll need protection."

Kelly looked between them again. "You're sure about this, Lainey?"

"Never been surer." She stepped closer to him and put a hand on his arm. "Will you come with me? Both of you?"

He covered her hand with his. "We've followed you this far. What's another forty miles or so?"

She sighed and spun around. "Then let's go today."

"Let's go before folks wonder what's going on up in this room," said Zane.

Kelly cast Zane another look. "That's the best idea you've had in two days."

Chapter Eight

Kelly shouldered his way between two big horses, tightening the saddle on a bay. A third horse stood on the other side, tied to the hitching post.

Zane stood on the boardwalk watching him. "Where'd you get them?"

"Leased them from a big Norwegian. Said he'd collect them again before the snow flies. Gets up toward Peshtigo pretty often I guess."

Kelly patted the whither of the bay and stepped up by Zane. He brushed his hands against his pants and pulled out his wallet. He sifted through it taking a cursory look at the thin stash of bills remaining. "Took a bit of dough. Gonna need replenishing when we get there."

Since the start of the fall logging season and harvest, more men disappeared into the woods or back to their farms. Others joined the push to get clearing done on the railroad line planned to link Fort Howard to Marinette. They only drifted back to carouse on the weekends. Most of the money Zane made off them he won on Saturday night. And sometimes he lost. It was the way of things.

"Still figuring on looking for a job?"

Kelly returned the wallet and put his hands on his hips. "Figure I'll be bored and broke if I don't. One's bad enough. I was going to ask the Norwegian for a job, but I reckon there'll be horses to work with in Peshtigo just as well."

"You still have a way with them. I don't suppose you'll have any trouble."

"I kind of miss it sometimes."

Zane's eyes pinched and he snorted. "Army life?"

"Nah. Just the feeling of a strong horse beneath me. Never thought a day would come when I didn't have a couple of them nickering in my ear at the end of a hard day, grateful when I gave 'em a handful of oats. Always made me happy when they survived a battle."

An odd mixture of joy and melancholy flushed through him at the memory. In a way, those army horses were his comrades, along with the soldiers who fought and died beside him. God had put a few different callings on Kelly's life, and taking care of horses, managing them, training them, was the only one left he believed he could still answer to.

His job tending horses during his time of service in the Union Army was the one thing about the war that didn't put him off.

"Think Lainey knows how to ride?" Zane asked.

"She says she does. My first impulse is not to doubt her. But I reckon we'll find out soon enough,"

Zane chuckled and shrugged. "She's kept up with us in everything else. Remember those three brothers she has back home."

Kelly laughed. Whenever they raised a brow at something she wanted to do, she reminded them she had three brothers to contend with back in the Chippewa.

"Let's hope she isn't stretching the truth about that. Forty miles is a long stretch in a saddle, and she is a woman after all."

Kelly threw him a sideways glance and a grin shot out at Zane. "That's one thing you don't have to remind me of."

He reflected on the nature of that woman for a while. No denying it, his first instincts and thoughts about Lainey Kade had been totally carnal. There wasn't much left of him that was pure since the war took its toll, and long years had passed since any conviction ruled him against finding his pleasure where he could. But she never returned any of his overtures toward her. Instead, she made it clear they were to be friends. But getting to know Lainey had begun doing strange things to the heart he'd thought shattered long ago. He let her in. He felt something stronger than anything else he'd experienced in his adult life. Sakes, the last time he thought he'd been in love was when he was fifteen! And that didn't even compare to the strength of sentiment that prickled inside him concerning Lainey.

He and Zane gathered up their bedrolls and bags and started strapping them onto the horses. Kelly thought about how he'd found her with Zane an hour earlier. He loved Zane. It was the one true thing he knew. But seeing the two of them sitting so closely together, and with Zane's hand on her skin, such an intimate gesture and look on both their faces, tore a hot streak of jealousy through Kelly he had to squash like the pain of loss as bad as the one he'd experienced during battle. Straining to keep his voice even, he pretended like it didn't bother him. He had no right, after all. Lainey wasn't his, and didn't intimate that she might become so. But she wasn't Zane's either.

Kelly glanced over the horse at Zane as he yanked on a strap securing his bedroll. Doubtless, Zane's thoughts about Lainey weren't far from what his own had been when they first met. Zane, too, found solace from dreams and memories and his own self-destructing anguish in cards, in whiskey, and in women. Lainey turned both their heads. If not for the fact that, after Lainey left their room, Zane reassured Kelly nothing was going on between the two of them, Kelly didn't know what he would've done. He loved Zane, and he trusted his word. Zane could see how smitten Kelly was.

"All set?"

Kelly nodded. "Let's go fetch her."

The biggest fact remained. Lainey never showed a romantic interest in either of them. Kelly only hoped that over the coming winter, maybe he could figure out why. Maybe he could get close enough to Lainey for her to share her secrets and hurts. The Lord alone knew that Kelly wanted to help her get over them.

*****

Bedrolls and baggage packed and tied down, Lainey, Kelly, and Zane rode north out of Fort Howard on the narrow, pitted wagon road. At least it wasn't springtime. They made their way along on dry ground. The abundance of autumn foliage whispering around them, and the sun dappling their shoulders through the branches of the trees brought a welcome sense of peacefulness to their journey.

They rode three abreast, with Lainey in the middle. They met a salesman, several loggers, and some farmers traveling along the way. One man hauled a wagon load of milk and cheese from one of the dairies springing up all over Green Bay. At certain points along the road they heard the ring of hammers striking steel and the muffled shouts of work crews some distance through the woods.

"It doesn't sound like a logging crew," Lainey said.

Zane gave a nod. "Railroaders."

"Oh, I suppose it is. They said there was going to be a new branch of the Chicago and Northwestern Railway connecting Fort Howard to Marinette inside of two years." Her notions began firing up. Kelly saw them in her eyes. "By then the line to Milwaukee will be completed, and folks all the way to upper Michigan will be connected by rail to Chicago and the rest of the world. Imagine what my property will be worth if I hold onto it until then."

Kelly leaned on the pommel of his saddle. "But what'll you do in the meantime, Lainey? It's none of our business where your money comes from, but how will you get by?"

She offered him a sly smile. "I have my means."

Kelly figured it to mean that her parents sent her money. Well, that was okay too. He was glad she had parents alive who cared enough to provide for her. There were plenty of times he missed his own parents. Why regret anything that Lainey's could do for her?

"I'll tell you about it sometime, maybe."

Zane smirked. "So long as I don't see you at the card tables on Saturday night, trying to bleed me dry."

"I can assure you that my means come from much more respectable sources."

Zane said nothing, and Kelly looked over to see her instant remorse. "I didn't mean it like that, Zane."

"No hurt feelings," he said.

"Truth is, if it wouldn't completely ruin my reputation, I just might try my hand at it."

"You stick to back room games with Kell and me... and maybe an occasional visit to watch me win." He grinned and leaned down out of his saddle to pluck a piece of timothy shooting up beside the road and stuck it between his teeth.

"Well, not that either of you gold diggers care, but I plan to find me an honest job when we get to this Peshtigo place that I can hardly find on a map," said Kelly.

"Oh?" Lainey leaned toward him, her gaze curious. "Do tell."

"I'm going to see about finding a job that will keep me from doing so much walking. I missed having all this horse flesh under me, and I think it's time I got back to what I'm good at."

"You worked with horses?"

"All my life, but more so during the war. It was my job."

"What about you, Zane? What did you do during the war?"

Zane spit out the grass. "Whatever they asked me to." The tone of his voice clearly closed the door to further investigation.

Kelly wasn't sure why Zane didn't want to talk about it. It wasn't as though Zane's job building railroads had anything to do with his ma and pa dying, or of any of the other bloody sights Zane witnessed back then. Perhaps Zane just no longer wanted to touch or speak of anything that had to do with his memories of war. For not the first time, Kelly thought about what a shame it was. Zane had both talent and skill when it came to railroading. He could be out there in the woods now, telling all those men what to do and how to do it right. He could've had any job anywhere in the country these last five years since the railroads started spreading like deep veins across the country, bringing life blood to every branch and limb of it.

Instead, Zane gambled and ran from the past and the pain. Just like Kelly did.

Dusk fell around them after many hours, and Kelly finally said they had to stop and let the horses rest for the night. He'd expected Lainey might complain of soreness by now, but other than a few adjustments in her saddle now and then, she never grumbled.

They found a place a few dozen yards off the trail to set up camp. It looked like a well-used spot. Remnants of a recently used fire pit and packed down earth made it clear that others stopped here frequently.

"Look at that, Zane, there're still coals under the ash." Kelly stirred around the pit with a stick, livening up the coals and adding some twigs and small branches. In only seconds, a small blaze erupted.

Lainey unbuckled her saddlebags. "I bought some rolls and dried beef for our supper."

"How come you didn't think of that?" asked Kelly as he glanced over at Zane pulling his bedroll down off his horse.

"Thought you were going to shoot us a squirrel or something."

"Don't have but two bullets. What if I missed?"

Zane smiled and laid his bedroll out on the ground. He glanced up at Lainey. "Where do you want me to put yours?"

"I'll take care of it."

"You fix us supper, woman," he growled then gave her a playful smile before stepping around her horse to undo her bedroll anyway.

"I'll fix you. That's what I'll do." She pulled out a chunk of jerked beef for each of them along with two soft rolls each, wrapped up in a piece of cloth. She watched as he spread her blanket out by the fire, angled away from the smoke which the wind wound toward them. Then he went back to his horse and took off the saddle and bags. Zane did the same to hers as Kelly began to ready his own spot near the fire then followed to settle his horse.

In a few minutes they camped around the friendly blaze, eating beef and rolls, and drinking from their canteens.

"There's a path that goes off that way." Kelly nodded toward the thicker trees. "Probably leads to a spring. Pretty popular place to camp, looks like. We can fill our canteens there in the morning, I bet."

Zane stared into the fire, his eyes unreadable. Kelly turned to Lainey. "Tired?"

"Mm-hm."

Her blue eyes looked dark and shining in the rising moonlight, her hair more ebony than the night. She'd pulled it loose and he'd seen her brushing it, then braiding it into a long smooth rope down her back. As much as part of him wished to be beside her, the other part of him liked being across the fire where his gazes could swallow her in long, relishing draughts.

"We may have to get used to camping out. Who knows if we'll find lodging when we get there."

She shrugged. "Always a possibility. But I reckon there'll be somebody willing to put us up if we pay them."

"They'll put you up anyway."

She smiled back at him, and her white teeth appeared luminous in the firelight, her lips soft and warm.

He glanced at Zane who stared quietly into the fire. Zane hated night. He'd try to sleep, but Kelly knew that once both he and Lainey had drifted off, Zane would be awake or up completely, fighting the dreams away until exhaustion swept over him.

"I think I'll go to sleep," she said, curling onto her side.

Only then did Zane look her way. "Good night, Lainey."

"Good night, Zane. Good night, Kelly."

"Good night," said Kelly.

*****

Zane listened to the wind hissing in the trees. Dawn crept up like that sometimes, causing a stir, waking the first of the birds. His eyelids drooped leadenly, and finally he slept.

And he dreamed.

Only this time -- finally, this time -- he didn't see blood or hear the screams and cries of men dying. He wasn't walking about without arms, or talking to someone with his face blown apart, words coming from a wide hole where the soldier's mouth should have been. This time he dreamed of Lainey. She ran along the banks of a river. It looked like the Fox. Giant pines hugged the edges with their roots dipping thirstily down over the banks. Water rushed like laughter over the rocks, and it mingled with the sound of Lainey's laugh.

Her hair flowed long and loose, and she started to pull it up, but Zane reached out a hand and told her to leave it, and she did. Her eyes shone brighter than the sky, deeper too. Her hands, long and white, crept around his neck and pulled him to her.

Her lips touched his, warm and soft.

"Lainey." He drank in her name with the taste of her.

"Lainey." Kelly's voice broke through the dream, calling him out of it.

Zane opened his eyes and rubbed a hand across his face.

"Lainey, I'm hanging the canteen on your saddle horn."

Kelly was up and so was she. The sun was near the tree tops.

She came to stand over him. "Hey, sleepyhead."

He sat up and flipped back the wool blanket, still trying to separate the reality of her from the dream. She squatted down beside him and held out an apple. Even now, with the dream still so close, he was ready to reach for her. He took the apple instead.

"Eat your breakfast. Then we have to go."

"Do I have time to wash my face?"

She pointed down the path. "Creek is that way. There's a pretty little spring feeding into it."

Zane wandered off into the woods.

Thankfully, the night had been free of the other dreams, but this one was just as real, and in its way, just as awful. He knew full well that Kelly was taken with Lainey, even if she didn't seem to feel the same way about him. But she might, given time. She didn't seem to be any more drawn to Zane; that was for sure.

If he didn't miss his guess, she'd been hurt in the past, maybe taken advantage of in some way. She was too pretty a gal not to have had a gaggle of men hound-dogging after her, especially in this Wisconsin country where men outnumbered eligible girls three or four to one. But all of her behavior told him something had happened. And now, unless Kelly could win her over, she planned to remain friends.

He wished Kelly luck. At least, he hoped he did. He hoped something happened this winter, because he didn't know if he could keep being haunted by dreams like that without doing something about them -- something unwelcome by both her and his brother.

*****

Clouds bound the sky from end to end when they rode through the bustling lumber town of Oconto and several other small communities, and finally found their way into Peshtigo City a little past supper time. They rode slowly, tired and saddle sore, up to the steps of the first inn they saw to seek lodging. Seeing as it was still early in the week, they found rooms in the Forest House available. Lainey spent her first two hours in Peshtigo taking a hot bath and resting her sore muscles. Kelly and Zane offered to brush down and bed her horse at the stables down the street, making her grateful at the moment she was a girl.

When she saw them later, however, they looked like they'd had time to clean up and rest a little too. The threesome ate dinner there at the inn not far from the river which wound through town, cutting it in two. Then they all retired early.

The next day Lainey rose promptly to find out about the location of her property. She expected they'd have to ride up to Marinette another half dozen miles or so away to locate it, but discovered instead the location of her land was not far from Peshtigo. It was only a couple of miles away in the area the locals called the Upper Sugar Bush. The man at the Peshtigo company office explained how to get there, knowing the area well, and easily recognizing the section she spoke of by the land description she gave him from her pa.

He pointed to it on his map. "Only about eighty acres. But a nicer little eighty you couldn't ask for. I've got a daughter and son-in-law who live out on a farm that way. Could make out real good on the lumber to be taken there. Soil's good too."

She asked him more about the town.

"Planning to settle out on that eighty?"

She smiled. "Well, I do plan to stay awhile and see what else Peshtigo has to offer."

He proceeded to fill her head with information about his fair and thriving town, and about the opportunities it afforded young people starting out.

When she left, Lainey's gaze roamed, taking in Peshtigo as a whole while she strolled back to tell Zane and Kelly, noticing the particular things the clerk had told her about the town.

Lots of lumber there? Why, the whole town was swallowed in pine land! There wasn't a road not shadowed by trees, and the town itself edged right up against the forest. Sawdust padded the streets six inches deep, and the sounds filling the town told of people making a living off the trees. No matter where she walked she could hear some of the ninety-seven saws at the Peshtigo mills, or the pounding and lashing and splitting of wood coming from the woodenware factory where two hundred men and boys turned out tubs, pails, broom handles, clothespins, and barrel heads.

She saw one man splitting shingles right in his back yard. He'd probably fill a wagon and haul them to Green Bay. Eventually he'd earn enough to buy a cow, and then a farm. Pretty soon he'd be a man of means. She could hear the whir of machinery coming from the foundry on one side of town, and from the sash, door, and blind factory if she walked to another side. Even the sound of plates clattering beyond windows bespoke of the men going to and coming from work in the woods. Delicious breakfast smells wafted from folks' kitchens, especially the kitchen of the big company boarding house where men gushed out, going to their work and eyeing her speculatively as she passed by.

She was nearly back to the hotel when she ran into Kelly. She gave an enthusiastic description of what she'd been told.

"So what'll you do, have it logged?"

"I might. It'll have to be cleared sometime, either to make way for the town to grow or for farming. Seems like the logical thing."

"So you're to be a lumber baroness then." He gave her a wink and a grin. "All those big lumbermen better watch their step." He tipped his head in an indication for her to follow him.

"I hardly think so, but for a while it'll be enough to keep me in the manner to which I've become accustomed, I should think."

"I should think so."

She put her arm through his. "Where are we going?"

"I want to take you for a walk, show you something."

They turned up another sawdust road and walked about three blocks. They crossed a wooden bridge spanning the rippling Peshtigo River, and came out close to the clamor she'd been hearing earlier. They turned onto a side street and stopped in front of a livery stable belonging to the Peshtigo Company.

The Peshtigo Company owned the nearby woodenware factory, the sash factory, the largest of the area's sawmills, a machine shop, a company store, and the big boarding house she'd passed earlier.

Kelly looked down at Lainey. "I got a job."

"What? Already?"

"Yeah." He beamed. "Right here. I'm going to be a teamster for the Peshtigo Company. What do you think?"

"Kell! I'm glad! When do you start?"

"Later today. First I have to head over to the store and get some work gear."

Lainey hugged him and he pulled her close for a moment. She backed carefully out of his arms.

His eyes clouded over when he looked at her. "Trouble is I'll be gone a lot."

She nodded. "I suppose so. But you'll be able to come to town on Saturday like the other fellows usually do."

He grinned. "And maybe steal a dance with a pretty girl."

"Maybe. What do you think Zane will say?"

Kelly shrugged. "He won't be surprised. We've talked the idea over."

"He'll miss you."

Kelly turned her by the arm and they walked along the street in the direction of the company store.

"You'll keep an eye on Zane for me, won't you?"

"I don't think he needs me to."

Kelly stared ahead. The clouds of the previous day had dropped a little bit of rain during the night, just enough to keep the dust down, and now the clear blue of the sky reflected in his gaze. "But it would be better for me to know he isn't alone all the time."

Lainey felt a growing puzzlement. "Why do you worry about Zane?"

He glanced quickly at her. "You won't tell him I said anything, will you Lainey?"

"Course not."

"Zane has had a lot of trouble since the war ended. We both have dreams sometimes." He paused then went on. "His are worse than mine. Sometimes they get so bad that he can hardly function for three days afterward. He doesn't sleep. He gets in a foul temper. Sometimes he sees things."

"What do you mean?"

"Like dreams, only he's awake." He looked at her and sighed. "Memories so vivid..."

"Kelly, I didn't know."

A small sigh slipped past his lips. "Course you didn't. I never expected you would. He'd be ashamed if he thought you knew."

"He sleeps a lot during the day."

Kelly nodded. "Has to. He has to wait until he's wrecked with exhaustion."

"What about you, Kell? You said both of you have dreams."

"Mine aren't so bad. I can cope. At least that's the way it is now. A few years ago it was a lot tougher. I think I'm starting to forget." He looked at her, closely. "I'm starting to heal."

"All because of the war?"

"That's about it. Do you know what it was like in Missouri during those years? Missouri was a border state. That meant we were a shredded state, a state torn by conflicting loyalties. In St. Joe there were riots, murders, martial law that was just as bad as no law. The battles..." He choked and tears glistened in his eyes. He blinked hard and she dropped her gaze.

"I'm so sorry, Kelly. I was pretty young. I never thought about what it was like for the soldiers who were off fighting, much less for those fighting their own neighbors."

"Zane fought in the same battle that killed our pa. He saw him cut down, and there was nothing he could do to save him. It about tore him apart. I think that's the dream that bedevils him the worst. He still sees our pa bleeding out his life, and all he can do is stand over him and cry out his name.

"Our mother never recovered from the ordeal either. She got sick and grew weaker and weaker toward the end of the war. Every time we saw her she'd wasted away a little bit more.

"My sister Suzanne carried a heavy share of that load. By the time Zane and I came home, Ma was too far gone to save. We watched her die, too."

"Kelly..." Lainey wasn't sure she'd spoken. Sorrow quenched her words.

"So look out for him, will you? Just don't let him spend too much time alone if he gets into one of his slumps."

She shook her head. "I won't."

He reached over and touched her cheek, and she placed her palm over his big hand. "Thanks, Lainey." He dropped his hand and they continued on their walk to the store.

They decided to wake Zane and tell him the news before it was time for Kelly to go to work. Together they pounced on the bed and jarred him into consciousness. Zane rubbed his eyes and listened to Kelly tell him about the job. Then he shook Kelly's hand and congratulated him.

"So get up, Zane," said Lainey. "We have to celebrate before he goes to work."

"All right. But if you're going to be making a habit of coming into my room and waking me up like this, then we'd better start telling people you're my sister." He cracked a teasing smile.

Lainey scooted off the bed. "Oh, get dressed!" With her hands on her hips, she strode out of the room.

After a hot cup of coffee to help Zane wake up and to send Kelly on his way, Lainey and Zane decided to take up the quest for more permanent housing. Kelly told them to see if there were rooms at the company boarding house.

Zane chewed his lip. "But I don't work for the company."

"Tell them you're with me."

"And Lainey?"

He had no solution to that, so they decided to address that matter separately. She would keep her room at the Forest House for the time being.

"You won't be able to afford it for long," Zane told her as they waved good-bye to Kelly from the steps of the Forest House.

She shivered. "You never know." Despite the bright sunshine, a nip clipped at the air that hung heavy with the autumn scents of leaf mold and pine resin.

"Getting cold?"

She nodded. "But I want to sit out here and sketch a picture of the town to send to my folks." She inhaled deeply. "It smells like home."

He smiled at her and tucked her close with a brotherly arm around her shoulders. "I'll keep you warm," he said, smiling into her eyes with a warmth she seldom saw there.

Chapter Nine

Lainey took one more glance around her room to make sure everything was as neat as a pin. It cost her seven dollars a week for her room and board at the Forest House, but by doing her own cleaning and laundry she managed to barter it down to five. When one of the cook's assistants left his job to move up to Marinette, the proprietor offered Lainey the opportunity to live there free in exchange for help. She leapt at the prospecty. She worked downstairs in the kitchen during the supper hour five nights a week. But she turned down the chance for extra pay by working on Saturday or Sunday, since that's when Kelly always came to town.

How she missed him! Mornings were lonelier with Kelly gone. Trotting her way downstairs to the kitchen she thought of him again. She'd grown used to spending her free time with the Beaumont men. Now it suddenly seemed as if a gaping, blank maw had swallowed Kelly away. She always fluttered with excitement during the Friday dinner hour, hardly able to wait to see him again. Fifty year old John, the Forest House cook and a retired camp cookee, teased her about her two beaus. But rather than argue with him, she just smiled and let it go.

In the kitchen, John mixed batter.

"Good morning. How about I put a fresh pot of coffee on the stove?" She whisked the pot over to the sink and thrust the pump handle up and down.

"You think I don't have time to do it. But I always wait for you to come down and put the second pot on." He whistled a tune while he poured batter on a cast iron griddle.

"Some morning you're going to run out, and the guests will wonder why you kept them waiting."

He laughed. "I will tell them Lainey overslept."

She gaped. "You would? You're mean," she teased.

"You have a swing in your step today."

"I have a swing in my step every day."

"I cannot argue that. I suppose it's one of your beaus."

"Now, John. You mustn't go getting me wed. The Beaumonts aren't my beaus."

He shrugged. "So you tell me. Clara and I think different."

"You like my friends. I can tell."

"I don't bother kicking them out of the kitchen anymore because you are a sweet girl who can use looking after by a fatherly person such as myself. I doubt this card player is worthy of you."

She scooped coffee into the pot. "You have no reason to worry about Zane. He's like one of my brothers."

She lost count of the scoops and tried to rethink. Wasn't he?

John harrumphed.

"I think you better give me a pancake and keep your opinions between you and Clara."

He chuckled as he slid a pancake and two eggs onto a plate and handed it to her.

She took her plate to a stool and ate in silence while John whistled and fried cakes and eggs. His words niggled inside her. Most folks would think she had two beaus, but it didn't really bother her. She still spent as much time as she could with Zane, partly because of her promise to Kelly, and partly because they shared a companionable misery over missing him. And, partly, just because their time together was the best part of her days.

Whenever Kelly arrived in town -- usually on Saturday but sometimes on Friday night if he could get away -- her world changed. The three of them spent the weekend carelessly, taking up each hour and new adventure as it presented itself. Since the weather turned and snow began to fall, they entertained themselves with picnics by the fireplace in the great room of the boarding house. They played cards all night long. They watched Zane trounce lumberjacks and railroaders at the tables in any of the dozen or more saloons scattered around town. Sometimes they watched him lose. Then she and Kelly spent the night trying to lift his spirits.

Sometimes they drank. At first Lainey only watched and shared a polite glass of wine at dinner. But there came the time she tried Zane's whiskey. Privately, of course, where no one else saw her when she coughed and choked and sputtered.

She decided pretty quickly strong drink wasn't for her. She stuck to an occasional glass of wine with her supper after that, but the experience made it clear she was willing to go even further than she thought to drown her past and any of the convictions she'd been raised to own.

With Kelly gone, she spent most mornings performing her simple routine. After cleaning her room, Lainey meandered to the kitchen for breakfast knowing Zane would sleep for hours still, unless for some reason he'd not had his usual trouble drifting off. But when that happened, he usually turned cranky and buzzed with anxiety. So most days she had breakfast in John's kitchen then spent the rest of her morning alone, waiting for the day to wind on.

"How are the eggs?"

"Very good, as usual." She jumped up and hurried to pull the coffee off the back of the stove before it boiled over.

"That was close." She stood rinsing her fingers in a tub when suddenly Zane slipped in the back door, startling her.

"Zane!"

"Morning, Lainey." He brushed her cheek with a kiss. "Got any coffee left?"

Warm and puzzled, she looked at him again. As comfortable as they were with one another, almost as though he really was her brother at times, he'd never greeted her with the familiarity of a kiss before.

He looked handsome this morning, and surprisingly rested. He'd shaved and combed his hair back neatly, though it was growing a little long. His face had lost little of its summer ruddiness, making his washed-blue eyes even more mesmerizing when he greeted her with his dreamy smile.

She took a cup off the shelf and filled it for him, offering him a pancake besides.

"You're looking in fine form so early in the morning." She allowed a hint of teasing to creep into her voice. Lonely thoughts dissipated like melting snow, and in its place a tendering of excitement grew.

"It's not too awful cold outside today. I thought maybe you'd like to get a couple of horses and go see what your trees look like in the snow."

"My trees?"

He smiled and blew on the steaming coffee. "Yeah. The ones you're going to cut down."

"Well, I haven't contacted anyone about buying them or cutting them yet."

"That gives us time to see them in their glory."

She grinned at him and sipped her own coffee. "Where are you getting all this energy from?"

He shrugged and set down his cup. "Hurry up. We don't have all day."

"Just about."

"Yeah, just about. But you have to be back to serve dinner, and I don't want to rush."

"All right, all right!" She waved a hand at him and rinsed her empty cup at the pitcher pump coming up into the sink. "I'll go get some warm clothes on."

"I'll be waiting on the porch. Don't keep me freezing."

She rolled her eyes at him and hurried back upstairs. It was good to see Zane so cheerful this early in the day. He must have slept well. She remembered Kelly's comments about the healing from his own bad memories taking place. She hoped that maybe the same was true of Zane. Apparently confident that she'd agree to go, two horses stood saddled and hitched at the rail outside. Zane helped her find her footing in the stirrup and eased her up into the saddle, then mounted the horse beside hers.

Turning their horses up the street, they followed the road along the river. They passed a saloon where Zane often played, but he didn't glance that way. A little further on, they passed the partly built Catholic Church. In fall, Lainey had often seen the priest, Father Pernin, working outside his little parsonage where he kept a small garden. Today they saw him vigorously shoveling a path up the walk. He gave them a friendly wave and they returned it.

"Are you Catholic?" The sudden question burst out of her.

"Nah." Zane shook his head. He glanced her way. "Haven't you figured out that I'm not much of anything?"

She waited a moment before answering, thinking about it. "But you were once." She didn't let her words sound like the question they were.

"Why would you think that?"

"I don't know."

"Because *you* were?"

Conviction like a steel rod bolted through her. It felt like she'd been shot. She took a deep breath. "Once."

"What happened?"

God, what happened? You know. You killed my Bobby. Took him away from me. You may as well have killed me, God. In a way, You did.

She looked at Zane and saw the question hanging there, waiting for her answer. They crossed the bridge and headed past the factories. She sighed, hoping he would tell her to never mind, but he didn't.

"I'm a Christian, Zane." She was surprised to see his eyebrows rise. "I'm a Christian who's angry at God. You've heard of that before, haven't you?"

He adjusted himself in the saddle and tugged at his hat. He pursed his lips thoughtfully. "Oh yeah."

"You're intimately familiar with the condition?"

"Beyond angry."

"So you've just given up on Him altogether."

"You might say that."

They rode on out of town and into the wooded, snow covered lane silently for a while, each lost in their bitterest memories. Finally Lainey spoke.

"What about Kelly?"

"You'd best be asking Kelly about that. Kelly has his own struggles." He looked over at her in that speculative way he had sometimes, as if he was trying to read her thoughts, or to tell her something without saying anything verbally. "I'm pretty sure he'll tell you all about it if you ask him."

"Why should he?"

He didn't answer, just clicked his tongue at his horse and pulled past her.

Lainey tapped her heels into her dappled mare and caught up. She gave him a look of defiance and urged her horse harder, pushing her into a gallop through the blanket of snow on the wagon road.

"Lainey!" Zane called, but she flew like fury ahead of him. One quick glance told her he'd charged after her.

For a quarter mile further she raced, ducking branches bent with snow, clinging to the horse and experiencing the freedom of the mare's body lunging beneath her. At a place where a limb lay across the road Lainey pulled up short. The horse pawed and pranced, panting veils of mist out its nostrils. Lainey's breath looked ghostly on the air as well.

"Good grief, girl." Zane pulled along beside her. "You really are mad at something, aren't you? Did you make some kind of death pact with your Maker, or what?"

She giggled, as surprised and touched by his worry as anything. Zane was just as addicted to action as she. He'd always given Lainey her head, not treating her like some fragile female, and here he was now, worrying about her.

"Come on, Zane. You know I can ride a horse."

"She might have slipped. There's snow and ice."

Lainey burst out laughing. "Are you telling me what to do, Mr. Beaumont?" She smirked between catches of breath.

"Oh, Lord no." He rolled his eyes as he started along again. "I should hope I'd never be audacious enough to do that."

Lainey followed along, laughing but subdued, letting him lead the way.

*****

The woods looked like a crystal, mythical kingdom. She imagined it to be a place like those in the fairy tales her mother told her when she was little. Massive black columns of pine, oak, and maple rose stark against the muted white background. She'd seen this same type of scenery a thousand times, yet every time she longed to capture it in a picture.

They led their horses through the woods, no longer on a path, and a longing stirred inside her both melancholy and beautiful in its desire. Somehow, she knew it wasn't just the woods making her feel that way. She watched Zane and a flutter of life lifted its wings inside her.

"Tomorrow I'll give you a haircut," she said.

"Is it that bad?"

"No. But it's time."

He walked around his horse and reached into a saddlebag. Pulling out a stick of sausage, he handed it to her.

"Thank you."

They dropped their reins and sat on a log, brushing away the snow first. She pulled off her glove and chewed on the sausage, looking at him next to her. Without much thought, she reached her hand into the hair at the back of his neck and let it drift through her fingers.

"You could lose a good two inches." She rubbed a few of his strawberry strands softly.

He didn't say anything, but his expression changed. His gaze pulled her into its wintry Lake Michigan-like depths, and she began to sink. Awkwardly, she pulled her hand away and with it, her eyes.

*****

"I can borrow scissors from Mrs. Mattson, John's wife."

He heard Lainey talking, but Zane's throat clamped around a lump stuck there in the middle of it. The feel of her hand at the base of his neck not only caught him off guard, but it nearly plundered every ounce of his composure. That good-morning kiss on the cheek had seemed so natural, so easy. And now, this desire to pull her to him seemed just the same. But he couldn't.

He fought the desire down, nearly suffocating in the struggle. His palms heated up, his body burned. And she sat there, talking to him, as though she'd no idea that she'd just derailed him completely.

Kelly, you better get back here, or I'll make us both sorry.

He nodded, not even sure what she was talking about. "Time to go?" he finally asked, his voice sounding hoarse to his ears.

She nodded, but didn't answer. With much less exuberance, they walked back out to the road and mounted the horses, heading home.

"Look at that," she said after they'd ridden half a mile.

"What?" He tried to tell what she pointed at.

"That tree. It looks like a perfect Christmas tree."

"Did you have Christmas trees back home?"

"The home of Manason Kade of Kade Logging without a Christmas tree? Are you crazy?"

He smiled. "Yeah, what kid doesn't love a Christmas tree? My pa used to get one for us every year, and we'd decorate it on Christmas Eve with all sorts of fanfare."

"I bet those were good days."

Zane smiled at her gentle words. "Yeah, they were. Has Kelly told you about our family?"

She nodded. "I hope you don't mind."

Zane shrugged. "Why should I?"

"Just because of... what happened to your parents."

"So, you know about that?"

"Yes."

She rode over closer to him and reached for his hand. He nearly gasped. He'd held a lot of women over the last five years, but none of them could do to his heart what this girl did just by taking his hand and looking at him.

"I know you have bad dreams."

But she didn't know that lately they'd been dreams of her, not the war, and that he felt less inclined to call them bad.

"You do?"

She nodded.

"Kelly told you?"

She nodded again.

"You and Kelly talk about a lot of things?"

Again, she nodded, her hair blowing in charcoal tendrils around her fair face, her blue eyes looking like dark sapphires.

"Well... that's all right. I'm glad you talk to each other."

She sighed. "I suppose it is a good thing."

He didn't know what the tone in her voice meant. But Zane knew one thing. He had to stop his feelings from growing. This time with her alone was doing dizzying things to him, and if there was one thing he would never do, he would never risk losing his brother's love because of her.

Especially when Kelly deserved her more.

Zane might imagine he was falling in love with Lainey, but Kelly's heart had found her first. And the fact remained, she would always be safer in Kelly's heart than in his.

Chapter Ten

Lainey held her breath, steeling herself for disappointment as she considered the letter. She'd not heard from Arthur Frayman in weeks, so she took the risk of sending him a few of her recent drawings, unsolicited. There was one of some loggers in flannel shirts and tall jackboots standing around the huge ramparts of logs waiting to be rolled down the riverbank in the spring. Another depicted the two churches in town, their spires facing each other on the page. The Catholic Church stood on the west side of the river and the Congregational on the east. The last drawing showed an immigrant farming family and their six children. The man and one of his sons sat on a wagon full of milk cans, ready to take the long drive to the cheese factories around Green Bay. His wife and other children stood clustered around him, beaming as though they were having their portraits painted.

Now she stood with the envelope from Mr. Frayman in her hand. Carefully she slit the side and pulled out the enclosed letter. When she opened it, she unfolded some newspaper clippings, and several bills spilled out. She sighed with relief.

Dear Miss Kade,

Thank you for your recent drawings. My editor is able to use two of them for future editions of his paper. The third, the one of the two churches, he has no room for at this time, but I believe I can find another publication which will be interested. I will send payment as soon as a sale is forthcoming.

Hoping this finds you in the best of health,

Art Frayman

She counted the money. Twenty dollars! Not as much as before, but a good sum none-the-less. She picked up the newspaper clippings and was about to set them aside with the torn envelope when a glance at them caught her eye, and she looked more closely. Unfolding them completely, she saw they were published copies of her drawings on the printed page. Excitement ran through her, then satisfaction. There it was -- her name in tiny script in the corner -- E. Eastman.

She folded them up and set them aside. With cash to get her through the next few weeks, her mind freed to open the other letter that lay on her desk. It was from Ginny Gilbert. Lainey plopped comfortably on the bed and propped the pillows behind her. Tearing open the seal, she peeled the pages out.

She scanned the letter over quickly. Ginny wished her a Merry Christmas and mentioned prayers on her behalf. Everyone was all in a stir because Ginny's parents, Joe and Kasheawa, a couple as old as Lainey's own folks, were expecting a baby. Ginny was an only child, and she herself would be marrying next spring. It was a strange time in her life to finally be gaining a baby brother or sister.

Lainey paused and thought about it. How excited they must be. Joe and Kashe, another baby after all this time!

She read on. Stephen, Grayson, and Eldon were all working in the woods, of course, and they sent their love. Everyone missed her.

And then there was Katie.

The tone of Ginny's letter changed. Instead of Lainey seeing all the previous news as Ginny's way of reveling in so much delight, she now saw it as her way of putting off news that she didn't want to tell, but felt she must.

...hate to tell you... Jed Clark... Katie... was afraid you would react... doesn't want to hurt you... a serious courtship...

Lainey dropped her hand and closed her eyes. Tears pooled beneath her eyelids and she clenched them tighter. Her hands curled into fists, crushing Ginny's message.

Katie, how could you?

Reproachful words screamed through her mind. She threw the note across the room and flung a pillow over her face, sobbing into it, but hating that she did so.

Why cry now? She wasn't crying for Jed, surely.

No, she was crying for the truth. The awful reminder that she was nothing more than a termagant, and neither Jed Clark nor any other man wanted to face a woman like that every day of their lives. *If only Bobby... If only...*

Neither Jed nor Owen understood her headstrong ways or loved her for being decisive and sure of herself. But Bobby Braedon had. Bobby laughed at her purposeful nature. He didn't condemn it. Bobby's eyes lit with mischief and appreciation when hers spit fire. Bobby breathed the same kind of air she breathed. Bobby lived by the same rules. Bobby let her be herself, and didn't try to change her. No one else did that except maybe her family. Not Jed, not Owen. No one.

Zane and Kelly came to mind.

But how the tune would change if they wanted to marry her, just like it changed for Jed. Then suddenly they'd want to make her into something else entirely. She couldn't stand it!

Anger ripped through her. Bobby didn't want her to change, and that made it easy to think of submitting herself to him. She could have done it forever.

She struck her fist into the pillow at the thought that Katie would do such a thing to her. It made Lainey look even worse, didn't it? And yet -- she clawed the pillow -- how could she blame Katie for being attracted to a man like Jed? Most girls were.

Her sobbing ceased, but the tears kept running from her eyes, until finally, the rage inside her dissipated, and her emotions drained away. Mid-day spiraled away as she lay curled in her blankets, and finally the pale lavender of sunset flushed the sky outside her window. Suddenly the success with her drawings seemed small, and all Lainey wanted to do was sleep.

*****

Zane tapped on Lainey's door late the next morning, a little surprised to be up before her. Or had she gone out and he missed her? He didn't think so. John told him she hadn't come down for breakfast, and it was almost eleven o'clock. It was Friday, and men were starting to trickle into town already. By nightfall there'd be more itinerants than year round residents roaming Peshtigo's sawdust streets. By Saturday there'd be so many carousers in the streets that decent folk would keep their children in their own yards. The fourteen saloons in town would be doing a hale and hardy business, and Peshtigo's genteel society would be doing their level best to turn a deaf ear to the noise, coarse language, and foul behavior openly displayed. Kelly would be back in the morning.

He rapped on her door a bit harder, but she didn't answer. Trying the knob, he found the door unlocked and peeked inside. He saw her lying there, still abed, but fully dressed.

"Lain? Lainey?" He eased himself inside and tiptoed across the floor. "Lainey, you awake?"

She looked a mess. She didn't appear to be sleeping, but neither was she fully awake and alert. Her dress wrinkled around her. She obviously hadn't been out of it since yesterday. Her disheveled hair covered her face. Boldly but tenderly, he drew her hair aside and whispered her name again. Her face looked puffy as though she'd been crying, and she shrugged away from his touch.

Zane was well-acquainted with the effects of a bad night's sleep. He might have smiled at catching her so disarrayed if worry didn't make him wonder why.

"What's the matter?"

"Nothing." Her voice was hoarse and small.

"Lainey, what is it? What happened? Are you hurt?"

A bitter sound escaped her.

Zane looked around the room and back to her. "You want me to leave you alone then? I brought you something."

Silence. If he didn't know better, he'd say she was pouting. Maybe she *was* pouting. Then he noticed the papers and opened envelopes lying on the edge of the bed. He reached for one of them, but her hand shot out, halting him from picking it up.

"Don't."

"Letters from your folks?"

"No."

Zane sighed and stuffed his hands into his pants pockets. A ball of paper lying on the floor caught his eye, and since she wasn't looking at him, he went over and picked it up. He started to smooth out the wrinkled sheet of correspondence when she sat up suddenly and held out her hand.

"Give it to me!"

He couldn't believe how angry -- or hurt -- she looked. Her hair hung all about her shoulders in black ribbons. Her eyes, an almost unnatural deep blue, looked like turbulent dark water.

He didn't give her the letter. He looked down and started to read it instead.

Lainey jumped off the bed and lunged toward him as he caught bits and pieces of the passage. Family news. Christmas wishes. Something about a couple having a baby. Recognition of Katie's name.

He held the letter out of her reach and even put it behind his back.

Her eyes flashed. "Give me the letter, Zane."

"Who's it from? A secret admirer?" he asked, egging her on.

"No. It's from my friend Ginny. Now will you give me the letter, please?"

"Why did you throw it away?"

"Who says I did?"

She reached again for the letter, and if she didn't look so distressed he would have enjoyed her nearness.

"It was crumpled up."

She sat down on the bed and folded her arms, looking away. "You're right. I threw it away. It's not important anyway. Didn't you say you brought me something?"

She was trying to bluff him into giving up. "Not so fast." Zane looked at the letter again. He wasn't really reading carefully, but sneaking in peeks of her to catch her reaction. She fumed, trying to ignore him.

I hate to tell you this Lainey, but you should know. Jed Clark has been seeing Katie. Well, more than seeing her. Katie thinks she's falling in love with him. I'm sorry to be the one to tell you, but Katie was afraid you would react badly at the news, and she really doesn't want to hurt you. It really does appear to be a serious courtship. I thought you should know. I'm so sorry. Katie will write to you soon, herself, I'm sure...

Zane lowered the letter slowly, his eyes drawing less to the page and more to Lainey sitting there on the bed looking hopelessly forlorn. So much suddenly made sense; what troubled her past, why she didn't want to go home with her brother and cousins, why she was only interested in friendship with Kelly -- and him.

"I'm sorry I intruded."

She stared at her hands in her lap, picking at her fingernails mindlessly. "Why should you be? I'm not sorry. Jed Clark was never the man for me. Never."

"You're sure about that?"

Her stare bolted up at him. "You don't know anything about it, Zane. What you read there is nothing. It only reminds me of other things, that's all."

Zane set the letter beside her and sighed. "All right. Then I'm just sorry that I pushed you. I never should have invaded your private life."

Something like regret passed over her features. "It's not you. I know you meant well."

He felt like a failure. To "mean well" in Zane's way of thinking, was something a child would do for his grandmother when he picked all her prize roses and presented them to her as a gift.

"Yeah... well... I'll leave you alone if you want me to." He turned to leave.

"Didn't you say you came here for something?"

Hopefulness laced her voice; at least he hoped it was hopefulness.

"Like I said, I brought you something, but if you'd rather not--"

"Don't go, Zane. Come here. I want to show you something."

Hesitant, he glanced over the room as though someone might be watching them. "What is it?"

She patted the bed beside her and he sat down. He felt awkward now, something he'd never felt alone with a woman before. Without explanation, she handed him some newspaper clippings.

He looked at each one twice, recognizing the scenes as being like any number of those he'd seen between Green Bay and Peshtigo.

"Hm... Kind of like the drawings you do. Where'd you get them?"

"They were printed in a paper in New York."

He didn't ask her how she'd come by papers from New York. "Why do you want me to see them?"

"Don't you notice anything?"

He looked at them again. "They look like yours." He held them toward the wintry daylight sifting through the window. "The name on this one says E. Eastman." He looked at the other clipping. "This one too." He raised his brows and harrumphed. "You can draw just as well as this. Somebody should buy your pictures."

She turned those amazing eyes on him again. "Somebody did."

He waited, stared back. "What are you saying?"

She didn't smile. Didn't express joy or anything else for that matter. "These are mine."

"What? Lainey!" He looked at the pictures again, narrowing his eyes, then opening them wide. "Lainey! These are yours? How?"

Briefly she told about meeting Arthur Frayman and how a few drawings sold to him had been providing her an income since they'd left Fort Howard.

He listened intently, amazed. "You don't seem excited."

Lainey shrugged, but the beginnings of a smile tweaked at the corners of her lips, and Zane knew that something about the news in the letter he'd read struck her heart's chords in a deeper way than he understood. Still, she did want to smile, just a little. Finally he asked about her reason for using the pseudonym E. Eastman.

For a moment she looked shy, embarrassed almost. "My full name is Elaina. I never told you. It's Elaina Eastman Kade. Manason Kade is my adoptive father."

A jolt ricocheted off his insides. Studying her, he said it very softly. "Elaina." Her expression when he said it wore a question. "Elaina," he said again, almost melodically, and her smile broke through.

He set down the clippings and took both of her hands in his, tugging her to her feet.

"This calls for a celebration, and it so happens that I have just the thing. Come on."

He pulled her into the hall and down the stairs to the front door. Outside, at the hitching rail, leaned a small evergreen. Her blue eyes dazzled to life.

"Do you recognize it?'

"It's the tree I admired in the Sugar Bush."

"Yes it is." Zane walked down the steps and stood the tree up straight. It came to his shoulders.

"It's kind of big for a small room, don't you think?"

He grinned at her. "Who wants a little Christmas tree?"

The smile he hoped to see stretched across her face. She hugged her shoulders and shivered. "Well hurry up and bring it in."

For the next three hours he helped her decorate the tree. He'd come prepared with paper, scissors, paste, three small paint tins, a needle and thread, and popcorn. "You can fashion some ornaments and paint them. I'll pop the corn and start stringing."

As night fell and Lainey lit the lamps, her little tree came to life.

Zane watched her in the glow of the lamp light and admired her dedication to the task, her creativity and thoughtfulness. Their friendship deepened as they talked and laughed the afternoon away, eating popcorn and drinking cider from John's secret supply, and Zane's heart was full.

He never expected to feel this way. Not in a hundred years. Zane had been devoid of love for anyone but Kelly and Suzanne ever since the war had created its vacuum inside his rib cage. His heart bled away its desire to feel anything ever again. Now something new stirred inside him, spiraling like a whirlwind. And it came with Lainey.

She'd found out something about his past, and now he knew something about hers. Maybe not everything. For sure, not everything. But given more time, perhaps she'd trust him to know, and then she'd be able to step out from behind the firewall that surrounded her heart.

He caught himself, remembering as he looked at the way her hands delicately held the paintbrush, and the way her eyes glowed like nightfall over Lake Michigan, that even if she opened up the secrets of her heart, it could never belong to him.

Chapter Eleven

Kelly leapt the stairs by threes. He went to the boarding house, but really wasn't surprised Zane was not there. It was Friday night. He'd probably already eaten supper and was shuffling cards in the back corner of some saloon, waiting for a game to turn up. He'd find him later. First he'd clean up then stop in and see Lainey. Maybe she hadn't eaten yet. Maybe she'd want to take a walk in the snow or something.

Forty minutes later he rapped his knuckles against her door, glancing down the corridor to make certain no one noticed him coming to Lainey's room. Peshtigo turned into a rollicking town after sunset on Friday night, but it did no good to make people think less of her.

"Yes?"

"Lainey, it's me, Kelly."

A moment later she opened the door and smiled at him. "Kelly!"

He stroked the brim of his hat in his hand and switched his weight from one foot to the other. "Hello, Lainey. How are you?" He drank in the soft look of her face and hair and eyes -- all of her. She opened the door wider to admit him to her room. He looked down the corridor again, and the question, *are you sure?* formed on his lips. But then he saw Zane.

He sat in a chair with his arm resting on the little table she had in the corner of the room. The table lay littered with paper and popcorn. Next to Zane in front of Lainey's one window stood a Christmas tree, and no mistake. The sight looked mighty cozy.

"Zane?" Kelly stepped through the door.

"Hey, Kell." Zane smiled at him. "You're back. You don't smell like a horse, do you?"

"I took a bath at the boarding house." He walked over and shook Zane's hand. "What're you doing up here?"

Zane's eyes were hooded, veiled in that way he had when his thoughts were meant to be his own. Kelly tried now to read them, but it had been a while.

"Actually, I was just getting ready to shove off. I brought Lainey a Christmas tree and tried to help her pretty it up. As you can see, she's the one with the artistic touch."

Kelly smiled at Lainey before his gaze swung back to Zane's. "You're off to find a game, then?"

Zane nodded, rising to his feet and brushing popcorn crumbs off his pants. "Yeah. Got to make a living."

Kelly rubbed a hand across his jaw and nodded. "Maybe I'll find you later. Lainey, are you hungry?"

Her hand went to the back of her neck as if she was stiff, and she smiled. "Sure. John likely has folks to feed downstairs and I should go lend him a hand. We can grab a bite after everyone's finished. How about that?"

"Sounds good."

"I'll see the two of you later, or tomorrow," said Zane, heading toward the door. "Lainey, thanks for showing me how to make those paper snowflakes."

She laughed and touched his arm. "Thank you for the tree."

Zane put on his hat and left.

She offered Kelly the benefit of her smile. "Should we go down?"

He looked around the room again. "It's a nice tree. Zane got it for you, huh?"

She nodded. "We saw it one day when we went out riding in the upper Sugar Bush. He remembered and went back for it."

"That was thoughtful."

She agreed, opening the door and stepping out into the hall. Kelly followed her and she took his arm on the stairs.

"Zane can be that way sometimes..." He said it aloud, but almost to himself.

Kelly didn't worry that Zane would try to move in on Lainey. He'd made his own affection for her pretty clear, and he and Zane never let a gal come between them. Some boundaries neither of them crossed. But at the same time, being away so long and so often probably wasn't the best way to win the lady's affections either.

He looked at her again and smiled. "It sure is good to see you, Lainey."

She squeezed his arm, and for a moment all Kelly thought about was what it would be like to hold her, but not just for the feel of her in his arms. Rather, to hold her as his own.

Kelly sat in the corner of the dining room and watched her while she served the tables and cleared away the used dishes. Every now and then she glanced his way and smiled. She brought him coffee while he waited.

Once the supper crowd diminished, she hung up her apron and got them each a plate. They ate and talked together companionably.

"I wish I'd been able to get you a Christmas present," he told her, thinking again of the tree.

"Just having you here is present enough."

"Tomorrow's Christmas Eve, and Christmas Day is Sunday. The boss is giving everyone an extra day for the holiday, so I won't be heading back until Monday afternoon."

"What about the animals you take care of?"

"I'm not the one who lives there with them. That job belongs to another fellow who doesn't have to take care of a family."

Her eyes teased. "Like you do?"

"Well, there's Zane. And you're like family," he said, wondering how she'd take that remark.

She lifted her chin and eyed him in reply. "I don't mind being taken care of." Then she blushed and dropped her eyes. "I didn't mean that the way it sounded."

Kelly laughed.

"Well, Kelly, I'm full, but I have to go help wash up these dishes. It'll be a busy weekend for John and Clara."

Kelly watched her rise and collect their plates. He wished he could stay with her longer. "I guess I'll go sit in on a few hands with Zane. Maybe I'll stop by later and toss a few pebbles at your window to say good night."

She giggled, tilting her head in a feminine way Kelly doubted she was aware of. "You do that."

Lainey walked him to the door and as he went outside he turned to look at her again before she closed it. "Think of something you want to do tomorrow."

"I will."

She closed the door and Kelly stood there a moment, still envisioning her. *No,* he told himself, *you won't win her hand by hanging around only on Saturday nights, not with hundreds of other men coming in from the woods besides. They'll all be trying to catch her fancy, and one of them could do it. Lainey Kade is storing her heart away for some reason, and if you want to be the reason she unlocks it again...*

Kelly didn't know what he'd have to do, but he knew he was going to have to put some heavy thought into the situation.

*****

Kelly didn't find Zane in any of the first five saloons he entered. Not until he made his way to the far end of the business district did he finally discover Zane seated at a table with a small pile of cash in front of him and a half empty bottle at his elbow. He hoped he hadn't just started that bottle, but the glaze on Zane's demeanor told him differently.

Zane could drink quite a bit and still keep his head at the table, but he got ornery sometimes too. Kelly decided not to say anything to him at all. He caught his eye, knowing Zane saw him but didn't acknowledge him so that anyone sitting around noticed. Then Kelly walked over to the bar and ordered a mug. He poured it down quickly and ordered another. Then he sipped only slowly, taking a look every now and then at how things progressed at Zane's table. He lost two hands then quickly recouped his losses in two more risky hands. A glint of satisfaction lit Zane's eyes as he collected his cash and took several stiff swallows from the bottle.

Two players gave up and backed away, shaking their heads in disgust at how suddenly their fortunes turned. Kelly took the opportunity to approach the table. He spun one of the empty chairs around and straddled it, facing Zane.

"Got room for company?"

Zane and the two other remaining players nodded.

"Long as your money's good," said the big lumberjack Kelly recognized as a man named O'Sullivan. He was a popular fellow around town, the self-proclaimed champion of the Saturday night sprees.

The other fellow began to shuffle and Kelly cut the deck. His initial hand looked more than promising, two queens, a pair of tens and a six. He tossed in his bet, traded off the six and settled back in his chair with the seven of hearts. The betting went around and the players laid their cards down. His two pair was high, and he took a small pot. The next hand the dealer won. Then Kelly took a big hand with a full house.

He caught a brief glimpse from Zane. Surprise? Warning? Humor? Kelly wasn't quite sure. The liquor looked to be swimming in Zane's eyes, and Kelly worked hard at not appearing too surprised himself.

Zane took one hand in four, and then Kelly began making a killing. By that time, with his second mug nearly empty, Zane was drunk. So was the champion. The other fellow kicked back his chair and gave up. He apparently needed to save a little of his week's wages for the next day.

Big O'Sullivan scowled. "What's going on here?"

Kelly raked bills and coins together. "Looks like I'm winning."

The hulking lumberjack looked between Kelly and Zane. "Is 'at so? You brothers?"

"That's right," Zane slurred badly. "I taught him everything he knows."

Kelly's mettle stirred. It wouldn't do well for Zane to get them into trouble with O'Sullivan. Kelly was big, but the lumberjack was bigger -- and meaner too -- from what Kelly had heard.

"Why don't we call it a night while we're ahead?" He glanced coolly at Zane as he pocketed his winnings.

Zane came to his feet with a stagger. "I could teach you, too."

"Teach me?" Thunder gathered between the man's brows and Kelly noticed his thick fists balling up.

"Sure. I taught a woman, so I could teach anybody," Zane challenged.

"Shoot," Kelly hissed under his breath, just as the challenger's fist shot out and cut across Zane's chin.

Zane slung backward, tripping over the chair and landing with a crash. Kelly stepped in and laid a fist, wrapped around coin, into the bully's gut.

Zane shook his head, but Kelly figured it would take more than that to clear the mud from it as he yanked him to his feet with one hand and ducked a forthcoming blow at the same time. Big O'Sullivan lunged toward him, picking up a chair and heaving it over his head. Zane plunged into the man's belly head first, sending him flying back against the wall, but O'Sullivan grabbed onto him and began swinging him back and forth by wrapping his two giant paws around Zane's head. Kelly lunged in for a clip at him, and before long, a crowd gathered, then began pushing and shoving and brawling some between them.

It lasted for about five more minutes before the bar tender fired a pistol into the ceiling and the three rabble rousers got tossed out into the street, bleeding but painless in their drunken stupors.

Except for Kelly. He hurt pretty good, and it didn't help with the pure mad he was feeling. While O'Sullivan and Zane lay there in the snow, moaning, Kelly jumped to his feet and brushed himself off.

He stood fuming for a few minutes, breathing deep while he looked at Zane lying prostrate in the snow. Then he bent down and jerked him to his feet.

Zane shook his head and wobbled slightly.

"Had enough to drink?" Kelly hoped the accusation in his tone was evident enough.

"What's the matter with you?" Zane said, the night air possibly clearing his head a little bit.

Kelly slapped the back of Zane's head as they moved off down the street, leaving the champion staggering in the snow, bellowing for someone inside the tavern.

"How often do I win?"

Zane rubbed the place where Kelly had snagged him and laughed. "Not very?"

"Yeah, well I was beating you."

"Go figure. How much did you take me for, anyway?"

"Enough. Count yourself lucky that it was me."

"You going to give it back?" Zane asked, a glitter in his eyes.

"Not anytime this year. Why'd you have to get so suckered up so early? I just got here."

"I thought you'd be with Elaina."

"Who?"

"E-lain-a."

"What are you talking about?"

"I'm talking about Lainey. You left her to come and beat me at poker?"

Befuddled, Kelly felt as though he'd been drinking more than he actually had. "You're drunk. I'm taking you home. Maybe you'll sleep."

Zane shrugged free when Kelly's hand shot out to steer him toward home. "Let's go wake her up."

"Who, Lainey?"

"I told you," Zane said, weaving down the street in the direction of the Forest House.

"Lainey's probably not asleep. It isn't that late. You're only drinking early."

Zane didn't reply, but kept winding on toward the hotel where she lived. They reached the place and Zane was about to totter up the front steps when Kelly pulled him back.

"All right. We're here. We might as well say hello, though I doubt if she'll want to see us like this."

Kelly pawed in the snow until he reached the mushy layer of wood dust and chips buried beneath. He picked out a handful of wood chips and began tossing them up at the corner window overlooking the street.

Tick. Tick. They hardly made a sound, but after a minute the curtain drew back and Kelly saw the shadowy figure of Lainey looking out, trying to focus on them in the darkness. The sash slid up and she leaned out on her elbows.

Her voice fell down on them louder than a whisper, but not much. "I thought you were kidding."

Kelly smiled up at her and tilted his head toward Zane. "We came to say good night, as promised."

"Okay."

"Hello, Elaina," said Zane unsteadily.

"Hello, Zane," she answered, while Kelly tried to figure things out.

Zane grinned stupidly. "Her name is Elaina Kade Eastman."

"Elaina Eastman Kade," she corrected. "Wait there."

The window closed and a candle's glow moved through the room and then went out. A couple minutes later she appeared at the door, wrapped in her coat and wearing a warm hat and gloves.

Kelly quickly ran the name through his mind, trying to piece this information into place as she came toward them down the steps.

"Your name really is Elaina?"

She nodded.

"I like it."

"He likes everything about you," teased Zane. "He'd like it if your name was Matilda."

Kelly blushed, glad for the darkness.

Lainey wrinkled her nose. "Matilda! How awful."

Zane frowned. "We had a cousin named Matilda."

"It was Ma's cousin," said Kelly. "She was nice. Makes me feel kind of bad for laughing at her name."

"Called her Mattie. She and Ma were devoted." Zane crossed his fingers and pinched his eyes nearly closed. "Like that." He grew silent, his expression stony.

Kelly watched the course of Zane's thoughts as clearly as if he were putting them in his head himself. He, too, could see their mother, nothing more than a skeleton of the beauty she'd been in her youth, lying frail and weak, her flesh colorless and thin like wax.

"Want to walk with us?" he asked, reaching for Lainey's arm. "Come on, Zane."

Zane looked at them. He studied them for a moment as though a flash of clarity had overcome him. He nodded.

Slowly they strolled up the street. Music and laughter poured out of the saloons. Kelly caught Lainey peering toward the people inside. She was noticing the women dressed in gaudy, low-cut dresses, taking their warmth on this cold, Wisconsin December night from the abundance of male company and the liquor. He tucked her arm more tightly into his own and smiled at her when she looked up at him. She returned a wan smile.

"Will he be all right?" she asked, peeking at Zane on the other side of him.

Kelly nodded. "I think the liquor will put him to sleep."

"Let's hope so."

Kelly nodded.

They talked of other things as they strolled through the open streets. They discussed the neat architecture of the town, how folks painted their houses so quaintly and kept them up so well. Not like some towns they'd visited. They talked about how hard it was on the local families when the revelers came into town each weekend making a ruckus, and Kelly felt a moment of chagrin over their part in it.

By the time they crossed town and got to the Peshtigo Company boarding house, Zane seemed quieted and somewhat sobered.

"I can tuck myself in," he said as they came to the entrance. "I won't even get lost."

Kelly patted his shoulder, and he and Lainey watched him mount the stairs, his footsteps measured and slow. Successful at the top, he turned and smiled at them, tapped his hat in salute, and went inside.

"I'll walk you back," said Kelly.

"It's too bad I'm clear across town. You'll have to come all the way back again."

"I don't mind."

She hugged his arm with her own, and he reveled for a moment in her warmth and vitality.

He laid his free hand on hers. "I guess I'm not sorry we pestered you."

"Me either."

"It would have been a long night."

"Tomorrow's Christmas Eve."

He nodded. "Have you figured out how you'd like to spend the day?"

"Not really." She gazed up the street, and Kelly took the opportunity to admire how her eyes reflected the starlight.

"Does your family go to church on Christmas Eve?" he asked softly.

She nodded slightly, her face hidden now beneath her wool bonnet. "They never miss. Christmas wouldn't be Christmas..." Her breath came out in wispy white trails. "How about you, Kelly? Do you and Zane go to church on Christmas Eve?"

He thought when he'd asked her the same question, it might be returned, but to actually hear it pricked him to the core more deeply than he expected. Yes, he always went to church on Christmas, and every other time the doors were opened before the war. Zane didn't nickname him Preacher for nothing. He rubbed his hands together and placed one of them back over hers in the crook of his arm. He smiled warmly when she looked at his face.

"Sure."

Lainey nodded. "Zane said something one day that made me wonder."

"Did he?"

She nodded again. "I told him I was angry at God, and he made me think that he was too -- that maybe both of you were."

"Zane's been through a lot."

"You, too."

Kelly agreed, as wave after wave of yearning grew inside him, but he wasn't sure what for. Was it for Lainey? That was certain. Did he yearn for all the things he'd given up and cast away? He tried not to think so. But the longing increased. Part of him wanted to tell her everything. Maybe that was it. But part of him feared her reaction. Lainey -- or Elaina, it seemed -- regularly made it clear that she wanted all the fun she could squeeze out of life. If she knew everything about him, she might decide he could never be the type of man to satisfy her. Kelly knew what girls like Lainey thought about boys who grew up wanting what Kelly once wanted. They thought they were boors. He felt his way along slowly.

"Do you want to go back? Ever?"

"Go back where? Home, or to church?"

"Church."

Lainey shrugged. "Maybe. I guess."

He thought about her answer as the question rebounded. *What about you, Kell? Is it time? Would you go back there now, with Lainey?* He thought maybe, then *yes.*

Kelly looked up at the stars. "Would you like to go tomorrow night?"

"For Christmas Eve?"

"Yes."

He sensed her indecision. It was the same for him, but something was happening here, and it was as though the yearning inside him found its course.

She looked up at him and her eyes shone in the darkness. "All right. If you're brave enough to face the wrath of God, then I am too."

Chapter Twelve

Kenton Kade stretched to the top of the tree and set the star in place. Then he jumped down off the chair and brushed his hands together.

"Now it looks like a Christmas tree." He backed up to stand next to his mother where he could admire his handiwork.

She beamed at him. "It does, doesn't it?"

"Too bad Lainey isn't here to see it. She always liked decorating the tree. Course, now I get to put the star on."

"How come she always got to have that job anyway?" asked Eldon who stood near Manason munching on a cookie.

"Cause she's the only girl," said Nase. He snatched at the cookie and laughed when Eldon broke it while trying to protect it.

"No fair. Now I get to have another one."

"You save some for tomorrow when Robbie's and Joe's families come over," Colette warned.

"Oh, Ma," Grayson came up from behind and put his arms over her shoulders, "we all know you and Grandma have enough cookies stashed outside in the old icebox to feed an army."

"Oh you do, do you?"

"Sure." He whispered conspiratorially, "We've got spies."

She slapped his hand and he pecked her on the cheek.

Colette gazed dreamily at the tree. "I do wish Lainey was here. I wonder what she's doing tonight?"

"I bet she went to church in Peshtigo," said Manason, coming up beside her, but Grayson and Eldon passed a glance to one another indicating they thought otherwise.

"She's with friends probably," said Gray. "There'll most likely be a party. There usually is in those out of the way lumber towns."

"Like ours?" asked Kent, and the family grinned.

"Yep," said Nase, "like ours. You boys going to the dance in Peterson's barn tomorrow night?"

Eldon shoved his hands in his pockets and crowed. "You better believe it!"

"He's all excited because he's hoping to dance with Mary Atkinson," said Gray.

"You've never danced with Mary?" asked Colette.

Grayson laughed. "Ol' El's never gotten up the nerve to ask her before now. We'll see if he does this time!"

Eldon swatted him and they broke into a tussle of laughter.

"Watch out for the tree," said Manason, and Colette rolled her eyes.

Grandma Lavinia tottered with her walking stick into the

room." What's going on in here?"

"We're just playing around, Grandma," said Grayson, giving Eldon one more jab.

"Land sakes, sounds like the house is coming down. Boys. Never had them, never will understand them," she said, and they all chuckled. "Well, now, won't you look at that tree? Who put the star on?"

Kent stepped forward. "I did. It looks perfect, don't it?"

"Give me a kiss," she said. "If that don't look pretty, nothing does. What time is everyone coming over tomorrow?"

"Right after church," said Colette. "I've got the roast all ready to put in the oven, first thing in the morning."

The old woman's face lit with a smile. "I bet this will be an exciting Christmas for Joseph and Kashe."

"Just wait until next year," Nase added. "I can't wait to see old Joe chasing around a toddler again."

"Maybe she'll be good as gold, like Colette was."

"Or maybe *he'll* be full of mischief like his father!" Colette chuckled, leaning into Manason's arms.

The next morning they all sat in church and sang reminders of the day the Christ came as a newborn King. Then they piled into the wagons with plenty of blankets and rode home up the hill to Manason's house.

"It doesn't seem quite the same without Lainey," said Kashe, always thoughtful of Colette's feelings. They and Lavinia and Colette's sister-in-law Jean worked together at the meal preparations.

Colette paused as she whipped the potatoes with a spoon. "No, it doesn't. I hope and pray she's having a nice Christmas. The boys say she has friends."

Ginny came in just then, unusually separated from her beau, Archie Sattler.

"What's Archie doing?" asked Kashe of her dusky, dark-eyed daughter.

"He's helping the boys fill the firebox."

Colette gave her a teasing look. "I didn't think you two ever left sight of one another."

Ginny flushed, looking even more becoming. "Did Mama tell you we set a wedding date for early June, right after planting?"

"No!"

Ginny nodded. "It's all set. Archie's house will be ready and all his crops will be planted. We can take it easy for a week or two before he starts cutting hay."

"Well, that's just wonderful."

"I thought she would like to tell it herself." Kashe reached a warm brown hand out to her only child. "It will be so strange when she is gone to her own home."

Lavinia set a basket of rolls on the long oak table and patted Kashe's shoulder. Her eyes twinkled. "But you will be getting ready for a new little one to raise."

Kashe blushed. "It is still so hard to believe."

"I told Archie I don't want to wait to start a family, either," said Ginny. "Then our baby can grow up with my little brother or sister."

The older ladies laughed. "You don't know what you're asking for," said Jean. "You just enjoy one another as long as God allows you to, and then you rejoice when He decides to send a little one your way."

"I will, Aunt Jean."

Joe poked his head into the room. "Time to eat yet? The smell of all the food is just about killing us in there."

"Come and help us set the table," said Colette.

Joe slipped further into the room. His brown eyes shone. "You always put me to work."

Colette recalled some of the many times in her life Joe had been there to help her. "I do have that habit."

"All right," he said with a sigh, "but I get extra dessert."

All the ladies laughed.

*****

In Peshtigo, Lainey bundled into her muffler and wool coat. She didn't want to freeze in the brittle air while journeying across town to the Congregational Church on the other side of the river. Part of her still paralyzed with disbelief over attending there at all. But Kelly acted keen to the idea.

They had gone to church on Christmas Eve just as Kelly suggested, and for the first time in many months, Lainey didn't necessarily feel at odds with God. But, neither did she especially warm toward Him. Last night's Christmas Eve candlelight service had been filled with holiday ambiance, and she admitted that it was nice to sing Christmas carols with the congregation. Kelly wasn't shy about using his exceptionally fine baritone voice.

During their walk home after the service, they decided to attend again in the morning. It would be a lark, Lainey supposed, wondering what Kelly got out of it. They'd invited Zane to come along, but his slate-gray eyes dulled with disinterest. She and Kelly went alone while he stayed in bed, sleeping off a Saturday repeat of Friday's drinking binge.

Neither she nor Kelly expected the holiday would keep them coming back to the small, white church after the morning service. But the church folk told them about a Christmas social tonight, and anyone was welcome. A lot of people without families usually attended such events, especially young single men, and the church tried to make them feel like there was someplace they could go and feel at home on Christmas Day besides the noisy saloons and bawdy houses that were so inviting.

Lainey tightened her bonnet and talked to herself. "I must be crazy to go. Next thing you know, I'll be making friends and joining quilting circles and being matched up with some old auntie's nephew." She tugged the bow beneath her chin and slipped on her gloves. "It'll be just like old times," she growled, and marched out the door. She came down the stairs just as Kelly walked in.

"All ready?"

"I suppose."

Kelly looked askance. "You change your mind?"

"No. I'm just a little worried about where all this is leading us."

Kelly laughed. "What's the matter, Lainey? Worried you'll wind up at the altar instead of in the back row?"

For a moment she thought she might swoon. What made Kelly say that? Then it dawned on her that he was referring to repenting at the altar, not marrying at it.

"Come on," he said. "I got us a wagon so we don't have to walk."

"Oh, good." She forced a faint chuckle. "You never know when we might want to make a fast getaway!"

Kelly laughed, and they exited the hotel.

*****

Zane stood outside in the shadows of the boarding house ignoring the cold twisting up his spine. Before long he heard a wagon trundling along, this time carrying Kelly and Lainey. He watched them ride by, laughing and joking, she leaning into him for warmth.

He loves her. The truth hit him like a gale wind. *Kelly loves her, and I'm a sorry weasel for caring for her myself.*

Zane had nothing to offer Lainey, and he never would. He would always be just what the war turned him into. A drifter. A gambler. A drunk.

He spit in self-contempt, and the spittle crackled and froze in the air before it hit the ground.

Maybe not a drunk, he thought hopefully. But the facts didn't change. If he didn't get over this strange, unsettling infatuation soon, it could only come to grief. He could never look at Lainey as a sister-in-law with feelings like these. He had to flush them away. *I don't have any choice.*

He turned and walked away toward the raucous Christmas bash that called to him from the Timbermen's Saloon down the street.

*****

He didn't get as drunk as he had the last two nights, and he was wide awake when Kelly came in from breakfast on Monday morning. He heard his brother's whistle before the door opened.

"Hey!" Kelly caught his eyes right away. "You're awake. They got a big pile of flapjacks downstairs, and a tub of sausage just waiting for you."

Zane looked him over. The man was so clearly in love Zane could have been blinded from the happiness shining off him. He felt more like a crumb than ever.

He tried sounding positive. "I'll have to go down and get some."

"There's plenty. Lots of boys won't get up too early today."

Zane scrubbed a hand over his face and sat up. His head pounded and his limbs felt like rubber. "Thanks for putting me to bed the other night, if I didn't say so before."

Kelly smiled and rolled up his sleeves to wash. "I'm here for you."

"Yeah." Zane started getting dressed. "So you and Lainey went to church again last night, that right?"

Kelly's expression showed surprise at the notion. "Go figure, huh? It wasn't really church, though. It was a social."

"Have fun?"

Kelly shrugged. "Sure." He threw some clothing into a case. "It was sort of different, being around people like that again. It kind of makes a fellow feel like he never left."

"Lainey comfortable with that?"

"She did okay."

"She tell you that she's mad at God?"

"It don't take much to figure out."

"She tell you why?" Zane wondered aloud.

"I didn't want to pry."

Zane thought about Lainey's letter from her friend Ginny, and he wondered if he should reveal what he'd found out.

"Why?" Kelly asked. "Did she tell you something?"

"Not really."

Kelly stopped packing and watched Zane wash his face and bury it into a towel. "How'd you come to decide she was mad at God?"

"I'll feel sort of lousy if I say anything."

Kelly braced an arm against the wall and crossed one ankle over the other. He looked every bit like he didn't plan on moving until Zane spilled his guts, so Zane finally capitulated. He told Kelly about Lainey's reaction to the letter from her friend and about the little bit of it he'd read.

Speculation crystallized in Kelly's blue eyes. "She's been jilted then."

"Sounds like."

"And that's the reason she's closed her heart."

"Maybe."

"Maybe?"

"She said it wasn't anything. It just reminded her of other things."

"Such as?"

Zane shrugged again, and this time his face must have shown a definite unknowing because Kelly didn't doubt him. "She wouldn't say." Zane lifted one side of his mouth into a taunting smile. "And I didn't want to pry..."

Kelly straightened up and jerked his chin. "Come on then. You can get breakfast and I'll try to solve Lainey's mysteries."

"I don't think you will."

Kelly's chest puffed out a little. "I always like a woman who offers a challenge."

Zane couldn't help but laugh.

*****

Lainey carefully packaged the picture and set it on the desk in her room while she got ready to head out. A January thaw had stretched into February, and the idea of a walk to the telegraph office sounded inviting. She would get in touch with Mr. Frayman about the drawing, and while she was there she would send a brief greeting to her family.

As she walked up the street, she thought about what she should say exactly. *Doing fine* seemed hardly adequate. It would invite a scolding from her ma for more news. She could mention her plans to have her timber land harvested next fall, but that would do better in a letter. She could say that she missed them, but then they would worry about her. A bell jingled when she stepped inside the general store that housed the telegraph office. Lainey settled on *Working and busy. Sold another drawing through Mr. Frayman. Attended church with Kelly last week. Beaumonts send regards to Gray and Stephen. Will write soon. With love...*

After paying for her telegrams, she headed toward the boarding house. She thought about the church service she'd attended with Kelly. It was the only one since Christmas, but not the first time he'd asked her. Lainey finally agreed, seeing how he seemed so strangely compelled in his desire to go. It was a nice service, and she didn't feel uncomfortable. Apathy kept her from feeling much of anything at all.

Zane didn't go. He probably never would. Yet, Zane never said he didn't believe. Lainey frowned, trying to figure it out.

Kelly kept talking lately about finding different work. He didn't like being apart from Zane so much and, she knew, apart from her. His evident, growing affection troubled her. Lainey did care a great deal for Kelly. Given the time and the right conditions, Lainey admitted to herself that she might even be able to fall in love with him, after a fashion. But she steeled herself with the reminder that she once loved Jed and even Owen -- after a fashion -- hardly with the same fullness of heart that she loved Bobby.

Her handsome, hazel-eyed Bobby.

If she settled for only a part and form of love, she would drive Kelly away, just as she'd done to Jed and Owen. A man needed a complete woman, not just her shell.

And I don't have that to give anymore. I can never submit my whole self to someone else like I did with Bobby. I can't trust that much.

A woman's voice rang across the street. "Lainey? Lainey Kade, is that you?"

Lainey looked up. She squinted against the bright sun glinting off the snow and smiled. Mrs. Anderson waved and hurried toward her. She'd been friendly toward Lainey at church.

"Hello, Mrs. Anderson."

"I see you aren't letting the cold keep you trapped indoors."

Lainey smiled. "No. It's such a fine day I thought I'd take a walk and enjoy it."

"That's good. It was so nice to see you and your friend in church on Sunday. Did you enjoy the reverend's message?"

Lainey couldn't really remember what it was about. "Oh, yes."

"He's such a wonderful pastor."

Lainey nodded.

"Well, I'll be off. Just wanted to say hello. Hope we see you there again soon."

"I'll try to make it. I can't promise."

Mrs. Anderson nodded in her continual sort of head-bobbing fashion, her smile unwavering. "We'll see you, then," she said, and hurried away.

Lainey turned and crossed the bridge toward the east side, wondering what Mrs. Anderson would think if she knew Lainey was on her way to visit a gambler in his private quarters. She smiled wickedly and picked up her pace.

Chapter Thirteen

Little snow fell over winter. Locals complained that they ought to hope for a rainy spring. It did snow more in March, and the wind whipped it about ferociously, but spring arrived with mild glory in Peshtigo and the surrounding Sugar Bush region. And, as the rafts of logs rushed down the rivers that emptied into Lake Michigan, Kelly Beaumont said good-bye to the men and animals he'd grown acquainted with over the winter, and made light feet toward home.

Home. When had he last thought of any place in that way? Not in almost ten years.

He joined up to fight against the rebellion when he was just seventeen. Now, going on twenty-seven, he realized he'd only been a youth the last time he'd had a home worth coming to.

The family farm in St. Joe never seemed like home after his ma and pa both died. Suzanne was already married and having children, and even though she and her husband lived in the old place, it never seemed the same. Even when Kelly and Zane talked about going home, Kelly knew that neither one of them believed there would ever be such a place again.

But that was changing.

Even though he quartered at the company boarding house, just having a regular place to drop his bags, and knowing Zane and Lainey lived there in town, made Peshtigo feel more like home than anything else had in all this time.

He wanted more.

Kelly stuck to his job all winter, and he managed to lay a fair amount of his earnings aside once he decided not blow everything on the Saturday night binges. He figured he'd held onto enough to start up his own small livery, and he and Zane could build a room in the back for living in while he earned enough money to build a house.

The urge to settle struck Kelly like never before. Even though desires came and went to do other things with his life, he never felt so much like planting roots. Not until he met Lainey. He fully intended to marry that girl, and he wanted to have some stability to offer her when he did. He knew she wasn't ready yet, but maybe by the end of summer she could have a change of heart. He'd be busy, starting up his business, building a place for him and Zane, then her, but there would still be plenty of time to be with her. Not like now, not just seeing her for a few hours each weekend.

Zane always had lots more time with her than Kelly had. It was a good thing Kelly trusted him. Zane stayed close, keeping other fellows from moving in on Lainey, even though they tried. After all, men outnumbered women in these woods five to one. But Lainey didn't show an interest in any of them. She acted content just to spend all her friendship on the Beaumonts. Well, that was fine with Kelly.

Kelly bought a buckskin gelding from a horse trader coming through the area selling stock to the company. Now as he rode towards Peshtigo, he thought about the things he and Lainey would do together. He would romance her the way she ought to be romanced. He'd let her know that she was the girl for him.

Ah, the town looked just like he remembered it, only the newness of spring made the colors lighter and brighter. The houses appeared clean, fresh, and inviting. Townsfolk worked their gardens and swept the sawdust and mud from the plank walkways lined along the storefronts.

He smiled and nodded at strangers he passed on the street, riding straight to find her. He saw the priest, Father Pernin, standing outside his home in a yard covered with wood violets. Kelly pulled his horse up short.

"Good morning, sir."

Father Pernin turned around and smiled at him.

"I wonder if it would be wrong of me to ask a favor?"

Father Pernin approached his white picket fence. "You have only to ask, and I'll tell you if it's in my power to help." He adjusted his spectacles with a smile.

"I couldn't help noticing the posies in your yard."

"Ah, yes. Beautiful, aren't they?"

"Would it be all right if I picked some?"

Surprise crossed the priest's features at Kelly's request, but quickly faded into understanding.

"Just home from the camps?" he asked as he opened the gate and invited Kelly in.

Kelly dismounted and swung the reins over one white picket. "Yes, sir."

"I'm sure your lady will be thrilled with a bouquet."

Kelly bobbed his head. "Thank you."

"My pleasure. You're going to see the young lady who lives at the Forest House?"

Kelly stooped to pick the delicate short-stemmed flowers. "Yes. Her name is Lainey."

"That is good to know. I often wave, but I didn't know her name. Now I shall be able to say 'good morning, Lainey,' the next time she passes."

Kelly continued plucking flowers, and the priest stooped to join him. "I appreciate your letting me do this," Kelly said again.

"Is she expecting you?"

"Not exactly, though she knows I'd be coming any day. I want to give a good impression on my first day back."

"You're definitely off to a good start, I'd say." Father Pernin handed him the flowers he'd plucked. The two straightened up and shook hands. "Blessings to you on your courtship."

"I'll need all I can get," said Kelly, and he headed back to his horse.

"Do you have a brother?" the priest asked unexpectedly.

Kelly nodded.

"I thought I must have seen the two of you with Lainey before."

"Yes, you probably have. His name is Zane, and mine is Kelly, by the way. Kelly Beaumont."

"It's a pleasure to know you, Kelly Beaumont."

Kelly nodded and turned his horse away. He put the violets to his nose and inhaled deeply, excitement stirring him at seeing Lainey in only minutes.

When he came to the Forest House, he thought about going inside, but decided instead to approach her the way he had last winter, by throwing a few wood chips at her window.

Hitching the horse to a rail, he clutched the violets in one hand and tossed handfuls of chips with the other. In only a few moments, the window slid open.

He held the flowers to his chest as though they grew straight from his heart. "Hark, what light through yonder window breaks?"

Lainey grinned, her black hair shining almost blue in the sunlight. "Not thinking of breaking my window, are you, Romeo?"

"It is the east, and Lainey is the sun."

She smiled at his flattery.

"Or is it the moon?" he asked, still smiling, but drowning in the sight of her. "For her eyes are blue like twilight, and her skin radiant in the night. Her hair like the shimmer of dark velvet..."

"That's enough, you."

He held up the flowers. "I missed you."

"Meet me in the kitchen in back."

His heart skipping, he strode around the building and up to the back door which she opened a couple minutes later. John was in the kitchen with her, preparing for the next meal. He eyed them both, but Kelly tried to ignore his presence. He offered her the sweet bouquet, and she inhaled the scent.

"Mmm. The first flowers of spring. Thank you, Kell." She put them in a glass of water and held it in her hand.

"I'm home, and do you know what I'm going to do now?"

"What?"

"Stay."

She waited for him to explain.

"I've had enough of life in the woods. I've saved a little money, and I'm going to approach the town council and see about buying a plot where I can build a livery."

"There already are two."

"Which are filled beyond capacity every weekend. And there's enough work available in harness repair and such to keep me busy during the week. I'd like to eventually buy a few animals and a wagon to lease out."

"That's wonderful, Kelly. It'll be so good to have you back, permanently."

"Course, I won't be able to keep living at the boarding house. I thought I'd build a room in the back of the livery for me and Zane. How is my brother doing by the way?"

"You haven't seen him?"

Kelly shook his head. "Not yet."

"He's doing fine, I guess. He hasn't mentioned any trouble with dreams or anything."

"He wouldn't."

"How about you? Do you still have them?"

Kelly looked at her closely. How could he tell her that she had chased all the sorrow and bad dreams away without such explanation scaring her off?

"No. Not anymore," was all he said.

"Should we go find Zane?"

"Will he be at the boarding house this time of day?"

"It's past noon. He might. But it's more likely we'll find him at the Timbermen's. That's his favorite haunt lately."

"All right. Do you want to put those flowers someplace?"

She set them on a windowsill near the sink. She turned to John. "Is this okay?"

"Sure. Long as the Mrs. doesn't think you brought them for me." He gave her a wink.

Kelly held the door for her, and they walked out together into the sunshine.

They found Zane an hour later coming out of the Timbermen's just as Lainey predicted. She was glad to see he hadn't been drinking.

The two brothers fell into a back-slapping bear hug. "Kelly! You just come in?"

"About an hour ago. Had to find this lady to tell me where you were."

Zane shifted his jaw and grinned. Kelly could sniff him out like a hound dog on a coon. He hadn't needed Lainey's help. He just couldn't resist seeking her out first. By his grin, Zane realized it.

"So what've you got planned, now that you're back?"

Kelly filled him in on his ideas about the livery. Zane nodded, appreciating all the thought Kelly had given his plans. "When do we start building?"

"Right away, I guess. I'll go to the town board members tomorrow, and if they can get me on a piece of land, I can get the lumber by Thursday."

"Let's do it," said Zane.

"All right." The two shook hands.

*****

Lainey's roots settled deeper into the Peshtigo soil. So much deeper she sometimes forgot she lived here on her own, apart from any family. She occasionally needed to pinch herself to remember that the Beaumont brothers weren't her family, even though she depended on them like kin.

She cheered for their success as they worked together to build Kelly's livery, just as she would have cheered had it been Gray or Eldon starting a business, or Kent training his mare. She marveled at how quickly the two brothers erected the frame for the building. They showed more talent for practical things than she credited them for. Kelly knew exactly what he wanted, and he certainly put his back into the task.

And Zane -- well, there Lainey discovered a surprise. Putting his mind to Kelly's success, Zane acted like a different man than the one she'd grown used to over the months. He surprised her with his sharp eye for detail and an acute insight for planning she'd never guessed at. He solved whatever puzzles arose with the practiced eye of a foreman just like her father or Uncle Rob or her family's woods cruiser and good friend Tom Durant. She thought it a sorry waste Zane didn't put his talents to use in a better place than the gambling halls.

But, she had no business telling him to change the direction of his life. She had her own problems to consider and moon over.

Wearing a dark, blue-checked dress and matching bonnet, Lainey swung a picnic basket on her arm loaded with leftovers from John and Clara's kitchen, her conscience feeling only the weight of Ginny's recent letter tucked inside between the sausages and Clara's rhubarb pie. Bringing Zane and Kelly their lunch and offering them a break from the mid-day heat, she also wondered if she might drum up the courage to tell them about her dilemma.

She walked past the still-unfinished Catholic Church and turned on Peck Street, crossing Maple and going two more blocks until she came to the corner where the distinct echo of hammers rang louder and louder. She shaded her eyes and found Kelly and Zane both on the roof, beating nails into wooden shingles. Kelly was a picture of brawn and sweat, his blonde hair plastered against the side of his face, his bare back and shoulders rippling and burned in the sun. Zane looked just as hot and uncomfortable, but he wore a blue shirt, the sleeves rolled up over his forearms and perspiration sticking it to his skin. His hair looked darker, more red than blonde where it showed under his hat. For a crazy moment Lainey wondered who cut his hair since she'd never followed up on her offer to do it.

"You boys thirsty?" she called.

Looking down on her, they both split grins, Kelly coming to the ladder first and bolting down with a grace that belied his size. Zane followed just as easily, but with less haste.

She set down the basket and pulled out a jug of cold water, handing it over to them. They took long draughts. Lainey smiled, inwardly pleased with herself for bringing it.

Zane wiped his sleeve across his mouth. "Thanks."

"It's getting pretty warm out."

"Hotter up there on the roof," said Kelly. "But you look fresh."

His eyes twinkled with the compliment, causing her smile to widen.

"It'll be nice when we get our own well dug."

Zane eyed the basket on her arm. "You bring us some lunch, did you?"

Lainey pulled out an old, thread-worn quilt and spread it over the ground. Sitting on it, she laid out their lunch. "Sit down before you faint."

Kelly took to his knees next to her. "This looks like a feast."

"Well, it's not bratwurst."

Zane pulled out some cold chicken and tore off a bite. "It'll do." He smiled a lazy smile.

"I can't believe how much you've gotten done in less than two weeks," she said. "I didn't know you boys were so talented."

"That's Zane's doing," said Kelly. "I just do what he tells me."

Lainey glanced at Zane who didn't deny it, but he didn't look at her.

She looked back at Kelly. "But you know what you want."

Kelly nodded. "That I do." He held the water jug out to her as though he were offering something more.

"I would like to know where you learned how to build things. Did your father teach you?"

Kelly shook his head, but Zane looked away at the building as though his thoughts were elsewhere. Lainey let her eyes swing his way every other moment or so, just to see if it was true.

"No, our Pa wasn't much for building things. But we learned a lot later on."

"During the war?" She watched Zane while she said it, and for a moment a smoldering pall filled Zane's far-away look.

"Yeah," Kelly said softly.

She decided to say no more. Clearly Zane was uncomfortable and still unwilling to talk about his military experiences.

"I got a letter from my friend Ginny," she said, changing the subject and wondering how to tell them of its contents with her own demons haunting her, but determined to try.

Zane darted a glance at her that reminded her he'd been listening, and that he knew something about her past, and in a way she hadn't expected, it gave her courage.

"She's getting married soon." A breath escaped her along with the words.

"It that good news or bad?" asked Kelly.

"Oh, it's very good news. She and her husband-to-be are a perfect match." Lainey pursed her lips.

Zane spoke softly. "You don't seem glad."

For the first time ever Lainey was able to read his eyes clearly.

He understands.

She reached into the basket and pulled out Ginny's latest missive. She handed the pages to him. "See for yourself."

He took the letter, unfolded it, and read silently while Kelly looked on. Passing the page to Kelly he said, "She wants you to be there for the wedding."

Lainey nodded.

"Your cousin Katie will be there."

Her voice dropped, and she fought a swell creeping up her throat. "Naturally."

"With Jed," Zane added.

She swallowed hard.

Kelly finished reading and set the letter on the blanket. His blue eyes filled with concern and question. He touched her arm. "Do you still love him, Lainey?"

"Oh, heavens no!" she burst out, rolling her eyes.

Kelly's shoulders relaxed, but Zane kept a close watch on her. "Lainey." The way he said her name called her gaze back to his. She sniffed. "What is it that makes you so upset about Katie and this -- Jed Clark -- if it isn't that you love him?"

She plucked at her dress, worrying the fabric between her fingers. The moment for truth had come. The moment she'd both dreaded and longed to be free to tell about, and it burned in her chest like a physical thing. "It's not the sort of thing you tell a man."

She noted Zane and Kelly's quickly exchanged glances. Then Zane offered her one of his rare grins. "Aw, Elaina, by now you must think of us as brothers."

She wondered how he could be so right. She gave him a doubtful smile. Maybe Zane considered himself to be like a brother to her, but Kelly didn't, and she was not exactly one of the boys.

"We know it's serious, at least to you." Kelly patted her hand. "We won't make fun or anything, Lainey."

She took a deep breath and let it out slowly. "It isn't just Jed. If I ever go back, I'll have to face everyone, and the idea just never seems to get any easier than it was the day I went away."

"Who is everyone?"

"Jed, Owen Steckler, everyone who says Lainey Kade is

unmarryable."

Zane's eyebrows shot up. "Un-*what*?"

She looked straight at him and poured out the truth. "Jed jilted me, just like you read in that last letter from Ginny. But to tell the truth, it wasn't the first time. First there was Owen. He broke off our engagement just days before the wedding. Jed thought he could do better with me, but he couldn't. I drove them both away."

Kelly's head dropped so that his gaze stayed on his hands folded in his lap. But he began to shake his head. Zane kept watching her as though somehow the story was going to change.

"You boys know how I am," she said, miserably. "Or at least you should by now. I'm stubborn and opinionated. Nobody can tell me what to do if I don't want them to. Not even the men I was supposed to marry -- either of them. My reputation is widespread. 'Lainey Kade, the shrew able to make any man miserable who has guts enough to come calling.'"

Kelly looked up, finally, and took her hand, squeezing it in his until she thought it might break. "They couldn't be more wrong."

"Kelly, you don't know what happened. I--"

"It doesn't matter. I know you."

"Kell, a woman has to be able to submit to a husband's authority. I... can't."

She glanced at Zane who still watched her stonily. What thoughts wound on behind his dusky gaze?

"Is that it?" The words came out of him softly, as though he'd figured it all out, and found nothing wrong.

She blinked and looked from him to Kelly and back to Zane again. "What do you mean?"

"Kelly's right. We do know you. You're a girl who doesn't care what others think. You are opinionated and headstrong."

She didn't feel better to hear him agreeing with her.

"So why does it matter to you what your reputation is with them? You break the rules. So what? You live your life."

Confusion assaulted her. "Here, I do."

"Here with Kelly and me you are Lainey. Who are you back there with them?"

She shrugged. "I don't know what you mean."

"Lainey, you do whatever you want, all the time. You break boundaries and have your drawings published in big city papers. You swim like the boys, with the boys. You beat Kelly at cards fifty percent of the time."

A small smile crept out at the corners of her lips. "And you sometimes."

"Not very often." He smirked then leaned close. "Lainey, you are no match for them. Why does that bother you?"

"I want to be loved!" A stab of pain ripped through her chest and tears welled up to blur her vision. She quickly wiped them away. "No.

No... That's not it. I want to be *able* to love."

Kelly's fingers caressed hers. "So why can't you?"

She turned to him. "Because there's nothing of that kind of love left inside me. It died. All of it. Forever."

Kelly sat back, uncertainty and confusion clouding his face, but he still held her hands.

"Because of those fellas?"

She breathed twice, then three times, quickly, trying to stop the assault on her emotions, but it didn't help. The tears she tried to stanch rolled out. "I can't tell you anymore. I just can't."

Zane's eyebrows rose and his jaw worked as he puzzled. Kelly looked beaten.

"I'm sorry." She swallowed more tears and wiped her face on her sleeves. "I didn't think I'd cry. I've wanted to tell you, but I didn't know how. I... I just couldn't be with Jed or Owen. They wanted to love me, but I couldn't give them all of me in return. The pieces were gone that needed to belong to one of them. You understand, don't you? If you married a woman, you'd want her whole heart, right? You'd want her to be able to yield it to you completely."

Zane nodded slowly, and Kelly stared, rubbing the knuckles of her hands in his.

"Is there a reason that the pieces were gone?" Zane asked quietly.

She nodded, her whole being filled with a wretched ache.

"We're sorry, Lainey. You don't have to tell us about it." He gathered the letter and tucked it back into the basket. "We didn't know."

"Thank you." She watched the care he took to gather the remnants of their lunch together.

Kelly's jaw tightened. "I'd like to go to your friend's wedding, just to have it out with any fool man who'd jilt you."

She sniffed. "Aw, Kelly."

"You do have to go," said Zane.

Her head shot up. "What?"

"You have to go. Your family needs you. Your friend Ginny needs you. Even Katie needs you to be there. You may as well go."

"Why?"

"Because this isn't about Jed or Owen or any of the people who mean to say hurtful things. It's about you getting over someone you cared about, and whom you can't let go of." He finished packing up their picnic and stood up while she stared at him, trying hard to figure him out.

"But how can I?"

Zane reached down and pulled her to her feet. "It'll be all right. Kelly and I will go with you. And your folks and your brothers will be there, too."

Nonplussed, she took in his words, wondering if Zane was serious. But if there was one thing she was beginning to discern, it was when

Zane meant what he said. She opened her mouth and fumbled for words. "You'd do that?"

"We aren't going to fight with anyone." Zane zeroed in a glance on Kelly. "We're just going because we're your friends, and you need us to be there. Your folks wouldn't want you traveling alone."

She looked between the two of them, wondering how she could feel so much better already, just hearing what Zane had to say. "My brothers were there to look out for me just days before I left home and it caused a bit of a stir, I can tell you."

Zane chucked her under the chin and smiled. "Kelly won't be able to stand it if you go away without him. He'll be afraid you won't come back," he added, drawing out a long smile that made her blush and unable to look back at the big blonde man standing beside her, who slipped her hand in his again.

Chapter Fourteen

"No horseback for you this time," said Zane. "You're traveling in pure luxury."

The second day of June found them loading a wagon with Lainey's bags and getting ready to set out on the road to Green Bay. They settled Lainey on the wagon seat between them, with their luggage in the back.

Lainey snorted. "I've taken plenty of wagons over roads carved out of the woods. I can't say that luxury ever described a one of them. I think we should have gotten tickets for the stage."

"Don't worry. Kelly has a delicate hand at these things."

"That's right." Kelly took the reins and snapped them over the horse's back. "I used to haul wounded men to the field hospitals during the war."

"You did?"

"Sure enough. I was in charge of the General's horse, too."

"All right. I'll trust you."

Endless tracks of tall pines hid the sky along the road to Green Bay, but they noted the progress of the clearing going on and the rail being laid northward. Again, they discussed how good it would be when they wouldn't have to endure a wagon ride at all. Economically, the railroads coming north to places like Peshtigo and Marinette likely spelled rising fortune for the lumber barons. They would be able to tap deeper into sources of timber which could then be loaded on freight trains and taken to the mills. But for this trip, at least, Lainey and the Beaumonts would have to endure the jostling journey in the buckboard.

"You just lean on us if you need to," Kelly said. "We'll act as your cushions."

Still, Lainey felt the soreness of the ride. She ached with relief when they finally boarded the train going west the next day.

The trip to the Chippewa country went so much faster than the one she'd taken leaving home. Certainly traveling a direct route made a difference, and they didn't make tourist stops along the way. She did, however, keep her drawing paper handy, and she sketched several scenes along the journey.

"Look there," she said once, pointing out the window to the north.

"Looks like fog," said Kelly.

"Smoke," said Zane.

Lainey leaned back against the seat. "It must be a fire. It may be a farmer clearing land. If it's a wildfire it'll likely burn itself out at some point. Either way, the farmers will be happy that it's done their work for them."

Fires licked away at the perimeter of civilization frequently enough, especially in places where trees were king. Sometimes they started with a campfire left to burn itself out. Sometimes a spark from lightning or, as Zane noted, from some careless railroad worker, though smokers were rare among any of the men who worked in the woods.

They passed many such crews of both lumbermen and railroaders, men strong and wild in body and spirit. They wore the careless masculine beauty of men who lived free lives in the open air.

Zane watched as Lainey tried to hurriedly harness their images on paper while the train chugged by. "You're both good and fast."

"Thank you. But partly it's because I've seen their like so many times before. It's not a new scene."

"No, I suppose not. I guess I could say the same thing. This whole country's going to be covered with track before we know it."

She nodded. "I wonder where it'll stop."

"Wherever there's a town to grow and money to be made, track will be laid to it."

"Even in Wisconsin?"

"I reckon so."

Fatigue dogged Lainey, and three days' grime and train soot embedded her skin by the time they reached Eau Claire. Yet, an unexpected anticipation at being home and seeing her family again took happy root inside her. She'd wired them to let them know they were coming, but there hadn't been time to wait for a reply. Kelly set the last of their luggage on the train platform just as she saw Zane looking toward a tall, dark-headed man approaching them at the station. Stephen Gilbert held out his hand.

Stephen gripped first Kelly's hand, then Zane's. "Welcome to the Chippewa country." Then he saw Lainey and a smile stretched across his face. He picked her up off her feet and spun her in a circle. "Well just look at you. An independent woman! Gray's over there with the horses and wagon. If we can carry all these bags, we'll go find him and get you home."

"How're my folks?"

"They're fine. Can't wait to see you."

Closer to the wagon, Grayson let out a whoop calling attention to their group. He jumped down off the buckboard and kissed Lainey's cheek before saying hello to the others. "It's about time you came home."

"Ginny was pretty happy when she heard you planned to be here for the wedding," said Stephen as they all climbed in and headed toward the northeast edge of town.

"How about Katie?" Lainey wondered aloud.

Stephen patted her leg. "Katie's more than glad. She's just a little worried."

Lainey gazed ahead up the road. "She doesn't need to be."

"I'll tell her you said so."

She looped her arm through his and hugged herself against him.

"Thanks, Stephen."

*****

Manason sat on the edge of the bed and pulled his socks off. On the other side of the bed, Colette sat brushing her hair. Leaning back, Nase gently took the brush from her hand. He came to his knees on the bed and began to brush her hair in long, even strokes that glided through his hands in the way he loved. She tilted her neck and he brushed the side, giving her a soft kiss on her cheek.

Her eyes closed dreamily. "So what do you think of them?"

Nase paused with the brush. "I don't know. I'm keeping my eye on them." He caught her smile and continued brushing.

"Kelly's in love with her."

"What makes you say that?"

"Can't you tell?"

"I'd like not to notice."

She turned around and faced him. "I don't want to see her hurt again."

"Well, then, she shouldn't be traveling alone with men who aren't her brothers or family. Lainey brings these things on herself. She's headstrong."

"She just doesn't always know her heart."

"She'd better start knowing it. There are two strange men staying in my home who don't seem like the types to tag along after a girl just for her friendship."

Colette frowned. "Nase, don't say such awful things."

"Well? Speaking as a man, I know it's true."

"You think they're trouble, then?"

"I didn't say that. Lainey could be trouble to them."

A shaft of pain stabbed Colette at the thought. That's what the talk was. Lainey was trouble to men. Now it came out of her father's mouth.

He seemed to hear what he'd just said. "I'm sorry, Honey." He held her against him. "How's a father supposed to trust men where his daughter's concerned? Especially when the daughter is a girl as wonderful as ours."

"You think this time will be any different?" Worry tinged Colette's voice.

"Well, I'm going to talk to these men while they're here. I'll get the lay of things figured out. Don't worry."

"Don't scare them off."

Nase chuckled and looked down into his wife's eyes, cupping her face in his square palm. "I'll try not to, but I can't promise," he said, lowering his lips to hers.

*****

"Lainey, I'm so glad you came." Ginny's eyes shone. "You'll stand in the wedding with me, won't you?"

"I thought you'd asked Katie."

"I want you both."

Lainey hesitated. Standing with Katie didn't bother her. She'd thought long and hard about her feelings where Katie and Jed were concerned and realized she no longer hurt from it. Pain still pricked at not being thought of as the marrying kind, and Bobby's memory clung in deep places, but it no longer mattered about Jed or Owen. She was over and done with them.

Ginny's brow lifted. "Please?"

Lainey hugged her. "Of course I'll stand with you."

"That's wonderful. You'll be standing opposite Archie's brother Raymond. He's nice, you remember?"

"I remember Raymond."

"What about your friends? They'll be coming, too, won't they?"

Lainey nodded.

"I wish you'd tell me about them. Katie says they're gamblers, but loads of fun."

Lainey laughed. "They are that."

Ginny's doe-like eyes held mischief. "So you're quite close with them."

"Ginny..." Lainey warned.

"Any closer to either one of them in particular?"

Lainey laughed again. "Ginny! Stop it!"

Ginny shrugged. "One can't help wondering. What do your ma and pa think of them?"

"I don't know. I suppose Pa's got his eye on them, but he shouldn't worry."

"Shouldn't he?"

"No. I'm not the marrying kind, remember?"

"Who said anything about marrying?"

Lainey slapped her playfully. "I can't believe you'd say that."

"Well, they're both very handsome. And we can't help noticing that they don't seem to regard you absolutely as a sister."

"Well, maybe not Kelly. But I'm not doing anything to lead him on. I hope you don't think that."

"No. I don't. What about the other one?"

"Zane? Zane is..." She shook her head. What about Zane? His heart had been abused, too. It was as much locked away as Lainey's was shattered. "Zane has his own troubles. He doesn't have any interest in adding me to them."

"What kind of troubles?"

She wondered if she should say, but trusted Ginny's confidence. "Soldier's heart."

"Oh... the war still?"

"They say it takes years. Sometimes soldiers never get over the things they've seen or done."

"And Kelly?"

"He says that he's doing better than he used to. He talks a little bit about it now. I think that helps. He used to handle horses during the war and carry wounded soldiers. All that besides fighting."

"And now he's starting his own livery?"

"Yes. He's got ambition."

"But not Zane?"

Lainey shook her head.

"Does he talk about the war?"

"No, never. I don't know what he did besides fight and watch people die. He saw their father die, so Kelly says."

"How terrible."

"Yes, I can't imagine it."

Ginny took both her hands in her own. "Well, enough sad talk. I'm so glad you're here, Lainey. So glad!"

*****

The wedding took place the following week. Lainey's grandma and mother fixed her a new dress of pale cream chiffon, and wound her hair up in shining black curls and ringlets on her head. She felt absolutely regal, but agreed the bride was stunning in her white gown with her dark complexion and deep brown eyes.

Joseph and Kashe Gilbert beamed on as they watched their girl marry her only love, Archie Sattler, and Lainey thought how handsome they looked as well -- Joe ever carelessly handsome, and Kashe like an Indian princess, burgeoning with child.

A party followed the wedding, and most of the town showed up for it. Katie, the maid of honor, promenaded now on Jed Clark's arm. Lainey spoke to her before the wedding day, and assured her she held no grudge. She wished them well. Such a nice looking pair they made.

Katie urged Jed to ask Lainey to dance, but Lainey told her younger cousin it would only cause talk, and declined her cousin's gesture of good will. She sensed relief from Jed as well.

Kelly held out his hand. "How about a dance with me? We haven't practiced up in a while."

She slipped her hand into his, aware of how her family and old friends watched them.

"They've all got their eyes on you," he said, waltzing her across the floor.

"No, sir. They're watching you."

"Well, then, let's give them something to watch." He wiggled his eyebrows and twirled her around the floor at a pace that left her laughing and breathless. "See how all that practice last winter paid off?"

He stopped in front of Zane who held a cup of refreshment out to Lainey. "Dizzy?"

She nodded and took the cup. "Thank you."

"People are staring."

She darted a glance from side to side. "I think that was Kelly's idea."

"May I, once you're rested?"

"I'm ready if you are."

Zane took her out to dance. He didn't fly with her like Kelly had, but held her gently, respectfully, never looking at anyone else, but only at her.

"You're a good dancer, Zane. You should spend more time dancing and less time playing cards."

"Who would I dance with? You and Kelly usually do that at the Sunday night jigs and forget all about me."

"Well, I never knew you danced so well, or I might have asked you to come along."

He seemed to consider her remark as he held her. "You just stick to Kelly. He'll take you places."

"What's that supposed to mean, Mr. Beaumont? Are you trying to play matchmaker between your brother and I?"

He grinned, those likeable lines around his mouth creasing. "I might be."

"Well don't wish that on him, all right?"

"Kelly doesn't scare easily."

"Neither did Jed, at first."

"How is it, seeing Jed with Katie?"

She shrugged, holding his shoulders tighter. "It's not a problem."

He changed subjects. "I don't think your father trusts me or Kelly."

Lainey smiled and cocked one eyebrow at him. "Then you just better take a care, Zane Beaumont."

*****

Zane's pulse quickened. Was Lainey flirting with him? She blushed and turned her head to spy her mother on the side of the room. Zane wanted to pull her closer, but he didn't dare. There was Kelly and her parents and brothers to consider. There was his own nature, his own slavish impulses. He didn't say it was his heart.

He considered this thing, this whatever-it-was compelling him toward Elaina Kade, and he finally convinced himself that it wasn't his heart doing the longing. He'd bludgeoned out his heart on the battlefield. It was there he learned that love brought pain. The two were inseparable entities. He wanted nothing more of love since those days when he buried his parents.

But there were still desires... base desires. Lainey fit so perfectly into his arms, her tall, slender body next to his. That's what this feeling was, wasn't it, just desire trying to take him over?

He let her go at the end of the dance and wandered outside, looking for a place to cool off and clear his head. He passed a group of men who looked his way but didn't stop him, and noticed a couple of young women casting him smiles. He walked downhill toward the dark swirling waters of a river he'd forgotten the name of. All these lumbering towns had a river running through them. One was the same as the next in some manner. The moonlight shone off the water and the sound of its gentle rushing brought calm to his thoughts.

"Elaina Eastman Kade," he murmured, tasting the syllables of her name like sweet candy.

He'd been paying close attention since coming to the Chippewa. The day she'd told them about her reputation she'd as good as said that someone else had stolen her heart -- and broken it -- someone besides Jed Clark or Owen Steckler. He hadn't pressed her then, and now, even though he watched closely, no one appeared who unsettled her. Maybe whoever it was had left the country, taking those pieces of her heart with him.

Suddenly a hand touched his arm and he started.

She stood there like an apparition in the moonlight, her hair lost in the blackness around her, her eyes big and shining, her skin white in the cream colored dress, her bosom rising and falling in silent breaths. She didn't say anything, but slipped up beside him and stared out over the water. He didn't want to break the spell she cast, so he kept silent for a while, feeling calmer and more peaceful as he got used to her being there beside him.

Finally she smiled at him. "It's strange to be home." Her tranquil gaze fell out over the water again. "I realize how often I've taken it for granted. I've stood on this bank, not in this exact place, but on this river a thousand times. It looks the same. The night air feels no different. There's comfort in being with people I love and who love me. I lay in my bed last night and listened to the house creaking. I could still smell the pie Grandma baked in the morning. It was so familiar."

Zane didn't interrupt.

"I've lived without being thankful."

She looked at him, then away. She smirked. "I don't suppose you'd understand."

"I would."

"Then why do we do the things we do, Zane? Why do we keep dreaming of something new? Why are we looking for things that we can't possibly ever find instead of being satisfied with those things we have?"

"Because some things are beyond our grasp and they always will be," he said, trying not to look at her. "It's who we've become that keeps us from them. So instead we keep moving toward the next adventure, the next turn of the cards."

"You're right." Suddenly she gazed up at him, and he couldn't have pulled himself away if he tried. He didn't. Lowering his head to hers, he took her chin in his hand and kissed her, softly, achingly, and then with more longing.

When they parted she stepped back, her mouth open in a look of surprise, the wind moving the hem of her dress in the moonlight.

"I'm sorry, Elaina," Zane said gruffly, instantly feeling shamed at his lack of control.

"It's... it's okay. It's not your fault."

He laughed humorlessly. "It's not?"

She frowned, and he hated himself for the troubled look on her face. "I better get back. I told Ginny I'd be sure and dance with Raymond."

Zane nodded, but held her eyes a moment longer. "You'd better, then."

"Will you come back inside?"

"In a bit. You go ahead."

"All right." She turned away and walked back to the party, never once looking back at him, leaving Zane to wonder if he imagined the whole thing. But the warmth lingering on his lips and the sweet taste of her told him that he didn't.

*****

Lainey rode home with Eldon and Kent and the Beaumonts in a wagon behind their parents.

"So what'll you do now that you're back? You still going to keep drawing for the papers?" asked Eldon.

"What do you mean? I'm not going to stay."

"What?" asked Kent. "Gee, Lainey, nobody's been mean to you have they? Why you want to leave again?"

She put her arm around him. "I don't know. It's just that I've kind of made a life over in Peshtigo. I don't think I'm finished there yet."

Eldon adjusted his grip on the reins. "Ma'll take that hard."

She looked at her brother with new eyes. Not for the first time since she'd come home did she notice how much he'd grown and matured. He was fifteen now. She'd missed his birthday and Kent's twelfth.

"She's too busy to be missing me every minute. I bet it's been pretty peaceful around home since I've been gone."

Kent brushed a snicker across his fist. "Well, there hasn't been as much yelling with fellows on the porch."

"You better watch it, or I'll show you some yelling." She glanced over her shoulder at the two men in the back of the wagon. They both grinned at the conversation. She chuckled. "I can yell at those two back there if it'll make you feel better about sending me off again."

"No, that's all right," said Kent. "I can get by without it."

The others all laughed.

"I hope Pa'll let me come and see you if you stay in Peshtigo," Eldon said.

"I don't know why he wouldn't, El. You're getting old enough to do some traveling. You can bring Gray or Stephen."

"They're going to be busier than ever this fall. Maybe something will work out. Maybe Pa will let me go alone."

"Maybe." She wondered what she would do with Eldon in a wild town like Peshtigo. Temptations a-plenty lay in wait to beckon a young man like her brother down a wrong path. She felt a moment's conviction. "We'll see."

Tiredness claimed her when they got home and she fell straight into bed. Her thoughts, though, refused to let her settle. She thought about Ginny standing before the pastor saying vows meant to seal her for life to Archie Sattler. She couldn't help but equate it to the fact that had Bobby not died, they'd have already been married for a couple of years. There'd probably be a baby by now. She closed her eyes and tried to picture him, his big smile, his eyes sparkling into hers. But the vision kept obscuring and Zane's face kept interloping -- Zane's eyes, with their dreamy, unreadable look. His lips touching hers.

She curled onto her side and pressed her hand against her lips.

Zane had kissed her and she'd kissed him back. Even now, thinking about it, she felt shaken in a way she didn't think she could feel again. But what was it, really? Just another thrill? Another daring ride into the unknown and the dangerous?

Certain that explained it. She thought again of the wedding and how happy Ginny was, forcing her reflections onto her friend until a restless sleep came over her.

*****

The barn door creaked open and Manason called out as he came inside. "Boys, you still awake?"

Zane and Kelly bedded in the loft. They hadn't yet turned down the lantern.

Kelly threw a questioning look at his brother and called back. "Sure."

"Mind if I come up?"

"Come right ahead."

Manason passed the horses' stalls and climbed the ladder to the half-loft on the far end where Zane and Kelly had made their beds.

"You comfortable up here?" he asked, peering over the edge before climbing over.

"Fine," said Kelly, sitting cross-legged on his bed.

Manason set his own lantern on the solid floor near theirs and squatted down in front of the two men.

"Have a nice time at the wedding?"

"It was great. Your family is a nice bunch of folks. I'm real glad Lainey brought us along."

"Well, that's good. Actually, I wanted to talk to you boys about Elaina." He looked from Kelly to Zane who said nothing either verbally or in his indecipherable look. "How's she doing over there in Peshtigo, if you don't mind a father asking?"

"She's holding her own. You should be proud of her."

He looked directly at Zane. "What do you think?"

Zane was propped up on one elbow, his blanket thrown over him. "You know her well enough, Mr. Kade. She's your daughter. She's a strong gal. She can handle herself."

"Mm-hm. Would you say she's doing all right emotionally?"

"Why ask us that?"

"The way she talks to my wife, it sounds like she spends a lot of time with the two of you. Lainey had some hurts before she went away. We're concerned about how she's handling them. It's easy to come back for a wedding and act like everything is all right. But that could be far from the truth, wouldn't you agree?"

Zane didn't answer, but Kelly said, "She's told us a little about those hurts, sir. We're doing our best to help her through them."

"I bet you are."

"Not like that, sir."

"Why don't you tell me what you mean? You two are fine, strong young men. Grayson tells me you travel a lot. You've earned your living in some interesting ways." He tossed a pointed glance back at Zane.

"I won't deny that I feel pretty strongly about Lainey," said Kelly. "I'm working at starting my own livery. Maybe she told you about that. You can trust my intentions, Mr. Kade."

"And what about you," Manason asked Zane. "How do you fit into Lainey's life?"

"I reckon I don't, much," he said without expression. "You see, it's Kelly, here, who's hoping to heal your daughter's heart. I'm just along for the ride."

"But the three of you are close."

Kelly gave a nod. "I hope so."

Manason looked Zane's way again. "I don't want to see my daughter hurt any more than she has been. You wouldn't do that, would you?"

Kelly interrupted. "She's over that Jed Clark, if that's what you're worried about. The other fellow too. And I won't hurt her. I promise."

"Some promises are hard to keep. But if I can trust you boys to handle her carefully and not dally with her, I'll be satisfied."

Kelly stretched out his hand. "You have my word, Mr. Kade."

Manason shook his hand and turned to Zane.

"I don't really see how I fit into this scheme," Zane said. "Like I said, it's Kelly who wants her heart. I won't stand in the way of that." Zane held his gaze a moment longer.

"All right, then. Maybe we'll talk again." He picked up his lantern and backed down the ladder. "You boys sleep well."

"You too," said Kelly.

But Zane just turned over and pulled the blanket up over his shoulders without reply.

Chapter Fifteen

"Well, what do you think?" The whisper of Colette's breath touched Manason's face. She propped her head in her hand, facing him as they lay in the darkness. "Are they safe?"

"No one is safe. Lainey isn't looking for safe."

"What do you suppose she is looking for?"

"Her way back to God."

"Oh Nase... do you think she'll find it?"

"He isn't going to let her go, if that's what you're asking me."

"What about Kelly Beaumont? He hasn't hidden his interest."

"No, he hasn't. But I wonder if he's aware how interested his brother is."

"Zane? He's been kind to Lainey. But he seems to stay clear of her where Kelly is concerned."

"So it seems. But I wonder."

"Has he said or done something?"

"Not that I know of. But there's something in the way he is around her. He's a hard one to peg. He holds a good poker face."

"So I've been told. Do you know that he taught Lainey to play cards?"

Manason frowned. "No, I didn't know that."

"I think it's just been innocent fun. You know how competitive she is."

"As long as he isn't taking her into places she shouldn't be."

"She wouldn't do something like that, would she, you think?"

Manason looked through the darkness at Colette, imagining the outline of her face. "I'm afraid she might. She's trying to forget her ache, any way she can."

"Do you think they know about Bobby?"

"I don't know. Nothing's been said."

"Maybe they'll take more care if they know."

"If you think so, then maybe I'll have another talk with them," said Manason before he closed his eyes to sleep.

He cornered Zane as he was rinsing his head under the back pump the next morning.

"Breakfast is almost ready."

Zane flipped his wet hair back and picked up a towel hanging on the handle. "Sounds good. Don't know how I can be hungry after all the food we ate yesterday."

Manason smiled. "That's for sure." He rested his foot on a saw horse and leaned forward, crossing his arms over his leg. "Say, I hope I didn't offend you with my questions last night."

"No offense taken." Zane dabbed the towel across his bare shoulders and reached for his shirt.

"Mind if I ask you something else, then?"

"Go ahead."

By the pewter cast of Zane's eyes, Manason sensed the other man's defenses going up before he even said more. "I know you said that your brother has an interest in Lainey that goes beyond the friendship the two of you seem to have."

Zane's expression was guarded. "Yeah. So?"

"Has Lainey ever told you about a young man named Bobby Braedon?"

Zane shook his head.

Manason looked hard at Zane. "Bobby had her heart."

Zane started to step away. "You don't have to tell me this."

Manason dropped his foot and stopped him with a hand to his shoulder. "Yes, I do. You see, Bobby died. He was killed by a widow-maker in a logging accident."

"A widow-maker?"

"A dead limb, or in cases like Bobby's, a falling tree. He was buried there where it happened."

"Sorry to hear--"

"It was days before their wedding."

Zane returned his gaze. "Shouldn't you be telling this to my brother?"

"Should I? I thought maybe you both should know. Tell him for me, will you?"

"Sure." Zane stepped back. "Anything else?"

"Not at the moment," said Nase, trying hard to like this man who had somehow managed to become so much closer to Lainey than he was willing to admit. Nase was sure of it.

*****

Lainey slept on the train. Her head rested on Kelly's shoulder, and Zane watched it nod back and forth, trying to stay balanced. Kelly's own eyes were closed and his head lay back, but he looked like he was smiling.

"Hey, Kell," Zane said softly, trying not to disturb her. "You awake?"

Kelly nodded.

"Did you know there was another one, one she didn't tell us about on that day by the livery?"

"What are you talking about?" Kelly mumbled.

"There was Owen and Jed," Zane whispered, "but there was another one too."

Kelly opened one eye. "She told you that?"

"No. Her pa did." Zane's voice fell even further. "He said the fellow died."

Kelly's other eye opened. He frowned. "Pieces of her heart..."

Zane nodded. "Logging accident. Right before their wedding." His gaze flitted over her. She looked so peaceful. So beautiful. Tendrils of black hair brushed against her cheek like raven's feathers. "The wedding she wanted."

Kelly came more alert. He glanced down at Lainey and seemed to be considering her. "I would never hurt her like those others."

Zane smiled. "I never thought I'd see you like this. My big, little brother, head over heels."

"You should try it sometime. Feels good."

Zane shook his head. "No, thanks. You enjoy it while you can. Sooner or later there'll be pain. There always is."

"Isn't there pain in not having anyone too?" Kelly asked, his voice mellow, his head rocking against the high back of the seat.

"It isn't the same."

"I don't know about that, Zane. Permanent freedom isn't so great. I think maybe commitment has its own rewards."

"I didn't say it didn't, Preacher Boy. I just said I didn't want it."

Kelly shook his head. "Look at this, will you?" His eyes fell down to Lainey sleeping soundly against him. "Wouldn't you like just a little bit of what I'm after?"

"Careful what you say."

"You know what I mean."

"You don't even know if she'll have you yet. Figuring in what her Pa told me, it's going to take a while longer for her to be ready to make that leap."

"To listen to you talk, I can't help but think that there's hope for you, then, too."

Zane grinned. There was just no out-talking or out-convincing Kelly sometimes.

*****

Disembarking from the train in Green Bay, Lainey took a deep breath. She smelled the difference in the air by Lake Michigan. People spoke of a salty tang near the ocean. This was nothing like that. Lake Michigan contained a snap that smelled like something perfectly clean and fresh. Like her linens on the clothesline. It quenched her lungs like a draft from a bubbling spring. The lake opened up the sky.

It made her feel far away in a different, more exotic world from the one she left when she said good-bye to her parents and brothers. Even the numbers of non-English speaking immigrants living in the area testified to the feeling of foreignness here. Yet, at the same time, she tingled with anticipation of getting to her home. She could hardly wait to get back to Peshtigo, a place more like home to her than ever. She looked forward to sending more pictures to Arthur Frayman, to working again in the Forest House kitchen with John and Clara, even to visiting the Congregational Church again with Kelly and listening to Mrs. Anderson regale her with the local gossip. She fit there in Peshtigo.

Kelly reached for her bag. "What's that smile on your face?"

"Oh... I don't know. Just glad to be back."

"My ma used to always say it's nice to go away for a while, and always good to come back home."

She smiled and tucked back a wisp of hair blowing at her temple. "Yes, I'd say she's right."

Could this really be her, sounding so settled? Kelly gave her another of his warm smiles.

"It was a good trip," she said. "No one slighted me back home. Not a single person. They seemed to finally forget about all my... difficulties." Warmth crept up her neck. "I suppose that has a lot to do with Jed turning his affections to Katie."

She caught Zane's eye as he loaded luggage into the wagon and she planted her hands on her hips. "Or maybe it even had to do with the way I strutted back into town with not one, but two fellows on my arms." Zane threw her a grin and she laughed.

Kelly helped her into the wagon. "They'll all wonder about that for a while."

She settled between the two of them. This feeling of contentment meant something more. She'd spent a good deal of time thinking about Bobby both before and after Ginny's wedding, and somehow, in the midst of it, the awful ache had lessened. The reeling of sorrow that usually came whenever he entered her thoughts, dwindled. She missed him. She always would. But somehow, the strength of the feeling changed. The agonizing, paralyzing sadness had dwindled. She'd begun to accept.

Maybe.

These days her thoughts more often came to the here and now, the days filled with things to do, and who she intended to do them with. She thought about Kelly and the way he attended to her. He'd told her something just last night, something that surprised her. "I hope you never change, Lainey. You're perfect just the way you are."

She wanted to argue with him, but he placed a finger on her lips and stilled her. "Don't say anything. Just believe me."

Kelly was the kind of man she wished she'd met before her heart became calloused and broken, before Bobby even. If she hadn't loved Bobby, she'd be free to fall for someone like Kelly who was still here to love.

Zane's knee bumped her as he settled back. His arm draped against the wagon seat behind her. Her thoughts of him jumbled like a puzzle.

Aloof, and ever a loner, his heart rebuffed emotional commitment like a shield. Love was never going to be a craving for Zane. And yet he'd kissed her, and the power in that kiss caused her certainties about him to blow away like ash on the wind. It wasn't just the passion, because it held something more, and it frightened her.

Thankfully, he seemed to have put it behind them, so she did too.

"I don't think we should try heading back yet today." His voice jerked her suddenly from her from reverie. "It's getting to be pretty warm out. I would just as soon wait until tomorrow and start fresh in the morning."

"I like that idea," said Kelly. "What about you, Lainey?"

"What'll we do today? Find a hotel and lie around?"

"I feel like I could use a swim. How about you two?"

Lainey brightened. "I can hear the lake calling."

"Actually, I had something else in mind."

Kelly's chin rose. "Do tell."

"Remember that creek below the railroad bridge we swam in last summer?"

Kelly snapped his fingers. "Oh, yeah! It's a great spot, Lainey. You'll love it."

"We can swim there?"

"There's a nice hole of water in the creek. We can jump off the bridge."

Familiar fingers of excitement tingled over her. "Did you say 'jump'?"

"You don't have to," said Zane.

"Nah. But I bet you'll want to," Kelly prodded. "What do you say?"

"Sounds like an interesting afternoon. Let's find a hotel so we can change."

An hour later they rode a wagon down a track leading south of town, across the Fox River and through Fort Howard, then on toward Sheboygan. Turning off the main wagon road, they headed into the woods on little more than a trail which stopped abruptly along the edges of a wide, low creek cutting through a shallow ravine.

Zane led the way. "Don't worry. It's deep enough under the bridge." He and Kelly carried a blanket and refreshment down the bank to the water's edge. The frame of a high trestle rose above them.

Lainey gazed up at the masterpiece of engineering construction. "Is it used often?"

"Once or twice a day at most. Maybe not more than once every couple of days. Trains will run on it a lot more when Green Bay isn't the end of the line."

"It looks pretty high."

Kelly laughed. "Well, it does seem so. But we've jumped off higher."

"Where?"

"During the war," Zane said. It was the first time she heard him mention any connection to it.

They spread the blanket in the sun then Kelly waded into the creek. Toward the middle it dropped to about chest deep. He splashed water over his arms and neck, and finally doused his head. Coming up, he drifted a little further out where the water seemed to be over his head.

"Can you touch?" called Lainey.

"Not here."

Zane hollered out to him. "It's deep like that for about a dozen feet. I'll show you." Charging into the water, he first ran then dove in after Kelly. The two of them hooted and splashed and swam while Lainey looked on and laughed at them.

Zane slung his hair back off his forehead, spraying water in the sunlight. "Are you going to get wet? Or do we have to help you?"

"I'm coming... I'm coming!" She'd already undone her shoes. She tossed them aside and pulled off her stockings. Jumping to her feet, her toes curled against the prickly grass, finding relief in the slick grass along the riverbank. A moment later she plunged in the water with them, her black hair sopped down her back, her light summer dress floating up in billows around her in the water.

The current swept them downstream, and they made a contest of swimming up against it. Lainey couldn't seem to make much headway, and the two men grabbed her hands and pulled her along with them. Then Zane left the water and ran up the bank, climbing up the steep incline toward the top of the hill where the tracks of the trestle touched the earth. Running across the spaced ties he headed for the center of the bridge.

"Point me to the drop off!"

Kelly waved a finger at a spot only a few feet away, and suddenly Zane leapt free of the trestle, plunging a full forty feet into the water hole. He popped back up quickly, swinging his head to clear the wet hair from his eyes as he drifted down to them on the current.

Lainey gasped. "I can't believe you did that."

"It's not hard."

"I would be afraid."

"I bet you wouldn't."

"My turn," said Kelly. He waded in long steps from the water and up the bank. A minute later he jumped, landing exactly where Zane had. They caught his arms as he drifted downstream.

Zane steadied him as he found his footing. "How was it?"

"Great. Let's do it again."

Lainey shivered. "I want to come up."

Zane glanced at her behind him. "You going to jump?" He left the water and reached for her hand, pulling her along up the hill.

"I'll see. I want to watch you from up there."

The brothers scampered out onto the track, but Lainey moved

slowly, her body feeling light and dizzy with the ability to see between the ties to the water rushing below. It seemed so far away. She was breathless. Kelly came back to help her. He held her hand all the way to the middle of the trestle.

Once again, Zane jumped into the water, yelling out as he leapt. Seconds later Kelly followed. Both men gazed up at her.

"Well?"

She shook her head, giggling. "I'm too chicken." Looking at them over the side left a nauseating sweet taste in her throat.

"Do you want to come down?"

"Maybe."

"We'll come up."

Kelly made long, smooth strokes through the water into the shallows. She watched his arms moving synchronously in tune with his body. Zane emerged right behind him. They both breathed fast when they reached the top, but she felt better having them there with her. Her legs felt leaden, like she might not have been able to make it back off the bridge without them.

Suddenly a rumbling stirred beneath her feet. They stood a long ways out on the trestle, probably fifty yards or more, and as certain as she was that a train was about to appear around the bend, she also knew she wouldn't be able to make it to the end of the track before it reached them.

Panic screeched through her. "Oh, no!"

"Jump!" cried Kelly.

"I can't!"

"You can. Go!"

"I'll show you," said Zane. "Just aim for me."

"I'll hit you!"

"No you won't. Just do it." He leapt from the bridge and struck the water two seconds later.

The train rounded the bend. Its whistle blew, shrieking through the forest and her body.

Zane coaxed from below. "Jump, Lainey!"

"Go now, Lainey!" Kelly yelled. "I'll be right by you!"

"But, Kelly!"

Kelly pushed her forward and a scream ripped from her chest. The bridge shuddered with a noise that sounded like all the timbers might break free as she toppled into the empty expanse of air. Her heart let loose of its moorings and rushed up into her throat, and an instant later she hit the water hard, every inch of her body stinging with sharp, wretched pain.

But the pain told her she was alive.

She came gasping to the surface, and suddenly Zane's arms wrapped around her, his body like a warm pillar steadied her as she floundered to gain her footing on the loose, gravelly bottom.

She gulped for air. "Kelly."

Zane looked past her, his eyes wide with fear, his face white. "Kell?" he called. The train roared by over the timbers and beams above them, filling their ears with thunder as he searched for Kelly. Violent fear filled his eyes, and Lainey turned in his arms. Zane roared. "Kelly!" The wheels of the train screeched and clattered northward over the iron rails and off the trestle as Zane stood her on her feet and dove into the current, driving himself upstream toward his brother.

Then she saw him. Kelly lay still in the shallows, water rushing over him like some new rock formation.

"Oh, God!" Lainey wailed, and it really was a prayer. She staggered out of the deep water after Zane.

"Kelly! Kelly, do you hear me?" Zane pulled his brother into his arms and shook him. He took his face in his hand and turned it from side to side, slapping him. "Kelly, don't you dare die!" Anger seemed to rip along with the angst from some deep well within him. "Wake up! Do you hear me? Kelly!"

He picked up the big man and plodded up the shore almost doubled over beneath his younger brother's weight. Carefully he laid him on the blanket.

Lainey was afraid to ask. The look on Zane's face was treacherous. "Is he breathing?"

Zane nodded. "Yes. But for how much longer, I don't know. Kelly!" he called again. "You stay with him, Lainey. I'll go for help." He looked down at his unconscious brother once more, speaking as though he had his full attention. "I'm going to get help. Don't you dare leave me Kelly, you hear?"

Stunned and fearful, Lainey watched Zane run like a wounded animal up the trail to the wagon. She heard him whip the horses around followed by the sound of the wagon wheels churning down the lane. Moving closer to Kelly, she tucked the blanket around him.

"Please, God." She began to weep. "Please don't let him die."

He could just as well have been her Bobby lying there, or Zane's pa, bleeding away his life for all she knew what to do. There was nothing she could do. Not a solitary thing but pray. Did she even dare? Had it ever changed anything before?

"Please, God," she moaned again. "Just... please."

Chapter Sixteen

Lainey stared out the window of her room in the Forest House. Another hot day in a series of long, hot summer days pressed in on her. Everyone kept saying they needed rain. Mrs. Anderson's flowers were all drying up. The priest next door carried water to his little garden, giving it a few pathetic drinks each day. John and Clara continued to sweat their way through long hours in the kitchen, Lainey helping them when she could. A new newspaper office opened up in Peshtigo, a branch of the Marinette and Peshtigo Eagle. Lainey wondered if she could possibly sell them any of her pictures. Her funds were holding out okay. Though Mr. Frayman hadn't bought any pictures lately, her father sent her back to Peshtigo with extra money. He told her he didn't want to see her becoming too dependent on "those boys".

Ha. Those boys.

Bitter gall rose in her throat. As if she could become dependent on Kelly, when he had every need of her.

She wiped away a tear creeping out the corner of her eye and turned her mind to doing some cleaning. She already melted in the heat, what did it matter? Another hour or so of work here before she took a meal to Kelly at his place in the livery. Of course, it wasn't a livery now, and it probably never would be, no matter what Kelly dreamed. It would be a lucky thing if he ever got on his feet again. Every thought of him saw him lying there in the water, pale, with the river running over him, both his legs busted on the rocks. He was hopeful; she had to grant him that.

But everything had changed.

While Kelly lay in bed in his livery, unable to get around, unable to do his work, Zane became someone she never knew. She swept her room in a frenzy remembering how he rambled on before he left.

"*I'll take care of him from now on, only better than before. It's my fault... all my fault. Kelly, do you hear me? I'm going back to the railroad. I'll make enough money so that you can go to a doctor and get well. Don't look so surprised. It's time, that's all. Lainey will be here, Kell, while I'm away. She'll take care of you. You will, won't you Lainey? I won't let you down. Never again. I built railroads during the war. I surveyed and mapped them. Both of you, believe me. I won't touch the cards or the liquor. I'll give it up and help you get well. I promise, Kell... I promise.*"

Lainey wiped the perspiration off her brow and set her broom aside. Tidying up her desk and smoothing the wrinkles off her bed, she went downstairs to find John. "Anything I can take him today?"

Clara stepped out of the pantry and handed her a basket. "There's plenty. I packed extra."

"Thank you, Clara."

She and John both smiled sadly.

Lainey left by the back door and started on the walk to Kelly's. The sun blistered down on her uncovered head. She'd forgotten her bonnet. What did it matter? What did anything matter with Kelly crippled?

Well, one thing did matter. Zane had turned over a new, yet somehow tragic, leaf. To think of him hiring out as a civil engineer for the railroad -- to think he'd not only been part of the same kind of track crews she'd seen working in the woods, but that he'd been part of the surveying and mapping of many such lines during his time in the military -- astounded her. He'd pushed all his skill and talent aside and let it lie dormant until now.

Now his determination to go to work and make an honest living, to somehow come up with a way to help Kelly find healing, kept him away from them both. He blamed himself for what had happened. Lainey knew it, and even though it wasn't true, she understood how he felt. He was ridden with guilt, and she felt lost and useless without him. The one redeeming thing about the entire situation was that Kelly himself seemed to be keeping his hope and his spirits alive.

She turned up the street where he lived and knocked tentatively on the door.

"Come on in, Lainey."

She opened the door and stepped into the shadowed room. "It's so dark in here." She forced cheer into her voice. "Why don't I prop the door open?"

"No, it'll let in the heat. I don't mind the darkness. It keeps things cool."

She agreed and wandered over to set the food on his little table. Then she sat on a chair beside the bed.

"How are you doing today?"

Kelly smiled at her. "You ask me that every day. Do you know that?"

"That's because I want to know."

"I am feeling fine, Miss Kade. And you?"

"How is the pain?"

"Not bad. I'll cope. And you?"

"Did you need to take any powders last night?"

"None. And you?"

"Doctor Kelsey said to let him know if you need anything more. Do you?"

"No--"

"And don't you dare say, 'and you?' I am doing fine, I have no pain except this headache from being in the sun without my bonnet, and I didn't take any powders last night though I may need some tonight. Now, does that about cover it?"

Kelly laughed. "Thank you. You are pain killer enough."

She couldn't help smiling at him. How he could sit there with his legs and his very life wrecked up and smile, she didn't understand. But, Kelly was surprising like that.

"I brought you some lunch."

"I'm going to get fat with you feeding me every day and me not able to do a thing to wear it off."

"Well, maybe you'll be able to start some exercises before long."

"That's a thought. Have you heard from Zane?"

Lainey shook her head. "Not in over a week. I suppose he's working on the track up toward Marinette or someplace. He didn't think he'd be back for a spell."

Kelly reached for her hand and she let him hold it. He rubbed her fingers between his. "I'm sorry for getting you into this."

She harrumphed. "You're sorry? Think of me. I'm the sorry one. If only I had jumped."

"I never should have let you stay up there."

"You couldn't have stopped me."

"No. Maybe not. But that doesn't make you any to blame."

"Doesn't it?"

He reached up and pushed a strand of hair behind her ear. "Lainey, I've been lying here thinking, and I've finally figured something out."

"What's that?"

"Children of God do not mark out their own plans or determine their own destinies. That's His job."

"So God did this?" She heard her own bitterness rising.

"God allowed this."

She stood to her feet. "That sounds like Him."

"It's a good thing, Lainey."

Her vision grew glassy as she spun toward him. "How can you call this good? What's good about you lying there with your legs broken and twisted, unable to walk, maybe ever, and your whole life ruined? I don't understand that, Kelly."

He reached for her, hushing her. She stepped closer and sat back down. He took her hand again. "You know, I'm willing to sacrifice my life to see what's happening to Zane."

She stared at him, trying to understand. "Zane's lost. Zane doesn't know if he's coming or going he's so wracked with guilt."

"I wish you'd known Zane before the war."

"I was too young."

"Zane was my hero, and now he is again. Zane was the one with all the brains. He could build things, design things. He could manage and make decisions. He was good at everything. The war tried to strip all that talent out of him. He hasn't been interested in anything since."

"So I noticed."

"But with what's happened," Kelly glanced down over his weakened body, "the old Zane has a chance at redemption."

"But at what cost, Kell? He'll make himself mad with the guilt. Doesn't that worry you?"

"I think God is in control. I just wish I'd seen it sooner."

"You've changed, Kelly. Maybe it isn't just Zane."

His eyes slid from hers. "Maybe." He patted her hand and stared ahead into the gloom. "I think there's probably something about me I should tell you, Lainey."

"What? You have secrets? I find that hard to believe." She offered a weak smile.

He drifted back into her gaze. His eyes were blue like hers, only lighter. They opened up to his soul and she felt like she could swim there. He pulled her into them when he spoke. "When the war ended and we buried both our parents, Zane and I wanted nothing more to do with the past or the lives we'd once had. Everything was different. Suzanne wanted us to stay and be a part of her life, but it was just too hard." He paused in the telling. He took a deep breath and let it out slowly.

"I had plans before the war. I was going into seminary. I wanted to be a pastor."

Lainey felt the blood drain from her face, but she waited for him to continue.

He chuckled. "I know that's hard to believe. But you've heard Zane call me Preacher. That's why. Sometimes old habits come back."

"But you changed your mind. You didn't go because of the war?"

"The things I saw, the things I did... they hardened me. The pain and killing, all the brutality and hopelessness, was more than I could understand at the time. I blamed God."

"That's understandable."

Kelly shook his head. "No, Lainey. It wasn't God's fault. It isn't God who comes to steal, kill, and destroy. It's the devil. But nobody ever blames him. He gets a free ride."

"But God could stop him."

"God will stop him. But for now, God allows him his way because he is a spirit with a free will, just like us. We wouldn't have to go through half the trouble we do. We choose it."

She fought the lump of emotion rising in her throat. "You didn't choose this, Kelly."

"I chose to run, Lainey. I chose to turn my back on a loving God."

Tears crept into her eyes and she shook her head. Kelly reached out and wiped away a drop as it escaped down her cheek.

"Don't cry, Lainey."

"It's not that..." She looked away, but the silent tears leaked out.

"Is it about something in your own past?"

She looked at him again.

"I know about that fellow who died," he whispered.

"Bobby?"

He nodded.

"You know about Bobby Braedon?"

Kelly patted the edge of the bed. She left the chair and moved over next to him. He took both her hands in his and kissed one of them tenderly. "God didn't take Bobby to hurt you, Lainey. He's not that kind of God. It's just taken me so long to understand that myself."

"Who told you? Gray?"

Kelly shook his head again. "No. It was Zane."

"Zane... But--"

"Your pa told him. He didn't want you to get hurt again. He thought we should know."

"My pa told Zane about Bobby and me?" She stopped crying and stared.

"Don't be mad, okay? I might never have told you about my own secrets or Zane's if I didn't think you'd understand."

"I'm not mad." She shrugged, their hands kneading one another's. "I didn't think I'd ever get over Bobby. But it hurts less than it used to. Still, you're right if you think I blamed God."

"Don't blame Him. 'He knows the plans he has for you,' Lainey Kade, 'plans to give you hope and a future.'"

"What about Bobby's future? What about yours, Kell?"

"Bobby had you for the best part of his life."

She'd thought of that before. Her ma said something like it once. Bobby was a happy, carefree man. His life had been short, but good.

Kelly's serious gaze plumbed the depths of hers. "I'm not afraid of the future, Lainey. I'm glad God has shown me a way back to Him again. I'm glad for what's happening with Zane."

"Zane's running, too."

Kelly nodded. "Zane used to teach Sunday school. How's that for a surprise?" He laughed and she lifted her chin a little.

A shudder raced through her. Suddenly she dropped down on Kelly's chest and embraced him. "Thank you, Kelly. Thank you for being so strong."

His arms folded around her and the steady rhythm of his heart beat against her cheek.

*****

Kelly closed his eyes and reveled over the memory of Lainey Kade lying in his arms, embracing him. She had gone away, but the scent of her remained, and he could lie here in this bed forever, just remembering how soft she felt against his chest.

She came three times a day to bring him food, to help him adjust himself in the bed, to even empty his bed pan. He wasn't very comfortable with that at first, but Lainey proved herself a first rate nurse, and she didn't seem bothered by it in the least. His humiliation quickly gave way to deeper respect.

Sometimes she stayed for the better part of the day, talking and sketching, letting him ramble on about his plans for the livery when he got better and could walk again. The doctor didn't promise he'd ever have his full mobility back, but with the right kind of exercises, he thought Kelly might at least have a minimal use of his legs again. Kelly looked forward to that day, because if God willed it, he wanted to marry Lainey Kade, and he wanted to offer himself as a whole man.

There was no reason, he decided, that he should wait to win her over. When she admitted the pain of her past was lessening, Kelly saw a fissure crack open in her heart. She told him that she didn't think she could get over Bobby Braedon, but Kelly knew better. Lainey was the embodiment of love. She loved all the time, whether she realized it or not.

She takes care of me even now, like this. She worries over Zane. She puts up with Mrs. Anderson's rattling on about everything. She loves. Her heart is like a fine jewel, perfectly cut, made all the more beautiful for what she's been through.

Sometime later Kelly realized he'd been praying.

Later that day, Pastor Beach of the Congregational Church stopped by. He knew of a youngster in the congregation willing to be Kelly's legs for him for the summer. If anything further needed doing, all Kelly had to do was have young Jacob Collins take up the task. Furthermore, after learning of the accident, Pastor Beach spoke to Dr. Kelsey and made arrangements for a wheel chair to be shipped up for him. It was an expensive piece of equipment but the church would help with that, he'd said.

Kelly acknowledged the gift with humble appreciation, saying he and his brother intended to pay the church back for their generosity.

"That's all right," said Pastor Beach. "It's the least we can do. The most is to pray for your healing."

"I can't thank you enough for that," said Kelly as the pastor shook his hand and departed.

It suddenly seemed to Kelly that, everywhere he looked, the hand of God moved in his life. How childish he'd been not to see it until now.

Fourteen-year-old Jacob Collins brought Kelly the gift of wit and energy. He seemed to think hanging around Kelly all day was a piece of cake, even doing little errands or cleaning bridles with the older man. When Kelly's chair arrived, Jacob and Lainey helped him into it and took him on a summer tour of the town, at least as far as they could travel on the boardwalks. Most of the roads themselves were too heavily rutted to push the chair over, even though the mud had dried.

"I've got me a real hankering to get out of town for a while," Kelly told them. "I've been cooped up for weeks. What do you two think about taking a little trip?"

Lainey looked askance. "How will we do that? You are heavy, you know."

"Well, Jacob here will have to find us some extra help for what I've got in mind."

"What do you have in mind?"

"You just wait and see. Next Saturday I want you to put on your prettiest dress, and bring a shawl and bonnet too in case you need it."

"It's hot out."

"I know, I know. Just do like you're told for once, Lainey, and don't argue with me."

She grinned and gave him a hard push, bouncing over the rough boards. She only went a dozen yards before she was winded. He laughed. "You always have to have the last word, don't you?"

"You should know that by now."

"Girls..." mumbled Jacob, and laughed with them.

There was no question of waiting around to see if Zane would return on Saturday. He stayed away more often than not, his work keeping him very busy where a crew cleared land for the rail line north toward Marinette. So, at eight o'clock Saturday morning, Jacob arrived at Lainey's room to take her to meet Kelly.

"You know what's going on, don't you?" she asked.

He only grinned.

"Why don't you tell me?"

"Wild horses couldn't drag it out o' me ma'am. If they did, Kelly would give it to me for sure."

"You aren't scared of him, are you? He can't even catch you."

"He will when he gets back on his feet."

"Let's hope that will be a possibility."

"My mam and pap are praying for him real hard. He'll get better, just you wait."

She tucked her hand through the young man's arm and followed his leading to the wagon waiting in front of the Forest House. He blushed, but walked beside her with a beaming smile.

"Where are we meeting Kelly?"

"He went on ahead with the help of my two cousins. They got a head start so they wouldn't hold you up."

She wondered what that could mean, but figured it didn't pay to ask. Jacob would keep his silence and relish every minute of it.

They met Kelly waiting at the edge of town in another wagon. Jacob helped her climb up onto the seat while Kelly sat behind her in his chair. The cousins jumped down and traded places with Jacob who climbed up into the driver's seat beside Lainey.

"Goodness, Kelly, what are you up to?"

"We're going to get away for a while, the whole day in fact. We won't be back until late. I hope you're okay with that."

"I made arrangements. It'll be fine."

"All right, then. Let's go." He nodded at Jacob who clicked his tongue at the horses. Slowly so as not to jar Kelly roughly, they headed out of town. Forty minutes later and six miles down the road, the way opened up to a view of marshes and sand and, on the horizon, the line of Lake Michigan. Along the shore the familiar sounds of sawing and construction echoed, and up ahead the long line of a dock stretched out into the harbor. The steamer *Union* lay anchored there, with its captain Thomas Hawley waiting to take on passengers and supplies.

"Kelly, are we going on that?"

A warmth coursed down him, even into his aching legs, at her excitement.

"You!" She swatted his shoulder playfully. "Where is it going?"

"Just north to Marinette. I thought you'd like to see a new town for a change."

"Kelly!" She leaned back to kiss his cheek.

She turned forward again to look at the harbor, giving Kelly a chance to get over his blush. Jacob gave him the eye and a grin to boot. Kelly winked back.

With the help of some shipmates and Jacob, they wrestled Kelly's chair up the gangplank, and Lainey stood beside him near the rail. A cool wind blew off the lake, a good fifteen degrees cooler than the inland air. Facing the wind, she loosened her bonnet and let it fall back, turning her face to the sun.

"Smell that?"

"It's the clean smell away from all the humidity back in town. And away from the livery," he added.

She took a deep breath. "This is a wonderful surprise. But is it too much for you? Do you hurt?" More than six weeks passed since Kelly's fall into the shallows, and it would be several more before Dr. Kelsey removed his casts. Lainey said many times how thankful she was he hadn't lost his legs completely. The skills of Dr. Kelsey and the surgeon in Green Bay had spared Kelly amputation. She'd told Kelly about her grandfather who'd lost a leg in a dynamiting accident years before.

"I'm fine. It's so nice to get out that I doubt I'll feel anything but goodness today."

She offered him a smile. "Then I hope we can go out more often."

It was an hour and a half trip from the Peshtigo harbor to Marinette. Docking in the small Michigan town, Kelly and Lainey made their plans while Jacob tagged along to help out in any way they needed. They visited some shops, ate at the best restaurant they could find, and fed the ducks in the river.

In the afternoon they went to the beach on the big lake and sat together on a blanket in the sand. They arranged themselves far enough up from the water to find shade under a stretch of trees lining the shore. Jacob took the opportunity to have a swim.

"You can join him if you like." Kelly wanted her time with him to be as full.

She smiled, drawing her fingers through the sand. "I'm not dressed for it. You told me to wear my best dress."

He looked her over, appreciating the way she looked in the pink and white flowered summer dress. "So I did."

"It wouldn't be fun with you sitting up here. You are the best swimmer of any of us, you know."

"You offer a pretty strong challenge, if I remember correctly."

She laughed, brushing her hands together to clean off the sand.

"I'll swim again, Lainey," he said softly.

"I..."

"You can express your doubts. I don't mind."

"I... wish I was as sure as you. What if you don't?" She searched him with her gaze.

"If I don't swim here, then I'll swim in heaven."

"It's not the same."

"You're right. It'll be better. No rocks in the swimming holes," he said, hoping to make her smile again.

"I want you to walk again, and swim again. I want you to build your livery and have a life. You can even be a preacher if you want to."

"I can do that without legs."

She threw up her arms in mock frustration. "You never get discouraged, do you, Kelly?"

Her blue eyes were dark and mysterious, like Zane's sometimes, filled with pools of possibilities and depths unfathomable.

"Course I do. If that were the case I would never have stopped trusting God in the first place. But I have to keep what I've learned front and foremost in my mind. God has a plan. It's better than our own foolishness. No matter what happens to me -- no matter what -- it's a good plan."

She studied him and he let himself be swallowed in her gaze, studying her in return.

"I do want that life you spoke of," he said finally. "But what about you, Lainey?" He brushed a piece of sand off the bridge of her nose. "What does Elaina Eastman Kade want?"

Her voice and expression turned wistful. "She doesn't know."

He leaned toward her and took her chin in his fingers. Gently, he brushed her forehead with his lips. "Maybe she does, and she just doesn't want to admit it." He sat back and tweaked her chin.

Her velvet blue eyes shadowed as she looked at him, and it was a long moment before she finally shook her head. "No, Mr. Beaumont. I really, really don't know."

Chapter Seventeen

Zane knocked on the door and lifted the latch. No one seemed to be about the living quarters in the rear of the unfinished livery when he went inside. "Kelly?" he called, but the bed where Kelly spent hundreds of hours lay vacant. He walked through the empty building wondering what could be wrong and where his crippled brother could be. And where was the boy whom he'd been told was taking care of him?

It was late. Ten o'clock on a Saturday night. Where could he possibly be? Going outside and securing the door behind him, Zane looked up and down the street. Competing musical tunes blared raucously from two nearby saloons. Men staggered in the street calling foul things to one another and to no one. A gunshot cracked in the distance followed by a growing row. He leapt down off the boardwalk and into the dusty street, making his way toward Lainey's place. He passed another fellow stumbling out of the doorway.

"Watch it, mister," the man growled, a nasty odor drifting off him.

Zane ignored him and went inside. He took the stairs of the Forest House two at a time and rapped on her door, not worried at all if he woke her. No answer. He knocked again and tried the knob but it was locked.

"Lainey?" he called, knocking one more time.

A door opened across the hall and a woman stuck her head out. "Some people are hoping to get some sleep. Besides, nobody's come out of that room all day. I think it's empty."

Zane trotted back down the steps and into the street. He stopped and put his hands on his hips, looking up and down each way. Where could they be? She wouldn't have taken him to one of the saloons, would she?

The fact that she might nagged at him. It was Lainey he was talking about, after all. He thought about checking them out, one by one, but hesitated. It would be easy to get inside and be pulled in to a quick game of chance or a cool drink. The air hadn't cooled down much since nightfall.

Just then he heard a woman's laughter. Lainey. He squinted into the darkness up the street catching the jangle of harness and creaking of wheels as a wagon made its way up the road past the Catholic Church and closer to where he stood.

Yes. Lainey. He heard her talking and Kelly's voice answer. Slowly they became more visible and his heart slowed.

He stepped forward. "Kelly? Lainey, is that you?"

"Zane?" Lainey peered into the darkness, focusing on him.

"It's me."

"Kelly, it's Zane!"

Jacob reined the wagon to a stop, and Lainey turned to climb over the side. Zane moved in quickly and lifted her down. "You're back." She hugged him.

He stepped away from her and looked up at his brother.

"Where've you two been? You had me worried crazy. I was about to go running all over town to find you."

"Oh, Zane, we had such a day. We went all the way to Marinette on the boat. It was wonderful! Kelly so needed to get out."

He tried to take in everything she said as she continued pouring out all the events of their day and went on about Kelly's health and what the doctor had to say and what a good sport he was being. But as much as he tried to listen, he had difficulty thinking beyond how she looked in that dress in the moonlight with her hair all falling like ribbons over her shoulders and her eyes lit up like the stars.

"You could have gotten there in a quarter of the time by stage. You went on the boat?" he finally asked, as though understanding for the first time.

"We did," said Kelly, "A pleasure trip. I half expected to see you up there."

"You did?" asked Lainey, surprised.

Zane rested his hands on his hips. "I was in Marinette yesterday, but I had to head back out to the Sugar Bush today. I just got in."

"Well, I don't want to call it a night now that Zane just got here," Lainey said. "Let's go back to the livery house. Kelly can get settled in and we can all have a good talk."

Zane took a long look at his brother. "You up to that, Kell?"

"Sure I am. Let's go."

Zane hopped up into the back of the wagon, and Jacob swung the rig around to head it back up the street. A bit of remorse struck Zane like it always did since the accident as they arrived back at the livery. Even in the darkness he noted the unfinished state of the building -- another dream ended tragically. But while he and Jacob got Kelly propped up in his creaky bed, Lainey went around lighting lamps to chase away the shadows and the gloom. His spirits started lifting. They sent Jacob off home. Then they talked for another two hours, even playing a few hands of Red Dog.

It was good to see Kelly laughing, even though Zane thought he might be wearing himself out for the worse. It was even better to see Lainey's smile.

Those first weeks after Kelly's fall, her smile hardly showed itself. He couldn't say he felt any like smiling either. But now, with Kelly doing better, the danger of infection decreasing day by day, and the hope that one day he might walk again all bringing bright possibilities, they'd all been able to smile and sigh with relief.

Of course, Kelly had changed. He'd been turning back to God. More and more often he quoted Bible verses to Zane and talked about God's mercy and compassion like he did before the war. Zane admitted there was maybe something to it. Kelly didn't talk about his nightmares reoccurring anymore the way Zane's still did at times. But then, Kelly had Lainey, or at least he probably would have soon.

He watched her there, across the wobbly square table pushed up by Kelly's bedside, laughing and joking, and a hard lump rose into his throat that he tried to quickly push down with a drink. But then, just about the time he thought he could survive this unwanted barrage of emotion, she'd reach over and touch his hand, or her eyes would wander like two mysterious jewels into his.

What are you thinking when you look at me, Elaina? What's behind those deep blue eyes I'm drowning in?

At last they called it a night. Kelly's head fell back on his bolster, and the sleep he fought began taking him over. Zane pushed the blanket up over him and moved the table out of the way.

"I'll walk Lainey home. You get to sleep."

Kelly gave a haggard smile. "Leave a lamp burning so you can find your way back in."

"I'll do that."

Kelly watched with drooping eyelids as Lainey and Zane turned down all the lamps but one. Then Lainey whispered good night and they quietly slipped out.

They strolled slowly, as though it was a Sunday afternoon and not the dead of night, though neither of them spoke for a while. Finally Zane said, "You're mighty good for him."

He knew she understood what he meant, so when she didn't answer right off, he just waited.

"Kelly's good for us, too, Zane. He's so determined."

Zane nodded, though she probably couldn't see him. "He doesn't want anybody taking responsibility for what happened to him. He doesn't want me to blame myself, even though I instigated the whole thing. He doesn't want you to feel bad about not jumping."

"It's hard not to."

"I know, but he's right. We didn't expect you to jump, either of us. Forcing you to do it when the train came, well, it's just something that a woman shouldn't have to be faced with."

"You take good care of him."

He glanced quickly at her, but she wasn't looking his way. "I have to. He's my brother. He's all I have. The fact is I nearly failed there, too."

"What do you mean?"

Zane felt the darkness around him like a shield, making him able to admit what he felt. "That day when he fell, I almost -- I almost couldn't do anything. I pulled him out of the water and when he just lay there and didn't move, I nearly froze."

"You didn't though. You knew what to do. You told me and then you went for help."

"Barely. For a moment I almost gave up. I almost crawled back under the poplar trees and covered my face and quit." His voice sounded rancid with self-incrimination. Then he felt her hand touch his arm, comforting him.

"You didn't quit on him, Zane. And that makes all the difference."

He sighed, thinking again about the horrible anxiety and panic that had threatened to immobilize him. Panic came so easily. It charged into his heart and made him anxious, ever since those days in battle...

"What about your sister?" Lainey said suddenly, pulling him back from the brink of horrific memories.

Zane thought a lot of Suzanne lately. Neither he nor Kelly ever mentioned getting in touch with her about the accident. It was one thing that they couldn't bring themselves to do -- not yet.

"We haven't told her."

Lainey paused in her step. "You haven't sent a telegram or anything?"

"No."

"You should do it."

"Have you told your folks?"

"As a matter of fact, I wrote them almost a month ago."

That surprised Zane since she hadn't mentioned anything about it. But, then, he'd barely been around. He'd thrown himself into railroading. Lately he'd been supervising clearing in the upper bush region where they used axes and fire to make way for the new line to connect Peshtigo to Michigan's Upper Peninsula.

"I should write to Suzanne." He glanced her way again and found her looking at him, so he smiled. "Since you'll make me feel guilty if I don't."

She grinned back, and suddenly she stumbled. Reaching out, he grabbed her arm to catch her. His heart thumped, but his hand slid down smoothly into her palm. He clasped her slender fingers in his, steadying her.

"Thanks. I think I caught a rut."

A teasing note lightened his voice. "Out here?"

"Well it's dark as anything."

"It'll be light out in a few hours."

"Kelly wants to go to church. Maybe you and I can get him there."

"Maybe." Sure, Kelly would love to get him there. "We'll see." He smiled at Lainey approvingly. She'd probably done more wonders for Kelly than any doctor ever could.

Finally they approached the Forest House, and Zane knew that their midnight walk together was ending. He thought of the night he kissed her back in June, two months ago. For a moment he wished he could go back there, to that time. She looked at him, her eyes pupiless

142

and deep in the darkness, and he wished her good night. Her small, unreadable smile made him wonder if she was thinking of that night too. But she turned to go inside. He didn't want to walk away. He wanted to stay there and wait for her to come back out again. As he watched her stride up the steps and go inside the Forest House, he wished he didn't ever have to leave her side again.

But his hand still tingled with warmth where hers had nested into his, because he hadn't let it go.

*****

Lainey jerked upright and flung the covers to the floor. Her long legs flew over the side of the bed and she lurched to see how high the sun had risen. Gasping with relief, she fell back onto the bed, her heart thudding hard, but slowing gradually to its normal pace.

She didn't oversleep.

Kelly wanted them to go to church today. All of them. Even Zane. She stood again and dressed as quickly as she could, knowing there was plenty of time, but feeling the urge to hurry back to the livery. Wearing her dark blue dress sprinkled liberally with pink rosebuds, she wound her hair around in a bun and tied on her bonnet. Springing down the steps as lightly and quickly as she dared, she cut through the kitchen to grab a sausage, and hurried out past John and Clara with a cheerful wave. She found Zane up and dressed at the livery, but Kelly still slept.

She kept her voice low. "Is he all right?"

Zane stepped out into the sunshine. "Just tired out. He needs to get some more rest. I told him I'd go along to church the next time."

"He must be let down."

"I think he's okay. He knows he might have overdone it yesterday."

While she listened she found herself captivated by his expression. His eyes were clear, his face ruddy from the sun, the creases around his smile filling her up with happiness.

She dabbed a finger across his nose. "I thought people outgrew freckles."

"Those aren't freckles."

She waggled a finger at his face. "Well they aren't age spots."

"How do you know? Maybe they're pock marks from a war injury." He took her wrists in his hands, grinning as she laughed.

"Some war injury. Too much sun," she giggled.

He pulled off her bonnet, knocking her bun askew. "There. Let's see who'll have freckles now."

She grabbed for her bonnet and he held it out of reach, one hand still gripping her wrist. Finally she settled. "All right mister smarty. I give up. And you can go ahead and gloat, because I don't usually give up so easily."

"I'm gloating." He flourished her bonnet before her. She snatched it away.

Zane glanced back in through the open door and smiled. "I think he's awake again."

"*You* did it," she said, laughter still in her voice.

"Hi, Kell. How are you feeling?"

"I'm still pretty tired. My legs hurt today. I think I'll have you give me some pain powders, if you don't mind."

Lainey fetched the powders. She mixed them in a glass of water then brought them to his bedside and gave them to him. He leaned his head back into the pillow.

"What'll you two do today?" he said with a grimace.

"I think I'll take Lainey for a stroll so you can sleep. Is that all right?"

Kelly nodded. "Stay out of trouble."

"We will," Lainey answered. She and Zane headed back outside and shut the door.

She faced Zane. "Well?"

"Want to get some ice cream?"

"Ice cream? Really?"

"I hear they've got some over at George Robinson's Meat Market."

"I haven't had ice cream in ages."

"Then let's go."

George Robinson's Meat Market boasted at being one of the only places in the region to make ice cream available. Lainey and Zane enjoyed theirs for breakfast. Afterwards they walked to the bridge in the middle of town and tossed pebbles into the river, then sticks, watching them rush along downstream with the force of the water flowing through the locks on the dam.

Zane watched their sticks bump and swirl away. "River's low."

"We haven't had enough rain."

"No. Do you realize that there hasn't been a drop since the eighth of July?"

"Has it been that long?"

"That's what they say."

"Well, that can't last."

"It does have its good points," Zane said. "There are hardly any gnats or mosquitoes to contend with when we're working in the woods. Burning is easy."

"I bet it is. The loggers will be worried about the coming season. They'll be hoping this doesn't carry over into winter. The water needs to be rushing for a good spring flood that can carry the logs downstream."

"Once these railroads are built, that won't present much of a problem. Track will be able to bring logs right out from the cut to the market."

"It's hard to imagine progress like that." Lainey sighed. "My pa's probably dreaming about it."

Zane grew thoughtful as he leaned with his elbows on the rail of the bridge. "Kelly figures I'll do pretty well if I stick to the railroad."

Lainey turned her back to the railing and studied him. "He says you're a lot smarter than you've been letting on."

He snickered. "Oh he does, does he?"

"He's told me a few things about you, Zane. I have to admit, I was shocked at what I learned."

"Well, Kelly always did think too highly of me. Try and remember that he's my little brother, despite his extra four inches."

His smile deepened and she laughed. Somewhere in the recesses of her memory Bobby Braedon's smile flashed before her, but her thoughts didn't stumble or even weave.

"You have a nice smile." She tilted her head to look at him more directly. "You're liable to catch a young lady's attention with that smile and your railroading brilliance." She giggled. She couldn't help it.

"Yeah, well, don't get your hopes up. I'm more liable to be plaguing you and Kelly for a long time as a bachelor."

"Well, that will be all three of us, then." She turned to stare out at the swirling brown water. "Two confirmed bachelors and a spinster. That'll be us."

Chapter Eighteen

Kelly lay awake by himself, his hands tucked under his neck. He'd slept the day away. Out in the stable, Zane packed his saddlebags to return to his job. Lainey was already back at the Forest House getting ready for the new week. She promised to stop by for a few minutes tomorrow morning with his breakfast before going to work on a sketch of the pilings being planted in the river where the new railroad bridge would cross. After that, she'd be needed in the Forest House kitchen, which meant Kelly would be sharing his next evening's meal alone with Jacob.

He lay thinking about his plans. Then he fished a silver ring out of the pocket of his pants, slit up both legs. He held it between his fingers -- a thin band etched with an intricate vine design. He leaned toward the oil lamp at his bedside to read the inscription, a smile pulling at his lips as he turned it around and around. He slipped it back into his pocket as Zane came into the room.

"I'm ready to go. Anything you want before I leave?"

"I have everything."

"Good. Are you sure?"

"I can get by. I'm learning to get myself in my chair. Did you know that?"

"Just be careful, all right?"

Kelly nodded. He wanted to tell Zane about the ring, but didn't want to ruin the sacred feeling. Maybe he could just tell him what he had in mind.

Zane flipped his satchel over his shoulder. "I'll see you later, then. Maybe in a couple of weeks."

"Sounds good." Kelly hesitated. "Zane?"

"Yeah?"

Kelly grinned. Only Jacob knew what he had in mind. As Kelly's cohort in love he'd pushed Kelly in the chair all the way to the jeweler's to pick out the ring. He said his sisters would all be jealous to have a ring like that.

"I... uh..."

Zane frowned. "What is it, Kell?"

"I'm going to ask Lainey to marry me."

Zane didn't say anything. He stared then blinked. Kelly grinned.

"I think I knew that," Zane answered finally.

"I mean soon. I'm going to ask her soon. I just have to get my nerve up."

The bed creaked as Zane lowered himself onto the corner. He tucked his arm into the handle of his satchel. "Are you sure about this,

Kelly?"

"I love her."

"But to get married..."

"That's what people do, Zane. They fall in love and get married."

"Well, yeah." Zane adjusted himself on the mattress edge. "But how do you know she's ready?"

"I think she is. And I'm not going to be bound to this bed forever. Or that chair, for that matter. I plan on being able to walk inside of two months. I won't run, and I'll probably need crutches to do it, but I'm going to use my feet. I'm going to open this livery and work with the horses, and... I might even take up preaching."

Zane bit his lower lip and nodded twice. "I don't doubt that you will."

"I wanted to tell you before you left."

Zane rose to his feet. "I'm glad you did."

"Zane." Kelly stopped him again. "David went to Gath."

"Who?"

"David. The king."

Zane smiled. "What are you saying?"

"King David went to Gath. Remember Goliath the Philistine?"

Zane nodded, raised his eyebrows. "Sure."

"Well, David went to Gath, to the king of his enemies, the Philistines. He was so beside himself with despair and anxiety he didn't know what to do, so he went to them for refuge." He had Zane's attention now. He listened patiently.

"We did that, Zane. Bars, brawls, and brothels -- we fell into all of them. We went to Gath. Instead of going to God, we went to the enemy, just like David. It's been all wrong. Do you see?"

Zane looked down at his hand in his lap. "And now we're seeing things clearly?"

"I think I am. I hope you are. I think Lainey is, too. Living life only for the moment, jumping from one thrill to the next, we all got so caught up in it we didn't see it for what it was. Just a place to escape, like Gath. Only we didn't see or care about the danger there. Hiding from despair has never been the way out."

Zane stood up and looked at Kelly. Kelly saw his thoughts in his eyes. Readable.

"I love you, Zane."

"I know you do, Kell. I love you, too."

Kelly smiled. "Just think about it, and if you think I might be right, we'll talk."

Zane grinned and nodded. "Okay. If you say so." He walked to Kelly's side and held out his hand, gripping Kelly's.

"I'll be seeing you, Kell." He turned and headed out the door.

"Anywhere but Gath."

Zane's laughter carried back to Kelly as he closed the door behind him. "Anywhere but there, Kelly. Anywhere but there."

*****

Rain didn't come. The stagnant days of August dragged on as lawns and gardens wilted, and even the trees looked dogged and thirsty. Bees crawled over the wild blackberries, consuming them for their moisture, competing with the women and children who hurried to pick them for canning. But they tasted very sweet this year.

Lainey popped one, bursting with juice, into her mouth as she walked to Kelly's. She and Jacob went out picking early that morning before the day's heat grew too intense. She gave some berries to John and Clara for baking a pie, and now she carried a small dish to Kelly's place for a treat with milk and sugar.

How simple life had become.

A year ago she and Kelly and Zane would have been heading off to picnic or swim or to find some other adventure to occupy these hot summer days. They would've given no other care to life, sure in Zane's ability to win at the poker tables, and her own security nestled in her capability to draw for periodicals or to sell timber off her land. Now here she was, finding a degree of satisfaction in such simple pleasures as picking blackberries and sharing a pie with John and Clara. But even so, her thoughts troubled her.

A letter from her mother rested in her dress pocket. She pressed her palm against it as she stepped under the eave of the livery out of the hot sun and rapped on Kelly's door before entering.

Lainey found Kelly perched on the edge of the bed, a flush to his cheek, rings of sweat showing under the arms of his shirt sleeves.

"You're not overdoing it, are you?" She hurried to set down her basket. "You should have waited so I could help you into your chair."

"I can do it all right. You don't have to be so bossy," he said with a grin.

"And people say I never listen."

Kelly leaned back onto his bolster, hefting his legs onto the bed with a grimace.

"I saw that. You're in pain."

"It's not bad. Just a little discomfort, that's all."

"I shouldn't even let you have any of these blackberries." She popped one into her mouth. "Boys who don't behave shouldn't have treats."

Kelly listened to her upbraiding with a smile. "Then you shouldn't come, Lainey, because you're treat enough."

His outright flirtation caused her to blush, and she handed him the berries. "You shouldn't say things like that."

"Why not? It's true. You're my cool breeze on these hot days."

His smile didn't look so careless now, and Lainey turned away to hide her face. She pulled up the square table and chair and sat down across from him at it. The more quickly she changed the course of their conversation, the better off she'd feel.

She reached into her dress pocket and pulled out the letter from home.

"Want to hear my letter?"

"If you want to share it." He began snacking on the berries.

"Do you want cream and sugar on those?"

"They're good enough like this. Go ahead and read."

She started in on the contents of the letter. "Dear Lainey, It's been a long time since I've written. After the wedding our little world suddenly got very busy. We'd no sooner heard from you when Kashe Gilbert delivered her baby. It's a boy, and my, but he's a handsome, plump baby. He is dark, like his sister Ginny, with a covering of fine, black down. They named him James, but everyone already calls him Jamie and he's quickly capturing all our hearts.

"However," Lainey glanced up briefly from the page and sighed, "Kashe isn't well. She had a difficult time birthing little Jamie, though she never had any such difficulties with Ginny. Still, that was years ago. Jamie came into the world with a struggle, and Kashe has not regained her strength. In fact, she seems to be losing more stamina as the days go by.

"Joe is so tender with her. I'm reminded of when Ginny was born, and how surprised I was to discover what a doting father he turned out to be. Well, nothing has changed in all these years. And Ginny came home to help too, leaving her new husband on their farm while she nurses her mother and ministers to the needs of her baby brother. Even so, Kashe is not flourishing.

"Truthfully, Lainey, I wonder if something more is wrong than simply having given birth to a healthy baby boy." Lainey settled the letter in her lap.

Kelly shook his head. "That's too bad about Mr. Gilbert's wife. I hope she gets better. We'll ask the folks at church to pray for her, and I will, too."

"Thank you, Kell. Can I get you anything? A wet towel perhaps? Your fingers are purple."

Kelly laughed. "Sure." She set down the letter and went to the dry sink where a pail of water sat next to a bowl and a towel. "What else does your mother say?"

"She asked about you and Zane." She came back with a cloth and handed it to him. "She's worried about how Zane is handling the effects of your injury."

Kelly wiped his mouth and hands on the towel. "I like your mother. She's intuitive. She sees what sort of man my brother is, how he runs deeper than he lets on."

"I think he made my father nervous."

"He makes all fathers of pretty girls nervous."

She chuckled. "So do you, I'm sure."

Lainey took the towel from him and returned to the sink. She rinsed it and hung it neatly. Added onto Zane's war experiences, how horrific it must've been for him to see Kelly lying in the river, his body broken. She imagined seeing one of her own brothers in that position. The thought made her shudder. Zane told her he'd almost given up in panic, and she'd felt it too. But Zane had taken charge. He'd saved Kelly's life and worked hard to give him a new one.

If only someone could save Zane's...

She shook her head. "I hope Zane is okay. I worry about him all alone up there, working so hard."

"For me."

She turned to face him. "For all of us, I think. He does it for the bond between the two of you, and that somehow always includes me."

His eyes softened on hers. "Yes, it does." He lifted himself higher in the bed. "Zane promised me he'd come to church with us when he gets back."

"He did?" She sat at the foot of the bed, toying with the edge of a blanket. "Sometimes I wonder if perhaps the only piece missing from Zane being a whole person again is letting God back into his life. But, then, I'm not in any position to hold an opinion."

"Why do you think that?"

She stood again, anxious in the heat. "Oh, Kell, I'm glad you've made peace with God, but I'd be lying if I didn't admit I still find trust difficult. Yet, I imagine the kind of man Zane would be if he had your faith."

A man unlike any she'd known, Zane held himself distant and aloof at times, and so close at others, a strange quivering pulsed in her chest where her heart used to be, just being near him. All the time when he seemed like nothing more than a gambler and a shiftless drifter, he'd been a skilled civil engineer. He took a careless, detached approach to life, when he really had all the competence to grab onto it and make something of it.

With effort, she pushed her musings of Zane aside. She moved back to the sink and made a pretense of tidying up, though nothing much had moved out of place since her last visit. "I wish he could be here and that things were like they used to be, don't you?" She stared out the window over the sink.

"Sure, Lainey. Say, why don't you stop worrying for a bit and just come over here and play a game of cards with me. I'm so out of practice that I won't even be able to offer Zane a challenge."

She turned back to face him and smiled. "All right. Just one more question. Do you know if Zane wrote to Suzanne?"

"Suzanne our sister? No, why?"

"I told him he should. You can't keep her in the dark about what's happened to you, Kell. At the very least, I'm sure she'd just like to hear from the two of you."

Kelly nodded reluctantly. "You're right. It's not just Zane's fault. I should have written, but it's hard to tell somebody something that's going to bring them hurt."

"But you know how important it is, just the same. I wouldn't want to be lied to about Kashe."

"You're right, of course."

"I thought that maybe it should come from Zane. It would ease his guilt, I think, to get it out."

Kelly looked at her but said nothing. He studied her, seeming to be trying hard to reach a conclusion. "You're a smart girl, Elaina Kade. Smarter than you want to let on sometimes, just like my brother."

She let out a little laugh and felt a blush come to her cheeks again. But this time she didn't try to hide it.

*****

When Lainey left, Kelly wanted to get out of bed. He'd learned to pull himself up on the crutches, and with a great deal of sweat he could drag himself several feet before collapsing on the end of the bed. If he worked hard enough at it, by the end of the week he intended to stand up and propose to Miss Elaina Eastman Kade.

He reached for the crutches leaning against the wall by the head of his bed and, moving to the edge of the mattress, he tucked them under both arms. He looked to his feet where they hit the floor, willing his legs to hold his body up.

Then he saw it lying there, Lainey's letter, poking out from beneath the edge of the bed. It must have fallen while they visited and been swished aside when she returned the little table to its place beside the wall.

Switching the crutches to free one hand, he carefully leaned over the bed and retrieved the lost sheaf. He was about to fold it in half and set it aside, but memories surfaced of what Lainey had read about her mother's good friend Kashe. He opened the letter and read about her again, praying for the woman's recovery and the baby's continued health, praying for the father, Joe's, encouragement, and young Ginny who'd left her home to care for her mother and baby brother.

Lainey knew good people. She came from a fine home and family. Kelly prayed for her, too. He prayed God would do whatever it took to bring Lainey's heart back to Him, and he asked that if God saw fit, He'd bring a piece of her heart to Kelly as well. He smiled as he prayed for it, his heart overflowing with love for the young woman who'd swept into his life and Zane's, and captured him with her spirit.

Saying "Amen", he was about to continue in his mission to get off the bed, but his eyes fell onto the lower half of the page where Lainey had ceased to read.

I hope that Zane is doing all right with all that has happened to his brother. Your father thinks that he's a troubled young man, and I want you to know, Lainey, that we've been praying for him especially.

The words gave Kelly an almost supernatural comfort. Yes, Lainey came from good people indeed, people who were sensitive to the leading of the Lord. He read on.

You may be surprised at that, given that Kelly is the one who's suffered the injury. Rest assured we haven't ceased to pray for him, either. But, to be honest, both your father and I wonder if there might not be some special reason we should pray for Zane. It's not my intention to meddle, Sweetheart, or to put notions into your head that aren't there, but we think Zane is very fond of you. And, Lainey, we wonder if your feelings for Zane might run more deeply than you let on? Your behavior with Zane while you were here was different than with Kelly. We know that Kelly cares for you, but we don't know if you're aware how much his brother might care as well.

Stunned, he wanted to put the letter away. It wasn't his to read, but he couldn't stop. No matter how much his brain screamed at him to put it away, his eyes locked to the words, and he kept reading.

Don't brush this off as mere friendship, Honey. Your father thinks Zane's feelings for you might run much deeper than that. He's a peculiar young man. But we sense a rod of iron in his backbone that could strengthen him for good or bad. We hope if the time comes when you should recognize something deeper than friendship for Zane, you will use wisdom and discretion.

Now, I promise not to speak of this again unless you wish it. We love you, Elaina. Your brothers send their love. Auntie Jean and Robin as well, and of course Joe's family. How my heart yearns for he and Kashe. He has need of a love like hers.

All my prayers and all my love,
Mother

The letter quivered in Kelly's hand. The weakness washing over him made him tremble, and any thought of getting out of bed dissolved. He hadn't the strength to hold the letter, much less his body, erect.

Carefully, he folded the pages and put them under his pillow. Then he returned the crutches to their place against the wall and hoisted his legs back into the bed. Crunching down into the pillows he thought over Mrs. Kade's words.

...his brother might care as well... we wondered if your feelings for Zane might run more deeply... something deeper than friendship... use wisdom and discretion...

Had he been so blind in his infatuation he'd missed seeing something glaringly obvious to Lainey's parents? Was Zane in love with Lainey? And did she think of Zane with greater affection than Kelly knew?

Recollection blazed across his consciousness, bits and pieces of past events, like sketches being drawn out on the pages of his memory.

Splashes of color imprinted on his brain -- Lainey laughing, Zane watching her with his unreadable gaze, laughing back. Zane's hands reaching out to help her. His mind working in tune with hers, teaching her things.

Kelly shook his head. No. *No!* It had been the same with both of them, Zane and Kelly. Lainey had made it clear she wasn't interested in romance.

But Zane hadn't.

Kelly remembered how they looked, talking and walking and laughing together on the sandy Lake Michigan shore. He'd seen them together like that a hundred times. Had Zane's heart reeled with feelings for Lainey every time he took her hand to help her down from a wagon, or every time his gaze connected to hers? Zane had had ways with women forever. Kelly grew up admiring Zane's savoir-faire with the girls in St. Joe, and later, after the war, with women they met during their travels. After Kelly walked off on God, he learned a lot about dealing with the fairer sex from his older, more-worldly brother.

For a second, raw anger clutched sharp nails into Kelly's throat as he thought about Zane attempting to take advantage of Lainey like he did other women he'd used over the years. Then just as quickly his anger ebbed. It wasn't fair. Zane hadn't treated Lainey like that, and Kelly didn't believe he would if given the chance. Lainey was more to them than that, more to Kelly and to Zane.

He remembered how he felt coming home last Christmas and finding Lainey and Zane together in her room at the Forest House. There was nothing indecent. Zane had given her a Christmas tree and the two of them were decorating it, cutting out stars and snowflakes like little children at a Christmas party.

Only, in the lamplight it had looked cozy to him at the time. A hot wind of jealousy blew over Kelly now, just like then.

Did Zane love Lainey?

And then, like a flash, the recent past attacked. He remembered just days ago, lying on his bed, overtaken in weariness, more asleep than awake, he saw them outside the door. They were standing in the shade of the eave with the door hanging open. Kelly thought nothing of it at the time, but now he thought again. Zane had his hands wrapped around Lainey's wrists, and he was teasing her. He'd taken her bonnet and she was trying to get it back, but not trying very hard, if Kelly remembered correctly. His eyes narrowed as he tried to see it again, clearly. *Freckles.* That word came to him. Lainey said something about freckles, and she brushed her hand familiarly across Zane's face. Her voice sounded light, teasing, flirtatious almost. Zane followed her lead, snatching the bonnet, holding it just beyond her reach.

Lainey's bun tumbled askew, and Kelly saw her in his mind's eye just as clearly as if he'd been Zane, standing directly in front of her, the way her eyes brightened with challenge, the smile that turned his heart over. She was looking at him -- Zane, and Zane was looking back at her.

Kelly hadn't seen Zane's expression, but it made him wonder, because he was sure it was the kind of expression Zane often wore around Lainey, only Kelly had been too lost in his own cloud to pay any attention to it.

Kelly tucked his hand beneath the pillow and felt the letter there. Why hadn't she read the whole thing? Of course, because the content troubled her, and because something about it rang true. Maybe Zane did love Lainey. If it didn't disturb her, she would have said, "Listen to this," and read it all the way. Together they would have had a good laugh about it. But they hadn't. Lainey had put the letter aside and talked about her worries for Zane. Whether he was well, whether he'd written to Suzanne, what his prospects for the future were. She was more than concerned about him.

She and Zane spent a thousand hours together when Kelly worked away as a teamster and now since his accident. They went riding, took walks, and shared long talks. Zane had even taken her out for ice cream. They spoke over his head, sharing secrets when he was asleep. They'd grown intimate...

Truth rolled over Kelly like a freight train rumbling on a trestle. The pillars of his being shuddered, and in the wake of all the noise in his head, he lay shaken and weak. It was probably true that Zane had had his heart split open by Lainey, just as Kelly had. He threw his arm over his head, trying to block away the facts.

"But Zane knows how I feel," he cried aloud. And at the same time an inner voice reminded him, *"Zane blames himself for your crippled legs, and he would do anything he had to, to keep from hurting you more."*

He breathed deeply, trying to make sense of this truth. Yes, Zane would try desperately not to hurt him. Maybe that's what he'd been trying not to do all this time. Zane had no desire to love anyone since the war. Love hurt, is what he said. Yet, Zane loved him, and would love him to the death. Zane would take Kelly's place at that bridge if he had it to do over. And Zane would never interfere with someone whom Kelly loved. Never.

But still, she'd not shared the letter. Did Lainey herself know how Zane really felt?

His mind went through all the scenarios again. For another hour he replayed all their times spent together and all the ways Lainey responded to Zane, and every time Kelly fought with the facts. Her countenance thrilled when Zane was near. She always spoke anxiously of when he would return. Given the choice, she always looked to him for comfort and assurance before Kelly. He'd known she was getting over Bobby Braedon and her heart was mending, readying to move on. Could it be mending because of Zane?

Sore truth pummeled him like a bare knuckled boxer, and inside, his soul began to bleed as he understood what Lainey probably hadn't as yet -- what she would recognize soon enough with her mother's insights to prompt her.

She loves him. She loves Zane. Kelly's heart gasped, gushing truth like blood out an open wound.

Chapter Nineteen

Zane wiped the sweat off his brow and stuffed his kerchief back into his pocket. His shirt clung, ringed with sweat, and steam worked its way up around his neck. The sun blazed down on the workers, and to make matters more stifling, they'd started another burn to open up the right of way for the track.

Carl Stauber barked at Zane for the fifteenth time as he rested on his axe handle. "We ain't working tomorrow unless we get some decent water for drinking."

"We're working on it, Carl."

Zane had been named foreman of the small rank of men clearing the route where his map indicated the new line was to be laid. They'd been working hard until now. Lack of rain had dried up creek beds and they had to dig ten feet below the swamp for the first sign of moisture. Now the men began complaining of the lack of water for coffee and drinking. Around them the countryside broiled. The only thing good to come of the dry season was the ease of burning the brush standing in their way. With the swamps drying up, it made laying railroad beds easier, too.

"Henry left with the wagon hours ago. He'll be bringing water back in barrels from the Peshtigo."

Carl looked doubtful and cast a glance at the railroad embankments like he might just drop down there and wait for the return of the water wagon. But the sand of the embankments was like hot ash beds to step in, and what minor relief there might be from the heat would have to be found farther in the woods where leafy shade could be sought.

"If he don't get back soon we're just going to have to lay these axes and shovels down and wait for him."

Zane hardly took notice. The men kept threatening to quit, and there wasn't much he could do to stop them. Once the water got there, things would be better. He'd have the cook boil up a big pot of coffee with their dinner and maybe even turn out a barrel to wash in. Henry could go back for more water in the morning.

Zane looked once more at the descriptions and map he'd been perusing, then rolled them back up and tucked them into his pack.

"Once you boys top that ridge we start northeasterly. Make sure you pay heed to the tree marks."

Men nodded and kept on shoveling and picking. A sultry burning smell filled their nostrils as they sweated on.

They all laid down their implements before the water arrived. They swore they couldn't hew another tree or haul away another pile of brush. They took the fresh water down in gasps and gulps, their parched throats moving like the gills of fish out of water. Some slung ladlefuls over their heads and necks, smiling with relief.

Henry watched them with amusement. "More tomorrow, boss?"

"More tomorrow," said Zane.

He wished that night for a bath. He'd grown used to living comfortably over the past few years, staying in hotels, dining well, sleeping in comfort with only the occasional campout to break the monotony. Now he felt like he was back in Missouri during the war. Dirt and sweat embedded his every pore. The good fortune was that the bugs weren't bad this year, or he'd have been bug bitten too. His hair hardly looked its strawberry blonde color, but rather turned dark and greasy. Grime laid hold of his hands beneath his fingernails and covered his skin. He wished for a bath and a good meal in the Forest House with Lainey seated across the table.

The end of August neared, and it had been almost three weeks since he'd seen either her or Kelly. He missed them both. Creeping into his thoughts wormed the notion that by now Kelly might have asked Lainey to marry him. Would she do it? He wondered and found he couldn't speculate. There were plenty of reasons why she should. Kelly loved her. First and foremost there was that. Kelly loved her and he would take care of her, whether or not he ever got the use of his legs back. He wouldn't let that stop him. Not Kelly. He was already talking about taking on some work, just as soon as he had a little more of his strength back. Kelly believed he could do it in his chair if he had to.

Zane took a damp rag and, in the lamplight, wiped away as much dirt and sweat as the small square of cloth afforded, which wasn't much. He tried to dampen his neck and face enough to strike up the illusion that he was clean. It was hard to fabricate the idea, but he tried.

He'd stripped off his shirt, boots, and socks earlier. Taking off the jeans stiffened with dirt, he fell onto his cot and tried to sleep.

Maybe he could go back on Saturday.

He'd stayed away from Peshtigo since Kelly told him of his plans. Somehow knowing that Kelly was going to press his suit of Lainey made the idea of going back there with them that much more difficult.

Why?

Didn't he want the best for Kelly? And wouldn't Lainey be the best woman -- the very best -- whom Zane could hope for his brother to love?

Yet, as much as he fought admitting it, it tore at his guts to think of them wed. Not with the way he felt about Lainey himself.

You don't love her. You desire her, that's all. Isn't that it? So what if she makes your heart kick like a train piston. Lots of women can do that to you, can't they? So what if she pulls you into her blue eyes like quick sand and you never want her to release you. That's just fire in your blood, isn't it? So what if you want to protect her. You're a man, and that's natural, right?

He sat up and went to his meager box of belongings to pull out a pint of whiskey tucked away there. He pulled out the cork and drew it to his lips, but stopped. Barely had the fiery liquid touched them when he put the cork back in the bottle, stuffing it away.

You can't drink these thoughts away. Forget about it. Just make yourself forget.

He went and stood in the open doorway of his tent. Most the men in the camp had dropped off to sleep. The heat and hard work drove the night life out of them, at least until Saturday. Then they'd head into town to gamble and carouse and get all their fill of every vice they could find.

Crickets sang in the grassy places, and a whippoorwill set up a lonely call in the darkness. He loved the sound of it, the haunting, desolate call of the night bird. Retrieving his blanket, he spread it out on the grass next to the tent and lay down. A soft breeze blew over him bringing cool relief and calm.

Kelly deserved every good thing he could get. Wouldn't God reward him for coming back? Wouldn't Lainey say yes? She said she was through with love, that she would remain a spinster. But Zane saw something there in her eyes sometimes when she talked about it, like maybe she didn't really mean it, like maybe she was healing. Wouldn't she see how Kelly loved her better than those other men, and that he'd never want to change her?

That's what Zane wanted her to see.

If she was to be his sister-in-law soon, he'd just have to deal with it. He wouldn't get in their way with his own self-interests.

I'll go and see them on Saturday. I won't get in the way of what they might be to one another.

Still, his self-assurances felt weak.

He stared across the tree tops, noting the pale amber glow in the west where summer fires burned almost constantly, thinking about them simmering even as he built a firewall around his heart.

*****

Woodsmen roamed the streets of Peshtigo already well into their cups by noon on Saturday. Riding in past the boarding house, drunks called out to one another, and a tussle began taking shape in the sawdust on the street out front. Tinny sounding piano music plunked a discordant rhythm from a nearby saloon, and the high pitched laughter of a woman twanged in Zane's ears. Turning his horse to head across the bridge, he noted how low the water flowed. He nodded at a stranger in a wagon that passed him going the other way. Leaving the bridge, Zane instinctively wanted to turn his animal toward the Forest House, but with reluctance he clicked his tongue and reined the gelding toward Kelly's unfinished stables.

How quiet the little building looked.

He pulled in and put the horse in a stall of freshly bedded straw, hauling him a bucket of water and some grain before turning in to see Kelly. Kelly's sudden presence behind him startled him.

"Man, Kell, you snuck up on me."

"Getting pretty handy at this chair," Kelly answered with a grin as he held out his hand.

Zane shook it, clamping another on Kelly's shoulder.

"You've been gone a long time. You're not that far away. Why don't you come home more often?"

"Oh, you know..."

Kelly's eyebrows rose in question.

"They got lots of work for me up the line."

"They let everybody else have a day off. How come not you?"

"I get time. I just use it to rest, that's all."

Kelly stretched forward and gave him a good-natured punch to the arm. "You can't rest here?"

Zane shrugged and stepped around Kelly. "It looks like you've been doing some work. You got these stalls finished."

Kelly wheeled around to the side of him. "Jacob's been helping me a lot. I can do a fair share myself, too, now that I'm feeling stronger."

"Not walking yet?"

Kelly shook his head. "Nah. Not yet. Like I said, I'm feeling stronger though."

"That's good." Zane nodded, appreciating the work Kelly had accomplished as well as his brother's hopeful disposition. "I reckon I can give you a hand today if you like."

"You sure? I don't want you to stay away again for weeks on end because I don't let you rest."

Zane chuckled. "Well, I'll see about that."

"It's about lunch time now. In fact," Kelly wheeled closer, looked at him squarely, "you just missed Lainey. She dropped off a basket of chicken. It's in the room."

Zane thought there was something odd-sounding about the way Kelly mentioned it, or maybe it was his own stifled desire to see her. He'd waited to come into town until late in the morning, hoping he wouldn't catch her there at Kelly's home. He wasn't ready to see them together, to hear her say that she and Kelly's relationship had changed. He wanted to hear that from Kelly -- alone.

"Good. I'm hungry. I have to admit you're liable to get more work out of me once I've eaten."

"You think I've forgotten that? Come on. Follow me."

Kelly led the way and urged Zane to sit down while he wheeled about and set out their lunch. Zane admired his brother's deftness at handling the chair. It seemed even without his legs, Kelly was a whole person. Some deep sense of relief washed over him to realize it, to know Kelly was the same, maybe even better for all the change.

The chicken, even cold, tasted better than anything he'd eaten in the railroad camp lately. Or maybe it was that the flavor alone evoked a rail car of memories, mostly of Lainey with him and sometimes Kelly.

"How's she doing?"

"She's the same," Kelly answered, seeming to know intuitively not only who Zane meant, but that he'd been thinking of her. "She drew me a picture to remember you by."

"She drew a picture of me?"

"Of all of us together. It's over there on the wall above the shelf."

Zane glanced up from his chicken and turned around to look over where Kelly pointed with a chicken leg bone. He wanted to stare at it -- at her -- but shrugged and turned away. "Where's it supposed to be?"

"I don't know. I didn't ask her."

"Looks like the bank of the Fox, down Green Bay way."

"You think so?"

Zane nodded and dove into a spoonful of potato salad.

"You didn't look at it very long. You sure?"

"Seems like I remember that big rock she's sitting on. I think she sat just like that there once."

Kelly smirked. "You have a good memory for detail."

"That's why I'm the card player and you're not."

"God blessed you that way."

Zane laughed softly and wiped his greasy fingers on a linen napkin Lainey had tucked into the basket with their meal. He sat back and took a drink of milk. "I suppose He did, if you say so."

"God's blessings are all around us. Take Lainey for instance."

"I thought that's what you were going to do..."

Kelly grinned and pointed at him. "You got me there. But don't you agree? She's a blessing?"

"The best kind."

Kelly smiled at Zane but said nothing. Zane was about to push away from the table, to get to the work he'd promised to help with, but Kelly's gaze and the next few words out of his mouth stopped him.

"What if she's not meant for me?"

"What?" Zane settled back into his chair.

"What if God's not meant Lainey for me?"

Zane looked down at his hands. "Did she... did she turn you down?"

Kelly studied him. "I haven't asked her yet."

Air rushed out of Zane's lungs. "Well, why not? I thought that was your plan. I stayed away so you could."

Kelly grinned. "Is that why you haven't come home? I don't get it."

"To give you time, just the two of you. Couldn't you work up the nerve?"

"I've got nerve a-plenty."

"Then what?"

Kelly shrugged. "I just wanted to be sure, that's all."

"You sounded awful sure the last time I saw you."

"Oh, I was. And I am. I meant that I wanted to be sure about you."

"About me? How's that?"

"If I marry Lainey, then things will change between the three of us."

Zane nodded, thoughts swarming around his brain. Lainey as Kelly's wife. A sister. No flirting allowed. "Yeah, I suppose they will."

"Do you have any trouble with that, Zane? I guess I never bothered to think about it before. I never wondered until just lately if maybe you weren't ever a little bit interested in Lainey yourself."

Kelly couldn't have stunned Zane more if he'd hit him on the head with a horse shoe. He sputtered for words. "What are you preaching about?" he asked finally, not unkindly. He smiled even though his head felt like it'd been laid against a grindstone.

"I just wondered if -- maybe -- you weren't ever a little taken with Lainey yourself."

"Course I was -- at first," Zane answered quickly. "Who wouldn't be? You remember the day we met her and her cousin Kate in the restaurant in Chicago. It was like anytime we'd met a stunner before. I'll admit I had my hopes up."

"But what about later? What about since we've gotten to be so close to Lainey?"

Zane shook his head and gathered up their plates. He pushed back his chair and took the dishes to the sink, his back turned to Kelly. He felt hot, hotter than normal even for a stifling summer day.

"Lainey's a fun girl." He poured water into the tub and started to haphazardly wash the dishes. "But I've known for a long time that you wanted her as your girl. She is your girl." He looked back at Kelly, trying to impress him with the forcefulness of the statement.

"Well, not yet."

"You've only got to ask."

"Then you're sure?"

"Yeah." He tried mustering up a more confident sounding tone than he felt as he turned to the dish tub again. "Yeah, I'm sure."

It was wrong to come here. He would help Kelly out today, but tomorrow, as soon as dawn lit the sky, he would go back to the camps where he belonged. He would go back and stay there until he got word that Kelly and Lainey were wed, just like he should have done in the first place.

*****

Manason Kade handed a sealed letter to Kenton and sent him on his way to the post. He turned to his wife. "How do you think she'll take it?"

"I don't know. How can she take it any better than the rest of us?"

"She's had so many shocks. Now another."

"Maybe she'll come home," said Colette, hopefully.

Manason put his arm around her and they walked out to the barn where he began oiling a harness.

"You think she won't?" Colette asked after a bit.

He gazed at her. "I wouldn't want to venture a guess, but if you insist, then no."

"But won't she know she's needed?"

He dropped the harness and put his arms around her. "I think she believes she's needed where she is."

Tears rolled down Colette's face. It seemed so hard to keep them at bay these days. "But--"

"Ssh. Come on. I don't have to do this now."

Manason took Colette's hand and they strolled back to the house and went inside. Together, seated on the sofa, they held one another.

Chapter Twenty

Lainey read the letter again, dampening it still more with fresh tears.

Kashe was dead. Some kind of tumor, the letter said. Joe was beset with grief but hanging on, leaning on Lainey's family and his brother Rob for strength, as was his daughter Ginny.

How could it be, God? How?

No answers came, not for questions like these, but still she asked.

She folded the letter and put it away. Someday, perhaps. Someday God might let her understand losses like those of Kashe Gilbert and Bobby Braedon, or the senseless injuries of good men like Kelly Beaumont or her own grandfather. Someday, in heaven, as Kelly and Pastor Beach both promised, she would understood these things, and those who believed would see each other again, whole, complete, without pain. For the first time ever, Lainey clung to that.

She thought of Zane, out there somewhere, and worried something terrible could happen to him before she ever saw him again. She wanted to rush to him with her letter and show him. *See? See how fragile life is, Zane? We can't take it for granted anymore! Why did you leave again without seeing me? Without letting me see that you're all right?* He would have been able to comfort her, to reassure her.

But for some reason he went away two weeks ago without ever talking to her. She hadn't seen Zane in over a month. He'd not gone to church with them, and now it seemed like he never planned to come back.

A frenzy swept through her thoughts, and she allowed it to have its sway. *If I'm not important to you, Zane, then so be it. But you're important to me, and I will see you whether you like it or not.*

She stormed around her room, throwing a few needed things together and dashing at the tears creeping out for Kashe. If she stopped to tell Kelly where she was going, she might not make the afternoon stage. There just wasn't time. She apologized to John, telling him she wouldn't be able to work for a day or two, before she headed out the door.

Fall didn't arrive with the intense beauty common to northern Wisconsin that year. The flaming red on the distant hillside was created not by the glow of red oaks and sugar maples turning color, but by the fires. Folks working out of doors complained often about the smoke from distant peat and brush fires stinging their eyes. A hopeful sprinkle on September fifth came to nothing, and even Mr. Kuchenberg the stagecoach driver commented on the situation as he helped her step into the coach.

"Think it'll ever rain again?"

"You know how things change," she answered with a smile. "We'll probably get a downpour, and then have so much snow next winter we'll wish for a few dry days come spring."

"That would be a heap of wishing. The air's so dry that if a man just touched a match to it, I swear it'd burn."

Lainey laughed. She'd heard that said before. People everywhere made similar remarks, at church, in the hotels and saloons, and on the street.

"I reckon those boys at the lumber camps wish it would rain. The river's so low they can't float the logs down. There're huge ramparts of 'em stacked up. Have you seen them?"

"No." Lainey shook her head, knowing what a disaster the dry spell meant for the loggers.

"Sure enough. I bet they're hoping for that snow you spoke of." With that he tipped his hat and turned to take the bags of a second passenger. A middle aged man with a round face climbed aboard and sat down across from Lainey.

"Mr. Noyes?" Lainey caught his attention. He smiled and she stretched out her hand. "You're Mr. Noyes, the editor of the Eagle?"

He smiled. "That's right."

"My name is Lainey Kade. I've wanted to meet you all summer, but I haven't made my way over to your office."

"Well, it's always a pleasure to meet someone who's interested in the Eagle."

Lainey beamed. "Yes, I'm a faithful reader. I don't subscribe myself, but I live and work at the Forest House and I read every issue there."

"Oh, the Forest House. That's the one near the church."

"Yes."

"Do you attend there?"

"No. I go to Reverend Beach's Congregational Church."

The coach lurched forward.

Noyes smiled. "Then you must know all about his prize winning tomato."

"I read about it, yes. I haven't seen it."

"One pound, ten ounces, I believe it was."

"So it said in the Eagle."

"Yes." Mr. Noyes removed his hat and set it on the bench seat. "Everyone enjoys reading about the local successes and blessings. This week I'm running a story about a woman here in town who's just birthed her twenty-third child."

Lainey's eyes widened. "Twenty-three children? I can't imagine!"

Mr. Noyes took off his spectacles and began to clean them. "Some women are stronger and more able than men. She must have the stamina of six men."

Lainey giggled. "Well, I know that children are a blessing, but it will probably be best if the Lord doesn't bless me ever quite so fully!"

"So you say you work at the Forest House."

"Yes. I help out in the kitchen. I also sketch," she added.

"Sketch?"

Lainey reached beside her and unwrapped the drawing pad she always took with her. "These are some of my sketches."

Mr. Noyes took the pad and spent several quiet minutes examining the drawings.

"These of the mill are very accurate," he said. "The logs are beginning to play out now, you know. It won't be very long before the mills are shut down and the boys are off to the woods."

"Yes, I know. My father is a lumberman over in Chippewa County."

"Is that right?"

"Yes. Mr. Noyes, I wondered if you could use any of my sketches for the Eagle. I've been published before under the name E. Eastman."

A light came into the editor's eyes. He snapped his fingers. "E. Eastman, why, yes. I've seen one or two of your drawings in a paper my friends out east sent me. I thought I recognized something familiar about the scene. Well, I tell you Miss -- Eastman, or Kade?"

"Either one. Kade is what most people know me by."

"I tell you, Miss Kade, the Eagle is a small paper. We don't have room for large drawings. But if you can help out with a few small images from time to time, I would compensate you. It would have been nice to have a small sketch of Reverend Beach with his tomato," he said jovially.

She laughed. "Yes, it would have."

He shook her hand again. "Stop by and see me when you can. We'll talk more."

Lainey took the drawing pad and wrapped it back in its cloth. "So you must be visiting your Marinette office today."

"That's my headquarters of course, yes. But I have a meeting with some men from the Sheboygan paper which I started some years ago."

"I heard you used to be a judge."

"Indeed. Judge of Monroe County. Before that a war captain, a lawyer, and now a journalist."

"You've lived an exciting life."

"I'm only forty-one. It's not over yet."

Lainey blushed. "I didn't mean--"

"Of course not."

"You said you were a war captain. Do you know of many soldiers who suffer with after effects of the war?"

"Oh my, yes." His voice took on a serious tone. "'Soldier's heart', or 'irritable heart' they call it, or sometimes 'nostalgia', or Da Costa's Syndrome. It's all related to the stress of horrors they've seen. Soldiers complain of chest pain, palpitations and dizziness subsequent to exposure to battle scenes. They suffer from nightmares, flashbacks, paralyzing memories."

"How long does it last?"

"Oh, I'm no authority of course, but I've seen it last months or a lifetime. There are so many factors. Some men live with it, try to ignore it. Others give up. They turn to alcohol or even take their own lives."

Lainey's heart churned. "I have a friend who struggles sometimes."

"Well," Mr. Noyes smiled warmly, "he can be thankful to know a young lady like you who cares for him."

A warm flush returned and she dropped her eyes. "Thank you, Mr. Noyes."

The trip went slowly. The stench of fire remained ever present, and in some stretches smoke sifted like a haze through the trees. They reached Marinette and she said good-bye to the genial Mr. Noyes. Then she went to the nearest livery to procure a horse.

"I need a horse to take me to the railroad camp on Pine Creek."

"Pine creek's dried up."

"But the camp is still there?"

"Sure. You're going alone?"

Lainey nodded.

"Hmph."

"I'll thank you to keep your opinion and just rent me a horse."

The stable hand eyed her doubtfully, but took her money and set her up with an old mare. Half an hour later she followed directions to Zane's camp. She knew when she was getting close. Smoke from the brush fires wove thicker through the woods, and pretty soon she saw movement of shirtless bodies between the trees. Before long she came upon the dirty white tents of the camp. Whistles and catcalls followed her as she road straight in and dismounted.

She straightened her shoulders and ignored them, letting out a holler. "Can any of you men tell me where I can find Mr. Zane Beaumont?"

"What do you want with him when you can have me?" someone called back, and the onlookers laughed.

Another fellow leered up a bit closer."How about me, sister?"

She put her hands on her hips with a show of authority, feeling little worry about these men. "I'm sure you gentleman don't want to hold me up. You've got better things to do than keep a lady standing in the sun without answering her direct question."

She looked them squarely in the eye, one by one. Many of them were barely more than boys. Some were older then her, Zane's age likely. Many would be married, and though their thoughts betrayed them, they were unlikely to cause trouble.

"Zane? You around here?" she yelled, and they started to back off.

"He's probably up at the shack with the boss man," one fellow said. "If you like, ma'am, I'll take you there."

"Thank you. That's very kind." She led her horse behind the lanky young man.

The tents stood in two long rows amid stumps and trampled brown grass, and at their end stood a shack where the manager or foreman's office was located. She tied her horse to a post nearby as the man went up and pounded on the door. "Zane, you in there? Somebody out here to see ya!" He smiled back at Lainey.

"My horse could use some water if you've any to spare," she said.

"I'll see what I can do."

"Thank you again," she said, just as the door flung open.

For a moment Zane stared dumbly as though he didn't recognize her. In fact, he was nearly unrecognizable. His face was whiskered and dirty, his hair dark with grease and sweat. After he realized she wasn't an apparition, he acted embarrassed. He pushed his hair back out of his eyes and darted a glance over the camp.

"Lainey, what are you doing here?"

She stepped forward and stopped, feeling unwelcome. "I-- I just--"

"Is Kelly all right?" Concern propelled him down the single step.

"Yes, he's fine. I only wanted to see you."

Now she felt a flush flooding her. Why had she come here? Why had she appeared in this camp as though she had a right to be here and embarrassed them both?

"Come on inside," Zane murmured, sweeping in the stares of the men by the tents. Just then the dinner bell rang and they all dispersed. Lainey followed Zane into the office.

Another railroad man closed a desk drawer and picked up his hat. "I'm about finished here. I think I'll head on over for dinner. Want me to send you a plate?"

"That would be great. And something for Miss Kade, if you don't mind."

"My pleasure." He smiled at her as he left the building.

"Have a seat, Lainey."

"I'm a little saddle sore," she said, rubbing her hip. She looked at him then. "I'm sorry, Zane. I shouldn't have come. I just didn't take time to think how awkward it might look."

"It's all right. I'm getting used to it." He chuckled, and her shoulders dropped in relief. "Why did you come?"

She shook her head and shrugged. "I don't know. I guess... well, I guess just to see that you were all right."

"Why wouldn't I be?"

"You left without a hello or goodbye last time you came to Peshtigo. I thought something terrible was the matter. Then there's been all this talk of fire danger and troubles in the woods..." she wrung her hands.

"What talk?"

"Oh, nothing. I just worried about you. I... I missed you, Zane."

She looked at him, wondering what about this man caused her

heart to beat like it hadn't in over two years, like there was life inside. Then she started to smile. He was such a sight!

"What? Oh..." Zane ran a hand over his face. "I guess you're sorry you found me. I'm such a mess."

A tease crept into her voice. "It's nice to know what you look like when you have to work for a living."

He grinned, his smile unusually white in his ruddy face. "Well, it isn't what I'd prefer. I'd covet a bath."

"It's Friday. Why don't you come to Marinette and have one."

"You're staying in town?"

She flushed further. "I guess I have to, now, don't I? I haven't taken a room yet."

"Then let's skip supper and get you back to town before they all fill up. We'll eat dinner someplace nicer than this."

"Are you sure? Aren't you starving?"

"I can wait for a steak."

An hour later they checked into rooms at a quickly filling inn, and Lainey paced the floor of hers while waiting for Zane to finish bathing. He paid extra for the bath, the price having jumped with the shortage of water and people's wells drying up.

But the wait was worth it. When she finally opened her door at Zane's knock, he looked even handsomer than she remembered. Rugged and tanned, the freckles she once teased him about were still visible. But he'd shaved, and his hair shone with soft highlights, combed back off his face to touch his collar. He wore clean clothes including a starched, white shirt, and she wondered where he got it. And he smelled good.

An effortless smile fixed on her lips. "You look ready."

"As do you," he said, and she noticed he looked at her with an appreciation he hadn't shown two hours earlier. He held out his arm and she put hers though it, but slid her hand down a moment later and let it fall into his.

They walked down the boardwalk hand in hand, a strange warmth and glow pouring over Lainey she didn't want to stop, with his strong, square hand wrapped over hers. He opened the door for her to his favorite restaurant and pulled out her chair. Finally, they ordered their food, and while they waited, Zane voiced the questions he must have been aching to ask.

"What did Kelly have to say about your impetuous decision to come up here?"

She toyed with her napkin on her lap. "I didn't tell him. There wasn't time if I was going to catch the stage."

"So you really did just decide to come on impulse? You didn't think of it yesterday, or the day before?"

She shook her head. "You know me, Zane."

His head fell back and he laughed before gazing at her again. "Yes. I think I do. But don't you think he'll be worried?"

"Zane--"

"He loves you, Lainey."

His gray-blue eyes settled and held hers as strongly as he'd held her hand a while ago.

"I know," she whispered. "He hasn't said so, but I know."

"And you?"

Lainey didn't answer right away. She didn't know how. She cared about Kelly more than she thought she ever could care about someone who wasn't really her family. Kelly... he was one of her brothers... They went to church pretty regularly these days, and she considered him a brother in Christ as dear to her as any earthly relation. But love him romantically? She thought, once, she might learn to love him after a fashion. But such a notion eventually slipped away. And it had nothing to do with his physical condition. She thought about it many times, and decided Kelly was as whole to her as he'd ever been. Not being able to use his legs didn't make him any less a man. But to be in love with Kelly was an entirely different matter.

Her heart was healing. The fact that she'd come here today gave testimony to that and stood as the real reason she couldn't be in love with Kelly.

She remembered for the thousandth time the notion her mother shared in the lost letter. Her parents wondered about her feelings for Zane. She told herself the idea was impossible at first. Zane was a brother to her too, like Kelly. But day by day her thoughts roamed to him, and she at last faced the fact that her heart had mended more completely than she dared believe.

She stared at him, recognizing why it was she didn't love Kelly.

I love Zane.

A spasm shot through her chest and she heaved a sigh. Love. Pain. They went together. How could she ever crush Kelly with her love for his brother? Zane himself wouldn't let it happen.

She gave her head the smallest shake. "I... I can't."

Zane sighed too. "Kelly's patient. He'll wait until you can."

"And if I can't ever?"

"Someday you may, Lainey. Don't give up on that." He reached across the table and laid his hand over hers causing her heart to swell. Then their food came and he drew it away.

*****

Zane watched the delicate way she brought each bite to her mouth and thought he could sit here like this every day, watching her. He never tired of the mischievous sparkle in her velvety eyes, or her exciting, impulsive nature. She was not the kind of girl to make him grow tired.

She'd come all this way, just to set her mind at ease that he was all right. No one but Kelly had ever done that sort of thing for him before. What a wonder she was. She gave him courage, just by being herself. Zane believed she would do the same for Kelly once her heart mended. Maybe she could heal him too.

"I wrote to Suzanne," he said, knowing it would please her. "Not a telegram, but a whole letter."

"You did? That's wonderful, Zane. She must be so glad."

"She sent me a telegram. She sounded pleased."

"She took it well, about Kelly I mean?"

"It distressed her, but she's a strong girl, like you."

Lainey smiled at the compliment, just as he knew she would.

"I'd like to meet your sister some day."

"Maybe you will." Already his thoughts flew to them going to Missouri, and the idea intrigued him rather than pained him. He and Lainey and Kelly. Whether or not Kelly married her, why not take her there to meet what little remained of his family? Why not get to know his niece and nephews? Why not let Suzanne feel like she might have a sister?

"We should talk to Kelly about it. Maybe next summer--"

"Kelly will want to go," said Zane, nodding. "He misses Suzanne and doesn't have the dread of old St. Joe like I do."

"But you're better now, right?"

He nodded. He was better. It was uncanny.

"What else did you tell her in your letter?"

"Just about the past year, mostly. I told her about you and how Kelly felt."

A rose bloom flooded her cheeks and he pushed down the urge to reach over and stroke her chin.

"You did? Wasn't that premature?"

"I suppose given what you've told me, maybe it was."

They finished their meal and strolled along the boardwalk in the twilight. Once or twice they side-stepped rowdies making their way from one saloon to the next.

"Have you been playing cards at all?"

"Only a hand or two in the tent with the fellows now and then. Nothing for money."

"You've turned over a new leaf."

Zane grunted. "Well, responsibility has a way of forcing your hand sometimes."

"We're proud of you, Zane."

He looked over at her. She wasn't many inches shorter than he, and he tried to read her thoughts. It was difficult. He thought he knew her better, but Lainey's dark eyes were as unreadable as people said his own were. Maybe he'd taught her that.

He thought of the way she'd answered him, or hadn't answered him, when he asked about her feelings for Kelly. There was something there. He was sure of it. It was the something keeping him from sweeping her into his arms now.

She said she couldn't love Kelly, implying that she couldn't love him *yet*. Just like she'd said so many other times -- her heart wasn't healed enough for love. But Kelly was wearing her down. Zane felt it. And he meant it when he said she might love Kelly someday.

I'm sorry, Kell, his thoughts admitted dizzily, *but I wish I were the reason she couldn't love you. No matter how wrong that would be.* Because for the first time ever, Zane knew that it wasn't desire or lust that drew him to Lainey. It was love.

Chapter Twenty-One

By the third week of September, Peshtigo was nearly cut off from Oconto and Green Bay. Constant strings of fire burned to the west and southwest, and the telegraph line burned as well, so there would be no forthcoming greetings from Suzanne or Lainey's family for a while. Each day at dusk the sun fell through the haze behind a curtain of distant red, yet it portended more than a sunset. A strange, amber glow held the western sky all night long. Women came out to their porches to toss their supper dishwater and looked at it, a frown on their brows as they wrung their hands in their aprons and scooted children off to bed.

Kelly watched it too, but life went on. His livery picked up work and his plans moved ahead, even as he wondered what would become of his feelings for Lainey.

The horse he worked on now whinnied as he poured a few oats in the bucket hanging on the wall. He stroked the horse's flank and spoke calm words to the animal, then leaned over in his wheelchair and picked up the horse's foot to examine it.

"You need a trim, but you're all right." He pushed himself back in the chair to reach for his hoof clipper.

He worked mechanically on the animal, his thoughts elsewhere, always going back to Lainey.

The day she went off to see Zane confirmed his every suspicion. He knew that not only did Zane have intense feelings for Lainey, but she loved him too. She might not know it, or be willing to admit it, but Kelly knew it to be true.

"Zane doesn't want to hurt me, and he doesn't think he's good enough for her," he said, still talking to the horse as it munched on the oats, its ears twitching slightly as though it took in every one of Kelly's words. "So what do I do, pal? Let her go?"

His muscles strained as he wheeled himself around to the other side of the horse and began work on its left feet. "Or do I just press on and let her decide whether or not to have me anyway? Maybe if I out and ask her she'll think twice about what she feels."

Moon-shaped crescents of hoof fell to the ground and Kelly moved to the hind leg, repeating his procedure. Finally, some minutes later, he sat back and patted the horse's rump. "I guess if she loves him and not me, well then..."

Kelly couldn't say what he believed -- that forcing her to think of his feelings for her would be wrong. It would put her in an even more awkward position than she already found herself in. Or worse, maybe she would indeed respond to her true feelings for Zane and thus change her relationship with Kelly forever. That thought was almost too much to take. As much as Kelly loved Zane, he wasn't ready to lose Lainey completely to him just yet.

"I'll just let it ride... wait and see if they come to their own conclusions or not. Maybe..." Kelly shook his head and tossed the clippers into a wooden bucket. Wheeling himself away from the horse, he gazed out the door into the paddock behind the livery. "Maybe God doesn't have her for me." Tremors moved through his tired body.

*****

Mrs. Anderson sat across the dining table and rattled on. "I tell you, Lainey, it just isn't right the way this town carries on. The Judgment is coming! You ask Pastor Beach if it isn't so. Why -- all the drinking and carousing -- it's getting so that decent folks can't step out their own doors on a Saturday night without the risk of being verbally accosted by some drunken lumberjack. The things I've heard -- it burns my ears! I can't even get the words out of my mind. They're planted there for good. That's how the devil works, you know, through the ear-gate and the eye-gate."

Lainey sipped her cool tea and agreed with Mrs. Anderson. She rubbed her ankles together beneath the table, anxious for the woman to wind up her visit and go home. Lainey liked Mrs. Anderson, but sometimes the woman's tinny voice grated on her nerves. She tried reprimanding herself for thinking such impatient thoughts toward the woman, but it was hard to hear her go on so.

"You know, out east there are women marching against such things. I wonder what these rabble rousers would do if the upstanding men and women of this community banded together to pass ordinances that would force them to give up their wild ways? Good heavens! I would be glad for just a quiet night's rest before I had to get up for church on Sunday morning. What do you think?"

Lainey set her cup gently on its saucer. "Everyone wants to feel safe, of course, Mrs. Anderson. But I wonder if Peshtigo is really ready to put a stop to these kinds of activities. Most of the men who come in from the woods really mean little harm. They overdo it, certainly, but they work very hard--"

"Are you defending their behavior?" Mrs. Anderson's eyes opened wide as silver dollars.

"Of course not, I'm just trying to understand them. They're unlikely to react kindly to forcefulness and prudishness--"

"Prudishness!"

"I mean, what they perceive to be prudishness. Kindness and charity on the other hand..."

"Humph!" Mrs. Anderson slurped on her tea. "I'll have to talk further to Pastor Beach. I'm certain he would believe in taking a firm hand with the likes of the riffraff pouring into our town every Saturday night."

"You may be right," Lainey conceded.

Mrs. Anderson nodded matter-of-factly as she set down her cup and rose. "Well, I'd best be getting home. Mr. Anderson will want his supper as soon as he finishes work at the mill. Will we be seeing you in church on Sunday?"

Lainey offered a bright smile. "I'll be there."

"Good. It's nice to see you and Mr. Beaumont coming so regularly. Shame about his injury though. Any hope of recovery?"

"He hasn't given up."

Mrs. Anderson "tsk-ed" a few times as she picked up her reticule and headed for the door. "All things work together for good," she reminded Lainey. "We have to encourage him with that."

"For those who love God and are called according to His purpose," Lainey finished the context of the verse from memory. "You can be sure Kelly hasn't forgotten."

"Very well, then. See you tomorrow. We'll serve coffee after service."

"Thank you. Good bye, Mrs. Anderson."

"Good bye."

Lainey closed the door and breathed a sigh. Kelly expected her in fifteen minutes. She'd wasted the entire morning listening to Mrs. Anderson's dire warnings and shotgun application of Scripture verses. No doubt the woman dearly loved the Lord, but when it came to ministering, she hadn't quite grasped the concept of what it meant to "be all things to all men". Still, Lainey upbraided herself for harboring harsh thoughts. Who was she to talk anyway? She'd ministered to no one, nor did she feel a calling on her life to do anything significant for God so as she noticed. Her one concern hung on Zane and Kelly's welfare. That was all.

She hurried to take the tea service to the kitchen and pump some water into the suds in the sink. She didn't care that it was cold. It was more of a nuisance that bits of silt drew up from the well. She gave the cups a quick washing and stacked them on the wooden rack by the cutting board to dry. Then she dried her hands and hurried up to her room to check her dress in the mirror and pick up her drawing pad before heading to Kelly's. His note sent by Jacob said that he had something important to talk to her about and she wondered what it could be.

She was twenty minutes late getting to the livery. Perspiration had gathered along the tendrils of her brow from the quick walk in the sun, and stepping under the eave of the building brought only minor relief.

She peered inside the door. "Kelly?"

"Back here."

She stepped into the darkened room and glanced toward the back where Kelly's frame sat shadowed in his chair in the doorway leading into the stable. He pushed himself closer so she could finally see him.

"It's hard to see after stepping out of that bright sun," she said, untying her bonnet and tossing it over a chair. She smiled at him. "How are you?"

He didn't speak, he only watched her, until after a long moment she grew concerned.

"Kelly?"

"I'm fine. How are you?"

"I'm fine. Are you sure?"

Finally he smiled at Lainey and the familiar ease she loved lit Kelly's blue eyes. He wheeled closer still and held out his hand. She took it and gazed at him. "What, Kelly? What is it? Is something wrong? You said it was something important... Oh, no. It isn't Zane--"

"No, no. Zane's fine far as I know."

Relief sailed over her and she let go of Kelly's hand to drop onto a nearby chair. "You scared me for a moment."

Kelly watched her again for just a bit longer then he sighed. "I have something to tell you, and I'm not sure what you'll think."

"Are you planning to shock me, Mr. Beaumont?" she teased.

He grinned. "I've tried that on any number of occasions and found it impossible, so no. Then again... maybe you will be."

"Why don't you just tell me, and I'll let you know."

Kelly smiled again, his teeth showing white against the tan of his face. "All right. Enough suspense, right? Well, Lainey, it's like this. I love my work here in the livery, but I'm thinking about doing something else with it."

"And that would be what?"

"Preaching."

His eyes locked on hers as if to see whether she would challenge his notion, but she couldn't. She could only try to register what he was saying.

Preaching? Was this God's idea?

She stumbled over words. "Kelly... I--"

He threw back his head and laughed, his silky blond bangs falling over his face. "I really did shock you!"

She chuckled. "You did."

Kelly sobered. "Well, what do you think? Do I make a poor choice for a preacher?"

"God is in the habit of surprising people that way, isn't He?"

He nodded. "So it seems." He leaned forward in his chair, getting as close to her as space allowed. "I know this has got to be a lot for you to take in. Believe me, Lainey, I'm not quite used to the idea myself, but I think that's what He wants." He sat up straight. "I've been selfish. For almost seven years it's only been about me. Everything has been about my pain, my desires, and my urges. Well, He's made it clear to me that enough is enough. It's time to put my attention back where it belongs."

Her heart raced. "But preaching? Are you sure? Where? How?"

"Get us something to drink, will you, while I tell you?"

Lainey nodded and rose to pour water from a pitcher by the sink. She handed Kelly his glass and sat back down, but she didn't drink.

"I thought I might start out with a little bit of circuit riding. You know, reach out to the men in the camps. Do some discipling. Try to get them to come to town for what's offered at church on Sunday morning rather than what they can get on Saturday night."

Lainey didn't know what to say. She opened her mouth, but nothing came out.

"It won't be easy, but the rail line will be going through soon, and that'll help. I'll have to learn to get on a horse again."

"Do you think you'll be able to?" Almost as soon as she said it she was sorry. She might as well hew down his hopes with a broad axe.

Kelly frowned, but the creases on his forehead quickly smoothed. "Sure. I've got lots of upper body strength."

"Kelly, I'm sorry. I didn't mean to imply you wouldn't get well."

He held up his hand to stop her and wheeled backward toward his bed. He lifted his cane from its resting place against the wall by the head of the bed.

"Watch this, Lainey."

Kelly scooted forward in his chair. He took a breath and steadied himself. Lainey moved to the edge of her chair and gripped the seat as Kelly's face strained, and beads of sweat began popping out on his brow. Haltingly, he lifted himself to his feet. She wanted to rush to him, to keep him from falling, but with nerves of steel she held back, only rising slowly to face him.

His body shuddered with the strength it took to hold himself there, but hold himself he did, though Lainey could tell that it pained him.

"Kelly," she gasped. "That's amazing! You kept it a secret!" She walked to him and held out her arms, grateful he didn't deny her as she hugged him gently and helped him lower himself back into the chair. His breaths came out hard from the exertion and she felt his heart thudding as she steadied him. Her own heart thumped hard, too.

"It's work," he admitted, "but I'm getting stronger every day. It may take a long time yet to learn to walk, but I'm hoping I can mount a horse by spring time."

"I think you will." She smiled and laid a hand on his shoulder. His hand came up to hers. He caressed it lightly until she pulled away.

Lainey sat back in her chair and took a long drink of water. "I still can't believe it."

"I hoped you'd be surprised, but to tell you the truth, I hadn't planned to show you yet. I just wanted to tell you about my plans to preach. I guess the Lord prompted me. His timing is always best."

She nodded. How could she disagree? Despite her life's experiences, here sat a man who had every reason to be angry and spiteful towards God, but he wasn't. In fact, his injuries and heartaches seemed to increase his love for the Almighty.

"Want to take a walk?" he asked.

"Sure. Where to?"

"How about to that place where you and Zane got the ice cream. I'll buy."

"All right. If you're buying then let's go." She got behind his chair to push. "As long as you don't mind me pushing you a ways. You should rest up a bit after that performance."

He didn't argue with her, and by that Lainey knew the exertion had been extreme. She tied her bonnet back on and they headed out the door and down the dusty road. When they reached the plank boardwalk, a couple of men stepped down and helped lift Kelly's chair up onto it. Lainey and Kelly thanked them and pushed on.

"Mind if I ask you something, Kell?"

"Go ahead."

"How is it so easy for you to have faith?"

Walking behind his chair, she couldn't see his expression. For herself, she was glad he couldn't see her either. She might not have been able to ask if she could see his penetrating blue eyes looking into hers.

"It's not so hard, really, Lainey. We can't live our lives under our own little clouds. Not when the Son is shining right behind them. Do you know what I mean?"

She nodded first, then said, "Yes, I suppose."

"God knows the plans he has for us, Lainey, for you and for me and for Zane. He has plans to give us hope and a future."

"It's the hope part that eludes me."

"That's faith."

"I'm afraid to hope and have faith. I've been foiled by it before."

"But even though you've suffered, isn't it true you've found reasons to live fully again?"

She shrugged, knowing Kelly couldn't tell. But his words hit closer to home than she wanted him to know. She had found reasons to live fully. Yet--

"But I can't forget the past. I can't forget that while I'm out here trying to live, Bobby is still dead, and so is Kashe. Her little baby doesn't have a ma. Folks have rifts, like me and Katie and Jed. You and Zane lost your parents and you saw so many others die, horribly, I'm sure. It's hard to wade through all that mire to find hope or faith."

"But, Lainey, those are the best reasons to have faith. God promises hope and a future. The future is the mystery, but it's something to look forward to. You don't have to dwell in the past."

Thankfully, a ramp angled off the end of the walkway so store owners could wheel their goods up. She descended it and moved up the next ramp onto the next block, stopping to wait for a lost cow to wander past with its bell clanking.

"I don't want to dwell in the past. Don't think that I want to wallow in self-pity, okay, Kelly? It's not that anymore. But I feel like I don't have any right, in some ways, to try for happiness."

He reached back for her hand and she stopped pushing the chair as he tugged her around in front of him.

"You have every right to be happy." Love poured out of him, and in some way that, too, broke her heart.

Her nose tingled and a tear crept into her eye. She brushed it away but another took its place. "But what if the future hurts too?"

He squeezed her hand. "Truth be told, it probably will. Life will always have its pains. But there's a better future. The one God is preparing for us that we can't see. We have to live with that future in mind above this earthly one."

She wiped vainly at tears tumbling down her cheeks. "You're so strong, Kell."

Kelly reached into his pocket and handed her a hanky. She dabbed at her face and nose. "If every bit of pain I've ever experienced was designed to bring me to this place where I want to do His will and can do it with greater understanding and compassion, then it was worth it."

"Really?"

Kelly nodded. "My suffering and loss will make me a better minister. And besides, without the pain of the past, I'd never have gotten to meet you. Did you ever think of that?"

Lainey nodded, though she considered it for the first time. Without Bobby and Owen and Jed, there'd have been no Kelly and Zane in her life. Without the war and all its sorrows, the three of them would never have met. But what did that mean to her future? Her eyes dried and she tucked Kelly's handkerchief into her sleeve.

"I'll wash this for you."

He grinned. "I'll let you."

Lainey laughed. "You'll be a good preacher, Kelly."

He lifted her hand and gave it a quick kiss before releasing it. "Well, that kind of compliment deserves ice cream."

She pushed him two more blocks and turned the corner to the meat market where they hoped to find ice cream still available so late in the year.

"I want to have faith, Kelly," she said as the store came in view. "I really do."

"Then step into it. That's all. Cast all your cares on Him, Lainey. That's all He asks. Because, you know, He really does care all about you."

Again she nodded, unseen, and Kelly leaned forward to push open the door of the store, a tiny bell jingling above their heads as they went inside.

Chapter Twenty-Two

September was almost over, and still no rain fell. The tenor of Pastor Beach's sermons changed. Like the itinerant preachers popping up everywhere in the Bush, waving their Bibles and warning people of impending judgment, he replaced his gentle words with powerful readings from Scripture about Sodom and Gomorrah, and admonishments to the people of Peshtigo to repent before God rained down fire and heaven upon them. Lainey expected to hear it again this morning.

The preaching scratched at Lainey like nettles. The carousers continued coming into town on Saturday nights, flaunting their debauchery, but conviction for her own behavior, like a rash in her thoughts, stung. *If judgment comes, it will be for the likes of people like me who know God and stop trusting Him.*

Wheeling Kelly's chair toward the church, she used one gloved hand to rub her itching eyes against the smoky, red haze pressing down the air. She recalled a verse Pastor Beach proffered from Isaiah 42. It clung to her mind where other verses had blown away, perhaps because it offered rescue more than judgment... if she chose to heed admonition: *"Fear not, for I have redeemed you; I have called you by name, you are mine. When you pass through the waters, I will be with you; and through the rivers, they shall not overwhelm you; when you walk through fire you shall not be burned, and the flame shall not consume you."*

That verse caught up on a whirlwind in her thoughts after last night, for fire truly had fallen from heaven. Sparks and cinders came down out of the sky from the northeast. They blew across the Peshtigo River and ignited a pile of sawdust and wood slabs next to the woodenware factory. When the warning whistle blew, Lainey ran out Kelly's doorway and stared as every available man ran to the riverbank. She followed at a distance and watched briefly as they formed a chain and passed water hand over hand to douse the flames, praying that the fire wouldn't reach the factory building. Then she hurried back to Kelly's.

He already sensed the strength of the danger. "We need to fill the troughs. Hurry."

She wheeled him out the door to the well, thankful it hadn't dried up though water levels stood low. They raced to pull out silty bucketfuls, one after another, and she rushed to dump them into the troughs so it would be on hand to protect the animals and the stable. When as much mud began coming up as water, she dropped onto her knees beside his wheelchair and clasped his hand.

He squeezed her fingers gently. "All we can do now is pray." Then she remembered the verse.

But fear also leaped like flame in her heart. Father Pernin, the priest, just two days ago escaped a fiery death trap in the Bush when he and one of Jacob Collin's young friends went out to minister to his parishioners. Jacob's friend said that they decided to hunt pheasants on the way back and got lost when they suddenly found themselves ringed by flame, cut off as tongues of fire snaked among the roots and leaves along the ground and erupted in a blazing circle about them. They would not have escaped, except that men who heard their cries for help beat the fire with strewn tree branches which caught like matchsticks, churning the currents of air and diverting the flames in another direction.

The entire country sat on a powder keg. How did Zane manage to stay safe? Mr. Noyes's *Eagle* assured them all that the railroad work was progressing rapidly, though they couldn't quite hear the whistle of the Chicago & Northwestern Railroad's locomotive yet. She hoped it was true. With travelers' stories of fires burning everywhere in the bush camps, and smoke and ash ever present on the wind, how could they be sure?

What if the dire warnings of the preachers' came true?

She and Kelly were supposed to have gone to hear the Italian minstrels serenade Peshtigo's citizens last night. Instead they heard the sharp cry of the whistle, calling them to fight God's judgment.

She shuddered as she walked to church, pushing Kelly's chair. The long night's vigil had wearied him a great deal. It had taken hours for men to douse the pillar of fire at the woodenware factory, but even so, sleep had come uneasily to everyone. Today, she'd no doubt that every pew would be full. The strong call to repent and fear God overcame the weariness they all felt.

As she shouldered toward the building with dozens of others making their way into the crowded church, she heard them talking about the strange occurrence of the birds which the men had witnessed while fighting the fire.

Thousands of birds, they said, flew up out of the trees like ghosts, their bodies shrouded in white ash. They fluttered maddeningly, bumping into one another, screeching, their instincts abandoned. The men watched as, for a few moments, they hovered there over the fire lapping up trees in the dusk. Then, instead of escaping, they suddenly plummeted back into the flames, sucked into the hissing, burning branches as the tall pines were consumed.

The preaching was just what she expected. She hoped she wasn't fidgeting under Pastor Beach's fiery words, but even if she had been, she wouldn't have been alone. Little girls dressed heavily in pantaloons and dresses trimmed in lace and flocking, with pretty ribbons trailing down their long, loose hair, twitched and rocked their legs. Their mothers and fathers frowned and worried their lips between their teeth. Boys craned their heads about looking for escape should the very walls of the church burst into flame at the thunderous preaching. Kelly clasped his hand over hers.

She caught his eyes and he smiled. It sent a wave of calm through her, and for the first time in hours, she captured a deep breath.

And then it happened. As Pastor Beach's voice lifted to a crescendo, the whistle screeched, signaling another fire. The crowd jumped to their feet and pressed to the door. She looked to Kelly who hadn't let go of her hand. He squeezed it.

He seemed to think immediately of the livery. "We should wet blankets, too, to put over the boards of the building."

*****

Zane's throat scalded. He imagined a tall, cold glass of water, but knew he'd be lucky to get a sip or two from the water wagon if and when one arrived. He nearly laughed, but not with any humor, as he considered that it was strange to wish for water when less than a year ago he would have been wishing for something a lot stronger. But the thirst of these past days he couldn't seem to slake.

Any more than he could slake his thirst for news of Lainey and Kelly.

He left the railroad at a standstill to dig trenches, as was the new order of the day. A blaze had erupted south of Marinette along the Peshtigo road, and if they wanted to save the rail line as well as the town of Marinette, the crew needed to step out and help. Usually his mind was filled with orders to the men under him, charting for the next stretch of rail, making drawings and listing supplies, keeping the crews on task. But now, shoveling dirt beside them, he was free to think of other things, and his thoughts went straight to the place his heart rested. If only it didn't rest on her.

Had she begun to love Kelly? He hoped so. It was a strange, sordid hope, because Kelly loved her, and they were good for each other. *Better than I could be for her. Kelly deserves a woman like Lainey.*

He brushed a sweaty arm across his forehead, caking his hair down. He wanted to hear word from Kelly that he'd proposed and a wedding was planned. Only then would it be safe to see Lainey again.

Finally the water wagon pulled up. Not much there. Just a few small gulps for each of them, then they'd be back to digging.

A man standing next to him in line swatted the dust off his hat. "Sure hope it rains pretty soon. Don't know how much more we can bear."

Zane nodded. The men echoed that sentiment often enough. How much more could they bear? How much longer would God hold out on them?

His break barely over, he went back to the shovel, digging with a fury and thinking about the preachers traveling through camp. Just this morning another one of them had barked out that they were all under God's wrath. Zane doubted it. He didn't need a drought or threat of fire to feel God's rod. He felt it every time he looked at Elaina Kade and knew she'd never belong to him.

That night he fell onto his cot exhausted, but sleep fled. For once when he might have fallen into it dreamlessly, he couldn't even shut down. Finally he rose and lit a lantern on his desk. He rapped his knuckles as he tried to decide, then yanked open the desk drawer and pulled out a sheet of paper and a pen. He uncorked the cap of his inkwell and dabbed the pen to his tongue.

Dear Kelly,

I've been working like a dog lately. You'd be proud of me. But don't think I'm complaining. I'm not. Freedom like we had before isn't so great. Commitment has its own rewards, and I think you knew that a long time ago. I'm just writing to say that I finally know it too. What I'm getting at, Kell, is that I want you to marry Lainey. I know you love her. When she's ready, don't you wait. You marry her, and don't wait around for me to show up.

Zane leaned back and stared at the words, then underlined the last part with a heavy stroke of his pen, <u>*don't wait around for me.*</u> He continued, his pen moving slower on the page:

I'll come visit after the honeymoon. Maybe I'll steal a kiss from the bride.

He thought about the kiss he and Lainey shared earlier in the summer. He thought about the shape of her lips and how easily they'd molded to his. Had she wanted that kiss as badly as he did, or was that all part of his meandering dreams? It must have been. He re-read the words he'd written. To say anymore would risk giving his true feelings away. He added only one more line.

Take care of each other.

Zane

*****

Late Sunday afternoon Lainey finally found herself back at the Forest House. She stripped out of her layers of woolens and poured a scant amount of water into a basin to sponge the sweat and dirt off her arms and neck. Slipping a clean shift over her head, she fell onto the bed and closed her eyes. She just started to doze when the blare of the fire whistle ripped her back into the present for the third time in less than twenty-four hours.

*****

Another week passed before Mr. Noyes wrote that the fires had finally abated. The standing timber, black as pikes pointing into the air, offered little in the name of more fuel to burn, so life in Peshtigo proceeded at its regular pace. Fears subsided, and the anxious tenure of the town calmed down. Perhaps they'd finally established an uneasy truce with the Almighty.

Kelly whistled a tune as he curried the horse named Othello. Even Pastor Beach opined with less fire-breathing in his sermon this morning. The atmosphere this Sunday, as compared to that other one, held more of thanksgiving after realizing how close they'd come to feeling God's wrath.

Kelly still wondered if God truly intended to judge them so harshly, or if it was more of an overall result of living in a sin-cursed, fallen world -- a continual reaping and sowing since Adam -- thorns and thistles, as it were.

The stables reeked of an acid odor intensified by the sickly, sweet smell of burned hay and pine needles, and the sharp tang of charred pine surrounding the town. But after a duel with nature, the citizens of Peshtigo seemed to have won.

God had really spared them, after all.

When the whistle sounded on Sunday night, and Kelly joined the ranks of those fighting the blaze, passing water down the line from his chair, they held out small hope of success. But then the wind had shifted almost miraculously toward the south, sweeping the flames with it and sparing Oconto Avenue and the town itself. God be praised.

Now October arrived upon them, bathed in a mottled glow void of autumn colors, but one which the scorched forests stood starkly against. Hope revived the citizens of Peshtigo and for Kelly no less so.

He set out to commence full operation on the livery. He'd arranged to purchase a new horse for leasing out, along with the two he owned, and he could now manage boarding up to a dozen others. He housed seven already. He contracted for hay from a Mr. Henke north of town, and oats would arrive from down south by wagon once the roads were clear of burned and fallen timber. It cost a fair piece. Fires had raked a lot of farm land. Crops and hay fields had been lost. But there, too, God had blessed him.

Which meant he could propose to Lainey soon. He'd be able to provide for her, even crippled as he was.

He thought about it and prayed about it even harder. He'd given both her and Zane time to discover their feelings, but it seemed they refused to acknowledge them. Perhaps it wasn't meant to be. Maybe, Kelly decided, God wanted Lainey for him after all.

He limped forward and continued brushing the horse. He wasn't on his feet often, but tried a few steps each day. As long as he had a means to rest or lean on something, he felt secure. Othello didn't seem to mind bearing his shoulder from time to time.

He tossed the brush into a bucket and lowered himself back into his chair. Pushing himself around the cleaned out stall took strength, but his upper body swelled with muscle since the accident. If his legs couldn't hold him for long, his arms could at least handle most tasks.

He wheeled back to the room he lived in. A blast of wind rattled the window frame above the dry sink. It would be nice when he could build a little house separate from the livery. There was no escaping the smell here. It wouldn't be ideal for a bride, but Lainey never showed any aversion to it.

He pulled Zane's letter out of his pocket and read it again.

It held the answer to his prayer.

Zane may care for Lainey, just as she cared for him. But Zane had as much as given Kelly his blessing to pursue her. So pursue her he would. He took the ring from its hiding place in the little drawer of his bedside table and looked at it again. He held it up, read the inscription, and smiled.

If Zane wanted them to be married before he returned, then he wouldn't keep his brother waiting for long. When Lainey came this evening with their dinner, he wouldn't hesitate. He'd ask her. He'd convince her somehow that they should be together always.

Tucking the ring into his shirt pocket along with Zane's letter, he poured enough water onto a cloth to dampen it then scoured the dirt off his neck and the smell of horse off his hands.

He had just run a comb through his hair when Lainey knocked on the jamb of the door and stepped inside.

Chapter Twenty-Three

Lainey set the dinner basket on the table and pulled plates off the shelf. She loved Sundays as long as they never had another one like that day two weeks ago. On Sundays she could escape the Forest House. It was almost like old times when the day held nothing more than time spent drawing and lounging about with the Beaumonts. Of course, lately it meant she'd go to church with Kelly. She didn't imagine it a year ago. But taking these small steps to renew her faith almost made her feel as though her freedom had grown.

She longed more to escape the Forest House lately. The edges of her nerves sharpened around the people there. John and Clara were worrisome. The guests talked only of fire and wind and the need for rain. Yet they all expected an eventual gale. Why, even today, the temperature had been climbing since morning, and the wind was winding up like a battering ram. She had to hold the cloth cover over the food basket tightly on her way to Kelly's so it wouldn't be ripped off and blown away.

Clara continued stocking food and blankets in the storm shelter. Having grown up through some of Wisconsin's fiercest storms, Lainey understood why. She thought about encouraging Kelly to make precautions. He didn't have a storm shelter, but he should make a plan for his safety in the eventuality of a whirlwind touching down.

She frowned. Even leaving the Forest House for the day didn't quell her nagging thoughts. Today she just wanted to put them all out of mind and spend the hours with Kelly. She smoothed her features and turned from her table preparations to give him a smile.

"It's almost set. I hope you're hungry. I have smoked ham and potato salad. And Clara parted with one of her coveted jars of pickled beets. They're sweet as can be."

"I can't wait. Preacher got my appetite worked up this morning."

"You mean you haven't eaten all day?"

"I had a roll and some cheese, but I wanted to get the horses curried and buttoned down in case we get a storm."

"Well, then let's eat."

She watched as Kelly shifted himself from his wheelchair to a regular seat where he could sit closer to the table.

"You're getting pretty smooth at that."

"I don't plan to live in the wheelchair forever."

"That's good. Sometimes I feared you'd have to."

He gazed at her, his blue eyes smiling and mischievous. "I have to keep up with you, Lainey Kade. Can't do it in that." He flicked his head toward the wheelchair. "Can't expect you to wait on me until my dying day either," he added with a drop in his voice.

She laid a napkin on her lap and held out a bowl of potato salad. "You're easy to wait on."

He caught her eye, and she knew she treaded on dangerous ground, or at least she imagined it so.

She cleared her throat as she forked a beet. "The wind is searing. It just about blew me over on the way here."

"It's picked up. The sky looks strange."

"I heard that's from all the fires in the west. I hope things are all right in the Chippewa and at my folks'. I haven't heard from them in a while, but according to the paper and the talk, it sounds like they've been safe from the Minnesota fires."

Kelly shook his head. "You suppose the whole prairie's burning?"

"It certainly seems like it. I saw Father Pernin digging a trench outside his church. It seemed so strange, the conflict between his present concern and the feelings of others that fear is in the past and that life can carry on. Why, right next door to where he was digging I heard the neighbors laughing through the window and carrying on over tea."

"Should we be following the priest's example, do you think?"

Lainey shrugged.

A sudden gust of hot wind slammed the door open and a swirl of dust and ash flew into the room, coating the cupboards, the floor, and even settling on their plates. Lainey jumped to close the door. Her gaze flicked out into the street where sawdust, dirt, and ash pelted down the street. The few autumn leaves remaining rustled and gave way. She was about to latch the door but stopped at the sound of a low moaning far in the distance.

"Kelly," she opened the door wider, letting the wind and dust pull at her hem; "do you hear that? I heard it on the way here, but it's getting louder."

He bent his head to listen, then pushed himself up from the table and limped closer. "It must be the wind."

"It could be trees."

"I suppose it is."

Both their gazes pulled upward at the sky, at the strange red glow in the west rising out of the twilight.

"Come inside," said Kelly.

She closed the door and followed him, but this time he sat in his wheelchair. His face was taut, and his eyes seemed to deepen in their color.

"Maybe the priest has the right idea. I think I should take all the new harnesses and hang them in the well. They might be safer there."

Alarm bells rang in her head. "You don't expect another fire, do you, after practically everything's already scorched and burned?"

"It's best we prepare, just in case. Could be we'll get a twister. I don't want to risk losing any equipment if I can help it."

She gathered up their dishes and food remnants while he wheeled away to the stable. He took first one trip to the well, and then another. She met him there and helped him hang the harnesses deep inside while the wind whipped at her skirts and blew her hair loose. A long rope hung over the side of the well.

She spoke loudly into the wind and smirked a little. "It'll burn if we do catch fire."

"But the harnesses will fall in and be all right."

"And who did you have in mind to fish them out later?" she asked, grinning.

"Why, you of course. Zane if you're not up to the challenge."

Her smile vanished. She looked up at the darkening sky again. *Lord, keep him safe*!

She frowned. "Kelly, the wind." The wind had died suddenly and almost completely, but the moan which had sounded so soft and deep and far away began growing to a subtle roar. Her voice fell to a whisper "What is that?"

"It sounds like... a train. Or ten trains."

A giant flake, like snow, settled down at her foot. Then the sky thickened with it. *Ash*.

A flagrant breeze began again, hot, scorching even. Then... silence.

Kelly looked up at her. Their gazes caught, and panic bolted like lightning between them. "The horses."

Kelly wheeled himself forward and she ran ahead to fling open the stable door just as a whirling slab of fire shot down out of the soot-darkened sky and caught in the sawdust on the street. The rumbling grew.

Kelly's arm muscles bulged and his shoulders heaved as he charged forward with his chair. "Hurry!"

She did. She flung open stall doors along one side while he did the same on the other. She slapped the rears of the lurching animals, urging them loose. Once, she turned toward the door and saw fire raining down from heaven.

"What do we do?"

"Get blankets."

She ran into his room, her heart pounding as she scooped the blankets off Kelly's bed. Sparks jumped with a sharp crackle and shot across the room in tiny darts of flame. Lainey screamed. Thoughts of gas emanating from the stables pushed at her fear, thinking the entire building might burst into a blaze at any moment. She ran outside where Kelly waited by the water trough, arms outstretched. Together they plunged the blankets under water as fire pelted at them like streaking birdshot. Lainey screamed again when a cinder caught her sleeve.

Kelly slapped it away and pushed a sopping blanket into her arms. "Wrap yourself!" he yelled above the growing roar. His own wet blanket lay across the rim of the well, steaming. He gripped her arm, yanking her face toward him. "Run to the river, Lainey. Run there as fast as you can."

On the street, people hurried by as if the very devil himself raked their backs with claws. Some scrambled on foot, some in wagons. Some led children by the hand, others tugged at the reins of frightened horses. Screaming and panic ensued, carelessness too. Lainey ducked as more cinders whirled and whipped all around her and a sudden sheet of flame leapt across the sky.

A fireball flung into a nearby roof top and sent a flurry of fire racing across then wrapping over it. It jumped and leapt and sprinted over the crown of the trees to the next roof.

"Lainey! Listen to me! You have to run. Don't stop for any reason until you reach the river."

"Kelly!" A sob of horror wrenched out of her and their arms clasped. He held onto her and she tried to pull him with her. "I'll push you."

"No!" He shook her. His fingers pinched into her arms, forcing her to pay attention. "You have to run. We've waited too long." His voice nearly disappeared against the growing rumble. It was as if they stood inside a waterfall beneath the tracks of a train trestle while a train rushed overhead.

"But--"

"It's your own best chance." His eyes glistened as dark and gray as Zane's in the furious red darkness. They compelled her to look at him. "The well is mine." He looked to the side of the well and her eyes drew to the rope.

Smoke, thick and black as snakes, coiled over them and filled their lungs. A deer, bounding in from the forest, stood on the street. Dogs ran past, ignoring it. The church bells pealed in a mad cacophony.

Heat seared her throat and she began to cough, her eyes stinging, closing against her will. She wanted to look at him, to see him safely in the dark, deep well, but she couldn't. She fell against him and he held her for a moment.

"Look."

She turned and pried her eyes open against the smoke. More great tongues of flame headed toward them above the treetops.

"You have to go."

A ball of fire, like cannon shot, crashed into the livery. Other rooftops ignited as the fire, like a running, twisting sheet, rolled overhead, reaching down to eat everything it touched.

He pulled her close for only a second more, and she felt the roughness of his kiss before he pushed her away. She stumbled back and watched, dumbfounded, as Kelly clawed at the rope and pulled himself over the side of the well.

"Go!" he roared above the tumult, and she turned around and ran.

Fear choked her as badly as the smoke, and all around her people plunged terror-stricken toward the river. They jostled and crashed into one another without exchanging a word or a look. A pack of housecats ran down the street between their legs.

As most people hurried toward the river, others ran from it. Vehicles crashed into each other. They tangled. Some tipped. Horses threw their riders and ran off. Trees crashed and houses crackled, blazed, and fell. Chimneys tumbled into the tumult of screeching flame and whirling wind. The wind pushed her. It felt as though she might be picked up and carried into the fire.

She beat frantically at the cinders alighting on her clothes, barely able to peer through her eyelids as the wind howled along with the shriek and crackle of the fire. A thousand noises bawled together, dissonant, deafening, adding chaos and confusion to the stampede.

She stumbled and fell. As she pushed herself up against the mob, she saw the priest, Father Pernin, pulling a cart like a horse. She forced herself against the current of burning wind, struggling to remain on her feet. The current had become a flaming cyclone, a fiery, burning twisting devil. Black soot, ash and smoke clogged her throat and eyes, and she turned in a circle, unable to tell where she was. A few feet away a woman suddenly burst into flame, her layers of woolens torching like the dry wick of a lamp in the eerie light.

Lainey saw the priest again and headed in the direction he was going. Screams rent the air. Wails and shrieks and panic caught tide as people fled, their clothing and hair catching fire. Some sank to the ground as though praying before suddenly being overcome by flames.

Lainey pulled the blanket close. It was dry. She held the edge over her face and tried to find a breath, but she could only suck in tiny dribbles of air without choking.

Balls of fire burst around her. The boardwalks ignited. People screamed for help. Figures, lit like candles, staggered forward, collapsed.

Flames from the woodenware factory soared high into the air. A terrible screeching rent the roaring air as the roof lifted. Moments later, burning tubs and wooden buckets exploded through the top. Lainey looked up. Fiery coals beat down around her, catching at her blackened blanket and clothes, sending shards of pain through her body as they caught her clothing and melded to her skin.

"God!" she cried as she stumbled again. And then she fell.

*****

Kelly tucked his head down, curling forward as best he could in the mere inches of water at the bottom of the cramped well. He'd had no trouble lowering himself, and now he buried his head in his arms, sucking for wisps of air as the inferno roared above him. He looked up only to see flashing sheets of flame. Smoke, thick and black as tar, sucked downward to fill his tiny space like an inverted chimney. He drenched the blanket in water and mud and pulled it over his head.

"Get her to the river, Father," he begged, his voice a hoarse rasp against the rage and roar of the beast. "I don't care what else you do. Take me if you must. I'm yours. But get her to the river." He gagged. Heat burned deep into his lungs squeezing his chest. Dizziness and nausea swept over him. He coughed and wretched but couldn't get a breath.

He panted, pinching his eyelids shut, his prayers a jumbled mix including everything and everyone at once. He prayed for air, for rain, for deliverance, for Zane, for Lainey... for Lainey... for Lainey.

He clawed inside his pocket, his thoughts swirling like hot mist, until he found the ring -- Lainey's wedding ring. He clasped it in his fist, searing her face in his mind. Ignoring the hiss and sizzle of embers landing on his blanket and burning tiny holes into the flesh on his back, he held her in his thoughts and heart and prayed again, until his eyelids felt pasted shut, and his thoughts could no longer hold themselves together. They disintegrated into bits of memory and longing as he gasped and choked, his body craving air, his chest heaving for it.

*****

Fireballs sailed through the air. Explosions fed the whirlwinds of flame with debris then spat it out again, raking the throng of Peshtigo's fleeing citizens.

Lainey lay for a moment unconscious despite the burns until someone fell against her. An arm grasped about her waist and pulled her painfully upward. She made out the sound of someone, a man, calling to her and urging her along. She allowed him to pull her, her mind a maze of confusion as he rushed them toward the river.

Sheets of fire curled like waves. They rolled over the ground like breakers on Lake Michigan. Anyone they touched burst into flame. Fire pelted down from above. The clothing it bit combusted in the instant. Yet, below it all, the darkness smothered like molasses, thick and breathless.

Suddenly she stumbled at the river's edge. Icy cold water shocked her body even more as the man wrapped his arms around her and pulled her in. She fell back. Water closed over her head and sucked what little air remained out of her lungs. The remnants of her dress wound like cloying rags around her legs and she couldn't gain her feet. Then strong arms pulled her up at the waist and clutched her.

"My God." The man gaped at her with wide, horrified eyes. "You're not my wife. I've saved the wrong woman." He dropped his arms and floundered to the bank leaving Lainey alone in the river. She blinked.

Silhouettes of people covered the banks as far as the eye could see. Some plunged into the river. Others dropped there on the edges and lay still, as though having come so far they could not take another step and waited to be swallowed by the red monster. Many others stood motionless as though petrified, with tongues protruding and eyes staring heavenward.

For a moment the wind lifted the smoke. She blinked again.

She saw the bridge catch. Men and women, children, wagons, horses, cattle all crammed the span, crushing together in panic. People jumped. Skeletons of the Peshtigo Company sawmill and the large company store glowed in ravaging orange plumes. Flames blew across the water and she had to drop beneath again to drift with the current. It was safer than standing there where blazing timbers from the burning bridge could crash into her, where she might be swept off her feet by cattle or beat against the wooden damn which also caught fire. Burning logs floated by from the supply kept at the woodenware factory.

She recognized Father Pernin on the bank, pushing people into the river. She could still hear their screams, some crying out that they could not swim.

She closed her eyes and ducked again, thankful for her ability, her mind swimming back to Kelly and wishing he were here in the river with her.

Chapter Twenty-Four

Gusts of hot air and sparks periodically sucked her breath away and forced her beneath the river's surface, but they eventually lessened as the hours passed. For a long while everything was aflame. The trees, the houses and buildings, the very air itself bellowed and rolled with fire. Then, sometime in the middle of the night the blaze began to smolder, and sulfuric darkness swallowed those in the river. Perhaps she was in hell, just as Reverend Beach warned.

She recognized no one. Occasional, fitful flames leapt to cast a glow on the shore, but nothing existed in the gaping darkness and no soul moved beyond the water's edge.

The water was very cold. Her body trembled and her teeth chattered. As she clung to the mud in the shallow water on her hands and knees, her bones and joints ached.

Then she saw someone rise up and move toward shore, collapsing on the embankment. Lainey tried to stand, but tripped and fell. She pushed herself out of the water again, and stumbled against the slow current toward the bank. A convulsive chill shook her. There was no controlling her limbs as she stumbled again and again, hardly aware of crying or the deep fear still shocking her body along with the cold.

She fell onto the bank, her face and body caking with dirt and ash as her hands clawed into the warm sand still spread with beds of burning embers. She curled into the dirt, her mind as numb as her fingers and toes. Burns along her arms, neck, and back, taken during her flight to the river, began to sting again. But despite the throes of conflicting kinds of pain, exhaustion won the battle, and Lainey fell in and out of sleep. She drifted somewhere between the nightmares of unconsciousness and the hellish realm of reality.

*****

Zane hadn't slept. As dawn broke six miles north over the town of Marinette, he strode into the dusty street and looked around at the damage. A dozen or so buildings had burned as the residents fought a tide of fire beating the town. By some miracle -- one Kelly would claim to be a real, God miracle -- most of Marinette stood unharmed. Now Zane wandered about restively surveying the scene and wondering what they'd do next. Likely the rail lines they'd laid were burned up, unless the fire had danced around them.

But he doubted it. The fire was like nothing he'd ever seen -- a tornado of fire, twisting over the countryside, digesting everything it touched.

God, what was he doing here? Somewhere in the cold places of his heart, he meant it. Why did he drift so aimlessly when God claimed to have a plan for him? Why wasn't he with Kelly?

Why aren't I with Lainey?

Life was short and hellish. Had he made the biggest mistake of his life by letting her go?

Up ahead on the street he saw a man everyone around knew to be Ike Stephenson, one of the biggest lumber mill operators in the country. He stood talking to a man who, from the looks of things, must've just ridden in. He wore only a shirt and pants, holding a rope for a halter as he stood next to a horse that had no blanket or saddle. He looked weary and distressed, as though he might fall down right there at Stephenson's feet.

Stephenson frowned, his hands hanging limply at his side as the man spoke and made weak gesticulations. He pointed behind him, south toward Peshtigo, and shook his head.

Zane's chest tightened, and for the first time that morning his thoughts traveled beyond the inferno that threatened Marinette to what might have happened further south. Kelly and Lainey were safe, surely. He dare not let unfounded fears creep in.

But Stephenson nodded and grew more animated. His expression held questions. The man looked like he might break down. Maybe he was a farmer whose home had caught fire outside of town. No -- not a farmer. Just big and strong like a farmer... Zane suddenly remembered. He'd seen him in Peshtigo last winter. Claimed to be a boxer. Worked in one of the camps.

He strode forward as the man pulled himself up on his horse and Stephenson headed off in a hurry up the street. The man's face was blackened by smoke.

"Hey, Mister!" Zane called.

The man lifted a vacant gaze.

"You been to Peshtigo?"

"You got folks there?"

Zane nodded. The white's of the boxer's eyes, rimmed in red, sent a licking of terror through him.

"Peshtigo's burned up. Folks are lying dead in the streets. The ones that aren't need help." He glanced down at the rope in his hands then looked back at Zane. "I hope yours are all right." He tugged at the makeshift rein and walked the horse past Zane up the street.

Zane stared at the ground for a moment, his thoughts twisted like a rail line caught in a dynamite blast. They screeched and clamored, and Zane squeezed his eyes shut to get hold of them.

He had to go to Peshtigo and he had to do it now.

*****

Lainey's shoes had burned off during her flight to the river. She awoke at dawn on the bank of the Peshtigo feeling the deep sting of burns blistering her bare soles. The tiers and ruffles on the lower portion of her dress and petticoat had burned away too, and her sleeves hung off her arms in singed, ragged tatters. But she fared better than some who wore practically nothing at all. They wandered about too numbed by loss to be ashamed of their nakedness.

The world was gray. The sky and earth spread before her like a charcoal drawing. Stark shapes in black outline marked the rigid forms of twisted metal protruding from the ash and people moving about in slow motion. Bodies lay prostrate upon or bent over some of the blackened objects. Lainey found it impossible to tell if they were dead or only warming themselves there on the heated metal. Actual corpses lay everywhere, some nearly whole but burned to a crisp, others reduced to small indistinguishable clumps of ash. The tornado of fire hadn't discerned between elderly or infant, man or woman.

Lainey saw the carnage and faced the horror without sensation. She only responded to her body's demands. Slowly she made her way through the ruins to a heap of coal still burning outside the smoldering ruins of the woodenware factory. Her gaze swung slowly to the left and the right. Nothing else about gave her a bearing as to where, exactly, she was. The whole town was gone. Yet it would be only a few hundred yards to walk straight back to Kelly's livery or at least to the plot where it once stood.

Her eyes shifted to those around her. Methodically some began to remove their wet clothing and spread it out on the ground or over the hot metal to dry. Lainey unbuttoned the waistband of her skirt and removed it, followed by her blouse. Her teeth still chattered as she stood in the cool air in her chemise, drawers, and one torn petticoat.

"Have you seen my wife? Her name is Dorcas." A red-faced man beseeched her, the edges of his mustache, eyebrows and lashes clearly singed off. His eyes stood out like half-ripe cherries, and bags hung beneath them.

The group gathered around the coals shook their heads.

A young man, blackened with soot from head to toe spoke softly. "I can't find my mother. She was next to me, and then she wasn't. I said, 'hold my hand, Mother,' but suddenly she wasn't there."

Murmurs rose around the fire, this one and that asking the same question. *Have you seen the one I love?*

Lainey craved the heat. Slowly it soaked into her skin and dried the front side of her body. Slowly her awareness returned.

Her voice cracked, sounding foreign and far away to her ears. "Have you seen a man..." She thought of the wheelchair, and looking out again at the flat, gray landscape, knew it no longer existed. "Have you seen a man who is crippled in his legs? His name is Kelly Beaumont. He's a stable keeper." She glanced in the direction she thought was Kelly's residence.

Hope leapt up in her throat when she said his name, and just as quickly vanished at the mute silence and blank gazes of the group.

She turned her head and looked back at the river. What was that? Someone knelt down, fishing things out of the water. She watched for a moment as he pulled a blanket out of the water and added it to a pile of odd objects on the bank. She stumbled toward him.

He looked at her suddenly. "Yes?"

"Would you like me to dry that by the fire?"

She was startled by his sudden sob as he nodded his head. "Someone may be able to use it. Take the clothes too, if you can."

She nodded and picked up the wet, cold things, soaking her front again. She spread them by the fire and hung them over black stumps. Then she huddled back by the others again, hoping for heat. Could it really have been over eighty degrees just two days ago? Now, suddenly, October had arrived with the cold promise of a winter no one would ever be prepared for.

An hour later she'd dried completely. Her stomach growled. Some men set off to look for something they might eat. Lainey watched them walk away, a new fear tightening along with the hunger in her stomach. She realized as her thoughts cleared that the rope over the well would be burned and that Kelly would still be inside unless someone had found him to help him out. How cold would he be, there in the water below? Shame filled her for her selfishness and mindlessness. She donned what remained of her dress and wrapped her blanket, riddled with holes, over her shoulders. Slowly, she picked her way across the landscape toward Kelly's, and with each step her trepidation grew. She gazed about at the others she saw, like living dead searching for signs of life, for family, for food and shelter and hope. There remained little of any of those things.

She saw no one she recognized. Not Clara or John, not young Jacob or Pastor Beach or even Mrs. Anderson. There was no sign of the busy priest or his wagon. Faces smudged with ash, some of them hairless, made them unrecognizable. She tried to hurry faster on her blistered feet, anxious for one face alone.

She stood on the corner she supposed to be where Kelly's livery stood. With everything so bleak and strange, she felt like she was no longer in Peshtigo, but someplace short of hell. Not in Wisconsin -- not in the world -- at all. She looked down when her foot touched something hard. A horseshoe protruded from the ashes. She looked closer and found the wire handle of a bucket, more melted lumps, the smoldering beam of what she thought might be the center post inside Kelly's room where he hung an iron skillet. She saw a straight object poking out of the ash and brushed it clean to reveal a handle. She gripped the skillet, black but whole. She picked it up and held it like a treasure.

She turned and looked beyond the place where the stable used to stand, into the gray nothingness of debris and blackened cinders, and she knew where the well was. She walked toward it, careful not to burn her feet on live coals, steadily so as not to trip. Rocks that formed the wells circumference had tumbled to the ground. Many had split, burst in two by the heat. They formed a ringed heap, covered in ash. The hole gaped in the center.

Lainey choked back a sob. It caught her throat in a grip, and then spilled out. "Kelly!" She flung the pan aside and fell to the ground on the still-warm rock pile. She bawled out his name. She pulled her face to the edge. Tears fell over her cheeks into the ashes. "Kelly!"

She stared, her eyes burning, weeping into the blackness below her as she tried to make out a sound, a face peering back, his hair blonde and long. "Kelly!" she screamed, weeping.

Light filtered down and ash floated over the hole like dust motes. Her eyes focused until the image could clear.

She saw him.

A howl rose out of her throat and then clamped off as she reeled over onto her back and gagged, sobbing. She pulled at her blanket and clothing as if by tearing it free she could get at her heart and jerk it out of her chest. Wails followed, then tears, upon tears, upon tears.

*****

The sun stood high in the sky, its eerie light filtered by layers of smoke. Lainey prevailed upon a stranger to help her bring Kelly's body up from the well. She laid him on her blanket and folded it over him gently. She refused to let the cold have him, even in death. She didn't cover his face. Not yet. She cleaned it and found strange comfort in touching his unscathed skin. Except for a few small burns on his back no larger than any of her own, he was untouched. He'd smothered in the well.

She pushed his hair back and let it fall like silk through her dirty fingers. She ran her hands over his arms and chest, feeling like somehow she must, to be able to hold him forever in her heart.

Oh, it was there all right, her heart. It was there and whole. If it hadn't been, it could never hurt so much now. She'd let Kelly in, just as she'd let Zane in, though differently. She wouldn't let him out, anymore than she had let Bobby out so long ago. They were all going to stay there where they belonged.

She touched his shirt pocket and felt something inside, a piece of paper. She unfolded it, and her heart lurched as she read Zane's letter. Fresh wounds struck her, and yet without surprise. Zane never implied that he might be in love with her, and here he confirmed it quite clearly by saying Kelly should make her his.

What would she tell Zane? How could she tell him about his brother? He'd break in two. A quiet tear rimmed her eye and fell on Kelly's shirt.

She looked at the ring on her finger, shining with unexpected brightness against the black smudges on her skin. She'd found it in his hand, or the stranger had. When the man hoisted Kelly up and laid him on the ground he said, "Look. He's holding something," and she found the ring clenched in Kelly's palm.

She turned it around on her finger as she gazed at his peaceful countenance, thinking again of its inscription. It was a Scripture verse. *"Perfect love casts out fear."* It was Kelly's hope for her, his promise and God's. He never wanted her to be afraid of risking her heart again. She understood that.

Would she have said *yes* to Kelly? No. She was in love with Zane, even though Zane made it clear from the letter that he didn't feel the same. So she wore the ring. She could at least give Kelly that. And she could always remember what he said. Somehow she would learn to trust and not be afraid.

*****

Zane headed out ahead of the supply wagon that was supposed to bring aid to Peshtigo. It wouldn't be much. Marinette's citizens endured enough of their own damage but committed to send what they could spare. Surely Peshtigo's damage couldn't be so much worse than their own. The man who talked to him on the road certainly exaggerated. If only the telegraph lines weren't down, they could send for help from Green Bay.

He clucked at his horse, moving her forward into a cantor. Hopefully Kelly and Lainey were all right. Zane comforted himself. Kelly had survived the worst during the war. He'd know how to take care of her.

But as he got closer to Peshtigo thoughts of comfort fled. He met a man leading a horse with a woman and a small boy hunched on it. The boy coughed in his mother's arms, and the look of death hung on him. Zane recognized it. He'd seen it often enough. The woman shushed the boy, soothing him with her burned and badly blistered hands.

The man lifted his eyes Zane's way with a hounded look. "You come from Marinette?"

"Yes."

"It's still there?"

"Most of it."

The man nodded and looked at his feet. He only wore one shoe. Then he lifted his head and moved on, toting his little family with him.

A fist grabbed Zane's gut. He picked up his pace. Still about two miles from town he passed a field, or what used to be a field. There used to be a house there, but it was gone along with the barn and the fences and everything else. Burned carcasses lay strewn about, but Zane could not tell if they were animal or human. He covered his face with his hand when the smell of roasted flesh struck.

Everything he saw had burned flat. More stone foundations began to dot the barrenness where houses had disappeared. Foul-smelling columns of smoke crept upward into the gray sky. The road blended in with the surrounding area. Only the iron wheel rims and axels sitting amid clumps of ash remained to mark the way. As he drew nearer, he was forced to skirt smoldering debris.

He made the mistake once, of finding a wagon only partially burned and glancing into the bed as he passed. Four bodies lay curled together in a calcined lump, black, shapeless, and almost indistinguishable from one another.

A sudden burst of emotion climbed into Zane's throat. He pushed his hand through his hair and sucked in breath that reeked and made his shoulders heave. He pulled his horse away and flung himself off, burying his face into the horse's shoulder, striking his saddle with a fist. Repulsion and fear burned hot and disgusting in his chest. Vomit filled his throat and he turned aside to spew it out.

He closed his eyes, trying to breathe, but images of the war came back, hitting him like the repeat of a rifle cracking off in his brain. Blood. Smoke. Men crying out. The acrid pall clung inside his nostrils -- the very real smell. A vision of the bodies in the wagon came again, assaulting him with a new horror.

He flung himself back up into the saddle. "God... let them be alive." He broke into a gallop, spurring the horse on for another mile, past more destruction, refusing to gaze down at more cremated remains along the road.

He came over the final rise in the road and saw it was true. Peshtigo was gone. Every building was leveled, including the huge boarding house. The mills and factories. He passed what should have been a rail line only to see the wheels of the railcars melted into misshapen globs of metal. Train cars lay hurled onto their sides a distance from the tracks. Blackened stumps and trunks of trees were twisted and torn from the ground before they'd been reduced to beams of charcoal. The company store, the churches, the houses spread out as mere piles of smoking powder. Even the bridge and the dam had burned to wreckage.

How could anyone have survived?

But somehow, some had. Once he got past the initial shock, Zane noticed the people milling about like ghosts, silently wandering the rubble. Here and there a child's or infant's voice whimpered, the only sounds he heard.

He slid down off the horse and led it gingerly across the ground. Some patches were still hot. He guided the animal down to the riverbank and into the water, half walking, half swimming him to the other side. In the river he dodged flotsam and jetsam threatening to sweep into him, but he came out safely on the other side where he came across more survivors searching through the ashes.

A man squatting by the water kept rinsing his eyes and murmuring, "I'm blind, I'm blind, I'm blind."

Zane offered him his hanky. "Your face is swollen. You've been burned. It's just your eyelids that are closed."

The man dipped the cloth in the water and continued washing. "I'm blind... I can't see... I'm blind."

Zane looked on for a moment. He wasn't sure if the man even realized he was there, or that he'd been spoken to. He continued along the bank.

A dead woman lay halfway in the water, her upper body charred. Had she been more afraid of the water than the fire? Why wasn't she saved?

Zane reached for his hanky to cover his nose then realized he'd just given it away. His heart fell still when he looked ahead and saw a flash of blue dress. Lainey? He hastened forward as he watched her sifting through the ashes where a trade goods store used to stand. She found something, brushed it off, and dropped it into a kettle slung over her arm. No. It wasn't her.

His heart rising and plummeting down again, Zane turned away. He looked across the ruins toward the place he now had to go. Dead or alive, he had to find them.

Chapter Twenty-Five

Lainey wrapped her arms around her shoulders. The man who helped her get Kelly out of the well returned with another fellow, and they carried him to a spot with some other bodies awaiting burial. She refused to keep the blanket. It was all she had to give him. Then she saw a woman wandering around the dead with a small child curled in her arms. They appeared unharmed but clearly suffered from shock and despair. She told the men to give the blanket to the woman. She watched as he carefully removed it from around her beloved friend. She took it from him, caressed the dirty folds, and tucked it close. Approaching the woman, Lainey held it out, saying nothing. The woman stared at her for a moment then nodded her thanks and wrapped the blanket around the shaking child.

Lainey cried again. Kelly's body lay neatly alongside a dozen or so others, and more were being brought. She'd said her goodbye, but the pain still felt like a fresh knifing every time she gazed in the direction of the dead. Still, it ached too greatly to walk away.

And where could she go? What should she do now?

Nothing remained. The livery would never come back. The Forest House was gone and she could find no trace of any of the people she'd come to know there. She'd not seen the bodies of Clara or John, but neither had she found them alive.

The churches were gone, and about the only one she met still alive was the priest. She saw no sign of Reverend Beach or any of the folk she'd come to know from his congregation. Surely some of them lived.

She thought of young Jacob and a prayer nearly formed in her mind, but it rustled in her heart as more of a hope that she couldn't find words for. *Not Jacob.*

She couldn't remain here by the communal grave site. She had to move, to find heat, to search for shelter.

Her body felt old, heavy and aching. The blisters on her feet had swollen and burst, and now felt raw. Each step pained her more than the last, and she limped a few yards away, going nowhere. She should walk north toward Marinette, if it hadn't burned up, to look for Zane. But she didn't know if she could even make it as far back as the river a few hundred yards away. She clenched her eyelids and hardened her jaw against the smarting and the rush of weakness flooding her. Would she faint?

Her stomach cramped, reminding her she hadn't eaten since the day before. She wondered if they'd all starve. Perhaps she would just lie down -- somewhere -- and sleep. Maybe she could sleep it all away and wake tomorrow to find she was in one of Zane's dreams and that the fire and Kelly dying never really happened.

She swooned and stumbled. Nausea crept up the inside of her ribs. She shuddered and stumbled again. Blackness closed in, shutting off the daylight, and she fell forward just as someone's arms wrapped around her.

*****

Zane quietly wept as he held her. *Thank you, God.* Her beautiful black hair was singed several inches shorter, and the smell of scorching clung to her body and her ravaged clothes. Still, he buried his face against her neck and breathed deep of the wonder of her. She lay in his arms asleep, but trouble clouded her face. He picked up her hand and saw the burns on their backs. Glancing at her bare feet, blackened with soot, he saw the edges of redness and deeper wounds.

Scooping her up, he glanced around, wondering where he could shelter her and tend to her. She began to groan and then whimper. He stroked the hair from her forehead and whispered her name.

"It's okay, Lainey. I'm right here. I've got you."

Her arm curled around his neck as she struggled to open her eyes, but clearly exhaustion held her in its grip. She blinked hard. He could see she was trying to make sense of him.

"It's Zane. I'm here now. You're all right."

As she came back to the present, he hoisted her onto the horse and climbed up behind her. He didn't need to tell her to lean against him. She melted back into his embrace, allowing him to be her strength.

He took the reins in one hand and glanced around while he kept his other arm wrapped firmly around her. "Do you know where Kelly is?"

The sudden shudder of her shoulders jarred against him. Sobs came gurgling up from her throat and words spilled out, but he couldn't put them together. She turned into him and clutched his shirt, sobbing harder, the words a babble, yet their meaning clear.

Dread, fresh and new, crushed down on him, and suddenly he was aware of people passing by, some transporting the dead. He hugged her close and clucked at her until she quieted, her tears still wetting his shirt and shudders still running through her body. Up ahead he saw the bodies lined up along the ground, just like after a battle. Sights and smells were nearly the same, only this time women and children were added to the numbers. He moved the horse past slowly, looking at each scarred and dirty face. And then he saw him.

He reined back and stared. There on the ground lay his little brother. Kelly -- his mama's preacher boy. The one who'd seen him through a hundred battles and close calls and never left his side. The brother who deserved to live.

He could only stare as the wound twisted deep inside him.

"I'm so sorry, Zane," Lainey whispered.

He ran his hand over his face. "Me too."

She seemed to find some of her strength. "He was so brave. Brave enough for both of us."

He flicked his gaze back to her and then got off the horse. He walked over and stepped between the dead, kneeling at Kelly's side. He could see no burns to speak of, no real harm done. And yet his brother lay dead. He pressed a hand to Kelly's chest and squeezed the stiff fingers.

Zane shed his emotion a long time ago, but it came back now, like shards of metal biting into ragged wounds.

"I'm sorry, Kell. I'm so sorry I wasn't here to save you. You were always the one doing the saving. Who'll do it now? I'm so, so sorry."

Lainey appeared, dropping to her knees at his side, her hand reaching into his.

"What happened?"

She shook her head. At first Zane didn't think she'd be able to say, or even that she knew, but pretty soon her voice found breath. "He sought for safety in the well, but there wasn't any air." Zane cried, sniffling, but he listened as she explained. "He made me run. He said, 'run to the river, Lainey. Run as fast as you can. The well is my best chance.'

"I didn't want to leave him there, but there wasn't any other choice. He flung himself into the well, and just kept yelling at me to run. So I ran."

Zane put his arm around her shoulders and pulled her beside him. Kelly had saved her, just as Zane knew he would. Even crippled, he'd found a way to protect her.

"I wanted to push him in his chair to the river, but he knew we wouldn't make it," she continued.

"He wanted you to make it." He looked down at her and saw her blue eyes riveted on him. "He couldn't have stood it if you stayed behind and got trapped too. It was a kindness you did, just letting him know you'd do your best to live."

She nodded, and he was thankful she understood. He might never understand why God took his brother. But even in the core of him, where grief and questions burrowed the deepest, he thanked God for giving Kelly the strength and frame of mind to make Lainey run. She would never have gone to the river if Kelly hadn't convinced her to leave him at the well. Kelly had died for her, just as surely as anything. All because of his strength and faith and spirit Lainey was alive and next to Zane now. He would keep her safe until they decided what to do next. How could he be angry at God for that?

Take care of my brother, God. Tell him that Lainey's all right, and that I love him.

He held her close again as words to God spilled out his heart. A cool breeze stirred around them, and rain began to fall.

*****

Refugees flooded into Marinette filling the hospital. Victims also flooded the Dunlop House where Zane had stayed on more than one occasion. He heard about man named Eleazer Ingalls taking refugees into his home, and he finally found a place for Lainey there. She rested on a pallet in the corner of the parlor, her feet and other burns healing slowly, her heart slower still. Zane stayed as close to her as he dared, comforting her when she cried out at night. He slipped away during the daylight to help gather food and find ways to bring relief to the suffering community.

He forced himself to stay busy in order to quiet his grief, and to honor Kelly. While tempted to succumb to yet another new layer of pain, to seek escape, Lainey laid hold of his mind and his heart, and he wouldn't leave her. She was his sister now.

He thought about the ring she wore as he hurried back with some bandages donated by the women at one of the churches. Kelly's ring. Kelly married her, just as Zane had encouraged him to do. He ached for the devastating reality that Lainey lost Kelly just when her heart opened itself to love again.

She hadn't talked about it, or mentioned when the marriage took place. She must be too lost in grief to open up her heart about something so intimate.

He stepped into the Ingalls' house and found some of the residents sipping on a thin soup. They went through the repetitive motions of eating, sleeping, and waking with the blank expressions of those whose daily expectations had collapsed. Lost in a muddled space between hopelessness and not knowing, a spark only lit their eyes when they saw a loved one, someone who hadn't perished in Peshtigo's inferno.

His pulse quickened when she turned her head, and he saw that spark now. Her dark blue eyes sought his like a hunger, and she held out her unbandaged left hand. The other was still wrapped, as were her feet.

Zane knelt down beside her pallet. "I wondered if you'd be awake."

"I was waiting for you."

"Sorry I took so long. I got more bandages and I found a fellow with some vegetables. I bought them and gave them to Eleazer. Thought they'd help."

She nodded and offered a weak smile. "They will." She didn't let go of his hand.

"I have some news."

Her eyes held expectancy, or as close to expectancy as he'd come to see since the fire.

"Town leaders sent out a call for help all through Wisconsin. Turns out, though, we weren't the only ones to have a fire. Chicago burned the same night as Peshtigo."

Her eyes widened. "Chicago? All of it?"

He wondered if she pictured it just like he did, or if she thought of the little café where they first met and she'd pretended to be a married woman. Now here she was -- a real one -- or at least a widow.

He shook his head. "No, but it was a big one, 300 dead or more."

Lainey sniffed. The number paled in comparison to the losses suffered in the north. In the ten days since the fire, the numbers of dead continued to climb, and many more remained unaccounted for. Already more than a thousand, it seemed, had been lost in the destruction.

"The governor didn't know about us. He'd gone to help in Chicago. It was his wife Frances who took charge. They say she's just a young thing, but she commandeered blankets and supplies headed for Chicago." He paused and offered her a smile. "She must be a lot like you."

He hoped for a smile from her, something to help him know she would be all right, but her gaze drifted to someplace far away.

"Kelly gave me a blanket," she whispered, still looking off somewhere. "I wrapped him in it when I found him. His must've been left in the well. I'm not sure..."

Zane stroked her hand. He wanted to pull her close to him again, and feel her next to his heart like he had on the ride to Marinette.

His voice turned husky, raw. "I think it's time we change your bandages."

She looked back at him, and this time her eyes cleared. "Thank you, Zane. Thank you for finding me."

"You're welcome." He squeezed her hand again and scooted down on his knees to remove the bandages on her feet. He gently lifted each one and examined it. They were soft and pink where healing had begun. "I'm going to put some more ointment on and re-wrap them, but I think in another couple of days the bandages can come off for good. They look well."

"That tickles." Her genuine smile lit him up on the inside, and all he could think was *God forgive me, I'm still in love with her. I'm sorry, Kelly. I'm sorry.*

Her strength seemed to be returning almost hourly. She grew restless too. The next day she asked for something to do, something to keep her hands busy. At first he thought she might want to draw, but when he mentioned finding her some paper or charcoal, her expression closed, and she shook her head. Instead he found her some clothing that needed mending, some items donated to the refugees but needing repair.

She wiggled the fingers of her right hand.

"How's it feeling?"

"It's sore still, but it feels good to handle a needle anyway, like I'm doing something useful. I'm not much good at needle work. Leastwise, I don't have much patience for it. But it feels important to be doing something -- anything at all."

"You getting better is doing something important." He smiled at her and she offered him a wan curve of her lips.

He watched her as she sat there, mending a sock. Questions scurried through his mind, but none he dared ask. They didn't talk about what they would do or where they would go when she left Eleazer's house. Zane would still have work available with the railroad if he wished. He wondered if she'd stay in Marinette, or if she'd want to go home to her family. Maybe he should take her to St. Joe to meet Suzanne. They'd be sisters. Neither of them ever had a sister before.

Over the course of the next week, the idea grew on Zane. He decided it might be the answer for them both. He dare not tell Suzanne about Kelly in a letter or a telegram, not after all their shared losses. He purposed to return and give her the news. It was the very least he could do. And somehow, the thought of going home didn't fill him with the awful bitterness it used to.

Plans circled his thoughts as he rode back into Marinette at the end of a long day's work clearing burned timbers off the track route. Filth covered him from head to toe. He couldn't wait to have a bath and see Lainey. Sometime, he hoped, he could ask her about whether she wanted to stay or leave, or whether she wished to walk away from the past year or go and meet Suzanne. One of these days she might be ready to talk about what lay ahead. It might be in arranging for the future that she'd finally feel safe to talk about the events of the past. Maybe, for a change, he could help her find hope.

It seemed strange how everything that happened served to heal him from the tragedies of his own past. Losing Kelly hurt more than he could say. But Kelly was with their ma and pa now, and somehow Zane found peace in that. After Kelly's accident, he'd made it clear he no longer held tragedy against God. Though Zane didn't understand Kelly's simple acceptance, he was thankful for it.

His boots clunked against the boardwalk on his way to the public bath house. He could almost imagine the smell and feel of the soap. His gaze swept out across the street, taking in the movement of people coming and going, carrying on their lives despite the desolation lying just beyond the town's rim. And then his boots jarred to a stop as he spotted three men in conversation. Zane narrowed his gaze. It couldn't be, could it? One of the men turned sideways and Zane got a better glimpse.

His question answered itself. He looked at Grayson Kade, Lainey's brother, and her pa Manason next to him. Another, younger-looking fellow stood with them. In another flash, Zane recognized Eldon. He'd gotten taller since they'd met. He looked a lot like Gray.

Zane ran a hand over his mouth and pushed his hat back a little farther on his head. So Lainey's family heard about the disaster, and they'd come looking for her. They were probably worried sick, afraid they wouldn't find her alive. Zane put his hopes on hold. The future just changed. He hitched his shoulders and started across the street to talk to Lainey's family, and he knew already what they would do. They'd take her away.

And he would have to let her go.

Chapter Twenty-Six

Lainey studied the scars on her hand while she peeled potatoes for Mrs. Ingalls. She'd have them forever, but they were healing without infection. Zane rubbed them with ointment and changed the bandages every day. Now they felt nearly whole. He'd nursed her and fed her. She supposed he'd done the same for Kelly a time or two, and who knows for how many others during the war. Since the fire, Zane stayed by her side during the night, not lying beside her, but sitting there in the Ingalls' rocking chair ready to comfort her when she dreamed. He said he couldn't sleep anyway, but she didn't think that still held true.

He left for only a few hours each day, and she sensed he didn't like leaving her, but he always came back with news and something the Ingalls could use to help care for the convalescents in their home.

She didn't know how much longer she dare impose on their generosity. She was getting well, just merely homeless. Surely Zane would think of something though, of someplace for her to go. Ultimately, whenever she worried about it, she knew one answer lay in going back home. Her family would have heard about Peshtigo's disaster by now and they'd be anxious. If only it was easier to send them a message. She did want to see them, but what about Zane? The two of them alone, without Kelly, leaned on one another. They depended on each other for strength. Without Kelly there for Zane, how could she think of leaving him?

She stood and went to the sink, carrying the bowl of potatoes. Gripping the handle to the pump, she rinsed first one white potato, then another and another, her actions mechanical, her thoughts darting.

Without needing to provide for Kelly's extra needs, maybe he wanted to leave the railroad and go back to his old ways. She wouldn't blame him if he longed to get out of Wisconsin altogether, maybe head west to California or off to Texas or to one of the other places he'd been before. He surely wouldn't want to stay put here in Wisconsin where he'd lost his only brother, the one person in his family still close to him.

After bringing her to Marinette that day, Zane went back to see Kelly buried, to tell him a final farewell. It must have been terrible seeing him stretched on the ground again. It must have been like the war.

Lainey pumped water into the pan of potatoes. The ring on her hand glistened. The etching of the vine winding around it sparkled, reminding her she still hadn't told Zane about discovering it in Kelly's hand. She frowned, thinking again about the letter in Kelly's pocket. Maybe Zane knew Kelly bought the ring for her just as he obviously knew Kelly planned to propose.

When Zane rubbed ointment on her burns, he worked the cream around her fingers, around the ring, but he never mentioned it. Didn't he wonder? He had a right to ask -- to know. She should have told him about it, but neither of them spoke much about that terrifying day.

She rinsed her fingers beneath the pump. What if Zane thought she and Kelly had married? She shook her head against the thought as she dried her hands on a towel, wondering. No, he'd not think so! She bit her lip. Zane couldn't possibly imagine she would say yes, could he?

She rested her hands on the wash tub. Gazing at the ring, she rebuked herself for not telling Zane how she'd found it. The next chance she got, she would tell him how she only wore it as a memento, something to remember Kelly by. She would always love him as a brother.

The voice of Mrs. Ingalls called her out of her reverie. "You'd best get off your feet now, young lady. You've been standing here washing potatoes long enough."

"It's only been a few minutes. And my feet are doing fine. I can walk almost as good as new."

"Still, there's no cause to overdo." Mrs. Ingalls took the pot of potatoes from Lainey and set them on the cook stove. "I can handle it from here."

Lainey smiled and removed her apron. She might as well go back to some mending she'd left earlier. She left the kitchen and crossed the foyer just as the door opened. "Zane." Her heart felt lighter seeing him, despite the dirt imbedded into every pore of his face and arms. She couldn't help smiling. "You look a fright."

"You're up." His hand came out as though he might reach for her, but dropped back quickly to his side. He smiled then, not a big smile, not a truly happy smile, but a smile that seemed more of a concession. "Maybe you'd better sit back down."

"Why? What--" The door hung open, and suddenly another man stepped into the room. Her heart lurched. "Pa!"

She reeled forward, burying her face against his shoulder. Tears filled her eyes as she soaked in the smell of his flannel shirt and felt the strength of his thick arms folding around her. His square hand stoked the back of her head. He kissed her temple.

His shoulders dropped as though they'd been tensed for weeks."My girl."

"What about us? Don't we get any hugs?" Eldon stepped up behind Manason and grinned at her. She turned to her little brother and he nearly crushed her with a might new to both of them.

Gray stepped forward next, wrapping her into his embrace, then setting her back and staring into her eyes. "You had us scared nearly to death. Ma is overcome with worry."

She cried, unable to control the weight of her emotion. "I know. I know, and I'm so sorry. The post is down. The lines for the telegraph are burned. Everything is so confused..."

"Shh." Pa tucked her against him again. "We know. That's why we came. We'll get a letter off to your mama some other way. And we'll bring you home so she can touch you for herself."

Lainey nodded, resting safe against her pa, knowing now just what she'd have to do and what it would take to free Zane to go his own way -- if that's what he wanted to do.

*****

Lainey's pa took her with him to their motel. Zane came over the next day and stood by while they loaded up their own horses as well as the one they hired for Lainey. They faced a long trip down to Green Bay, and Manason wanted to get started right away, as long as Lainey thought she could handle it. She said she could. Of course she'd say that.

There wasn't a woman as strong as Elaina Kade. Nor one as feminine.

Zane agreed to ride with them. They planned to part at Green Bay. He didn't look forward to it. But at least his mind was made up. He'd go on to Missouri. Family waited there. There was no sense staying in the Peshtigo country, even though there was plenty of work to do. The thought of being there for only himself cut a lonely swath through him he couldn't bear facing. Maybe, before he and Lainey went their separate ways, he could broach the topic of having her come down to St. Joe and meet Suzanne sometime.

Or maybe she'd learn to be used to her widowhood before long, and then she'd forget the Beaumonts altogether. His thoughts wavered between sweet hope and bitter gall.

They spent one night camping in a clump of trees that somehow missed the scathing. When they passed the place of Kelly's accident, both he and Lainey looked in the direction of the train trestle hidden down the lane, but neither of them mentioned it. He wanted to talk about Kelly, and he thought maybe she did too, but it didn't seem like the right place. It was just another bad memory, and Zane figured they both needed to think of better days.

But time slipped away. A day later, Manason held train tickets in his hand, and Gray and Eldon already waited on the platform with their slight baggage.

Zane's mind felt like it moved through maple syrup. Yet the changes taking place happened at lightning speed. He wanted everything to slow down, just for a minute. When the ticket master announced the train's delay, he thanked God.

"Lainey." He stole up to her where she waited, seated on a bench with her father. "Mind taking a walk up the platform? I feel like goodbye is coming a mite fast."

She nodded and stood. A glance from Manason made Zane feel

exposed. Did he still think Zane cared for his daughter?

Well, he had been right that time, after all.

Zane touched the brim of his hat and Manason looked away at Eldon studying posters tacked on the side of the building. Lainey looped her arm through his. They walked a few feet in silence.

"I'm going to miss you, Zane," she said, surprising him.

"Are you?"

She tugged on his arm. Then he noticed her swipe at her eye.

"I didn't really see this day coming. I'm going to miss you, too."

"I have to say that I'm afraid I won't see you again. It doesn't seem possible after everything we've been through, but that's what I'm afraid of. I'm afraid you're going to disappear like a vapor, and well... that will be that."

"It's funny you should mention that, Lainey, cuz I've been thinking about you coming down to St. Joe someday. Suzanne's going to take it hard, about Kelly, but I think if she could meet you it'd be easier somehow."

They stopped walking at the end of the platform and turned to look at one another. Her forehead creased and her lips pinched. "How could I possibly make such a thing easier?"

He had to bring it up now. It had seemed a closed subject, unmentionable, but in the distance he heard the keening of the train whistle. There would be no other time.

"She'd want to know the girl Kelly loved, the girl he, uh... married."

She unhooked her arm from his and stared up at him, eyes wide. She brushed her fingers down the length of his forearm and stopped when they touched the back of his hand.

"You mean you think...?" She lifted her other hand and looked at the ring. Then she looked back at him. Her blue eyes became animated. They shone with a life he'd not seen since before the fire. He shrugged. Did she think he didn't know? Did she think he wouldn't notice the ring she wore? She'd never worn one before. Did she think Kelly wouldn't tell him about his plans?

She stepped even closer, and Zane's heart raced. They were talking about Kelly, for Pete's sake! And here she was, standing there so vulnerable, all he could really think of was pulling her against him and shielding her in his arms.

The whistle grew louder. Iron wheels clattered up the track.

She took his hands in hers, her soft fingers wrapping around his own. Couldn't she feel his pulse?

Her lips curved into a soft smile. "I would love to meet Suzanne. I told both you and Kelly that before. I feel like we are sisters."

His heart roared like the train engine whishing up beside them. Its whistle screamed and steam frothed up around them as the giant metal beast screeched to a halt.

"I think it would honor Kelly, maybe he'd even rest better if you came... someday."

"Lainey!" Eldon hollered up the platform. "Pa says it's time to go."

She glanced away and then back again. Her eyes looked deeper blue this time, and Zane realized they always did that when some bottomless emotion swept over her. Parting was hard for her, too.

"I hope she'd think it all right for me to visit. Zane, I -- I didn't marry Kelly."

If he'd stepped in front of a blast of steam straight out of the train's engine he wouldn't have been more blown back. He fumbled for words. People began filling up the platform. In a few more moments she'd have to board.

"You didn't? But I thought--" he caught up her hand and held it -- the ring -- between them.

"Kelly was holding it in his hand when we found him. I should have told you."

He shook his head, trying to figure it all out. "No, no you didn't have to."

Her brow curled, her pupils nearly invisible in the dark sea of her eyes. "I couldn't have married him, Zane. You know how I feel about that. I told you that day at the restaurant in Marinette. I loved Kelly, I really did. But I didn't love him that way. I know you hoped I would." She flushed. "I -- I found the letter you wrote to him. I didn't mean to, but I did. I know you wanted me to marry him and to love him like a -- like a wife. But Kelly was my friend, that's all."

"Lainey, time to go." Manason slipped up and touched her elbow, but she clung to Zane's hand. If Zane didn't know better, he'd think she loved him, too, maybe even differently, even more than she loved Kelly. He hungered for some sign, some word telling him truly if she did. But she didn't say anything else. She just stared at him and held his hand, squeezing it as though her life depended upon his understanding.

Suddenly she flung her arms around him. "Goodbye, Zane. Goodbye."

And with that she turned and hurried up the platform. He watched them board, Manason last of all. Lainey's father handed his tickets to the agent and paused. With a glance over his shoulder, he looked again at Zane then stepped up into the train.

And Zane could only wonder at Manason's look and at the things only a father like he might know for sure.

*****

"Are you sure you want to do this?"

Lainey sat next to her father in the coach seat. Gray and Eldon sat behind them. She flitted a glance at her pa, surprised. "What do you mean?"

"Are you sure you want to let him go?"

Lainey held her breath, then slowly her lips parted and she let it escape, hoping to be able to calm the sudden pulse of her throat. "Zane?"

She glanced at him again. Clearly he meant Zane.

"I said goodbye."

"You aren't answering my question."

Her fingers fidgeted in her lap and her pa's hand slipped over them, cupping them in his palm.

"I was surprised he let me take you away from him," Manason continued. "I could see in his eyes he didn't want to let me. I suppose after losing his brother and having his whole world turned upside down with the fire, he probably figured he didn't have a choice."

"I don't know what you're talking about. Zane is ready to go back to Missouri."

He squeezed her hand and the gesture compelled her to look at him. She didn't dare let her love for Zane turn into a hope that could never be. He didn't love her, not in that way. He felt responsible for her. He cared about their friendship. But his responsibility had come to an end. He was ready to go back to Suzanne and his true home and family. She needed to be happy for him about that. She needed to rejoice that he'd not let Kelly's death become the final spike in the long track of despair he'd been running on. He was going home.

Home to a place she had no part of, nor ever would.

Her pa said nothing, he merely looked at her a moment longer. In some way she wished he would keep talking, that he'd at least try to give an excuse for what he said. But he didn't. He just let his comment settle into her, making her crazy with speculation.

"I wish you'd explain yourself."

He feigned surprise and she narrowed her look at him.

"Don't give me that look, Pa. Explain what you meant about... you know... about what it was you saw in his eyes." She rolled her own.

"Hasn't he ever told you?"

"Told me what?" Her voice rose. She took a breath, resettling herself when an older couple across the aisle glanced over at them. "What should he have told me to make you get the notion he didn't want to let me go?" There. She'd spelled it out, just as she knew he'd been waiting for her to do.

"That he loves you."

She shook her head and gasped, a forced attempt at humor. "That's ridiculous. You don't know Zane. Apparently you don't know me either. You forget how unlovable men find me." She hadn't thought about it in a long time. Being as she was heading back to the Chippewa, she supposed thoughts of her dreadful past just naturally pushed up to the surface like rocks after a winter frost heave.

"If you say so."

She threw him a sharp glance. That was it? He wasn't going to try to convince her? "It's not as though I want to be unlovable," she said, stammering a little. "I want to be able to open my heart. I just don't know if I can. I've been through a lot and--"

"Lainey." He turned sideways and faced her. She felt like tumbling into his arms the way she used to when she was a little tyke. He'd always been there for her to be able to do that. She couldn't have imagined a birth father loving her more.

Her hands felt clammy even though it was chilly outside and the train wasn't really very warm. She looked up at him and then away. Why was he making her hope? Why would he do that? Especially now when Zane was lost to her? She couldn't even test her father's theory. She couldn't look once more into his stormy gray eyes and see if there was really something in them of the sort of feeling her father spoke of.

"Lainey." He spoke more softly. "Do you love him?"

She took several shallow breaths, her jaw working. To say it out loud and be denied the chance to be with him would be the hardest thing ever. Harder than losing Bobby, harder even than losing Kelly in some way. She flushed, shamed by such a thought.

"Never mind. I don't want to embarrass you." He tugged her to him and she laid her head against his chest. Before long her eyes grew heavy and she fell asleep, dreaming of seeing Zane, and watching for the storm in his eyes to calm, and love for her to make them bright.

Chapter Twenty-Seven

Winter wrapped Lainey in a cocoon, and she was glad for its onslaught, though it grew exceptionally harsh. The thermometer sunk below zero nearly fifty times. Often, when the cold seeped through the stout walls of her family's home, and frost managed to line the rafters, and ice dared to coat the windows on the inside so that even the fires burning hot in the fireplaces and in the kitchen stove couldn't ward it away, Lainey's thoughts sunk deep into worry for the people homeless in Peshtigo and the Sugar Bush. Doubtless, many would have moved away, and others would have been taken in by strangers. But, still, there would be those who tried to stay and fight for their lives. Only this time the attacker would be the cold and the snow instead of the raging beast of fire.

She didn't like to think about it. Sometimes she simply couldn't help it.

Stephen bought her new drawing supplies as a Christmas gift. She thanked him for his thoughtfulness, but Lainey rarely drew. Memories she loathed threatened to come out onto the page. Only pictures of Zane were safe. But what would she do with a stack of such drawings? They only made her lonely and embarrassed. So she didn't waste much time with paper or charcoal.

As spring finally found a foothold in the Chippewa, Lainey tried to turn her hand to other tasks. She'd spent the winter working in the house. Baking things kept her warm. Now she joined her brothers brushing down the horses and taking them up to some cleared land where the grass came in with greater lush. She helped her mother and grandma tend the kitchen garden. She even asked her pa to give her jobs to do, as long as they weren't tasks that set her near any of the millworkers. But she was glad to run errands, send telegrams, or even clean his office for him on occasion.

It was better doing all those things than to sit still and think, and her social life wasn't exactly bright. She avoided going out to parties, not that there'd been many invitations during the brutal winter. She didn't bother visiting her cousin Katie, for then she'd likely have to see Jed and hear details about their planned nuptials. That didn't appeal, even though it wouldn't bring the sting to it that it might have a year ago.

When she went anywhere for pleasure, it was usually for a visit with her friend Ginny. It was a pleasure to help Ginny care for her new baby Della as well as Ginny's baby brother Jamie. Ginny seemed quite fit for motherhood, even with two babies to handle most of the time. It amazed Lainey to watch her. Would she ever be able to handle the tasks of mothering half so well?

The thought sharpened. She'd probably never need to.

At least Lainey was content. She'd made peace during the long months.

It doesn't matter what *happens to me... God has a plan.*

Kelly's words came back to her often enough, and gradually she started to believe them. She might not like sitting still, but she certainly had no inclination to go running off looking for trouble.

But that didn't mean it wouldn't come courting anyway.

The lilacs bloomed bright and filled the air with a fragrance like desire. She twisted and bent the thick stems of the blooms off the bush beside the house as she inhaled the heady scent. It would be a grand thing to be married in spring with a bouquet of them in her arms and sprigs of them decking the tables. She paused to sniff one and chuckled.

"Why do you chase such thoughts anyway?" she whispered.

"Lainey, you out here?" Pa's voice carried over the yard.

"Cutting lilacs, Pa. Be right there."

She wrestled a final sprig from the bush and bunched it with the rest of the cluster as she strolled around the side of the house. Her father stood on the porch.

"You got time to run an errand for me today?"

"Sure. What is it?"

"I have to get to the mill, but there's a gentleman coming into town today on the coach to negotiate a contract. Do you mind taking the buggy down to the Falls to pick him up?"

"Sure, Pa. So he won't be going straight to the hotel then? You want me to bring him out to the mill?"

He hoisted a foot onto the porch rail and tied his boot. "No... no. Just bring him home here. Your mama's planning a nice dinner."

She grinned at him with a lift of one brow. "Must be a big contract."

"It sure is. I don't want to make any mistakes on this one."

She rolled her eyes. Her pa rarely made mistakes. She couldn't think of one. "As if that would ever happen. What time is his coach coming in?"

"Four o'clock. But be there early, just in case."

She stepped up onto the porch and stood by him while he tied the other boot. "But the coach is always late, never early."

He winked at her. "Just in case."

Lainey helped her mother set the table. Grandma fiddled around with a dust rag in the front room. Earlier Lainey had put a rhubarb pie in the oven for dessert and now she set it to cooling on the window sill. She admired the pleasant aroma mingling with the jar of lilacs centered on the table.

Colette slid a pan of rolls into the oven. "You'd better get going so you're not late."

"It's barely two-thirty. I'll have to wait forever."

Her mother reached into a jar in the sideboard and pulled out some coin. "Here's something to spend while you wait."

Lainey flushed. She felt like a child given permission to choose a stick of candy. "You don't have to give--"

"Take it." Mama pressed it into her palm. "Buy yourself a piece of ribbon or some new gloves. You haven't had anything new since the few things that were necessary when you first got home."

"You and Aunt Jean made me two new dresses for Christmas." She glanced down over the creation she wore. It was a simple day dress, but fitted her figure nicely, and the dark blue fabric complimented her dark hair and brought out the sapphire of her eyes.

"That was months ago."

"Well, maybe I'll buy a newspaper," she said, her voice sassy, but she accompanied the remark with a kiss on her mother's cheek. "Thank you, Mama."

She grabbed her shawl off the hook and flung it around her shoulders as she headed out the door. "I hope Mr. Moneybags isn't disappointed that Pa won't be meeting him."

"I'm sure he'll be enchanted."

Lainey threw a look over her shoulder and stuck out her tongue when her mother laughed.

It was a good day for driving the buggy into town. Birds sang, and the drive along the rushing Chippewa revived her. The days were getting longer between sunrise and sunset. Summer was about to burst upon them. It was wonderful and it was bittersweet. Sometimes, in the midst of such a glorious moment, pain stabbed her straight through, and she thought of all she missed, of last summer, of Kelly's warm smile, of Zane's teasing and the feel of his hand in hers, his fathomless gaze behind a deck of cards... of the three of them adventuring together. That time would never return again, and the memory turned to haunting.

*****

The coach rocked. Zane glanced down at the letter in his hands. He'd read it so many times he'd practically committed it to memory. But, still, he kept it, staring at it again and again as he did now just to make himself sure he hadn't imagined any of it.

It came from Lainey's father.

The letter arrived two weeks ago. He imagined Lainey's father had been busy at the mill with logs coming in from the spring rush like Lainey talked about so often and as Zane saw up in Peshtigo. Manason had probably been busy keeping the saws turning and the crews getting his logs out of the cuts and up the river. Yet he'd taken time to write to Zane.

The page was worn, the markings smeared from folding and re-folding the thin sheet.

Dear Zane,

It's been a long winter, certainly for you and your family too. I suppose it's not gotten any easier to be without your brother Kelly, but that you're trying to adjust. My wife and I continue to be sorry for your loss. He seemed to us a very good man, one you can eternally be proud to own as your brother.

He always paused reading right there and thought about Kelly. Yeah, he was proud to call him brother. Lainey's pa had no idea how much. Kelly had changed him inside and out, or at least Kelly's reminders of their Heavenly Father's love had.

Going home to Missouri had not been easy, but he knew a life full of running was not the answer either. He'd been to Gath. He'd fled straight to the enemy and found him wanting. Zane wanted no more of Gath's brand of comfort.

Kelly never blamed God for his accident. Neither would he have blamed God for taking him in the fire. Zane believed that. He wondered if, in fact, Kelly sensed the possibility of something like this happening. He remembered how his big, blond brother had studied him when he asked about the level of Zane's own interest in Lainey. He'd said *maybe God doesn't have her for me.* Could he possibly have intuited that something could interfere with his plans to marry Lainey, even to the point of it being his own death?

No -- no. He was carrying it too far. Kelly didn't know he'd die. Yet, Zane felt certain that he would have accepted dying as long as it meant safety and a future for Lainey. He kept reading.

Your brother was an open man. He seemed willing to reveal himself. My family felt as though we came to know him a little during those few days you both spent with us last summer. But we didn't get to know you quite the same way.

I have never been able to let go of the feeling that there was a reason why we should, and that the reason had completely to do with feelings on your part for Elaina. Then, when we came to find her last fall, and the two of you said goodbye at the train station, I knew it.

Son, I almost lost the best woman in the world because it took me too long to recognize what she meant to me. I know you mean a great deal to my daughter. At the risk of her heart, I'm going to tell you that she loves you. Both her mother and I believe it. We don't want to see her hurt again after all the things she's suffered. But neither do we want to see her lose you if, as we suspect, you love her as well.

Colette and I have the idea that there's a strength of character in you that you've been belying; and, we hope, a faith. Is that the way of it? If it is, then we'd love to have you come to us again. We're willing to get to know you still, for your own sake as well as Lainey's.

If time and inclination are with you, come up to the Chippewa. The railroad is coming this way too.

Sincerely;
Manason Kade

*****

Chippewa Falls grew while she was away. Not immensely, but in little ways. Or maybe it was she who'd grown. Lainey parked the buggy and wandered down the main street boardwalk. Entering the mercantile, she came out fifteen minutes later with a new comb, a stick of peppermint candy, and two newspapers, the Pioneer and the Eau Claire Free Press. She found an unoccupied bench outside the store and made herself comfortable. It was three forty-five, but she expected to have a wait. Her intuition didn't disappoint. She'd made it through the Pioneer and the candy stick, and was well into the main body of the Free Press before the coach arrived, almost half an hour late.

Lainey rolled the papers into her palm and stepped forward to meet the passengers. A lady stepped out first, a matron older than her mother. Lainey ignored her and watched as a gentleman stepped out, settling a derby on his gray hair. She took a half step forward and smiled. She was about to approach him and introduce herself when a third passenger stepped off the coach.

Her step caught and she gaped. She dropped her hand limply at her side. A clamor rose up inside her, but couldn't seem to get out. Zane's gaze swung her way. He stepped forward and stopped just as abruptly then stared at her as though she were an apparition, as though he'd no idea why she was there. She could safely say she understood exactly how he felt.

A giddy feeling lumped up her throat and finally burst out. "Zane?"

He walked a straight, steady course toward her, stopping only a foot in front of her and setting down his carpet bag. Then like a torrent of river, joy rippled out. He pulled her against him and hugged her fast.

Her voice fell muffled against his chest. "You're here. I can't believe it." His breath whispered against her hair along with the scent of soap -- some scent she'd never before realized as being distinctly Zane's -- filled her nostrils and heightened her senses with a power stronger than lilacs and rhubarb pie. She pulled back but clutched his arms.

His eyes gleamed -- blue and bright -- sparkling with pleasure. Is that what her pa saw? Was this the way he'd always looked? But it was only a simple happiness, wasn't it? She searched his face, longing to touch it, so she did. She put the palm of her hand against his cheek, touching the sparkling of whiskers he'd probably shaved off earlier in the day. His hair, shorter, but still touching the collar of his shirt, was brushed back except for the stray strands falling down over his temple. She fingered it and studied on.

So what if she was in the middle of the street. So what if people gawked. Who were they anyway? Every sense of propriety regained by returning home flew away with his coming. She cared not for it anyway. She just cared that he was there.

He hugged her close again. "I missed you." His voice sounded thick, gruffer than she remembered.

"Oh, Zane. It's been such a long winter."

They looked at each other, and Lainey thought of the time apart and of Kelly and the past, just as she knew he was thinking. They'd been to hell and back again. But they'd touched on heaven too.

"Oh my goodness!" Her hand flew to her cheek. She suddenly understood. "Pa knew you were coming. Ma too."

Zane tipped back his head and laughed. She should have realized everything the moment she saw him, but he'd stunned and confused her so. She was just a bit annoyed.

"How long have they known you were coming?"

"I sent your father a telegram last week."

"You sent it to my pa? Not to me?"

"We can talk about that later. Right now I'm starved."

She squeezed his arms again. "C'mon. Get your luggage. Ma's got a feast waiting and the stage was late."

So excited she could hardly steer the buggy, they headed home. More than once Lainey glanced up at him and nearly careened off the lane, or so he claimed, teasing her. They spoke of his journey and the countryside, they laughed when the buggy jarred over a rut, tossing their shoulders together. He asked her if she swam much in the Chippewa coursing along beside them. But they didn't speak of Kelly or Suzanne or any of the past. When the house came into view up the climbing drive, they fell silent.

Lainey flicked a glance at Zane and saw his face had drawn serious. Was he nervous about meeting her family again? Zane? She couldn't believe so.

Her parents stepped out onto the porch as Zane leapt to his feet first then helped her down from the buggy.

"You made it back. I was worried your brothers would eat all the food before you got here."

"I hope you didn't hold them back on my account," said Zane.

Colette waved the comment off. "I promise you, they aren't starving. Come on in and make yourself at home." She turned and called through the screen door, "Kenton? Come take care of the buggy."

They approached the house and Lainey's pa stepped down from the porch. He shook Zane's hand. "Welcome back to the Chippewa. Glad you made it." He gave Lainey a small smile. She tried to catch his eye with a bit of teasing glare, but he quickly turned and led Zane up the steps.

"Thank you, sir. It's good to be here."

The men sat at the table and Colette, Lainey, and her grandma quickly set out the meal. The screen door clacked as Kenton came in to join them, followed by Gray and Eldon trotting down from upstairs.

She watched Zane taking them all in with a sweep of his gaze.

"Glad you decided to come see us," said Gray. Eldon shook his hand.

"Yeah, Lainey sure missed you," said Kenton. She grazed him with a look. "Well, you did." He plunked down, grabbing a baked potato and juggling it between his hands before dropping it onto his plate.

She decided to change the subject. In an effort to pretend his surprise had been lost on her, she said, "I guess that fellow coming to meet you decided not to show, Pa. Guess he wasn't interested in a contract after all."

Manason chuckled. "Oh, he may be, after he finds out what I have to offer."

Her heart jumped. She hadn't expected her father's quick comeback. What did he mean by that anyway? Was he going to offer Zane a job? Perhaps. Yet logging wasn't Zane's forte. Railroading was. She caught her mother's smile. What, exactly, was on her parents' minds?

*****

After dinner Lainey rose to help clear the table, sending Zane a demure smile that made his heart leap off a cliff. Was her father right? Did she really love him, or was it only his own hope that made his chest throb when she looked at him like that?

Her brothers pushed back their chairs and Zane caught Manason taking note of him. His hands sweated like the first time he found himself in a real, high-stakes poker game. He straightened up in his chair.

He cleared his throat. "Sure wouldn't mind stretching my legs a bit. Been a long day of sitting."

Manason lifted his chin. "Why don't we go outside while the gals finish up?"

Zane nodded, denying himself a look back at Lainey. She must wonder. Zane hadn't gone out of his way to talk with her pa last summer. Why the sudden friendliness? That's what she'd be thinking. Maybe.

The two men wandered out into the yard. The early evening still rolled wide out across the sky in yellow and blue with touches of orange to the west. Below the rim of the hill where the Kades' house stood, a sea of trees sprawled, and a ribbon of silver river sparkled amid them.

"I take it your land stretches out quite a ways."

"Six hundred forty acres in this piece."

Zane whistled. "That's a nice size section of trees."

"Course we have claim to lots more, but this is what we call home. You remember my sister Jean and her husband Rob."

"Stephen and Katie's folks."

Manason nodded. "That's their place just down the hill."

Zane recalled the house.

"When Katie and Jed marry they'll probably build down on the southwest forty. We've got plenty of room for the whole family."

Was that some kind of implication? Zane wasn't so sure. "So the railroad will be cutting up this way any time now."

"That's what they tell us. We're hoping so. We can get the cut out a lot faster if it does. Gonna eventually end up way up north at Lake Superior. That's a lot of miles of trees and swamp to lay track through."

Zane imagined the work it would take. It would be like Peshtigo. He turned and looked squarely at Lainey's father. "Mr. Kade, I don't want to beat around the bush. It's not my way unless I'm playing cards, and I'm not doing that these days. So I need to come straight out with it."

Manason crossed his arms over his muscled chest and studied him, but Zane had been inspected hard by men before. He wasn't put off by this one, even if he was Lainey's pa. He just had to know where he stood.

"You know a little bit about me. I've been a gambler... a drifter. That's what I did after the war. But my folks taught me better than that, and if I can say so, I'm a hard worker, a good engineer. My family gave me their faith. I... I wandered from it for a while. Kelly--" Zane looked down and paused. Unexpected emotion punched him and he waited for it to pass. He sighed. "Kelly found his way sooner... and he reminded me of mine. I thank him for that."

Manason's arms loosened and he tucked his thumbs in his pockets. Zane sensed him opening himself.

"I knew that Kelly loved Lainey. He deserved someone like her. I figured he deserved her more than I ever could. What's even more, I believed she deserved a man like Kelly, a righteous man. I didn't want to interfere."

"But you did care for her."

Zane nodded, rubbed a hand across his face. "Took me a while to realize it, but I always have. I don't even know when it happened. I felt guilty and tried to stay away from them -- her and Kelly."

Manason grinned. "Love does that to a man. Sneaks up on him. Takes hold of all his strength and pins him down."

He tried to find the humor in Manason's words, but he still didn't know where that left him. "Sir, I came here with one objective. I plan to tell Lainey that I love her and to see if she'll have me. I've been through two kinds of war and lost most of those dearest to me. I don't plan to waste time. You said in your letter you wanted to get to know me, but I'm telling you now there isn't much time." He lifted his arms from his sides. "This is who I am, right here. I'm willing to pour everything I am into taking care of your daughter and being a good husband to her. I don't want to change her." He looked hard at Manason. "But as her family, you'll all have to take me as I am, too."

Manason settled his hands on his hips and said nothing for

moments. Zane wondered what he could be thinking. Maybe he would tell him to get packing now. Maybe he'd come off too strong.

But that would just have to be the way of it, like it or not. If Lainey really did love him, she'd take him that way too.

"Are you sure you don't want to change her?" Manason said at last.

Zane's lips parted in a smile. "Are you kidding, sir?"

Manason held out his hand. "Then I'd like to trust you."

"I'll give you every reason." He shook the man's hand, liking the steely grip that told him here was a man who's own love for Lainey would challenge and uphold him. "But though it's a really nice evening to be talking here with you, I'd much prefer a walk with your daughter now, if you don't mind me saying."

Manason scratched his chin. "You do mean business, don't you, son?"

Zane laughed and glanced back up at the house just as Lainey pushed open the screen door.

Chapter Twenty-Six

Lainey caught the look between Zane and her pa and knew that the conversation, whatever it was, hadn't been easy. But when both men cast a smile softly at her, she thought maybe it hadn't been too bad either. She let the door bang shut behind her and strolled down the steps out onto the grass.

"You've been enjoying yourselves, I hope? Pa, you haven't been telling Zane any stories about what a horrible child I was or anything, have you?"

"No, I'll leave that to your brothers."

She swatted his arm.

"What's your mother doing? She finished with those supper dishes?"

"Almost. She and grandma chased me outside." She flitted a look at Zane.

"Well, maybe I can lend a hand to speed things up. It's too beautiful a night to spend it in the kitchen." He walked away.

"Well," she turned to Zane, "how was your visit?"

"Well," he said, too, returning her smirk, "I must admit it is interesting, getting to know your family. Your father's a good man. I don't think I gave him enough credit when we met last summer."

"So, in other words, he didn't bite you. Or, maybe I've got that backwards. You didn't bite him, did you?" She laughed and he captured her hand in his.

The touch sent a jolt through her.

"How about you take me for a walk. I'm tired of traveling and sitting. I feel like I'm bound up with energy."

"All right, Mr. Beaumont. Where would you like to walk to?"

"How about that river in the distance?"

"That's a walk for sure, but I think we can make it there and back before it's too dark. There's a good trail. Maybe I'll show you my favorite swimming hole."

"Only if it means we'll go swimming there when it's warm enough."

She smiled. Did he intend to stay for a while then? "Absolutely." They started down the hill and she swung his arm with their clasped hands. "Zane, did my pa offer you a job?"

He snorted. "Is that what you think?"

"I don't know. You said you sent him a telegram. Why did you do that? And you looked serious talking to him just now. He joked about a contract, and he takes his contracts very seriously, I can tell you."

"You sure are full of speculation, Miss Kade." He squeezed her hand. "That's one of the things I like about you. You aren't afraid to ask questions, and I, for one, have such a good time watching your curiosity get the better of you."

Their stroll took them out to the main road. They passed her aunt and uncle's cabin.

"Careful what you say. Remember, I've been known in these parts to go beyond the pale with my questions, my opinions, and just about everything else. I'm sure my meeting with you in town today already has people talking. 'There goes that Lainey Kade, starting up again. Wonder how long this fellow will abide her?'" She heard the sourness in her own voice thinly veiled by the humor, and wished she hadn't said it. Maybe Zane would think she thought of them as... together. She flushed and led him off the road, down onto another trail, this one worn smooth but narrow through the woods.

"I hope they do talk."

She stopped short and looked at him. He didn't let go of her hand but caressed her fingers with his thumb.

"Why?"

He tugged at her fingers and moved on, taking the lead. She could hear the river up ahead. The trickle and splash of water played against her ears while Zane said nothing. They stopped when they came to the bank itself. Water in the Chippewa churned wide and deep. A big elm hung close to the edge where a fat old rope hung out over the current.

"This is the swimming hole?"

"Yes. Stephen and Gray hung the rope with my pa and Uncle Rob more than ten years ago. They wouldn't let me help, even though I was older."

He laughed and she grinned.

"What about Katie? Didn't she want to help too?"

Lainey rolled her eyes. "Don't you remember much about Katie? She barely learned to swim."

Zane released her fingers. He dropped down on the bank and leaned against the old tree. She settled down in the grass facing him.

"Your father wrote me a letter."

"He did?"

Zane nodded. He watched the current, tossed in a twig. "He invited me up."

"He did?" she repeated and frowned. Not usually at a loss for words, she upbraided herself. Why would her father write to Zane?

Embarrassment stung her. She knew why. Her behavior all winter long probably echoed of their departure last fall. She'd been sullen, languid. Memories of the fire plagued her through the long, cold season, yes, but her father had guessed how she felt about Zane that day on the train. He and her ma must have been reading her thoughts ever since.

She hesitated, her thoughts cringing. "What else did my father say?"

"He brought up a little of our meeting last June and some of the things we'd talked about then."

"I hadn't realized you spent any time talking with my father. Kelly seemed more willing to do that." She flushed. "I mean--"

"Kelly was ready. You know that. I told you about his feelings and you could see them for yourself." He glanced down at her hand. "That's why I thought the two of you had gotten married."

She leaned forward. "But I told you I couldn't. I meant it, Zane. I could never have married Kelly, dear as he was to me."

"But you might have healed from your heartaches eventually, enough even to marry my brother."

She shook her head. "No. You don't understand. It had nothing to do with my heart being broken by Bobby Braedon or Jed or Owen or--"

"Or?"

"Or anyone! Zane, I could not have married *Kelly*."

The sun dipped below the treetops. Dusk started settling in the woods. Soon daylight would fade completely and they'd be stumbling their way back along the trace. Like nightfall, Zane's eyes went dark, stormy with thoughts swirling through them. But what were they? Did he still not understand what she meant?

"Lainey, can I ask you something?"

She nodded.

He reached up and touched a strand of her hair hanging over her shoulder. His fingers ran down the length of it, sending a shiver up her side.

His voice dropped, slowed. "If the ring had been mine instead of Kelly's, would you have accepted it?"

She held her breath. "I -- I'm not sure what you mean."

"If I'd offered you my heart, instead of Kelly offering his, would yours have rebelled?"

"You mean would I have rejected you as someone *more* than a friend?"

His hand lifted to that strand of hair again and she tilted her head so that his fingertips touched the side of her face. Her eyelids lowered and her heart raced.

When she opened her eyes he was studying her, and his hand fully cupped her cheek.

Now was the time. He was asking her to be truthful, to tell him how she really felt. He might cast her aside, tell her she shouldn't think of him at all. But she didn't think so.

She blinked, her voice a whisper. "If you had offered me your heart and your ring I'd have taken them both."

Zane leaned close, his hand still on her cheek. His face inches from hers, he stopped. She could hardly see his eyes, but knew enough of their look to feel the fire stoking in them. His fingers gentled around her neck and drew her to him.

Like the night last June when he'd kissed her on another bend of this very river, he kissed her now. But this time he didn't draw away.

Not right away. His lips caressed hers with a gentle fervor, driving fears and nightmares away from the crevices of her memory. His lips moved over her face, kissing her forehead, her temple, the bridge of her nose, and finally her lips again. When they drew apart, he held her fast so that her forehead rested under his chin.

His voice rumbled softly. "I didn't want to hurt you. I was afraid of that more than anything. Afraid of hurting you and not deserving you."

She leaned away and looked at him.

"I wasn't whole. I didn't think God cared. I couldn't see anything good in His plans so I rejected them. But I was wrong."

She shook her head. The warmth of his fingers on her skin encouraged her to admit it all. "I was afraid you couldn't love me because I'm stubborn."

He chuckled, and it was as if she could hear the weight of a thousand bad memories breaking apart and crumbling off his shoulders.

"It's just the opposite. I started falling in love with you when you were pretending to be married to Stephen. I saw your back stiffen up with resolve not to let anyone in, and something got hold of me then that I couldn't let go of, no matter how hard I tried. Believe me, I tried. I didn't want to ruin that in you and I didn't want to ruin something else in Kelly." He took both her hands and held them. She could not mistake the gaze he steadied on her. "Don't change, Elaina. I love you just the way you are."

Tears clouded her eyes. She gasped and couldn't tell whether the tears or the laughter would break free first. "You do?"

"Yes. I do. I love you Elaina Eastman Kade." He leaned close and kissed her again, whispering her name once more.

*****

Zane was ready for one last gamble.

On Saturday the Kade house filled near to busting. Lainey's parents invited the whole Kade-Gilbert clan for a picnic to welcome him. The big kitchen swarmed with women going to and fro between the oven inside and the tables sprawled across the lawn outdoors. Lainey flitted between her mother, her cousin Katie, her Aunt Jean, and Grandma Lavinia carrying baskets of bread and pies, potatoes and greens. They put Zane and Gray to work setting up log benches and chairs at the tables. Lainey's pa and her uncle Rob roasted a pig out on the spit while Rob's brother Joe kept up the conversation as he held onto a squirming little boy. Joe's daughter Ginny looked after her own little one. Meanwhile, Eldon and Kenton kept the fire stoked, and Lainey's old beau Jed Clark and her cousin Stephen hauled a barrel of apple cider up on a wagon from Rob's house.

Zane took some time to observe Jed when he could. He was glad the fool had rejected Lainey, even though it hurt her. Because if he hadn't, well... if he hadn't, Zane might still be on the run, spending away his life on all-nighters.

Now, both their hearts were mended. It was as if God had collected all the torn up pieces off the forest floor and off the battlefield and molded them back together, then planted them back inside their bodies making them whole and complete and wise -- and able to be given to one another.

And they had.

Last evening he and Lainey walked home in the dark, their hands clasped and shoulders touching. They talked on the front porch late into the night, yet rose at dawn to see each other again. He had no need of sleep, it seemed, and it wasn't for fear of sleep and the dreams that used to torment. It was for joy of spending every moment together.

And that's how it would be.

She smiled through the picnic meal as he talked to Kenton about horses and about all the things Kelly could do with them. Kenton said how much he wished he could've gotten to see the stables Kelly and Zane had built.

Her father treated Zane like a welcome member of the family and bragged to Rob and Joe Gilbert about Zane's work on the railroad. He saw Lainey's mother wink at her from down the table. Between them, his confidence in his ability to play his hand grew. He knew they had it in mind to get to know him better. They didn't really know what had transpired between him and Lainey since last night, but they'd know soon enough. That's what mattered.

He intended to find a job with the railroad moving north. He aimed to offer Lainey a real home and a good life. With God's help, he'd make sure she got it.

He looked at the woman sitting next to him and his heart wanted to weep. God, she was beautiful, and he meant it like the prayer of thanksgiving it was. He didn't deserve her, yet she loved him. She said he was never her second choice. She told him about the day she first realized how she felt, and as she remembered back, how she'd known from their first time on the beach in Sheboygan, it had always been him.

Colette and Jean passed out pie. Lainey was laughing at some antics of the baby boy in Rob's lap when she looked up and saw Zane watching her. She blushed. She'd never been very good at holding a poker face. It was time he laid down his cards.

Zane reached over and squeezed her hand. He wiped his mouth on a napkin and stood.

"Where are you going? I can get you something," she said.

He shook his head. "You'll see." He looked across the group. One by one they began to notice him and realized he was going to say something.

"I just wanted to tell you all thank you for bringing me into your home and family like you have. I have a little family left down in

Missouri -- my sister Suzanne and her husband and kids -- but I've lost most the others. You all know about my brother Kelly and my folks. So it means a great deal to me to know you and be part of a day like this.

"But I really want to say that it's more than that. I've had a family for a while now. It's been Lainey." He glanced down at her, and as he looked back at the others, her blue eyes framed by her dark hair lingered in his vision. "For the past two years she's been a sister to me, or at least that's what I pretended. The truth of it is I've loved her."

He looked at her again and took a drink of her smile. "She's told me a lot about each of you, and about herself." He looked up and down the table, and his eyes flicked only momentarily on Jed's. "And with everything I've come to know and find out about Elaina, it seems we are one and the same. I never want to see her change, least of all for me."

His next glance down showed the sparkle of tears in her eyes. He turned to face her and drew her hand into his. Then he lowered himself before her, his knee on the grass. His voice was soft so that some of them strained to hear. "I want everyone to know what I think about that, Lainey. I want everyone to know you are the one for me, if you agree."

She nodded. He let go of one hand to dash away the tear on her cheek. Then he caressed both her hands again in his.

He spoke to her as if none of the others were present. "I did some research before I arrived. They're laying track north to places I never heard of. Ashland. Superior. I'm going to help them do it, but not without you. Will you come with me, Elaina? Will you marry me and let me build a life with you -- around you?"

Someone choked back a sob further down the long table, but he didn't turn his gaze from hers, nor did she turn away.

"Zane Beaumont..." she whispered, "I'll walk with you wherever you want to lead me."

She began to lean forward, and he rose and pulled her against him. Everyone started talking at once. He kissed her, and so only she could hear, he whispered into her ear, "I love you."

Manason stood and cleared his throat. The subtle roar died down.

"When did you figure on hiring on again with the railroad, Zane?"

Zane looked at him, squaring his shoulders. He'd make his intentions very clear. "I intend to be working by the end of June. So for that reason, I plan to marry your daughter before another week is out. That way we can take a honeymoon down to Missouri." His lips curved into a smile. "I'd like to take a boat for a change."

Gray and Eldon laughed, and he could see that despite Manason's concern, he was more prone to understanding.

Lainey's ma stood up next to her husband. "I think it's a wonderful idea. And I'm happy that Lainey will get to meet your sister."

"Yeah. It's about time," said Kenton as he reached across for another helping of pie. "Lainey's sketchbook is full of pictures of you. Maybe she can give some of them to your nieces and nephews since they don't see you very much."

Everyone broke out in laughter and Lainey blushed. He pulled her close beside him.

"Will you marry me next week?"

"I'll marry you today, if you can rustle up a preacher."

All he could do with words like those was kiss her again.

Epilogue

1875

Lainey closed her eyes and took a deep breath. Oh, yes. Rest. The window standing open to the front lawn ushered in a breeze. The scent of wild roses beneath the sill wafted into the room, filling it with perfume. She loved the wild roses. Even the array of roses she'd planted along the walkway leading up to her and Zane's two story house couldn't compare to the wild ones God allowed to crop up on their own.

She inhaled again, enjoying the wistful calm their scent affected. How wonderful her life was.

She and Zane had married at a small church in Chippewa Falls. It was very like the church in Peshtigo where they'd attended. Could that have really only been four years ago? On days like today, when the cool Lake Superior breeze pushed the summer air through her windows and stirred the scent of flowers, it seemed the fire was only a dream -- a nightmare that had since faded, thanks to the life God restored to her in Zane and her family, and in learning to trust His ways.

They'd married then gone to Missouri. Zane was right. She and Suzanne got on very well. She would always have a sister in her, no matter how many hundreds of miles of rivers and trees and plains lay between them. Someday, she hoped, Suzanne and her family would come to visit them at their home in Superior, the growing town on Wisconsin's northwest corner.

She curled onto her side, remembering.

She could draw again. She'd been drawing since settling up north. She used her pad and charcoal to purge the pain of the past as well. She drew Kelly and Suzanne, her brothers, and each of their families. She rekindled memories of Kelly's livery and the Forest House. Of faces lost, but not forgotten.

They never heard what became of some of their friends. Of young Jacob Collins, for instance, Mrs. Anderson, or Clara and John. They believed them all lost in the fire, but clung to the hope they'd escaped somehow.

Living amid the thick forests of northwestern Wisconsin, it was hard to believe there had ever been such devastation in other parts of the state.

Suddenly she felt a hand on her side, curving around her. She smiled and turned onto her back. With one knee on the edge of the bed, Zane leaned down and kissed her.

"How're my girls?"

"This girl is tired, but so glad to see you."

He kissed her again.

"The other girls are asleep, finally. Jesi has been colicky again."

He grinned and lay down beside her. "I think she's just willful."

"Like her parents, I suppose."

He dashed a finger over her nose. "I feel like holding them."

"You could probably hold Cori. She'll sleep though anything."

"I won't try. You need your rest."

The twins were a handful. Lainey often wondered how Ginny managed to care for her own daughter Della along with her little brother Jamie when they were tiny. It was easier now that they'd a few years behind them. She suddenly missed Ginny, Katie, Gray, Stephen and the rest. She did get homesick for them from time to time.

But ultimately her heart always came to rest. It settled in the safe place God had given her with Zane.

She nestled into the crook of his arms just as a whimper erupted from one of the cradles in the adjoining room.

Lainey moaned.

He kissed her ear. "Is that one Jesilyn?"

"No. Corianne I think. I'd better go see."

"Never mind." He rose up and went into the hall. A moment later he reappeared with a twin tucked in each arm. Sticks of red hair poked off their tiny heads. Cori closed her eyes and tried to suck on her fist, while Jesi's eyes blinked and she squirmed against the harsh afternoon brightness on the white walls.

Lainey and Zane laughed.

"This is just the beginning, you know," said Zane, his eyebrows raised as he smiled at her. "They're going to give us trouble I think."

She held out her arms for one of the babies. "Don't you dare say so. I'm barely done rebelling against the world myself."

Zane laughed. "Well, I guess they aren't going to be grown tomorrow. You can still be that wild Lainey Eastman-Kade-Beaumont for a while yet."

"For a while," she said, soaking up his love with every ounce of her. "For as long as we both shall live."

The End

About Naomi Dawn Musch

Naomi writes from the pristine north woods of Wisconsin where she and husband Jeff live as epically as God allows on a ramshackle farm near their five adult children and their families. Amidst it, she writes stories about imperfect people who are finding hope and faith to overcome their struggles, whether the setting is rich in American history, or set along more contemporary lines.

In non-fiction venues, she spent five years as a staff writer for the EPA award-winning Midwestern Christian newspaper, *Living Stones News*, telling true-life stories of changed lives. Naomi has also written dozens of magazine and internet articles for the purpose of encouraging homeschooling families and young writers.

She invites readers to say hello and find out more about her books, passions, and other writing venues at http://www.naomimusch.com or to look her up on Facebook (Naomi Musch - Author) and Twitter (NMusch).

Author's Historical Note - The Real Peshtigo Story

The events of the Great Peshtigo Fire surrounding Lainey's story are true. Details such as the previous fire scares at the woodenware factory, ash and smoke descending on the citizens of Peshtigo for days before the inferno, the fiery preaching of God's judgment by pastor Beach and other itinerant preachers, wells and rivers drying up, birds covered in ash flying upward into the sky, herds of cats fleeing down the streets as well as deer wandering into town are all actual recorded events.

So were others. The awful horror of people bursting into flame as they fled the inferno, of wagons crashing helter-skelter into one another during the chaos, of individuals falling to the ground to melt like wax, happened. The incident of the young man who ran with his wife into the river, but later found out he'd grabbed the wrong individual (in my story, Lainey), of Father Pernin's previous near escape while hunting as well the things he did on the day of the fire, and of those who spent many hours in the frigid waters of the Peshtigo River all occurred.

Most of what the characters see in chapters 23 & 24 is taken from witnessed accounts recorded of the actual event. Peter Pernin's book *The Great Peshtigo Fire: An Eyewitness Account* describes exploding balls of fire, raining slabs of fire, electrical currents jumping in the overheated air, the panic of flight, of trying to cart church items to safety and so on.

There were too many other events to mention. Bizarre occurrences even stranger than any fiction I could write are told in annals of Peshtigo's great firestorm. Some farm families in the Sugar Bush tried to hide by burying themselves in trenches they dug in their fields. One individual might be charred to a crisp, while someone right next to them remained untouched. Some citizens saved their lives but lost their sanity. Tale after tale of harrowing escapes and tragic mishaps are recorded. I was mesmerized by many of the stories retold in *Firestorm at Peshtigo (A Town, Its People, and the Deadliest Fire in American History)* a stunning account of the historical event by Denise Guess and William Lutz.

Today a cemetery stands next to the place where the priest's church stood. A different building eventually replaced the one which burned. It is now the home of the Peshtigo Fire Museum. In another location, a mass grave marks the place where up to 350 unidentified bodies are laid to rest.

The remains of many were never discovered, so complete was the disaster.

There are other, less traumatic things about the Peshtigo story I enjoyed incorporating into Lainey's story. For instance, Luther Noyes, the editor of the *Peshtigo Eagle* is a real individual, as is his report of Reverend Beach's prize-winning tomato and of the woman who bore 23 children. The stories of lumberjacks and railroad men coming to town to carouse on the weekends are Wisconsin lore. The building of the railroads into the heart of the pine country spurring productivity in logging is part of Wisconsin's history that inspired the *Empire in Pine* series. I included real places such as The Forest House, the Peshtigo Company Boarding House, and even George Robinson's Meat Market where Lainey, Kelly, and Zane went for ice cream.

As a life-long Wisconsin resident, setting Lainey's story in the real Peshtigo narrative was intensely compelling for me. My parents spent numberless hours fly-fishing on the Peshtigo River, and I wandered the banks of many rivers like the Wolf, the Fox, and the Wisconsin as a child. The great woods still stand in northern Wisconsin and I live in the midst of them. There, the places and stories thrive, but the forests themselves are forever changed by history.

Made in the USA
Charleston, SC
13 March 2016